READER'S DIGEST

CONDENSED BOOKS

FIRST EDITION

THE READER'S DIGEST ASSOCIATION LIMITED
25 Berkeley Square, London W1X 6AB

THE READER'S DIGEST ASSOCIATION SOUTH AFRICA (PTY) LTD
Nedbank Centre, Strand Street, Cape Town

Printed in Great Britain by Petty & Sons Ltd., Leeds

Original cover design by Jeffery Matthews A.R.C.A.

ISBN 0 340 22515 7

READER'S DIGEST
CONDENSED BOOKS

COLLECTOR'S LIBRARY
EDITION

In this  volume

BEL RIA *by Sheila Burnford* (p. 9)

The dog was a war refugee, rescued from
the beaches at St. Nazaire. MacLean, its saviour on
HMS *Tertian*, knew nothing of its origins.
He simply set out to shape it firmly to his own
no-nonsense idea of what a dog should be.
The task proved surprisingly difficult. . . . A poignant
new animal story by the best-selling
author of *The Incredible Journey.*

THE NAKED COUNTRY
by Morris West (p. 99)

Two men, the hunter and the
hunted, alone in the relentless
Australian outback: the one an
aborigine, wise in the age-old
ways of his people; the other a
European, armed only with the
skills of his western civilization. In
this vivid and fascinating story,
internationally-successful author
Morris West draws deeply on his
own personal experiences of the
Australian desert.

THE PHYSICIANS
by Henry Denker (p. 165)

When the little baby boy was found to be brain-damaged, his millionaire grandfather angrily accused Dr. Grant of malpractice. In the ensuing court battle both the career of this brilliant young paediatrician and the fine reputation of his hospital were endangered.

This unusual and compelling novel presents the human background to a dramatic medical-legal confrontation with touching authenticity.

CAPTAIN HORATIO HORNBLOWER
by C. S. Forester (p. 299)

Off the rugged coast of Nicaragua, in one of the most brilliant and exciting sea battles ever described, Captain Hornblower had managed to strike a decisive blow against Spain's power in the Americas. Yet for Hornblower perhaps a graver threat remained, from his passenger: the handsome sister of the future Duke of Wellington. . . .

HOME BEFORE DARK
by Sue Ellen Bridgers (p. 419)

For the fourteen short years of Stella Willis's life home had been her father's battered station wagon. Now, suddenly, the Willis family had a real house, with windows, and a porch, and proper furniture. Stella, fiercely possessive, was determined never to leave it. Not *ever*. . . . But Stella Willis was growing up. And so, in his own strange slow way, was her father.

BEL RIA

a condensation of the book by
SHEILA BURNFORD
Illustrated by Susan Hunter
Published by Michael Joseph

Nobody knew the dog's real name, the name its gypsy owner must have given it.

Sinclair, in the chaos of the 1940 evacuation from France, never thought of it with a name: it simply needed him, so he gave it what help he could. MacLean, on the destroyer *Tertian,* called it Ria: but then where he came from in the Highlands all bitches were called Meg and all dogs Ria. While in war-torn Plymouth old Mrs. Tremorne . . . well, she did her best, choosing Bel at last because that was what the little dog seemed to answer to most happily.

To the dog itself, of course, all this was of small account. It knew who and what it was, and that was that. It was obedient, and loyal to those who earned its loyalty, and affectionate too. But always it remained unalterably itself. The dog didn't change. But the people surrounding it did—and mostly for the better.

This novel, like *The Incredible Journey* by the same author, is an animal story with a difference. The people in it are touchingly real. They *live,* and their uncertain path to happiness makes heartwarming reading.

PART ONE

Its flaking red paint almost obscured by dust, an old swayback grey horse between the shafts, the caravan stood out even among the bizarre lines of transport that filled the last free roads of France that bright June morning in 1940. Alone it creaked along against the civilian refugee traffic, the endless frieze of handcarts and ancient perambulators, wheelbarrows and farm carts, the weary disillusioned people. All were on the open road, but only the caravan belonged there by custom: caravan people, from the Basque country, travelled the side roads of France as seasonally and independently as the onion vendors, as shrouded in antiquity as the gypsies. A few short weeks ago such passersby would have stirred interest, curiosity, but now there was only sullen resentment towards strangers who took a road leading back in the direction of the approaching enemy.

Hard-pressed after Dunkirk by the German spearheads thrusting to close this last escape route in France, an intermittent stream of military traffic headed south for St. Nazaire on the Brittany coast. On the northbound side, only a rare rearguard squadron of light tanks, or the occasional army truck being driven to the wrecking dump at Montoir pulled out to pass the caravan. Then almost always it was the civilian traffic opposite that had to give way or take to the ditches.

A little dark grey dog led the caravan. There were other dogs on the road that day, as dispirited as their owners, but this alien dog that passed the other way trotted along with important cheerful intent, head and tail held high. At a carefully kept distance ahead, it appeared to lead the horse, for the reins lay slack in the hands of an ancient man huddled in shawls on the wide seat with a tiny monkey perched on his shoulder.

Walking at the side, a tall, black-clad, granite-faced woman led a shabby bear, which occasionally sank back on its hindquarters, the muzzled head swinging low, and refused to move. Each time, after a brief glance back, but apparently unsummoned, the dog halted the horse by sitting down before it, then ran back to bark encouragement while the woman alternately tugged on the chain and prodded the brown bulk with her foot. When the bear was once more on the move, the dog returned to rouse the horse and the wheels creaked into action again. A young donkey tied to the back of the caravan completed the procession.

Corporal Sinclair, a Highlander of the Royal Army Service Corps, driving his empty truck back from the coast to be wrecked, had been inching along behind the high, swaying caravan for a mile, unable to swing out and pass. Then, at noon, during a long halt while a broken-down hearse was manoeuvred off the road, Sinclair dismounted and tried to communicate with the woman as he bent to pat the dusty little dog. A distant stare rewarded his sketchy French. He proffered a packet of cigarettes. After a moment's hesitation she took one and tucked it behind her ear, refusing another; but for a fleeting moment the Highlander saw a relaxation in the grimly set lips, and, as though taking his line from her, the dog stirred his short tail, eyes alert under a topknot of pulled-back hair.

The road was hot, dusty and noisy, the sun beating down from a cloudless sky. The woman took out a goatskin water carrier which she handed up to the old man. Then she drank. The tethered bear sank down on its haunches, the extended forepaws pressed together, begging. She filled a bottle. Clasping it like a child, the bear inserted the open end through the steel and leather of the muzzle and tilted it. A canvas bucket was set in turn before the horse and donkey. Finally she filled an enamel bowl and, after the monkey had drunk, the dog came running to lap.

10

A panting black mongrel crossed the road, thrust its head into the bowl and gulped avidly. The little dog moved aside, unaggressive, until the woman intervened and edged off the intruder. A young woman with a child on her hip crossed the road and held up a tin pitcher, asking for water. There was no reply. She shouted, the child howled, the dark woman continued to hold the bowl while her dog lapped. Only when the other spat contemptuously into the bowl, did she straighten up and, with eyes blazing, hurl it at the young woman. Quick as a flash, the mother picked up a stone and aimed at the little dog, who leaped for the shelter of the driving seat. The stone flew across the road and found a target on the bear's nose. It whimpered, and shook its head. Another stone followed to rattle on the caravan, and another.

Sinclair was outraged by the pitiful senselessness of this shabby bear pawing feebly at its bleeding nose. He was saved from action, however, by a northbound tank rumbling by to meet the last of a southbound convoy in the middle of the road. Chaos intervened. When the road was cleared, he returned to find the caravan lurched precariously in the ditch, the dog barking by the straining horse while the woman alternately pushed and hung on to the tilted side. Even the old man had been galvanized into flapping the reins. The sullen audience across the road, once more on the move, trudged by indifferently.

With the aid of a passing dispatch rider, Sinclair got the caravan back on the road. At the last heave, the back near wheel collapsed, the axle pin sheared. But, miraculously, the caravan remained upright. The woman suddenly looked exhausted, close to despair. Sinclair produced a wheel jack.

"All in the day's work," he said cheerfully, and showed her how to use it. "You might as well keep it," he added later, when the wheel was replaced and a spare pin fitted. She looked dubiously at him, then rummaged in her skirt pocket for a small purse from which she extracted a few coins. The soldier closed her fingers around the money with a smile of refusal.

They were standing by the driving seat, their heads on a level with the dog sitting up there, his bright eyes going from one

11

face to the other, as though trying to interpret every expression. The monkey, now perched on his back, peered ludicrously over the dog's topknot.

The woman's face suddenly cleared as she looked at them. She clicked her fingers. The monkey immediately transferred to her shoulder, the dog jumped down and rose up on his hind legs beside her. With the occasional slight motion of her hands, she put him through a small repertoire of tricks. Accompanied by the faint sweet tinkling of a bell around his neck, he strutted back and forth, turned three rapid backward somersaults, then finally sat up at their feet with one paw raised in salute. The woman gazed down at him, her face softened by obvious pride. The dog's sturdy little body quivered as she reached in her pocket and tossed him some small titbit which he caught in mid air.

The soldier applauded. Clearly this display was his reward. He turned to go. The monkey on her shoulder smacked its lips in an astonishingly loud kissing noise, and held out a pink paw. The soldier laughed and shook it. "Goodbye," he said. "And good luck—bonne chance, madame." But already she was hurrying to untie the bear tethered in the shade of the overgrown hedge.

She tugged, but the bear lay unmoving, its muzzle half-buried in leaves, the little eyes sunken and apathetic. She broke off a branch and raised it threateningly. The bear whimpered, closed its eyes and winced in anticipation. At this she threw away the branch, then, hands on hips, stared down, indecisive. Just as Sinclair was about to drive off, she ran towards him and pointed to his rifle. Somehow she made him understand. . . .

Sinclair did not hesitate; to his mind, this sorry beast would be better out of its misery. He slipped a round in his rifle and followed her back. She held the bear's chain, with no change of expression on her set face, and it was all over in a second. Thriftily she removed the muzzle and collar, and the soldier pulled some branches over the bear. She shook his hand warmly, then swung herself up beside the old man and took the reins herself. The monkey, chattering excitedly, jumped onto her lap. The dog had already taken up his station ahead of the horse. She accorded the soldier a brief nod as he drove past.

The retreating traffic petered out as Sinclair drove on to
Montoir to hand over his truck to the wrecking crew. After that,
he was to make his own way back to St. Nazaire for embarkation.
"Get there after dusk," the sergeant advised. "It's not a healthy
place in daylight."

Ironically it was at the very moment of departure, after weeks of
bombing and shellfire during the long haul back across France and
the frustrating absurdity of driving all those miles solely to
destroy his vehicle, that Sinclair was wounded; a tin exploded
from a burning NAAFI truck and tore a jagged path across his
ribs. Someone covered the wound with a field dressing and he left
to take his chances of a lift to the coast. The situation was totally
confused, he was told, and all communication had broken down.

He shouldered his rifle and started off. He was very tired. He
could not remember when he had last slept for more than a
snatched hour at a rest centre; he had lost a good deal of blood,
and now felt dazed and numb. He tried to take his mind off his
body, to think of other things as he plodded on down a side road
littered with the wrecked equipment of a retreating army. He
thought of his young wife, now working in a munitions factory; of
his father in the highland glen, a solitary old man in the white
cottage that had been home. He shifted the weight of pack and
rifle. It had been winter when he was last there, the red stags
awaiting his coming with feed on the windswept hills. . . . Sick
and giddy he paused at the side of the road, every breath he took
was a searing reminder of his wound. Slowly his knees gave way,
and he folded gently into the shallow ditch.

He came to, and with no sense of alarm found himself looking
directly into a pair of eyes only a few inches away. They were
interested eyes, one partly obscured by a few wisps of hair
escaped from a familiar topknot. As the dog's head bent closer, he
heard a faint tinkling. His eyes travelled peacefully over a pair of
feet in worn espadrilles, thick black stockings, and the hem of a
dusty black skirt. He felt no surprise; it was almost as though he
had expected her.

He raised himself and looked around, wincing at the stab of
pain. The caravan was drawn up on the verge. He tried to get to

13

his feet but the world went into a sickening spin. The woman helped him out of the ditch, speaking with an incomprehensible urgency as she pointed down the road. She slung his rifle over her shoulder; then, with an arm like steel around his shoulders, she bundled him inside the caravan and onto a narrow bunk that ran down one side. She thrust his rifle under the sagging mattress and, almost before the soldier knew it, bundles of sacks, blankets and quilts were placed on top. She indicated a tiny sliding ventilation grille in the side, sliding it fractionally open before dropping a musty pillow over his head. Something—a bundle of withies, he guessed—was thrown across his feet, then finally he felt the dog's light weight across his thighs. The door slammed. Seconds later the caravan swayed into movement. The soldier gave himself up to the musty darkness, the steady soothing clop-clop of hooves, and drifted away again.

An alteration in the weight on his thighs roused him and he heard the tinkle of the dog's alerted head. The caravan halted, and there were men's voices, the revving of engines, someone shouting harshly. They must have reached a German forward patrol. He heard the woman's voice, apparently arguing, and the sound of heavy boots approaching. As the door was flung open he lay rigid, his breath held. He felt the dog sit up, the quick movement of his tail, and heard the woman's voice again. Then, extraordinarily, the sound of laughter. The dog jumped down, the boots and voices moved off to the side, and someone closed the door. The woman's voice rose yet again, loud and audacious now, and once more the mystifying laughter.

He turned cautiously to the ventilation grille and put his eye to it. It was like looking down on a small spotlit stage, for in his circumscribed view he could see only a semicircle of boots and the grey-green of German uniform tucked into them. In the centre, now adorned with a small cluster of bells secured to the topknot and tinkling circlets on each forepaw, was the little dog. Below him he saw the black skirts and dusty espadrilles of the woman, the toe of one of them raised even as he heard three sweet flute-like notes close to his head. Evidently the old man was providing the music.

14

On the fourth note the toe began to tap, and the dog rose to his hind legs and began to dance. In perfect time he pirouetted in a circle, forepaws held out and head held high. The music changed in tempo, slower now, and at the end of each phrase the dog nodded his head so that the silvery bells accompanied its last three notes. Now he brought his forepaws into action, one at a time, each circlet of bells set at a different pitch to the cluster on the nodding head. It was the performance of a virtuoso.

Not far away, guns rumbled a reminder that three-quarters of the continent lay reeling in the wake of destruction left by these grey-green uniforms. Yet for this moment, in this one place, there was nothing but a silvery tinkling and a lilting tune and an audience who had become children again, spellbound before a dog who danced on a sunlit road to the bidding of an old man's flute.

The flute quickened in tempo and the little dancer spun in a small tight circle, the bells sounding wildly; and then, like a clockwork toy running down, the dog sank onto his haunches, shaking the bells on each extended forepaw in turn; then the paws lowered to the dust, the body following, until, finally, the last shake of bells to the final note of the flute, the head drooped and the dog lay still.

There was a momentary hush, then a ragged round of applause. The woman spoke one soft sibilant, and the dog leaped into life to make a comic bow to the semicircle of boots. The fingers clicked and he came running. The fingers removed the bells from the paws, then slipped into a side pocket to return with some small reward of food. Two arms now made a circle and the dog jumped through it and out of Sinclair's sight.

For a second he saw the monkey scuttle into view holding a tin cup, then, clear above the guffaws, the woman's voice rose, harshly reminding him of a huckster at a fair. He heard more laughter, then a tinny rattle of coins. The show was over. Shouted orders were followed by a crescendo of revving engines.

The encounter must have taken place at a crossroads, for when the caravan started again Sinclair felt it swaying to a right-angled turn, and the road surface was rougher. At least they were not travelling away from the coast now. He must get out as soon as

16

possible and rejoin the road. He lay still until he reckoned they must have covered a reasonable distance. Then he struggled up and retrieved his rifle from under the mattress.

He tapped on the forward door. It opened a crack and he peered through at an empty potholed road. But when he pushed the door wider, intending to jump, the woman pressed it back and spoke in an unexpectedly sweet clear voice, quite different from the harsh fairground tones he had last heard. The words were as incomprehensible as ever, but their message was clearly stressed; he must get under cover again. To his repetition of "St. Nazaire, *St. Nazaire,*" she merely nodded calmly. Then, as though to reassure him she cracked the whip above the horse's ears, and the pace increased.

Presently they turned off the road and creaked to a halt. The woman came through and opened a shutter, a shaft of sunlight falling on the bright red stain on the soldier's blouse. Gently the woman undid the buttons, her face concerned. The field dressing was soaked through. She replaced it with what looked like a wad of moss, smearing it first with some aromatic salve out of a rusty tin, then binding it firmly with a strip torn off the hem of her underskirt. The effect was extraordinarily soothing and comfortable.

They were halted on a sandy track under a clump of pines. The woman unharnessed the horse, then, when the shafts were down, she helped the old man down, reached up for a folding stool and seated him close to the wheel. He was still holding his flute; she stuck it in his pocket and substituted a clay pipe. Next she lit a small pressure stove which was soon hissing beneath a blackened billycan. Sinclair could barely restrain his impatience until he realized that whatever she was doing she remained wary as a poacher, eyes and ears alertly sweeping the countryside.

Lastly, accompanied by the dog with his little monkey jockey hanging around his neck, she walked quickly to the top of the rise and surveyed the land. Satisfied, she turned back and brewed bitter, strong tea, lacing Sinclair's mug from a small medicine bottle rummaged out of the old man's pocket.

The concoction flowed through Sinclair's veins like molten fire. As he sipped, she took a twig and made a sketch map on the sandy

17

ground; here was the road where they had picked him up, the crossroads where they had turned east; and here was a back road, that eventually met up with a secondary road leading into St. Nazaire. He followed her pointing finger to the south where, high up in the pale sky, puffs of gunsmoke expanded like parachutes. His arm rested on the donkey's back, the coarse, sunwarmed hair suddenly nostalgically familiar in this unreal world.

It was time to go. Unable to express his gratitude to this enigmatic, indomitable woman who had taken such risks for him, Sinclair simply patted the dog's head and felt in his pocket, luckily finding the remains of a biscuit. It was taken gently, then laid on the ground until the woman nodded.

The old man suddenly grunted and held out the medicine bottle. Only when he saw his offering stowed in the soldier's pocket did he sink again within his shawls—like a tortoise retracting into its shell. Sinclair said goodbye and set off up the sandy track. On the crest of the rise he looked back. The woman had her back turned as she fed the horse. Only the dog, and the monkey once more astride his back, watched his departure.

THE SOLDIER covered the ground in the easy strides of a Highlander, feeling surprisingly refreshed and alert. It could not be much more than ten miles to the coast and he reckoned on reaching the docks after nightfall, when the rescue ships could steal in under cover of darkness.

As he emerged into a narrow lane, he heard the engines of a Stuka, and almost immediately saw the plane sweep across the fields towards him. He wondered why, for there was nothing in the fields but a scattering of cattle. As he flung himself down into the ditch, with a gasp from the pain in his chest, the Stuka screamed over, its machine gun raising spurts of earth, pinging on the tin roof of a cattle shelter.

"Bloody lunatic," he shouted indignantly after it, then started off again, keeping a weather eye open for its return.

Presently, he was overtaken by his first military traffic—an RAOC sergeant pedalling along on an ancient bicycle. A slight young Lancashire Fusilier with grotesquely swollen feet, his boots slung around his neck, sat sideways on the crossbar. "Sorry, mate, full up," said the sergeant as he wobbled past.

Sinclair stepped out beside them for a few yards. "Watch out for a Daredevil of the Skies in a Stuka," he said. "The type that would shoot up a turnip field for the hell of it."

"*Him*—" said the sergeant, disgust flooding his face. "He conquered a couple of gypsies and a wagon back there. . . ."

"In a clump of pines—an old man and a woman?"

"I wouldn't know, but there were two bodies all right," said the sergeant. "The wagon was blazing—"

"They had animals?" asked Sinclair.

"I shot a horse," said the sergeant briefly, "and there was a donkey, but I missed it—it went off into the trees."

"There was a dog, and a monkey," said Sinclair wearily. "It was a little circus act."

"Probably copped it too," said the sergeant, and pedalled on down the road.

Sinclair walked on, reproaching himself that if they had not turned off the road for him they would still be alive—now they were all senselessly wiped out.

An hour later, as he turned to look back along the road, he saw, less than a hundred yards behind, a dog slinking along on the verge. Sinclair stood still for a moment. The dog stopped too, cowering. A tiny face with anxious eyes and wrinkled brows peered over the dog's head.

They were not ghosts; they were disconcertingly real. But they belonged to the dead, there was no place for them in his life, no time to spare for their plight. Turning abruptly, the soldier continued on his way, quickening his pace. Behind him the dog stretched out to maintain its imposed distance.

Nearer the town he saw a lone raider unload a stick of bombs across a field, the last bomb hitting the hedge and scooping a crater deep into the soft sands of the rabbit warrens there. The blast blew the rabbits out of their burrows like shells from the muzzle of a gun. They lay in a sickle-shaped cluster about twenty feet from the crater's rim, dead but outwardly unharmed, as though dropped there by some retrieving dog.

Sinclair stopped for a moment, unable to tear his eyes away. On the far side of the crater the dog suddenly appeared, standing utterly still, his head up as though pulled back by the monkey's hands around his throat. Two pairs of eyes stared unwaveringly at him. In a sudden blind rage he shouted and swore at them, desperate to drive them away. *They must not follow him into the seaport. They must find some other human—at some farmhouse perhaps.* "Get out!" he yelled. "Go back! Go away. . . . Shoo. . . . *Allez!*" He picked up a stone and threw it. The monkey buried its head, but the dog crouched steadfast, its eyes unwavering.

It was useless. Once more he turned his back. He set off at such a pace that he reached the outskirts of St. Nazaire shortly before sunset. Only then did he look back. They were still there. But in the town centre he lost his followers at last. Taking cover against the falling flak, he saw the dog momentarily, obviously terrified by the barrage, cowering against a wall; then, as shrapnel rained down, he bolted from cover, and the last Sinclair saw of him was the little grey animal streaking away down the cobblestones, veering wildly, the dark shape of the rider crouched low on the outstretched neck. Sinclair pressed himself into the stone arch of a garden wall, feeling both disquiet and relief. They had been incongruous enough before, but here their jockey-and-steed comicality was almost an outrage before the tragedy of a war-torn town. Behind the shuttered windows of a house, a crackling radio blared the Marseillaise.

The bombardment increased. It was dark before the first lull came and he found his way to the military control post. The blacked-out town was still full of troops, patiently awaiting embarkation orders. He had a mug of coffee at a canteen operating in a roofless church, then joined a file of silent men converging on the docks, but the bombardment started up again, and they scattered for shelter.

For hours he crouched within the sandbagged emplacement of a wrecked gun with a dozen or so other men. They dozed fitfully. Unable to ease his ribs into any comfortable position, Sinclair remained awake. Taking a packet of cigarettes out of his pocket he came across the medicine bottle. He drank to the generosity of the old man, and then to that fierce-eyed brave woman—and at that moment, almost as though summoned, he felt rather than saw the wraithlike presence of the dog, and the dark limpet blur that was the monkey. A nose touched his hand, then quested within his open battledress blouse, moving over the binding there. They had found him, the one tenuous link with their destroyed past; the old woman's scent on the strip of clothing that she had bound around his ribs.

The man beside him flicked a shaded lighter. "Cor," he said, "look what's here—" and a hand reached out to the monkey. But it gibbered fearfully and the dog whirled with bared teeth. Another hand proffered a piece of chocolate, but the dog, trembling violently, pressed closer to Sinclair, thrusting its head into the shelter of his arm. The monkey reached out to grab the edge of his blouse, then quickly thrust its head within. Sinclair knew nothing of monkeys, but some instinct caused him to cup a hand over its haunches and the little thing burrowed in. He did up the buttons, hoping that it would not sink its teeth in him later when he removed it.

But, when the order reached them to move, he paused, his hand irresolute over the buttons. The monkey was too small and human a burden to return to the shoulders of a small distraught dog. Even if he did so, it would not be easy to drive them away. He buttoned up his blouse. The medicine bottle had made him quite light-headed and carefree. Let them take their chance.

The dog kept close to his heels. Ahead groups of men were moving out of cover to the shaded pinprick of light that marked the gangway to a destroyer. As he awaited his turn he saw that two MPs on either side of the gangway were turning back with well directed boots the frantic attempts of a collie dog to board.

He bent down and felt around the neck of the grey blur at his feet. The bell was firmly attached to a metallic thread but he silenced it by wrenching out the clapper. The next time he looked down his shadow was no longer there. He shuffled forward in his turn and produced his identifying paybook, feeling the small warm stillness under his pocket as he did so. A naval officer, flanked by a keen-eyed master-at-arms, inspected his paybook briefly, glanced

21

up at his face, then down to the front of his battledress. Sinclair looked down too, resigned, expecting to find a tell-tale paw or tail sticking out, but "Wounded?" asked the officer.

"Not seriously, sir," said Sinclair.

"Report to the medical officer when you board the *Lancastria*," said the officer, his eyes already on the man behind him.

As he boarded the gangway, Sinclair could just make out a small form pressed against the canvas sides, only a few inches away from the gleaming boots of one of the MPs. Between the boots and the canvas was a space of some eight inches, and he marvelled at the strategic positioning of this extraordinary little dog. There was a momentary brushing, light as a feather, against the inside of one of his legs as he took the first step up the gangway, and as he stepped down at the end he felt it again.

It was impossible to move forward through the packed mass of humanity already on board the destroyer. He remained jammed agonizingly against the rail as they slipped away from the dock and headed towards the liner that lay at anchor three miles out. When they transferred to the *Lancastria*, it was impossible to distinguish anything among the boots milling in the darkness, but he had no doubt now that somewhere, at the end of his crossing to the liner, his shadow would attach itself to him again.

Everything on board the liner was proceeding with the calm efficiency of a peacetime cruise. White-jacketed stewards were everywhere. He was directed where to report, where to collect a life-jacket, where to stow his kit; he was allocated a mattress in No. 2 hold, and finally he was directed to the sick bay.

Scrub the sick bay, said Sinclair to himself, suddenly resolute. A medical officer would obviously take a dim view of the monkey. And scrub the mattress in No. 2 hold as well, he decided a minute later, feeling a strong revulsion against the constraint of walls and packed humanity. The upper deck might be packed too with huddled shapes, but above was the June night sky and fresh salt air. He made his way up and found a place beside a sleeping civilian at the end of a row of back-to-back seats; and even before he had wedged himself in, he was aware of a small shape slipping down the narrow tunnel formed at their base. After a while he put a hand down and smiled in satisfaction when he felt the touch of a nose. So far so good.

He had been handed two thick bullybeef sandwiches soon after boarding. He ate one, then took the meat out of the other and passed it behind him, but it remained uneaten on the deck. He pushed a crust inside his blouse, but drew no response from the monkey. It seemed to be asleep. Sinclair closed his eyes and dozed.

When he woke they were still at anchor, vulnerable, the men huddled under gas capes against the dawn chill. Sinclair felt around in his blouse—the slight bulge at his chest was no longer there.

The man beside him opened one eye. "The monkey which is emerged from your vestments is now there," he said in French-accented English, and pointed vaguely behind him. "It has sullied the floor," he added severely. "A sailor has expressed considerable chagrin." He closed the eye.

Sinclair was relieved; at least it was not his vestments that had been sullied. The chagrined deckhand must have dealt with the offence for there was no sign. Nor was there any sign of the offender or the dog; they must be deep in the fastness of their tunnel between the seats. He decided to leave well alone and went off to queue for a mug of tea and another sandwich. He had just emerged onto the upper deck again when, almost simultaneously with a shipboard uproar of alarm bells and gunfire, there came the scream of aircraft engines. The liner shuddered convulsively to two nearby explosions, and men flattened on the deck like a pack of cards as dark shapes passed over and veered off towards the coast before the gunfire. Grumbling, the men picked themselves up.

The morning wore on and still the *Lancastria* lay at anchor. Another raid at lunchtime was driven off, but two miles away a black pall of smoke hung over their sister ship, the *Oronsay*. She had received a direct hit. A sense of unease deepened and spread from group to grumbling group. Why didn't they push off now? There were reportedly over six thousand troops and civilians aboard—true, every now and then another handful of weary men would be brought aboard from a fishing boat, but was that enough to justify the risk to six thousand lives?

As though sensing the unrest, the dog crept out of shelter at last and pressed shivering against Sinclair's knees; woebegone and bedraggled with terrified eyes and tucked-in tail, he was almost unrecognizable from the jaunty little leader of the caravan. Sinclair noticed that almost the entire left flank of the close curled coat had been singed. The monkey, on the other hand, seemed quite unscathed. He sidled swiftly up to a nearby soldier, newly woken, about to light a cigarette. Quick as a flash, the monkey grabbed his lighter, then snatched the cigarette and stuffed it into his own mouth. Like a child showing off, the monkey rocked from foot to foot and gibbered triumphantly.

He made a lighthearted diversion, and the men around cheered him on. After a while Sinclair clicked his fingers as he had seen the woman do and, to his surprise, the little creature came immediately, running crablike over the deck to reach up and offer the lighter. Sinclair restored it to its owner. Someone produced a mouth organ and began to play. The monkey jigged around, deftly catching any pieces of chocolate or biscuit that were thrown—all of which he brought to Sinclair. The dog began to show a spark of interest; his eyes brightened and his ears crept up. But the interlude was all too short; minutes later the alert bells shrilled out again, while a voice came booming from a nearby tannoy speaker: "*Action stations! Action stations! Take cover—take cover. . . .*"

There was nowhere to take cover. Men flung themselves to the deck again, monkey and dog fled back into their tunnel, and, as the aircraft swept screaming towards them, the liner leaped and bucked to the blast of her own guns. Sinclair crouched at the end of the seats, hunching himself tightly. As though scoring some Olympian goal a bomb dropped down the ship's single funnel, exploding below the water line with such force that the *Lancastria* leaped like a mortally wounded animal.

A still second of shock followed, then the guns roared out again over the rattle of falling flak and twisted red-hot metal. The liner had listed sharply. Then, as the sea surged in far below the water line, she righted herself, wallowing in an ill-balanced roll. It could not be long before she turned turtle. Sinclair reached for his life-jacket. Clear above the bedlam of noise, a steady voice through a loud hailer directed men to remove their boots and jump now. Within minutes the deck angle began to tilt, so steeply that men, equipment, floats and seats avalanched together towards the rail.

Clinging onto the fixed seat as they kicked off their boots, Sinclair and the Frenchman waited until the area directly below was cleared; as they slithered down together the monkey leaped for his shoulder and clung on. The dog shot past, paws scrabbling.

"One, two, three, and over we go," said Sinclair, as the other man hesitated by the rail.

"As yet I am unable to swim," said the Frenchman in thin, precise tones, looking down with extreme distaste.

"You won't learn standing here," said Sinclair. "Here, put this on—" He pulled at the tapes of his jacket, trying to wrench it off: but the monkey had hold of his neck and clung on grimly.

The rail was within twenty feet of the water now. As he struggled to dislodge the monkey a lifeboat swung out on its davits a few yards away. There was a rush to fill it, but as the Frenchman climbed onto the rail Sinclair heaved, and the man was up and safely into the boat.

Sinclair was over the rail when he saw the dog, desperately balancing on the almost vertical deck. He scooped him up as he jumped. He knew he must get as far away as possible from the sucking vortex that would follow when the ship went down. He was mad to hinder himself with the dog. He released his grip and started swimming, encumbered by the life-jacket and breathless with pain. The dog paddled along easily beside him.

Behind him came a demented medley of noise, the hiss of escaping steam, sirens, whistles and shouts. Incredibly a machine gun was still firing. He heard the slapping crash as the lifeboat dropped free from the falls, and turning his head was suddenly aware that the monkey's arms were still wrapped around his neck.

A spar attached to part of a cane seat suddenly bobbed up in front of him; he grabbed it and rested for a moment. The dog's paws churned as he tried to get some purchase on the wood; he had almost succeeded when the spar rolled over. Choking, he bobbed up again, his eyes wild, his paws beating ineffectually.

Sinclair raised him by the scruff of his neck and rested the forepaws over his own forearm. If the dog had resisted him, he would have held its head under water then and there and put an end to it; but, almost as though recognizing the possibility, the dog hung on without struggling.

Sinclair turned to watch the last moments of the *Lancastria*. Her bows already under, she reared almost three-quarters of her length clear of the water, then slid inexorably to the depths, her siren still blaring.

Over the flat horizon, Sinclair saw an assorted fleet of boats converging on the area. The water was cold, but he felt confident he would be picked up soon—provided that he could swim out of reach of the oil, he thought, as he saw the first viscid blackness float up and begin to spread.

The grasp of the wood was comforting; he turned upwind, away from the oil slick, and paddled towards a distant destroyer. An empty lifeboat floated by, men clinging to the looped ropes on her sides. A small crate, empty and buoyant, both ends stove in, followed. He caught it, shoving the spar through until the cane seat jammed against the sides so that the spar now rode fairly steadily. He gave the dog a slight heave onto the half-submerged seat, and it crouched there shivering. At this, the monkey leaped onto the dog's back, then to the crate top, clear of the water.

Finally the oil reached them. The dog tried to scramble up beside the monkey on the crate top, still clear of oil. The crate rocked wildly; somehow the monkey hung on, but the dog slipped and fell back. Sinclair bent his elbow under its haunches, and the dog scrambled back onto the cane seat, the gleaming blue-black oil plastering his coat, all except the head.

Another lifeboat went by, dangerously low in the water. "What happened to your hurdy-gurdy, mate?" someone called. Then, "Hang on, lad," called another, "plenty of boats picking up now."

He could see them, the launches and lifeboats and whalers, zigzagging to and fro as they picked up survivors. But none came his way, although he waved and shouted, and he seemed to drift farther and farther away from the rescue ships. As the lonely hours wore on he became increasingly weak and at times light-headed.

His legs were numb with cold, and he knew that he must keep moving them, but all effort had become excruciating.

The monkey seemed to be shrinking; eyes closed, it looked impossibly fragile, huddled into its own enwrapping arms. But as he rested for a moment, it suddenly reached down and touched his eyebrow, withdrawing its fingers to examine the oil on them closely, sniffed them, plainly did not like the smell, and wiped them delicately on its as yet unplastered chest.

The dog crouched only inches before him, the oil-slicked coat sculpturing bone and muscle in shining blue-black relief. There were times when Sinclair felt the effort needed to hold on was too much, that it would be so much simpler just to let go and drift off into peaceful oblivion. Then always, just as he was slipping away, he would be jerked back to sharp lucidity, knowing that he must stay wakeful and cling onto the spar—even as these animals clung to their precarious raft—onto life itself.

He was almost unconscious, his legs still fractionally moving, his eyes fixed, when the dog began to bark. Close above his head, he heard a voice. He roused himself. "Grab the dog," he gasped.

He tried to take the scruff of the slimy black neck himself, but his fingers slipped. Arms reached out and he was hauled over the coaming of the boat, resting in agony on crunching ribs before he finally slithered down. Someone wiped his mouth and eyes, and eased off the cumbersome jacket. The whaler was filled with other slumped oil-black figures, and from all around came the sounds of retching and coughing. From these blacknesses, a small blackness detached itself and crawled to his side. He clung on to it in sudden fierce protectiveness and, still clinging, dropped off into unconsciousness at last.

PART TWO

Sick Berth Attendant Neil MacLean, of the destroyer HMS *Tertian*, was tending a group of walking wounded on deck when word reached him that the ship's whaler had been swung aboard and there was a man haemorrhaging in it. He called for a stretcher, and made his way forward through the jammed mass of soldiers. Only two men were left in the whaler. The one who was obviously the haemorrhage case MacLean sent as an emergency to the wardroom where the ship's doctor was working and turned his attention to the other man. The front of his battledress was stained bright red, a matching trickle running from his mouth. He bent down to take the man's pulse and his fingers suddenly came in contact with a warm slimy black mass. Part of the black mass split open to red and gleaming white, and a low warning snarl preceded the snapping together of the white gleam.

"*Mo ghaoil, an cu!*" said MacLean, reverting aloud to his native Gaelic.

The man's eyes opened and he answered in the same tongue: "Leave the dog be."

"I'll leave him all right," said MacLean with a sour look at the teeth so close to his hands as he investigated the Highlander's wound. "I need my hands the day."

The man struggled to sit up. "Stay where you are," said MacLean sharply, and called back for another stretcher. But the soldier suddenly strained up in such wild incoherence that MacLean had to hold him down.

"The animals—the monkey—where are they?" The man's words came in such panting distress that MacLean felt certain one lung must have been pierced by a rib fragment.

"Resting—lying back *resting*," said MacLean smoothly. He felt in his satchel for an ampoule.

"The horse—" panted the soldier, barely audible. "The rabbits —*all* those rabbits, they were innocent—I tell you, they were *innocent* . . . even the bear."

"All having a nice wee rest the now," crooned MacLean hypnotically as he slid in the needle.

When they came to move the man to a stretcher his hand groped wildly across his chest.

"All right, all right," said MacLean. "Lie still, for God's sake, the dog's there—no one's going to take it away."

He stood up; there were others awaiting him. From the throng of exhausted bodies, a civilian, fully clothed, clean and dry, eased

28

through, as though summoned, and squatted down beside the stretcher. "It is I," he announced formally, and the soldier's eyes opened and crinkled in recognition.

"You know him?" said MacLean, and the French civilian nodded. "Keep him from moving, then, until the drug takes effect. Rub his legs, and try to keep him warm—and watch out, there's a dog underneath the blanket—"

"Yes," said the helper, already busy. "*And* that one—*le singe*," he added, cocking an eye at a point overhead. MacLean looked too: on the superstructure, twenty feet above, was the tiny huddled figure of a monkey, one hand doubled loosely on its knee, the other stuffed in its mouth, its eyes fixed on the head of the dog below. At least there was no sign of the soldier's other innocents, the decks so far clear of horse, rabbits, or bear. MacLean departed.

An hour later he returned. The drug had done its work and the soldier drowsed. The Frenchman had managed to ease off his oil-soaked battledress, and had cleaned him up. MacLean looked down on the pale, clear-skinned face, black hair and dark blue eyes of a Highlander. The dog lay close by on the battledress blouse. But as the soldier tried to speak, and went into an agonizing spell of coughing, it crept on its belly to the head of the stretcher, there to lay its muzzle on the edge.

"I will do his talking," said the dry precise voice of the Frenchman as MacLean worked swiftly to change the dressing. "He wishes to tell you that he is not wounded, that he must walk off this ship, for he has these two companions who have come a long way with him. They have no one else apparently. He is obsessed. They are a trust. He must walk off, for if he goes to hospital he will be separated from them, and this is insupportable."

The dog lifted its head, and its inflamed eyes under the matted hair looked directly into MacLean's. He shifted his gaze to the soldier. "Ach, don't fash yourself so, man," he said with professional mendacity. "No need to worry—you just leave it to us."

"I have your hand on it?" the Highlander managed to whisper. His hand moved on the blanket, and the dog stretched forward to touch it with his muzzle. "You'll see to him?"

But there was a difference between the professional assurance and the binding promise of his word; for a moment MacLean hesitated. The dog's eyes watched him. A voice shouted urgently for him, and he rose. The dog rose too, still watching. "Aye," he said. The word was seemingly forced out of him. Then he repeated it firmly, "Aye, I'll see to him. You have my hand on it."

He passed by several times that night, each time half-expecting to find the blanket pulled over the man's face, but he seemed to be sleeping, and his pulse was stronger. The Frenchman was nodding beside him, only the dog watchful and suspicious as he bent over the stretcher.

Early in the morning, as he turned back the blanket, he found the monkey curled into a small tight ball between the soldier's arm and chest. MacLean's lips pursed with displeasure, but the dog growled fiercely when he tried to move the little animal. He left well alone—let it go ashore on the stretcher undetected; he wished the medical orderlies joy in its discovery. His promise had been for the dog alone. With that in mind his hand descended with practised skill upon its muzzle; he deftly inserted three pills down an instantly submissive throat, and bundled a jacket over it. The rails were lined with silent watching men as the shores of England loomed out of the mist. It would not be long before they disembarked. He would return for his bundle in good time.

BY THE TIME the *Tertian* docked at Falmouth the port health and quarantine officials were ready for the four-footed camp followers who trailed the British Army, even in retreat. A man with a large net on the end of a pole was stationed beside the police and an RSPCA van stood waiting.

The last of the wounded ashore, Neil MacLean leaned for a short respite over the *Tertian*'s rail and watched the scene below. Only minutes before the helpful Frenchman had waved back as he went down the gangway. Now MacLean saw an angry cat removed from a soldier's gas mask haversack, while several dogs that he had not even seen aboard were led off to the van. Then something that looked like a ferret or a white rat gave itself away by peering out of the blanket folds around the neck of one of the walking wounded, and was plucked out gingerly, despite its owner's protestations that it was British-born and only coming home like him.

There had been no inspection of the stretcher cases, however: the monkey would have made it safely ashore. MacLean watched the loaded ambulances speeding off with some satisfaction. As the bo'sun's pipe summoned all hands to clean ship, he turned to go, yawning, longing to get his head down for a few minutes. A small smacking noise attracted his attention; ten feet above his head, huddled dismally on the inner ring of a lifebuoy hanging over the bridge rail, was the monkey. It smacked its lips again softly and looked for a moment as though about to jump down.

MacLean scowled up at it, furious that it had outwitted him. At that moment the quayside siren, almost directly alongside, started on its first wailing crescendo and the *Tertian*'s alarm bells shrilled into action a second later. The monkey fled, swarming up the wireless mast, fouling the deck as it went. MacLean gazed gloomily after it; then he turned through the steel door and clattered down to the sick bay.

The doctor had gone ashore with some of the wounded. The cabin reeked, and looked as though a hurricane had hit it. He opened the scuttle wide, took off his jacket and rolled up his shirt sleeves. It was very quiet now that the ship had settled into the waiting silence of action stations, and he was safe from interruption at least until the All Clear sounded. Nevertheless, he drew the door curtain across.

From the cupboard under the bunk, he drew out a large cardboard box marked Boracic Lint and turned back the brown paper lying on top. Inside, on an evil-smelling oily blanket, eyes closed, but with its flanks moving steadily up and down, was the dog. The heavy sedative would ensure that it remained this way for several more hours—by which time he hoped he might have some more inspiration as to its future.

He threw the blanket on a pile of soiled linen in the corner, lifted out the limp bundle and laid it on a rubber sheet on the bunk. Then he went to work with swabs and surgical spirit. Towelling the result dry, he looked down on the small body with professional satisfaction. The coat was revealed as a closely curled blue-grey, the hair singed off in a large area on one flank.

He looked with a critical eye at the lines of the dog. It had the proportions and apparent fragility of bone that suggested poodle blood at first sight; but the hindquarters were exceptionally powerful and there was an unusual depth of chest; there was the high-domed forehead that he usually associated with present-day overbreeding—and the stupidity to go with it—but this dog had an unexpected width between the eyes. The muzzle was short, clean cut and pointed. He pulled back the lips and examined the teeth: shining white, but very slightly worn, and he decided that the dog must be about six or seven. A slight parting in the hair around the neck caught his attention: close against the skin was a strand of ribbon through which ran a single metallic thread. He cut it off, finding that it ran through the ring of a tiny silver bell with the clapper missing. He dropped the ribbon into a basin of solvent, wiped it off, and put it in his pocket.

The All Clear went, and he was galvanized into action. Scooping up the dog, he wrapped it in a dry towel, then laid it in the middle of the soiled pile, covering it loosely. As boots clattered and voices rang out, he drew back the curtain and was hard at work when the first figures passed by the open door. By the time the MO returned, he was seated at the desk filling in forms. Apart from the stained pile by the door, the sick bay wore its usual look of shining efficiency.

The doctor congratulated him, and told him to turn in for a couple of hours while he could—the buzz was that they would return to sea as soon as they had been revictualled. MacLean asked him a few questions about the shore evacuation of the wounded, then tied the four ends of a sheet around the bundle by the door and picked it up.

"If you will not be wishing anything further, sir, I will be taking this lot ashore," he said.

"Go and get your head down, man, and to hell with that lot," the young doctor said. "And that's an order—just lose it overboard, and we'll indent for more."

"We already have, sir," said MacLean primly, and departed.

He took the bundle down to the mess which he shared with the acting petty officers when the destroyer was in port. At sea, he slept in the sick bay. The mess was deserted except for APO Reid who was trying to clear the decks of litter. MacLean did not trouble to conceal anything from Reid; he was a close-mouthed individual. He slid the towel-wrapped bundle of dog out on the deck, turned back an edge to reassure himself, then lifted it into the bottom of his locker. After checking that the ventilation slits at the bottom were not blocked, he locked the door.

"Been liberating something?" asked Reid.

"A dog," said MacLean.

"Looked dead," observed Reid, fishing a pair of braces and three socks from under the table.

"Doped," said MacLean sitting down. "See here," he added, rare persuasion in his voice, "you never saw it—neither did I. When we're at sea, it appears and that's that—something else left behind by the pongos. No one's going to heave a poor wee dog like that overboard, is he?"

"Wouldn't put it past the buffer," said Reid, referring to the master-at-arms who was reputed to have a copy of King's Regulations instead of a heart. "What do you want a dog for, anyway? You must be barmy."

Useless to explain to this hard-headed Yorkshireman that he and that wounded soldier shared a common tongue and heritage, that their birthright alone imposed an obligation. "I'm doing it for a kinsman," MacLean said simply. "I might need a hand—there would be a pint or two in it," he added cautiously.

Reid put a boot to his heap of oddments. "Would there be a meal thrown in with the pints perhaps?" he said at last.

"Aye, there would be that," agreed MacLean, and went off to scrounge a mug of tea out of the galley.

"Didn't you do some kind of work with animals in civvy street?" asked the assistant cook. "Do you know anything about monkeys?"

"A bit," said MacLean cautiously.

"Then you'd better get up to the foredeck," said the cook. "There's one there and they can't get it down. The chief's in a proper tear about it."

Armed with some nuts, MacLean made his way up to the foredeck. The monkey was clinging to the wireless mast. The chief petty officer was directing two ratings to its capture, and there was a lot of encouraging banter from the rest of the work party. It looked infinitely small and pitiful, the skin loosely shrivelled, the oil-streaked face pinched and furrowed within its frame of fur. As he joined the ring of men, the monkey's head turned towards him. "Tch, tch, tch," he said and recognition came into the eyes. It reached out an arm.

"All right, you try, MacLean," said the chief disgustedly. "You try and get the little perisher down."

MacLean held out the nuts. The monkey dropped down at once and scuttled to his feet where he grasped a trouser leg and gazed earnestly up at his face. It put out a hesitant paw, then took a few nuts, stuffing them listlessly into its mouth with forefinger and thumb. The watching group to a man admired this prodigious feat with sentimental smiles, and even the chief's face relaxed for a moment before he recollected himself.

"Come now," he said. "Smartly now, before the first lieutenant comes along and says what the hell's going on."

Suddenly the monkey took things into its own paws; reaching for MacLean's hand, it swung itself up into the crook of his arm and clung around his neck. It was shivering, yet there was a dry heat to its body that MacLean's mind associated immediately with other ailing monkeys in other days.

"Right," said the chief petty officer briskly. "Now, MacLean, if you'll just double off to the harbour police with it, and you, Wainwright, swab that mucky deck down, we'll get on with the job of running this ship—" but the last of his words were drowned by the wail of sirens and, as the ship's alarm bells followed, the group scattered to their stations. The monkey burrowed its head deeply into MacLean's jacket.

"Hang on to it, MacLean," bellowed the chief against the uproar, "Get it below and . . ."

As MacLean ducked in through the steel doorway, he covered the monkey's head with his hand against the noise. It rewarded him by vomiting down his jacket.

34

The doctor was still sitting in the sick bay, his feet on the desk, his eyes closed. MacLean coughed gently. "The chief sent me down with one of the *Lancastria*'s lot that got left behind, sir."

The doctor opened his eyes and took in the monkey without any change of expression. "The army's really scraping the bottom of the barrel," he said. "What is it, and what's it complaining of?"

"A Capuchin monkey, sir, suffering from exposure and possible pneumonia," said MacLean with equal gravity.

The doctor sighed, removed his feet from the desk, and took a stethoscope out of the drawer. "Take a deep breath, Capuchin," he said. Then as the monkey bared its teeth, "*Your* patient, I think, MacLean," he added generously, and watched with sleepy interest as the patient submitted to having its eyes swabbed out, drops administered and M & B tablets crushed up in water and poured down its throat without a drop being spilled.

MacLean was a reticent man, and apart from once prying out the fact that he had worked for a vet and in an animal laboratory before joining up at the outbreak of war, the doctor knew little of him other than what he had observed. He spent his off-duty time in the sick bay, when it was empty, reading and knitting. Very much a loner, neither liked nor disliked by his shipmates, he ran the sick bay and dispensary with impersonal extreme efficiency. The lead-swinger got short shrift, but he could show unsparing gentleness towards the seriously ill. In the six months that he had been on board, the doctor could not fault him in any of his duties.

Finally the monkey was briskly and neatly cocooned in cotton wool and a towel. "Very professional," the doctor said approvingly, "and now what?"

"The boiler room," said MacLean as he departed, with a look of profound distaste at the bundle in his arms, to install it in a cardboard box with some holes punched out in the lid.

Three hours later, the *Tertian* cast off from the tanker and slipped away from Falmouth, heading for the open Atlantic. The *Tertian* was what was known in the navy as a "happy ship": from the day she was commissioned, her officers and men had shaken down into that mysterious chance medley that makes such a ship,

35

and into which the two animals were easily assimilated. Besides, she was only living up to her name of the Ark, a nickname that had followed inevitably when Lieutenant Commander Andrew Knorr, RN, was appointed to her command.

As well as being the "owner" of the Ark and a flaming red beard, Knorr also possessed the legendary Barkis, some seventy amiable pounds of solid white bull terrier who had conformed to life in a destroyer almost as though he had evolved there. And, while the officers and men of Knorr's Ark admired and respected their skipper for qualities such as unruffled seamanship and a unique—and contagious—general enthusiasm, Barkis regarded him merely as a willing, easily taken-in slave. So that, when Knorr eventually issued an official warning that any infringement of ship's discipline traceable to the new arrivals on board would result in them being dumped overboard forthwith, no one was unduly alarmed.

The dog had been discovered in the mess room locker, most fortuitously by none other than APO Reid, who duly reported its presence to the buffer, receiving the sole comment, "Flaming Ark is flaming right." The master-at-arms in turn reported it to the first lieutenant, who inquired hopefully whether it was large enough to devour the ship's fecund cat Hyacinthe, and then reported it to the captain, who instructed the officer of the watch to enter it in the ship's log. Finally SBA MacLean volunteered to assume responsibility. So, officially, one dog had been processed through all the proper channels, and was now on the ship's strength.

But, even if he had understood, this knowledge would have been little consolation to the small newcomer in the sick bay, straining to keep his balance, even his faculties, in a heaving nightmare of confusion and terror.

He had lived his entire life on the open road, safe within a small nomadic world of which he was the beloved and valued centre. In one flame-seared moment that world had gone, and with it all security. He had come through the terrors of fire and water to waken now in an unstable steel box filled with the hurrying boots of strangers and fearful incessant noise. It was an inhuman

36

metallic world. Above all, it was the loneliest of worlds, with only the slightest association of voice and smell between MacLean, the brusque stranger who now ordered his life, and that soldier who had been his only link with his lost world.

A rope collar had been fashioned for him to stop him sliding around the deck and he was kept tied up with only brief forays on the end of a line to where the depth charges were secured over the stern. Here, in an area frequently washed down by following seas, Barkis came to lift his Olympian leg or squat, and here, to this sterile, salty substitute for trees and fragrant earth, came the trembling newcomer, creeping low, hesitantly testing the deck as though expecting it to give way beneath him, or scrabbling desperately for purchase as it heeled. Barkis displayed a generous interest when they met there, but the exuberance of his greeting only terrified the little dog even more.

All the spark had gone out of him. He spent the hours tensely crouched in the dark obscurity of the kneehole under the sick-bay desk, or under the table. The engaging topknot had been cut off, the hair on his ears trimmed short: he was drearily unattractive in his misery, and he had become very thin. He had been taught never to eat anything offered by strangers. Only one familiar hand had slipped titbits into his expectant mouth. Food had always meant a shared intimacy at the end of the day's work or travel, the woman's plate or the pot to lick clean afterwards, perhaps a morsel fallen from the old man's fingers, a handout from the monkey—and, if there were any doubts over the rights, there had always been her smiling nod of reassurance. There had been no isolated bowl set before him, to be eaten alone.

MacLean attributed the dog's refusal of proper food to a combination of seasickness and changed environment. But as the days passed, and his charge continued to exist on a just adequate diet of porridge, gravy and cod-liver oil, all of which he lapped up with tidy apathy, MacLean tried seasick remedies, put sulphur in the drinking water; he mixed conditioning powders and emptied them down the unprotesting throat. Vitamin pills by the handful followed. He even tried feeding by hand: but his disapproval being communicated through his fingers he achieved nothing.

The dog's dejection and constant shivering irritated MacLean exceedingly: it went against his professional grain. For the first time in his life, he had encountered an animal whose will to resist his was unyielding. He even consulted the doctor.

"My prescription would be time," the doctor said, looking sympathetically at the abject huddle at MacLean's feet. "Time—and lots of TLC."

"TLC?"

"Tender Loving Care—plus, plus," said the doctor, happily writing "TLC" on a medical form. "Patient's name, rank, and number?" he asked.

"It hasn't got a name," said MacLean, stiffly.

The doctor looked up in genuine astonishment. "Well, you might start in right there with the treatment—at least give it a personality, poor little devil," he said. "I wouldn't feel like eating myself if I were nothing but an It," he added, half to himself, as MacLean departed. And he wondered, not for the first time, at the complex nature of his SBA.

In his job of censoring the crew's letters, among this week's batch there was one that the doctor read twice:

HMS TERTIAN
c/o GPO
July 1st 1940

Dear Corporal Sinclair,

It is my sincere hope that when this reaches you, you will be well on the road to recovery. I write this line just to tell you that I have your belongings in safe keeping. I found the enclosed souvenir among them and enclose it for luck. The clapper was missing, but I have fashioned another.

I would be glad to receive a line from you. There seems little likelihood that I will be able to dispatch the above mentioned article for some time as we are kept on the hop just now. But I will see to it that it reaches you in good condition one day as promised.

Yours sincerely,
Neil MacLean, SBA

It was the first letter of MacLean's that the doctor ever remembered. "*Very* interesting," he said to himself, wielding the censor stamp, and was immensely tempted to write "and bow-wow to you too!" under its imprint. "Very interesting but *why* . . . ?" He replaced a tiny brightly polished silver bell, neatly cocooned in a pillbox.

MacLean wasted no deep thought on a name. He had been brought up on a farm where each succeeding sheepdog had inherited the name of its predecessor. Thus there was always a Ria if it were a dog, and a Meg if it were a bitch. This was therefore a Ria. It was as simple as that. So, phoenix-like, and most sadly, this new dog, Ria, arose from the ashes of his former life; as unlike that other as it was possible to be: no hint of the vivacious little professional in this stricken-eyed cowering shadow.

In contrast, shipboard life was warm and happy for the monkey. Leading Seaman Lessing, who had owned a Capuchin monkey in civilian life, had interested himself in its welfare from the beginning, when it had been housed, a sick, listless bundle, in a cardboard box in one of the boiler rooms. Here it had received the best clinical attention from MacLean, but grew daily more apathetic. Lessing insisted that if the little animal did not have constant contact with a living being it would simply pine away, no matter how excellent the treatment.

He took matters into his own hands one day and removed the monkey to the mess deck. Here it almost immediately became a distinct personality, with a name, Louis, the beginnings of a wardrobe, and some fifteen willing subjects. For days, Louis was never out of someone's arms or stuffed inside the comforting warmth of a jersey or duffle coat, and by the time it was decreed that he was fit enough to be left to his own devices on the deck for a while, he was everyone's concern.

A seaboot stocking had been neatly tailored to make a pullover: he already owned one pair of knitted shorts with a second pair on the needles: and other hands had netted a small hammock.

Number Five Mess was an incredibly cramped and congested kingdom, directly above the ship's magazine. Yet in it some fifty men, divided between the port and starboard watches, lived, slept and had their comfortless being. Louis thrived there. There was always company, always something going on.

Even when all hands turned out to action stations and Louis was tethered by a collar and chain to a table, he was still not alone, for there were always two hands stationed at the ammunition whips leading up from the magazine. If nothing was happening he would occupy himself endlessly polishing the table with a much-prized yellow duster in one hand, an empty tin of polish in the other. At the first explosion of guns or depth charges, however, he hopped into his hammock and covered his head in the folds of a long woollen scarf.

ON LEAVING FALMOUTH, the Ark had proceeded to Gourock to find that she was now on Atlantic convoy escort duty. The first few hundred miles outward bound to Halifax were an exhausting grind, but the U-boats were not yet ranging right across the Atlantic, and there was an area of a few hundred miles, a Tom Tiddler's ground, where the convoy dispersed to continue alone or with Canadian-based protection, and the Ark turned back with the homeward-bound convoy. Before she steamed back into the range of the U-boats, there was a brief and blessed interlude when there was time to sleep, to eat a hot meal and for the off-duty watch in Number Five Mess to bring out a harmonica or a concertina and entertain—and be entertained by—their mascot.

The moment any music started, Louis would bob up and down until someone found his enamel mug, then break into a kind of shuffling dance. He expected applause, and when he got it would make the rounds with an enamel mug for reward. If the monkey was a relaxing diversion to tired, tense men, they in turn gave him everything he could have wished for: love, company, adulation, warmth and comfort. He even had his own place at the table where he downed thick cocoa or very sweet tea from his own mug, and picked at whatever delicacies the messman and his mates could heap upon his plate.

If he lacked one thing in his little kingdom of Number Five Mess, that was the other half of his life's act, his steed and companion, the dog.

MACLEAN NEVER intended that dog and monkey should meet, but he had not reckoned on Ria's nose. One day he returned to the sick bay after treating the monkey for a minor skin ailment. He laid his jacket over the chair, then turned to wash his hands. Under the desk, Ria stirred into sudden life as one of the jacket sleeves hung before him. He sniffed intently, his stumpy tail quivered and one ear went straight up. Somewhere in this steel maze was hidden another living part of him! Like a pinpoint of light glimpsed at the end of a long dark tunnel, there must come a time when his nose would surely lead him to it. . . .

Then, a few days later, a stoker was admitted to the sick bay, seriously scalded and in great pain. The Ark was in mid-Atlantic, still within U-boat range, and under attack most of the way. In such conditions, with a drip running into his arm, the stoker needed almost constant attention until he could be transferred at the turn-round point. APO Reid undertook the charge of Ria in the mess, and for the next five or six days MacLean took what sleep he could on a chair by the sick-bay cot.

The first evening, spelled off for supper by the doctor, he went to snatch a meal in the mess, only to find Reid asleep, Ria wedged in at his back, his ears laid back in dog guilt. "Get down, you," said MacLean sharply. "That's no place for a dog."

Reid opened his eyes and smiled up at him. "Why don't you just push off—and *quietly*, there's a good soul," he said gently. "We need our sleep—" He pulled the blanket over his face. Ria's apprehensive eyes peered over his back—then disappeared quickly before the look they received.

MacLean swallowed his warmed-up food, gulped a mug of tea, and returned to his patient. Reid lay awake for a minute or two, one hand absently fondling the dog's ear, then he huddled down under the blanket again, falling asleep almost instantly. Curled up to his back, Ria closed his eyes, heaved a long relaxed sigh of utter content, and slept too.

Perhaps because of the warm security of this first contact, and the cameraderie that came his way in the following days now that the dog was free of MacLean's disapproving eye, perhaps because he now had a purpose, Ria's confidence gradually returned.

41

First, and most important, he found his sea legs. Previously he had had to be carried up and down ladders. Now Reid, by encouragingly placing his paws one after another on the rungs, persuaded him to scramble up. After that he soon learned to come down again, using all four paws, head foremost.

His next step forward was to show some initiative. Fear and the ladder had imprisoned him in the mess. Now the second barrier was down, and he soon overcame the first. He climbed the ladder many times, staying at the top to survey the passing world and assay its scents for longer and longer intervals. Then, in the comparative quiet of the middle watch, he set off on his quest, urged on always by his nose. He traversed the familiar route to the stern, then step by wary step past the throbbing terrors of the engine-room hatch, up and down companionways, along passageways, hastening now to a growing certainty; and then down the final steep ladder. . . .

He crouched for a moment, unobserved, searching through the blue haze of tobacco smoke. A terrible journey, but at the end of it he had found a part of his lost self again—there, perched on a man's shoulder, eating a potato, was the monkey.

Lessing, sitting with his back to the ladder, thought for a moment that Louis had gone mad. The monkey suddenly jumped from his shoulder, squeaking and chattering, swung from the overhead pipes to another shoulder, where he rammed his potato into a sailor's open mouth in passing, then somersaulted off onto the deck and scuttled down the length of the mess.

Now Lessing saw the cause of the excitement—MacLean's dog. Louis leaped for him, clasping him tightly around his neck. The ship rolled heavily and they skidded down the slope coming to rest against the hammock rack from which Hyacinthe the cat had been surveying the vulgar human world before her. Hyacinthe exploded, Louis grabbed her tail. She turned—it seemed even in mid air—and raked his forearm so that he squeaked in pain, whereupon the dog went for her. The deck rose again, and the yipping, squeaking, spitting tangle of mixed fur skidded back and forth and finished up under the table where Lessing doused the uproar with a mug of water.

It was a spectacular first entrance, and received the applause it deserved. Hyacinthe stalked off to soothe her ruffled dignity in the galley. Lessing dried off the whimpering Louis, and Ria solicitously licked the scratch. The end of his tail quivered like a tuning fork, and every inch of him was vibrant and eager. Ria had come to life once more.

This monkey haven was where he wanted to be too, and in the remaining days of freedom he made his way to it whenever possible. Reid was well aware of what was going on, but as Ria was always punctiliously returned by Lessing or one of his messmates, by unspoken agreement nothing was ever said, and MacLean remained in ignorance of his charge's double life.

Now a bright-eyed eager little dog would appear in Number Five Mess, leaping down the ladder to be greeted with an enthusiastic welcome in general and with rapturous affection by Louis. Inevitably Ria was offered food and invariably it was refused—until the day he happened to arrive during a meal. Louis was guddling around in his own mess tin, picking out the choicest parts first as usual, and as Lessing watched he picked out a morsel that did not seem to meet with his approval, for he lobbed it over to the dog. It was caught and swallowed in a flash, and Ria moved closer, wagging his tail, his ears cocked expectantly. He was not disappointed: so engrossed in his plate that he did not bother to look up, Louis held out his paw with another reject, and Ria took it gently. When Louis had finished, he moved in and polished the mess tin clean. Lessing gave him some of his own dinner and that disappeared too.

Unaware that this was the first solid food the dog had eaten, his appetite seemed only natural to Lessing. But he was astute enough to recognize quickly that Ria would never eat unless he, Lessing, were having his own meal at the same time.

The day came all too soon when the Ark turned back on the homebound passage, and MacLean's stoker-patient was transferred.

And there Ria's freedom ended, for shortly afterwards, clattering down Number Five Mess ladder in an explosive mixture of anger and anxiety came MacLean, infuriated to find Ria, a look of almost besotted pleasure on his face, being groomed by the

monkey, the centre of a watching ring as absorbed as Louis himself.

He called twice but, beyond laying his ears back apologetically, Ria did not stir. MacLean strode over and picked up the dog, but Louis hung on determinedly. There was a titter of restrained laughter as scarlet-faced, he tried to prise the monkey loose.

Lessing came to help. "Leave him till the watches change," he suggested as he disengaged paws. "Louis always lets him go then without any fuss," and as MacLean's mouth remained closed like a rat trap, "I'll bring him back myself," he added hopefully.

"The dog has no business to be here, now or any time. Come, you," said MacLean, and turned to go. His reluctant shadow fell in at his heels only after being dragged the first few feet.

"Come on, Doc, be a sport—" wheedled the rest of Number Five Mess. "Give them a treat—poor little orphans, they don't get many."

For a second, MacLean hesitated. He was exhausted, and there was nothing he wanted to do more than get his head down for a few hours. But in that moment of indecision, Louis struggled free and scampered across to hang on to Ria's tail, so endearingly comical in his too-long shorts and white rollneck jersey that a roar of laughter went up, increasing as the dog's tail wagged furiously and the tiny body at the end of it quivered in rhythm, the shorts dropping lower and lower. Then they dropped down altogether, Louis trying to pull them up and out of the way with one hand as he held on grimly to the tail with the other.

"I'll thank you to get yon brute of a monkey off," said MacLean venomously to Lessing.

Lessing pried the furiously protesting Louis loose. He made one last attempt. "But why *not* let them be together when they can? He's sort of settled down here with Louis. Why don't you give it a try, anyway?"

"The dog's settled—with *me*," said MacLean. "*I'm* responsible, and I'll not have any daft to-ing and fro-ing all over this ship— free to make a nuisance of itself where it shouldn't be," with a meaningful scowl at Louis as he picked up Ria and left.

When he reached the upper deck, MacLean put Ria down and

45

made his way aft in the darkness to lean over the guardrail and watch the straight white wake roll out behind as the Ark steamed steadily on the starboard flank of the convoy. He was bitterly regretting his promise and the subsequent complications—the dog's baffling resistance and, above all, the disquieting intrusion into the ordered fastnesses of his mind. His thoughts churned over the humiliating episode with the monkey. An explosive "Come!" brought Ria slinking to his heels, and he turned abruptly and vanished through the hatchway.

Back in the sick bay, he filled the kidney basin that now bore the label "Dog only" with water and set it down before Ria, then shook out the daily ration of vitamin pills from a bottle and grimly dropped them down Ria's submissive throat. The empty dish was carefully washed and put away. He removed his shoes and jacket and turned in on the cot. Ria lay down by the open door. Two minutes later MacLean was asleep. Two hours later Ria still lay with his head on his paws, his dark eyes wide open and unseeing.

NEIL MACLEAN would have been astonished, even offended, if he had heard himself being described in Number Five Mess as a "little tyrant". He was merely discharging an obligation with the utmost conscientiousness.

He came from crofter stock in a thriving west Highland farm, the youngest son, the seventh, a sickly asthmatic child in a family of tall strong brothers. A strong aroma of Friar's Balsam from the steaming asthma kettle perpetually enveloped him, with pungent overtones of the eucalyptus oil with which his wheezing chest was rubbed. His family, therefore, did not find it altogether surprising when, as he grew older, he seemed to be able to subdue or dominate the farm animals by his presence alone: small wonder that before fierce waves of Vicks Vapour Rub, the most recalcitrant cow, the wildest of dogs, the maddest of bulls seemed to be almost anaesthetized into submission.

On account of his dread wheezing, he was sent to the drier climate of inland Morayshire to board with an aunt, and to go to school there. The improvement was dramatic, but a residue of his strange power over animals remained, and was recognized by an astute local vet who took the boy on to help in the school holidays at first, then later as a full-time assistant when he left school.

He became the most efficient and percipient handler of animals that the vet had ever experienced, and he helped the young man towards the goal of veterinary college. But after two academically successful years of college, he suddenly quit. He returned to his assistant's job, and the disappointed vet could get nothing out of him other than that "studying and the like was no the life".

He had married eventually. As mysteriously as he did most things, he returned from a holiday on the island of Mull with a sonsy, red-haired girl, who laughed at him and loved him. Two and a half idyllic years later, on a visit to her parents, Margaret was drowned crossing to Iona in her father's boat. Only her father's body was washed up; the sea kept for ever his Margaret and all that had been their life.

His face expressionless as stone, Neil MacLean gave his notice to the vet and with a letter of recommendation to the director of an animal laboratory in London, he left Morayshire for ever.

It was not long before he became the head attendant in charge of the laboratory animals; and the meticulous conditions in which they now lived became a byword. No animal ever bit his ministering hand, no animal cowered away from him; and no animal ever greeted him with pleasure. His uncanny but dispassionate power could not have found a better outlet. He treated the inmates as machines to be kept in perfect working order.

He volunteered the day after war broke out and, when his veterinary and hospital experience were revealed, the medical officer recommended him for training as a sick-berth attendant.

This, then, was the rigid complex little man, bitterly inturned, to whom fate had sent a cherished extrovert of a dog. If MacLean could have admired any dog enough to wish it for his own it would have been one like the captain's great barrel-chested Barkis, certainly not a small shivering animal who could not even face his food, and allowed a doll-sized monkey liberties.

So Ria, who was only what he was, a dog to amuse, grew increasingly bewildered by MacLean's disapproval. But his needs were too strong now. Time and time again, when MacLean was

47

occupied he would judge the moment to vanish. If tied, he slipped the collar or bit through the line, then went straight to the haven of Number Five Mess. Invariably he was retrieved, invariably he returned; and no appeal from Lessing or anyone could persuade MacLean to change his mind and permit the visits.

But the strain was beginning to tell. MacLean found himself dreading the trip to the lower deck. And his worry over Ria's lack of appetite increased too, for now this disconcerting animal was beginning to show distaste even for his carefully fortified porridge mix, and seemed to be living on water alone.

Inevitably came the time when he was confronted with the scene of Ria and Louis sharing a mess tin—worse still, the monkey was actually feeding the dog, his delicate little hands fishing out delicacies which were then tossed into the waiting eager mouth.

"He's right hungry today," said the innocent Lessing, looking up from his own plate. "Scoffed his own, and now he's after something from Louis. Meat, potatoes, beans—the lot. Did you know he could sit up and salute? He's a sharp one—"

But his last words were directed to MacLean's back; overcome with revulsion and mortification, he had said nothing—but so forcibly that for once Ria leaped with alacrity up the ladder before him and made straight for his proper obscurity under the desk, regardless of the fact that the doctor's feet were already there. He was only too well aware that once again he had offended.

"You look very guilty, my lad," said the doctor. "What have you been up to this time?"

He pressed against these friendly legs for protection. But it was Barkis who would be his saviour that day. Barkis's claws to be exact: they had to be cut. For this painless operation three men had to hold him down, while a fourth wielded the clippers.

"You're wanted on the bridge," said the doctor as a set-faced MacLean appeared. "Operation Toenails, you lucky chap. I did the job last time and it took me nearly a week to recover."

MacLean left Ria where he was and arrived at the day cabin off the bridge to find there the brawny yeoman signaller to whom Barkis was much attached, and the captain's steward. It was a sunny morning, the Ark steaming steadily, and the unsuspecting

Barkis slept peacefully on the bridge. The captain whistled him in, and he came to the door with his powerful rushing roll, paused, sensed his impending doom and backed out hastily.

"Grab him, Yeoman," shouted the captain, and the signaller leaped in a flying tackle. Barkis rolled over and waved his paws supplicatingly. Nothing would induce him to get to his feet again.

MacLean watched this performance. "If I might be making a suggestion, sir," he said at last, "it is that we knock him out and proceed with the operation while he is unconscious?"

The captain looked at him in shocked surprise. "I don't think he would like that," he said. "Apart from the fact that it would take a sledge hammer to knock him out."

"I am not meaning a blow, sir," said MacLean, his voice becoming more Highland with embarrassment. "I was thinking that we could knock him out with a wee whiff of something—"

Still faintly dubious, the captain sent for the doctor, who agreed, straight-faced and solemn, with MacLean's suggestion. A mask and ether were produced, and peacefully, quietly, in orderly ship-shape fashion Barkis parted with his excess nails.

Thanking MacLean afterwards, the captain asked about Ria— he was a fine-looking little dog, he had thought on the few occasions he had seen him. Most intelligent, and—he had been about to say "amusing", but for some unknown reason he substituted "and full of guts, too".

Taken aback by the obvious sincerity of this praise, MacLean was speechless for a moment. Fine looking? Intelligent? Full of guts? *Ria?*

As he swept the last neat crescents of claw onto a piece of paper, speech returned: "I had not thought on it, sir," he said politely, then added with considerably more conviction, "But, aye, he certainly is a determined wee beast." He turned his attention to Barkis, still lying on the table with a slit of eye open and a silly pleased smile on his thin pink lips. He folded back one of the white ears, then suddenly bent over it closely.

He straightened up and sniffed disapprovingly, "Dirty ears," he said. "I will be cleaning them out. Come with me, you—" Barkis slid off the table and laid the shameful ears back, a picture of abject apology. "I will return him in fifteen minutes, sir," said MacLean, straightening smartly to attention before exiting with Barkis rolling obediently along behind, looking for once almost bemused. Whereas MacLean looked rather satisfied with himself.

Later that afternoon as he sat at the desk, Ria suddenly came to him and pushed a cold nose into his hand. Reminded of Barkis's unsavoury ears, he lifted one of the softly folded ones under his hand and inspected the spotless convolutions within. Pleased with what he found, he let his hand lie for a moment on Ria's head. Then he inspected the shining teeth as grimly as if he expected to find signs of decay already from the illicit diet of Number Five Mess. "They'll do," he said.

Suddenly his mind went back to these same teeth gleaming from the black oil-slimed mass of the soldier: this same wee jessie of a dog had then endured over eight hours in the water, and heaven knew what else beforehand—yet still had fight in him. It occurred to him that the mighty Barkis would not have stood up to those hours in the water. "Full of guts," the captain had said —maybe he wasn't so far wrong. And intelligent, certainly.

"You'll do," he said, almost grudgingly. "Aye, you'll do."

Ria's tail was delighted at such praise. Head to one side, ears cocked, he searched the face above as though expecting something further. But at that moment eight bells sounded; time for MacLean's routine inspection of his first aid packs stowed on every gun turret throughout the ship. He secured Ria by a strong line and left.

He climbed the ladder to A turret platform, and found Ria immediately behind him, the collar slipped. Exasperated, he gazed down, but Ria, ears at a demure half-mast, gazed studiously into the distance. It was too late to return with him now—and at least this time he had not made for Number Five Mess. He continued his rounds, the dog close behind, yet never in the way.

They returned to the mess; time now, too, for Ria's meal and the routine battle. He set the dish down, already tense.

Reid, already eating, watched in silence. "For God's sake, man," he said in a rare burst of irritation, "if you'd stop looking as though you had a mouth full of razor blades, perhaps the dog would eat something—it's enough to put anyone off their grub!"

MacLean looked up. Then suddenly he smiled, almost shame-facedly: "Perhaps I am just a thing over-anxious," he admitted.

"And talk about a dog's dinner," said Reid, looking at the bowl in disgust, "Who'd want to eat that grisly-looking mush?" He ladled some of his own food onto the dish, stirred it around with a finger.

To MacLean's astonishment Ria set to and polished the bowl clean, so obviously ravenous that the Highlander gave him some of his own. It was interesting, he thought, that a dog should actually have preferences as to where or how it should eat.

From then on, there was to be no refusal of meals; a battle had been won. And there was no doubt in MacLean's mind as to who had triumphed. Dogs always came round in the end, he knew.

AS THAT DESPERATE summer of 1940 wore on into autumn gales, the most important adaptation shipboard animals had to learn was the art of keeping out of the way. The shrill of action stations meant instant activity to humans, to them it signalled withdrawal.

There were many hours of stand-by for the doctor and MacLean, and during these Ria became relaxed in MacLean's company, as knitting needles clicked and pages turned. All in all, MacLean reflected, the dog had settled in amazingly well, and had turned out to be no trouble even in the most exigent circumstances.

Then, one warm September morning, as the Ark swung gently to her buoy off the fishing port of Oban, a letter came from Donald Sinclair's wife. Her husband was now off the danger list, she reported, but one lung was permanently collapsed; he would remain in hospital for some time yet, and would be invalided out of the army in due course:

> Then, God willing, we will be able to take the dog off your hands at last. . . . One day we hope to repay you, if only with our thanks. . . . My Aunty knitted the enclosed for you. . . ."

The enclosed was a pair of socks. MacLean examined them critically. Aunty was an expert, but had been over-generous in length. They would do nicely for Reid.

He put the letter away, his feelings very mixed, and went out on deck. The mountainous island of Mull dominated the western horizon. This was the land of his forebears, and of Margaret's. Twenty-four hours here could only be twenty-four deeply disturbing hours.

The gentle rise of mainland hills stretched before him, vividly slashed with bracken's fiery russet and the deep purple of heather. It was a Sunday, and across the intervening water a light wind carried the peaceful sounds of church bells and sheep bleating—and, to a sensitive nose, all the exciting and tantalizing smells of sun-warmed earth. Ria stood by the rail, his nose twitching. The distraction irritated MacLean, stirred now to a sick nostalgia. "Wheesht," he said curtly.

Farther along the deck, Lessing appeared. A likeable youngster, he was going ashore on the next liberty boat; there wouldn't be anything doing in the town, he said; but he thought he'd walk over the hills and maybe have a swim—would MacLean like to go too? And take the dog?

MacLean seldom went ashore, only for dockyard stores, and he had never once taken Ria. He had rejected all overtures of friendship so consistently that his solitariness was now an accepted fact. But his defences were momentarily down. He smiled his rare transforming smile, and said there was nothing he would rather do more and it was a grand day for the walking; but the doctor was ashore, and he was on duty . . . and he thanked Lessing anyway for thinking of it.

Lessing seemed overwhelmed by this unusual spate of words. "Let me take Ria then," he said at last. He hesitated as the other's smile vanished but went on resolutely. "It'll do him good to have a run—get off this tin box for a while. Must be worse for a dog being cooped up—not even a blooming tree to think about."

For a moment MacLean almost reverted to his usual image and told Lessing to mind his own business, and then, despite himself, he heard his voice saying, "Aye, it's an unnatural life all right. I'd be glad if you'd take him—off with you then," to Ria who, sensing something different and exciting, bounded after Lessing.

MacLean watched as the liberty boat sped off to the shore. He had relatives here. He had only to go ashore and telephone. His father would take Ria for him, and in time despatch him farther north back to Sinclair. It would be as simple as that. . . .

On the horizon, MacLean could just make out the lonely dot that was the holy island of Iona. He watched it, and some of the lightness of heart that his Margaret had brought returned to him, as though her laughter came echoing down the years. Unconsciously he smiled then shook his head and went below.

Ria came back ecstatic, his eyes clear and shining, his whole bearing jaunty—a very different dog, as the man who greeted him on the deck could not fail to observe.

For once MacLean looked directly down at him. Suddenly he knew that Margaret of all people would have been the one for this dog, that from her extravagance of love and gaiety she would have encouraged and abetted all antic nonsense and found a counterpart in lightheartedness.

"Behave yourself," he said now with automatic severity, but Ria wagged his tail with unabashed enthusiasm and continued to look as though he were laughing with open mouth and lolling tongue. They turned and made their way along the deck to the stern, Ria scampering ahead unchecked.

To the rest of the ship's company there was no apparent change in the relationship between MacLean and Ria. They remained an undemonstrative pair. The transition from MacLean imposing his will to Ria anticipating his wishes evolved so naturally that he was unaware of it, yet the bond of communication had become so close now that sometimes it seemed that the image of the dog had only to pass through the man's mind before he would appear.

MacLean never thought other than that the dog had changed and conformed. But to the rest of the ship's company, Ria was the same amusing self-reliant diversion as always. His interests had become legion, ranging from seabird, convoy or iceberg-watching to the entire ship's company, for he was immensely inquisitive, and liked to keep an eye on everything aboard.

MacLean had not seen how much of his heart had been given to the dog until the Ark returned to Devonport in early March, 1941. He was looking forward with unusual pleasure to a forty-eight

53

hour leave, and had made plans to spend it walking on Dartmoor with Ria—the first time they would ever have gone off together. When the mail was distributed that first morning in port there was a letter for him. It came as the most profound shock.

Donald Sinclair was out of hospital and returned to his Highland glen, there to wait a final medical board before being discharged from the army. He would no longer be any good on the hills, he said, but eventually he would be running a farm instead, and now at last he could relieve Ria's benefactor of his obligation—". . . so thoughtlessly imposed upon you. Now at last we can give the dog a settled home. Any port that you are in—if you could dispatch him on to us . . ." He enclosed a postal order to cover expenses, the ticket, and the purchase of the obligatory muzzle for "an unaccompanied dog".

Suddenly the world seemed very bleak. And fate seemed indeed to be working against him, for within ten minutes of confiding this news to Reid, arrangements slipped easily into place. Reid had returned from telephoning a sister who lived in Plymouth: she was travelling home to Yorkshire in a few days' time. The same train would go on up to Glasgow. Ria could go ashore with Reid that afternoon and he would leave him with his sister.

It all happened so quickly that there was no time to brood. The morning was fully occupied with routine duties. At noon MacLean changed and went ashore with Ria who was only innocently excited at the prospect of a walk on dry land.

Once clear of the dockyard gates and feeling like a Judas, MacLean handed him over to Reid. "Away yon, go for a run," he said, forcing reassurance. Ria was very attached to Reid and had often gone ashore with him, but now he sensed something disastrous. As MacLean turned away down the street he whined and struggled to follow, straining at the end of the short lead.

Reid picked him up to soothe him, but as MacLean turned the corner he heard a sound he had never heard before—a high-pitched almost hysterical barking that was to haunt him for days.

He shut out the sound in the nearest pub and drank himself into a state of solitary gloom such as he had not attained for a very long time—and barely made it back on board.

54

They were anchored out in the Sound. Soon after darkness fell, the alarms sounded and the systematic Nazi destruction of the ancient town of Plymouth began. The *Tertian* was a Devonport ship and many of the men had families on shore, while almost all had friends. Next morning those who had homes or relatives ashore were given a few hours' compassionate leave. For some it was a thankful reunion, for others a nightmare search through rubble-strewn streets.

Reid went ashore, and found his sister standing in front of what had been her house, one of a terrace leading off the Hoe. All the windows were out, the roof was gone, and the kitchen extension at the back lay in a heap of rubble. That was where Ria had been, she informed him tearfully; fortunately she herself had been out for supper with the neighbour with whom she was now sheltering.

They could not salvage anything from the rest of the house for there was an unexploded land-mine at the back of the row. There was nothing further Reid could do. He returned to the Ark to break the news to MacLean, and the only consolation he had to offer was that Ria's death must have been instantaneous.

MacLean was standing by the rail. Without turning his head, he thanked Reid in a flat expressionless voice and continued to look across at the smouldering city. He never spoke of Ria again.

Soon those ashore were recalled urgently and all leave cancelled. A signal had come through that the cruiser *Admiral Hipper* was making a sortie out of Brest, and the Ark was to be part of the force sent to intercept. For days they played cat and mouse, but in the end the prey eluded them, and the Ark proceeded on to the Mediterranean to join the Fleet there.

She was never to return.

PART THREE

O n the night that Reid's sister's house was destroyed the sirens had sounded the red alert in Plymouth about nine o'clock. Almost before the first warning notes had ebbed away, the skies were filled with a deep multiple droning and the anti-aircraft barrage and searchlights came into action. A minute later the bombardment had begun.

Ria had become used to the noises of war at sea, but when the anti-aircraft batteries started up there was no familiar sanctuary to which he could make his way; there was only himself in a strange kitchen.

As the first stick of bombs screamed down, each earthshaking crump landing nearer, Ria cowered against the back door; then he bolted under the table. A bomb landed squarely between the two adjoining houses of the terrace, slicing a path between them as cleanly as a knife through butter, and as the bricks and masonry of the next door chimney cascaded onto the kitchen roof, the roof and wall disintegrated in a shower of bricks.

For a few seconds, a hush fell over the ruins of the kitchen. Then the mounting crackle of flames rose from somewhere just beyond the jagged edges of the roof. The ghostlike figure of a dog, white with dust, appeared from under the pile of wreckage by the table and drifted across the rubble, through the sagging door, and out into the yard. The last hinge on the door gave way and it crashed down. Ria bolted into the street, his paws scarcely touching the ground, clearing the fence with a foot to spare.

He smelled fear and death, an evil blend that sent him slithering across the rubble and glass-strewn streets, shying away from the running boots of wardens and firemen, until he reached the open spaces of the Hoe. He ran on madly, turning at last into the centre of the stricken town. A man, reeling drunk, whistled, but the dog fled on. In the back of a shop crouched a cat with a mewling kitten in its mouth. As the dog ran in, a lightning paw flashed out to rend an ear so that he turned and fled with high hysterical yipping. He ran throughout the night until, hours later, he veered crazily between the tombstones of a churchyard, and finally collapsed under the solid sheltering wing of a toppled marble angel.

The All Clear sounded in the dawn of a new day, and one by one the dazed inhabitants of Plymouth emerged from their burrows to survey the world that had been left to them. Ria stayed around the churchyard for a while until the terrifying wail of fire engines drove him on. He limped down a narrow street, picking his way between fragments of glass and twisted metal. He sat on the sunny step before the roofless shell of a house and scratched himself, watching with mild interest a large white rabbit investigating the shattered glass of a cloche in the next door garden.

He wandered on, limping and thirsty, in the hazy dust-laden sunshine. There was only one place he knew, and he returned to it at last, to the sheltering marble wing in the churchyard. He was there still when the nightmare started again soon after dark, and he pressed back into his refuge, shuddering convulsively, until at last the noise and terror drove him out into the madness of the night. This time he did not always run alone; there were other dogs that ran in terror-stricken circles too, instinctively forming a pack.

Once a runaway horse came thundering up a narrow cobbled street, an old grey carthorse, galloping heavily, its flying mane and tail gallant in the unearthly orange light, one opaque white eye fixed steadily ahead, the other rolling wildly. The little dog broke away from the pack as though drawn irresistibly, to run ahead, as he had once run before another old grey horse. He ran with unseeing eyes before the feathered hooves striking sparks from the cobbles, until at last they thundered up a street blocked with fire engines, and there the horse wheeled, skidding in the soaked debris, and was brought down to its knees. A fireman seized the reins and encouraged it back to its feet. He led it beyond the hoses and fire engines until he came to a house with a garage attached. The dog trotted along behind. The garage was empty; the man tethered the horse to a workbench and ran out. The dog stretched his forepaws up to the chest of the horse, almost as though from custom; at the first touch the horse shied clumsily, then stood, shuddering. The dog wagged his tail, and at last the horse lowered its head, whickering softly. The dog jumped onto the bench and curled up. Gradually the horse quietened. They spent the rest of the night there.

The owner of the horse traced his runaway early next morning, and led it off down the smouldering street to his scrapyard, followed for a while by the dog. Ambulances, fire engines, rescue units and mobile canteens edged past them; men shouted angrily at them to get out of the way. They plodded on, the dog's head low as the horse's, close to its dragging hooves, until they reached the scrapyard, and there the man led the horse into its stable. But when the dog would have followed, the man drove him off and closed the half-door. The dog drank from a trough, then limped out into the road again where he stood indecisively.

He stayed around the same area during the next three days, foraging in dustbins or wrecked shops and houses. In the late afternoon of the third day, cowed and slinking now, he wandered farther afield to a residential area on the outskirts of the town, and there, sorting through the already well-rifled contents of a dustbin blown into the orchard adjoining a large garden, he paused, one paw lifted, sniffing the air. He limped through the garden until he came to a building, a coach-house converted into a garage. The windows were blown in and some of the roof was down, but the walls still stood sturdily. To the right of the closed double doors was the original stable door, half open, and the little dog, after hesitating for a moment, edged in warily.

The interior was a tangled mass of beams, lathes and slates, and he approached it cautiously, his nose still working busily. Where a small inverted V of access to the pile had been formed by two beams he paused, his tail moving fast, ears cocked and head to one side, whining excitedly. Then he infiltrated the narrow tunnel. It widened out after a few yards to a small cavern, the roof formed by a jumble of precariously balanced timbers. An arm protruded from below, lying along a length of board, and as the dog crawled towards it the fingers opened and closed as though beckoning.

Delighted with his find, he licked the hand, then wagged his tail when a weak muffled voice from below responded to his action. Questing around, he tried to tunnel down through a mass of plasterboard, but as he dug, the vibration loosened part of the pile, and from somewhere above there was a groaning shift of weight followed by a heavy resettlement of timbers. The dog yelped as a heavy board pinned one paw; he pulled desperately, the yelping changing to a higher pitch with the pain. The paw tore free at last; whimpering, he fell to licking his mangled toes.

The weak disembodied voice below whispered for a while, then grew silent, but the hand still moved wearily as though in search, until at last the fingers found and closed upon the other forepaw. Ria licked the fingers perfunctorily and returned his attention to his injury. A glimmer of light high up in the tangled pile slowly faded as darkness fell. The bleeding staunched at last, exhausted with pain and hunger, he laid his head down, his muzzle resting lightly on the hand which held his paw. The fingers moved out and up past the matted hair on the crown of his head, then to the sensitive hollow behind his ears. Sometimes the arm was withdrawn for a while, but the voice continued, sometimes speaking, sometimes singing; sometimes it called out high and continuously, when he would whine or lick the hand as though in response to a call.

Gradually he and the hand grew weaker. By the evening the hand had withdrawn and the voice was silent. He could no longer lift his head, and his eyes were sealed with a yellow discharge. He lay without movement, only the occasional flick of one ear to sudden creaks above betraying the will to live.

On the late morning of the second day he raised his head—then suddenly he pushed back on one foreleg to his haunches and broke into a high wild barking.

ALICE TREMORNE had been trapped in the pit of The Cedars' garage for two nights and days when the dog found her. She had been alone in the house on the night it was hit as Janet Carpenter, her companion help, was away on a week's holiday, and the daily help had left soon after putting the evening meal in the oven. After listening to the nine o'clock news, restless and so bored with her own company that she had even cleared away the supper dishes for the first time in her life, Mrs. Tremorne suddenly thought of sloe gin. At the beginning of the war she had put up several bottles. They should be pleasantly aged by now, maturing in the work pit of the garage, a place which, she had found, maintained an excellent temperature for her home-made wines. She would tell Carpenter to fetch a sample bottle when she returned. . . .

But the more she thought about the sloe gin, the more she

59

wanted to try it now. Why should she have to wait five more days? Wincing, but still majestic, Mrs. Tremorne rose stiffly to her feet. Taking a small torch, a fur wrap, and her stick from the hall cupboard, she shuffled slowly down the path to the garage on stiff arthritic legs.

The Cedars' stable yard was paved and easy to negotiate, even for an elderly woman who normally never set foot outside without her companion's arm, but when she opened the garage door and shone the light around, she realized she had forgotten the fitted boards covering the pit and the steps down. Outside the sirens wailed, such a normal event now that she took no notice. Her knees twinged at the thought of removing the boards, but Mrs. Tremorne was not one to turn back; somehow, puffing and panting, giddy with the effort, she managed to lever up enough of the boards. It was at this moment that she realized the sirens had heralded business this time; the anti-aircraft defences ringing the town burst into an excited crackling, and now the naval guns from the dockyard joined in. Above all, there was another very unpleasant noise indeed, spaced and dreadful thuds which rattled her bottles in their straw; those unspeakable Germans were actually having the effrontery to bomb Plymouth.

Mrs. Tremorne switched off her torch. The garage door now framed a bright orange sky across which searchlights moved, and a garden illuminated as clearly as a stage setting. There was a sudden clanging as fragments of metal rained down on the path, then Mrs. Tremorne's world was filled with a rushing noise like an express train coming straight at her.

Arthritis and all, she dropped to the floor and lay flat, her head buried in her arms. The stone floor rocked, she felt as though all air were being sucked out of her body. Without in any way being conscious of her passage across the garage, she was neatly picked up and deposited on the straw on top of her own bottles at the bottom of the pit. At the same time the roof collapsed, the first beams straddling the pit, and so supporting the remainder that fell on top. Terribly shaken, her head spinning, her eardrums thudding, Mrs. Tremorne lay on her straw mattress and wondered if this was the end before she dropped off into unconsciousness.

When she came to some hours later, lying with her arms by her sides in thick black silence, she thought she was in her coffin, additional proof being that when she spoke up indignantly to say that there had been some mistake, she heard no sound. She resigned herself, with black fury, to eternal rest.

After a while, she became conscious of sharp things boring through the straw like fakirs' nails into her back, and memory returned: the tops of her wine bottles. She lifted her arms then each leg cautiously in turn; everything worked. Her shoes had been blow off, but she still clutched the torch in one hand. She saw now that there were occasional chinks of light in the otherwise impenetrable mass over her, but even if she had the strength to remove some of the obstruction, the balance was so delicate she might well bring the whole jumble crashing down. She would have to resign herself to waiting, conserving her light, her strength. Thank goodness she had put on her cape. She blamed those dreadful Germans for her predicament, this unnerving deafness, and she concentrated all her hate on them.

She did not know when the All Clear had sounded, she scarcely even knew if it was day or night, only that she was now very cold and ached in every bone. She shouted, not knowing that her voice had become a whisper, and tears of fury and weakness furrowed down her dusty cheeks. Falling silent at last from sheer exhaustion, she realized that the ARP post at the corner of the street where the listed occupants of all the houses around were kept would probably check the house only. Knowing that Carpenter was away—one of the wardens was her cousin—they would assume Mrs. Tremorne had gone out for the evening. They would never think of looking in the garage, for everyone knew she was unable to get around without assistance. But the daily would come at nine o'clock, Mrs. Tremorne reassured herself, she would come searching. . . .

But no one came. She had no idea of the passage of time for her watch had stopped. She moved some bottles to form a straw nest. Sometimes she fell into an exhausted sleep. Thirsty, she remembered the sloe gin and found a bottle of it. Taken strictly medicinally it was very comforting.

It was in one of her more lonely moments, during her second night, that as she clenched and unclenched her fingers against their growing stiffness, she suddenly heard an unfamiliar creaking in the timbers, and out of nowhere came the warm wet touch of a tongue on her fingers. Instinctively she jerked her arm back; then she heard a dog's soft whining. Her fingers moved again to touch a muzzle, ears, to be covered again by an eager tongue.

Unfamiliar tears of gratitude welled up in Mrs. Tremorne's eyes. When the pile shifted and high agonized yelps followed, she forgot her own splitting head and aching bones; she longed only to comfort this warm miraculous link with life, to show it by the soft stroking of her fingers how much she cared. From that moment, Mrs. Tremorne determined that if she had to spend another month here, living on gin in total darkness, she would somehow come out of it and see this small creature, the only living thing that knew or cared, apparently, that she still existed, that had risked its life to come to her out of the terrible night.

It was undoubtedly the sloe gin that brought her out alive, for it was to be another two days before she was found by the devoted Janet Carpenter, who had cut short her holiday. She had arrived only that morning. The daily help who had promised so faithfully to look after Mrs. Tremorne had vanished without a trace and for a while Janet thought Mrs. Tremorne might have vanished with her, to the country perhaps. Her mistress would not have gone out with friends that evening for the simple reason that she had no friends. But it never occurred to Janet to think beyond the house at first; Mrs. Tremorne elsewhere, solo, was unthinkable.

But when she came out into The Cedars' garden to survey the wreckage, she heard a faint barking. Puzzled, she traced it to the garage. Plainly there was a dog trapped somewhere in that pile. She sniffed the air; it smelled as though some Bacchanalian orgy had recently taken place. On top of a pile of broken bottles was a familiar shape under a coating of dust—Alice Tremorne's ivory-headed cane! Janet Carpenter turned and ran for the ARP post.

They uncovered the dog, a small white shadow who gazed up at them from thickly encrusted eyes behind a matted fringe of hair, dusty save for the red of a clean, licked, mangled forepaw. It acknowledged their presence by a brief quivering of its tail. The warden laid it on the floor and they set to again for the urgent, yet frustratingly slow, uncovering of Mrs. Tremorne's body.

It was unveiled at last. Alice Tremorne lay stretched out neatly on a bed of straw, her head pillowed on a square of empty bottles, her hands folded tidily on her chest under her sable cape, her stockinged feet together. The string of pearls on the massive shelf of her bosom moved up and down with peaceful regularity. Even as they gazed upon her, she hiccoughed gently, then a loud imperious snore fell upon their astonished ears.

She was taken to hospital, where—almost incredibly for a seventy-six-year-old semi-invalid—no damage other than bruising was found. The first thing she asked for when she recovered from her monumental hangover was the dog, her rescuer.

"It was a miracle," she said, her words still somewhat slurred, "I held ish paw and strength flowed out, poshitively flowed . . ." Her glazed eyes glared round, challenging anyone to dispute the source of the miracle-working flow, and Janet Carpenter left to track the dog down.

She was able to report next day that one of the rescue team had taken the dog home with him: its eyes were open, the wound on the paw was clean, but possibly there were internal injuries or severe shock for the animal seemed to have lost the will to live— it simply lay in a box without stirring, and was kept going only by spoonfuls of warm milk laced with precious whisky.

The man must be suitably rewarded, and a vet must be called immediately, commanded Alice Tremorne—two, three vets if necessary. A taxi must be summoned so that the dog could be installed at The Cedars straightaway. Carpenter must go forth and —here was her alligator bag—set the machinery in motion; a dog basket, the best, to be bought; leads, brushes, bones and tempting dog delicacies—dogs liked liver, she knew: fetch then, quantities of liver. . . .

Liver was very hard to get nowadays, offered Janet apologetically. But it was useless explaining. The war to Alice Tremorne was simply an interlude of personal inconvenience. Janet Carpenter departed dispiritedly to the shops.

"Good dog, good little doggie," mumbled Alice Tremorne, drifting off again. "Did it hurt then? Poor little doggie . . . never mind . . . Alice is here . . ."

IF MIRACULOUS strength had flowed out of the dog's paw to Alice Tremorne, now the procedure was reversed and strength flowed back through every means that the hand dipping into its alligator bag could provide. By the time Mrs. Tremorne was allowed home, still stiff and sore, he was installed in a basket in her bedroom, his coat brushed, his hair tied back from his eyes with a red ribbon that would have sent MacLean rushing for scissors. The hair around his delicate hocks had been shaved to match the area around the injured paw over which a baby's blue bootee was drawn to hold the dressing in place. He hopped on three legs, and several times a day Janet Carpenter, mouth buttoned into a thin line, clipped a leash onto the lightest and finest of red leather collars and took her charge for an airing in the garden. After the first day of Mrs. Tremorne's homecoming she no longer returned him to the basket, but lifted him—her lips by now almost invisible—into the fastness of Mrs. Tremorne's bed, who then drew her pink silk eiderdown tenderly over him.

At first he hardly stirred. When he slept briefly, his body twitched convulsively, and then Alice Tremorne would reach out to pat and talk the reassuring baby talk that she had never used in her life but which seemed to come naturally to her now, until he lay quiet again. As the days passed, his tail gradually stirred more and more, his ears rose fractionally—until one day she woke from a light sleep to find him lightly brushing her arm with one paw, his eyes bright with interest.

Now to find a name for him. Propped up against her pillows, she started off by running through all the fictional or traditional canine names that she could remember: none met with any recognition from the dog. She was about to dip into the telephone book when she remembered John Peel and his hounds.

"*Yes, I ken John Peel, and Ruby too, Ranter and Rover . . .*" She trailed off; no, it wasn't Rover, it was . . . ? She started off again, hoping to get carried along unconsciously: "*D'ye ken John*

64

Peel, With his coat so gay," she sang determinedly, only to get stuck again at Ranter. She was still at it when Carpenter arrived to take the dog out. Commanded to make a duet, she outran Mrs. Tremorne convincingly: *"Ranter and Ringwood, Bellman and True. . . ."* she continued in a surprisingly sweet soprano.

The ears before her flickered and the round eyes lit up in seeming recognition. Mrs. Tremorne repeated the names, and this time the dog jumped off the bed and sat quivering expectantly, his eyes never leaving her face. It was Bellman that excited him, but she soon found that the first half of the word had the same effect: "Bell!" she said, *"Bell*—good Bell!" and each time she spoke, the dog's tail wagged more furiously.

"You see," she said triumphantly, "that's his name—Bell! Time for walkies then, my darling Bell." She gazed down dotingly.

Carpenter produced an opinion of her own, which was almost unheard of. "I think Bell's a silly name for a dog," she said. "It sounds like a girl one way or a chime the other."

Mrs. Tremorne quelled the mutiny with cunning ease: "Neither the feminine nor the ding dong," she said with lofty dismissal, "but *Bel*, who—as I am sure you will remember—was the god of heaven and earth in Babylonian mythology." Many years addiction to *The Times* crossword had paid off.

Bel he became, the sound near enough to the one to which he must have responded for so many years before he became Ria. Measure for measure, he returned the love and care lavished on him, and all his uninhibited affection and natural gaiety, so long denied, returned. He filled out, becoming in the process the closest thing to a poodle to which the united efforts of his mistress and a kennel maid skilled in the art could clip and comb him, the dark hairs of the outer coat stripping down to a pale, almost lavender grey. The mutilation of his toes left him with a slight limp but did not seem to inconvenience him at all.

Soon, even the reluctant Carpenter fell under his spell. She no longer looked so haunted, for now that Mrs. Tremorne had an all-engrossing obsession, the spotlight of attention shifted, and an atmosphere of almost cosy warmth gradually permeated the normally gloomy house. Suddenly one day she became Janet. Bel loved her, and more and more she enjoyed his company and the interest he brought to her formerly solitary walks. But undoubtedly the one who received his full devotion was the one whom he had found himself, his own human bounty, Alice Tremorne.

He seemed to be completely content in his role of the perfect companion; obedient, fastidiously clean, with faultless manners, even towards food, for at first he would eat nothing, however tempting, unless she were eating too. To all appearances a dog for old ladies to pamper, who could fit right into a gentle purposeless life as though he had known no other; a chameleon little dog.

Yet there were times when he lay for hours on top of the garden wall, watching the world that passed below as though waiting to recognize some familiar form. Watching him herself, Mrs. Tremorne gradually discovered the pattern of his interests; the clip-clop of a horse-drawn milk van or coal cart always brought the most eager attention. Servicemen, and sailors in particular, also. But this knowledge only added up to a questionable composite of an equestrian sailor for a former owner, and that was not much help. He made many friends among the regular passersby. They would stop and have a word with him, and he would receive their attentions with dignified polite interest.

There were the occasional times too when he lay listless and unresponsive, his eyes infinitely sad and faraway. One afternoon, eerily, he had sat up suddenly, thrown his head back and howled, a high haunting sound that had rung in Mrs. Tremorne's ears for days afterwards. Sometimes he would sit before her, tense, searching her eyes, straining every nerve to get his message across. "Darling Bel, what *is* it?" she would implore. "What are you trying to tell me?" But a puzzled shadow only would flit over his eyes.

One day, when the wireless was playing Irish jigs, he rose to his hind legs. She took his forepaws and moved them in time to the music. "Come on, my darling," she said, "dance with me." She moved three stiff steps to the right, then to the left, and he followed her. "One, two, three," sang Alice Tremorne to her eager little partner, "and a one, two, *three*—" Breathless, she let his paws go, but to her astonishment he circled on, nodding his head and pawing the air in a quaint little dance.

Enchanted, she clapped her hands. Her pleasure was so patent that thereafter he volunteered this performance from time to time; but only, she noticed, when the need to communicate or demonstrate affection became so overwhelming that he had to make this unique bestowal of himself.

Because she wanted more than anything else to participate in his life, she forced herself to walk more, to go farther afield in the garden, hoping perhaps even to take him for a proper country walk one day. White-faced with effort, she persevered, and was rewarded in more ways than one, for not only did she begin to feel better physically, but through Bel she made daily contact with the outside world. She had actually been seen talking over the fence—about Bel naturally—to her neighbour.

One afternoon she and Bel had reached the far end of the garden at their customary tortoise pace when suddenly he stopped, ears pricked. Then he shot like an arrow down through the hedge, across the small orchard beyond, and leaped at the barred gate to the paddock. He paused there, poised on the top bar, clinging on with his front paws, his tail moving rapidly. He looked so like a fluffy hovering dragonfly that Mrs. Tremorne laughed out loud.

Now she saw the object of his excitement, her neighbour's donkey, the long-retired Fred who grazed her paddock from time to time. She watched Bel streak across the grass, then slow to a halt a few feet away, his excitement apparently diminished. However, he sniffed around as the donkey gently nudged his head. He crouched, sprang, and dropped lightly on the shaggy back. Fortunately, fifteen years of children had accustomed Fred to almost anything. Mrs. Tremorne leaned on her cane and revelled in the light-hearted spectacle of Bel, his pink tongue lolling, his forepaws rigid before him as Fred moved off slowly, cropping the grass, the small motionless rider still on his back.

When Mrs. Tremorne called at last, Bel came running, his eyes still alight with excitement. After this there was no problem about providing an outdoor interest; if not bound for a session on the wall he would trot off briskly in search of Fred, sometimes lying by his feet as the donkey whiled away the long summer afternoons in the shade of the trees, sometimes bounding in a beautifully co-ordinated arc onto the broad patient back, there to dream with head thrown back, erect and totally still.

The weeks stretched into months within the garden walls, the war news intruding only through the impersonal voices of the BBC. Thus it was not until Mrs. Tremorne was faced with the prospect of one egg per week from her ration book and two ounces of butter to spread over seven days of morning toast that the full impact of the war was brought home to her. She was unable to dismiss this inconvenience any longer; it was clearly here to stay.

Unable to do anything about the butter, she turned her attention to the egg problem: they would keep hens. Fortunately Janet showed unexpected enthusiasm for this project. Even more happily, yet another interest was provided for Bel. Six day-old chicks were bought; for the first few days they were reared in the kitchen under a lamp in a box, and under the unwavering gaze of Bel who appeared to be almost mesmerized by them. When they were let out they followed him around as though he were a mother hen; and if he lay down they climbed all over him. His retinue persisted even when they were grown birds and had the run of the orchard. They would converge on him with hysterical clucking whenever he appeared, and were greatly frustrated when their wings were clipped and they were no longer able to fly up and perch beside him on the donkey's back.

Now Bel's days were full indeed, and by the time a year had passed and the months of the second were marching on, he was indirectly contributing to the war effort as well, for in a combination of patriotism and the effort to arrest the stiffness of her fingers in order to groom him, Mrs. Tremorne learned to knit. Slowly and painfully she knitted for the Naval Comforts Fund, working her way up through the endless tedium of scarves to balaclavas and mitts, and then the ultimate triumph of socks. Months later she received acknowledgement of her labours from two of the recipients, and was strangely touched by their letters; for the first time she was in personal contact with the front.

68

If her life had been completely altered by Bel's coming, so was Janet Carpenter's—she looked ten years younger, within reach now of her actual thirty-four. Having cared for her elderly parents until they died, she had been untrained for any job. Unable, because of a slight congenital heart defect, to escape into the women's services, she had resigned herself to the grey future of a light-duties companion. Now that Mrs. Tremorne was so occupied, she had nerved herself to ask if she might join one of the voluntary services, and slaved happily two afternoons and evenings a week in a railway canteen. She proved to be an unexpectedly amusing raconteuse, and brought back a breath of outside life as she regaled Mrs. Tremorne with her various encounters over the coffee urns. Mrs. Tremorne, eager to expand her Bel audience, encouraged her to invite lonely or stranded young servicemen and women back to The Cedars.

At Christmas, by now well-launched into undercounter deals, she procured a magnificent turkey, wine, and even crackers, and eight young people sat down to an unforgettable dinner. Afterwards, one of them produced a pennywhistle, another a concertina, and they sang carols. Then, as though to put the final seal of pleasure on this happiest of days, Bel judged his moment and rose to perform his solemn little dance.

It had been some time since he had expressed himself this way to Mrs. Tremorne, and as she watched him circle now with nodding head and outstretched paws, she saw that his eyes sought hers with the same strange intensity of those first weeks. At that moment, with a sudden stab of jealous helplessness, she knew that this was only a part of a presentation: it should go on, but it could not, for something was missing. Everything else in his life she could provide, but not this release that belonged to someone else. She did not speak of this to Janet; if she had become such an absurd old woman that she was jealous of a ghost then it was better to keep it to herself.

INTO THIS HAPPY little Eden one day, nearly two years after Bel's arrival, came a stranger. He rang the bell, and asked to see Mrs. Tremorne. He was in naval uniform, small and slight, with a finely-drawn, almost ascetic face. Janet asked him to come in, thinking him one of the recipients of Mrs. Tremorne's knitting.

"What name?" she asked.

"Neil MacLean," he said, then added in a soft lilting accent, "but Mistress Tremorne will not be acquaint with it. I have been trying to trace a dog that was lost in Plymouth in 1941, and I had heard from a nurse at the hospital here that . . ." His voice trailed off: it was too long an explanation to give now, and he looked at Janet expectantly.

A terrible feeling of disaster closed in as she stood silently staring at MacLean. Oh, no, oh, no . . . she cried silently, seeing the grim vista of a future that held no Bel, life as it had been before. . . .

Even as she stared at his puzzled face, Mrs. Tremorne's voice floated down the stairs, "If that is the laundry," she said, "tell them we are now missing two pillowcases."

Janet found her voice. "It is a Mr. MacLean, wanting to see you about a dog," she called up.

Mrs. Tremorne was rather deaf nowadays. "God?" she said, puzzled, for Mr. Vane, the vicar, did not usually announce himself so baldly.

"*Dog,*" shouted Janet, almost wringing her hands. "*MacLean.*"

Mrs. Tremorne looked down and saw the dark blue uniform with some relief. She decided that he must be one of Bel's garden wall acquaintances. "Come along up, Mr. McVane," she said pleasantly.

MacLean followed her into the small upstairs room that Alice Tremorne used nowadays so that she could watch Bel with a pair of field glasses. She hobbled across the room on swollen feet, and sat down, motioning MacLean to a seat opposite. By the arm of her chair was a small table on which lay her knitting and some photographs of Bel. "You must be one of Bel's friends?" she said.

"I am not acquaint with the name," said MacLean. "As I was telling yon lass at the door, it was about a dog that was thought to have been killed during the blitz in 1941—" he paused, suddenly aware of a current of hostility in the room.

"How sad," said Mrs. Tremorne. "So many poor animals

70

then—" Carefully she tidied the photographs away, then took up her knitting and turned her hooded gaze on MacLean. She nodded with gracious sympathy. "A terrible time. We had no dustbin collection or electricity for a week, and my garage was hit."

"Indeed, now," he said, as graciously, but determined to get on with the business in hand. "It was in early March, and it's a long story, but I heard in a roundabout way that you had acquired a dog then, one that had found you when you were buried under your house."

"Garage," said Mrs. Tremorne. "It used to be the coach-house. . . ."

"Buried under your garage—"

"In the *pit*—"

"Buried in the pit of your garage that used to be a coach-house," amended MacLean, softly and patiently. Their eyes met, and he continued hurriedly, "and I thought from what I heard that it might well have been Ria—"

"Ria?" said Mrs. Tremorne, her fingers dropping a stitch.

"That was the name I gave him for I never knew his real one. He was brought aboard our destroyer off St. Nazaire with one of the survivors from the *Lancastria*. The man was badly wounded, and I kept the dog for him. There was a monkey too. Then I left the dog in Plymouth, and—"

"Monkey?" said Mrs. Tremorne, stalling for time, time to climb out of this bottomless pit that so suddenly yawned before her. Outwardly contained, inwardly surging with a fierce determination, and entirely untroubled by conscience, she decided that strategic attack was the best defence. "And what did this dog of yours look like, my man?" she said. Her voice was icily condescending.

"Ria was not very big," he said, "dark grey, with quite a thick coat, and his tail had been docked. He wasn't any breed, mind you, a terrier type, but you couldn't mistake him for his eyes— very large and bright they were. And he was the cleverest wee beast I ever came across—" Despite himself, his face had softened as he talked. "In fact," he confided in a sudden earnest rush, leaning forward in the chair, "when I heard that this dog had saved someone's life, I said that will be him for sure, that will be Ria, for he had the great courage." MacLean stopped, astonished at his loquacity.

"What a wonderful dog he must have been!" said Alice Tremorne with masterly earnestness. "How I wish I could say the same about mine! Like so many of these overbred small poodles nowadays my darling is very timid and highly strung."

"*Poodle?*" said MacLean.

"Poodle," said Mrs. Tremorne firmly. "You see, I'm afraid you've wasted your time, Mr. McVane."

Now or never. He must take this formidable old cow by the horns: "*MacLean* is the name," he said, "and I would like to see him."

"I'm afraid he's not here—he's with friends. What a pity. I am sorry," she added, searching busily in a knitting bag for another needle to pick up her dropped stitch. "I know how attached one can become—although I cannot understand why you did not direct your inquiries through the RSPCA. There is a very efficient branch here . . . Now, if you would not mind, Mr. MacLean, I am a very busy woman—" She nodded distantly at him, as though dismissing some recalcitrant servant, and reached for the bell on the table. The ball of wool rolled off her lap and under her chair.

MacLean bent, two dark spots of colour on his cheekbones, to retrieve it from under the chair. She looked down and saw a livid recent scar snaking up from behind one ear across the back of his head, the hair combed carefully across it. Pity and revulsion stirred simultaneously. And MacLean at that same moment, his eyes on a level with her grossly swollen feet and ankles in their gleaming buckled shoes, experienced the same reaction. He looked up at her as he handed back the wool, and she looked down, and, like recognizing like, an unspoken truce was called between them.

He stood with the ball of wool in his hand, picked up the knitting and examined it briefly, then laid it on the table. "It is the fine sock that you are making," he said, with only a momentary hesitation. In fact, it was a terrible sock, one that to his expert eye would produce blisters on the first foot it encountered, so loosely knitted that its present gargantuan size would shrink to tiny stiff matting at the first wash.

"There are many of my socks seeing service in the navy," said Mrs. Tremorne with a kind of complacent grandeur. "Balaclavas, scarves, mitts, too."

She looked down at his own neat navy blue socks with a critical eye. "Very nice," she said. "Very nicely knitted indeed. But no double heel?"

"No," said MacLean, "I am not liking the double heel, it is clumsy looking, yon."

"They last *twice* as long," said Mrs. Tremorne reprovingly. "You should ask your wife to do them that way—"

"I am not married," said MacLean coldly, "and I like them single—the heels, that is."

"They have to be darned," said Mrs. Tremorne, "and what looks worse than that? Double is the *only* way."

"I never darn," said MacLean with Olympian dignity. "It is a foolishness. I knit new heels." Torpedoed amidships, he thought with some satisfaction. "This is the second pair of heels these have had," he added, for a final salvo.

But far from going under, Alice Tremorne was staring at his socks with admiration. "*You* knitted them?" she said. "How wonderful—I wish I could turn heels like that—I always get a space there and have to darn it in. And a needle is such a finicky thing with these stupid hands of mine. Look," she said, holding up the knitting, "it's starting to form now—"

MacLean hesitated, momentarily defenceless before her admiration. "Here, it's like this," he said, and took the sock.

Mrs. Tremorne relaxed. Bel was safely in the paddock with his friend and would not return unless she called him, or until he saw her in the garden. She would make sure, nevertheless.

Janet, entering the sitting room a few minutes later at the bidding of the bell, resigned to fetching Bel's lead and watching him limp out of her life with this sinister visitor, found the stranger sitting on a chair drawn up close to Mrs. Tremorne's, their heads bent over something.

"Now, into the back of the next stitch, careful now," he was saying. "*Then* pass the slipped stitch over . . ."

Mrs. Tremorne looked up. "Ah, Janet, my dear," she said, and

paused meaningfully. "If that Mr. *Bell* should call this morning, tell him to come back later—I am not to be disturbed . . ." MacLean's head was safely bent over the knitting. She nodded at it and one vulturish eyelid dropped.

"I'll see that he gets the message," Janet said, almost skipping out of the door and down the stairs.

"And now, Mr. MacLean," said Alice Tremorne, "just once again—into the back of the stitch you said . . ." She was playing with fire, she knew: he should go now—but she could not overcome the terrible desire to speak of Bel, to hear something of his background from this dour, inscrutable, little man who gave no inch to her, who had once owned Bel. . . .

"I mind once," he was saying, "being sat on the deck, peaceful like in the sun, knitting, when Ria. . . ."

Helpless, avid for more, Mrs. Tremorne listened, and as Bel's life at sea unfolded so many of the missing pieces clicked into place; and something else, which she tried to push into the back of her mind, the unconscious laying bare of a man's life, and the gradual returning warmth to it from the coming of the dog.

"And so, you see," he ended at last, "that was why I left him here in Plymouth. I had promised Sinclair—"

Mrs. Tremorne could hardly believe her ears. "You mean to say that after all those months you deliberately left him?"

MacLean looked troubled. "You don't understand," he said at last. "There was more to it than just a promise. Sinclair seemed bound to that dog—I do not know how he acquired it—for it followed him from France and would not give him up even in the sea. He was a strange dog—how he affected people. Even me."

He stopped, looking suddenly old and defeated, but Mrs. Tremorne resolutely closed her mind's eye and spoke with brisk firmness. "At least you are talking about that poor dog in the past now," she said, "and I am sure that is the only sensible thing to do. Stop blaming yourself, Mr. MacLean, and lay the past to rest."

He stood up and looked out of the window across the sunny garden and paddock to the orchard beyond, his eye caught by the ambling figure of a donkey in the long grass between the apple trees. Close at its heels he could make out a small dog and some

75

hens. His eyes followed them until they disappeared behind a hedge.

Mrs. Tremorne had stood up too. "A beautiful view, isn't it," she said, and picked up MacLean's cap and handed it to him. "It has been most interesting meeting you." She managed to smile at him, trying to rivet his eyes safely away from the window.

Donkey and dog came into sight again. MacLean's eyes narrowed intently as he watched. The dog squeezed under the gate and ran up the fence line. As he came into full view, running with an uneven gait, MacLean saw an impeccable poodle with squared off jaws and trousers, a shaven tail terminating in a knob of hair, the clipped coat a pale grey. He turned away.

"I am sorry I troubled you, Mistress Tremorne," he said wearily. "I am owing you an apology. I will be going now."

Before she could ring the bell he was halfway down the stairs. He let himself out. And Janet, watching his walk down the path, hurried indoors to rejoice with Mrs. Tremorne.

But Mrs. Tremorne was leaning by the window, her face contorted in grief. "Don't stand there gaping, you dolt," she said. "Fetch me a handkerchief."

I would not have done it, *I would not have done it*—I would not have lied, Mrs. Tremorne told her conscience fiercely. I am almost sure I would not have done it if he had not been so ruthless in his talk of promises, his *own* feelings. . . .

Bel came running up just then, his eyes bright with love and interest. She put out her hand to him, the mesh bag with her knitting in it dangling from her wrist. He stiffened, sniffed her hand, and now the ball of wool, the half-knitted sock—and suddenly was off like a hound on a trail, swift as an arrow down the stairs, through the open door and along the path to the gate. And now he was jumping wildly at the gate, throwing himself at it, falling back, throwing himself at it again. Yet he could have jumped as he usually did onto the wall, and down to the lane below; it was as though he must go *through* the gate, follow the reality that had gone through it already.

Janet ran after him, calling, but he took no notice, only went on leaping and falling.

"Open the gate," said Alice Tremorne steadily. "Quickly, *run*— open the gate and let Bel go. . . ."

And Janet watched the little grey shadow streak down the road.

HALF A MILE AWAY, MacLean waited at a stop for the bus back to the naval barracks at Devonport. When it drew up, the small queue shuffled forward and he swung himself on board.

"Standing room only, move along there," said the conductress. "Pass along there, please now—and no dogs allowed, *if* you please." She touched MacLean's shoulder, "Sorry, mate," she said in a conspiratorial whisper, "the inspector's on board—". Then in a loud cheerful voice, "Come on, doggie—" and she smiled down.

Sitting at his feet, looking up at him with clear, unmistakable eyes, unblinking beneath a ludicrous topknot secured with a red ribbon, panting slightly, but otherwise in complete control was Ria. Together they got off the bus.

MacLean walked the miles back to the naval barracks and afterwards could not remember one yard of the way. Every few minutes he looked down to reassure himself: Ria, undemonstrative as ever, trotting at his heels with the slight limp and the ridiculous poodle cut. MacLean paused only once as they neared the dockyard gates, and removed the red ribbon.

THREE DAYS LATER, at ten o'clock in the morning, Bel returned to The Cedars. Janet heard him at the garden gate, and ran to let him in. He took the stairs in three bounds, pushed open the bedroom door, and jumped onto Mrs. Tremorne's bed. Mrs. Tremorne had been gazing blankly into a cup of cold tea, willing herself to get up and face the day.

She was possibly the happiest woman in England the following moment, with Janet a close second, while Bel in his excitement made the first clumsy movement of his life and upset the cup of tea. The dog Ria might be undemonstrative; Mrs. Tremorne knew only a Bel who openly demonstrated his affection for her, nudging at her face with his muzzle as though he could not get close enough. Janet and Alice Tremorne wept unashamedly together.

After that, Bel followed his usual morning routine as though he had never been absent. After his ten o'clock offering from Janet— a square of chocolate from her precious sweet ration—he trotted briskly down the path towards the orchard, checked on the welcoming hens, and, followed by his flock, continued on to the paddock. The old donkey broke into a trot towards him and Bel sailed through the air to land on the dusty brown back. It was as though he had never gone. The only difference was that he no longer wore a ribbon, and someone had clipped the long hair on the top of his head.

He was there when Mrs. Tremorne made her slow way to the orchard. Later Bel accompanied the old lady up to her room for her afternoon rest, and had a good sleep himself, under the pink eiderdown.

At teatime, after he had balanced biscuits on his nose, retrieved his ball and given it to Janet, Bel indicated that he had business elsewhere; he sat by the door, and then, when let out, sat before the gate in silent supplication, again ignoring the wall. Janet looked up at Mrs. Tremorne who watched from the upstairs window. This time she seemed almost happy.

"Yes, open it," she called down; and then had an inspiration, for she had no idea where MacLean was stationed, or how to get in touch with him. "Tie on a fresh ribbon before he goes," she said. But the hair was too short, and the ribbon had to be tied to his collar. He ran off without a backward glance.

So Ria, arriving back at Devonport barracks three-quarters of an hour later, was able to inform MacLean how and where Bel had spent the afternoon.

NOW BEL AND RIA merged into Bel Ria, a composed purposeful little figure who was often to be seen on the back roads between Devonport and The Cedars, intent only on reaching his alternative worlds. Communication was soon established between his two owners. Mrs. Tremorne tied a label on his collar with an invitation to tea. The deft-fingered MacLean fashioned a small waterproof capsule into which he rolled his acceptance.

It was at first a very formal tea party, with both sides wary, but by some tacit understanding no mention was ever made of their first meeting. Guilt was as unfamiliar an emotion to Alice Tremorne as triumph was to Neil MacLean, but disquietude was now mutual: the spectre of a third and rightful owner—rightful to MacLean anyway, but to be fought to the last inch by Mrs. Tremorne—hovered uneasily between them. This drew them closer together and the acquaintance flowered.

As MacLean's talent for fixing things around the house was revealed, urgent inquiries about what to do with a leaking U-bend or a Hoover emitting alarming sparks followed, with Bel Ria as courier. On receiving one of these SOSs MacLean would arrive as soon as he had time off and put things right. Once he turned up with a pair of overalls in his gas mask haversack. Then, armed with a saw and a bucket of tar, he "sorted", as he described the operation, the apple trees. From there it was but a short step to clearing choked gutters and drains and putting a coat of wood preservative on the henhouse. At first he had little to say; he would do whatever he considered had to be done and then depart, brushing aside any thanks, and refusing always to stay for any meal. It was as though he could not bear to see his Ria of the Ark behaving as the pampered Bel of The Cedars.

Alice Tremorne taxed him with this one day, and he admitted it bluntly: he didn't like dogs—or any animals for that matter—made fools of. She was silent for a moment, but when she spoke there was no sharpness in her voice. "I don't think it is we who make fools of dogs," she said slowly. "I am beginning to think that they make fools of us—they show up our needs and weaknesses somehow." As though embarrassed by this insight, she handed him a glass of her Elderberry '38 to try. She knew now that he was not the ghost of her jealousy. Ria could never have danced for this man.

MacLean sipped in silence. "Aye," he said non-committally. They were standing by the window upstairs, looking across the garden to the roofless shell of the coach-house. "Yon needs sorting," he said, with a disapproving scowl in its direction.

"Impossible!" said Mrs. Tremorne. "This dreadful war— carpenters nowadays are either so doddery that they'd fall off the ladder or charge so much that it would be out of the question."

"Indeed now!" said MacLean, his face brightening in a way she had come to recognize presaged the taking-up of a challenge. He left shortly afterwards, and she watched him walk down the drive to the gate, her heart turning over as always at the sight of her darling Bel following him, however temporarily, out of her life.

"Half a loaf is better than none," Janet had consoled with maddening logic. Indeed it was—yet she still found herself longing that MacLean might be transferred to some remote, dog-debarred posting, and his half restored to her in impeccable poodledom once more, his lovely topknot unsnipped. . . .

There had been bitter argument between them over Bel Ria's appearance. In the end a compromise was reached, engineered by the diplomatic Janet: why not let his coat grow out all over and then keep it short to something like Bedlington terrier length? Both grudgingly accepted this, both secretly admired the compact result; and both suffered the same stab of realization when they saw a few white hairs in the short curly coat.

MacLean had a fortnight's leave coming up that autumn, and Mrs. Tremorne had to admit that she would miss the dour little man's visits. And so would Janet, she thought with sudden amusement: there were times nowadays when she was positively skittish.

He took her unawares therefore on his next appearance when he put forward the proposal, presented with much delicate Celtic circumvention, that it might be a good idea if he were to spend his leave restoring the coach-house. Admittedly he wasn't a carpenter or a bricklayer but it was possible that he could overcome this handicap, and he knew a chippy chap who could lay hands on some timber and tools.

She was delighted. Janet could turn the yellow bedroom into a bed-sittingroom for Mr. MacLean's leave and of course it must be a proper financial arrangement with the proper going wage. . . . Suddenly she became aware of a coolness in the atmosphere. Bel Ria, sitting beside her, laid his ears back.

When MacLean spoke his voice was very cold indeed. There would be no financial arrangement; he would be doing it because he chose to do it. There would be no bed-sittingroom in the house, however yellow, however comfortable. The harness room was still weatherproof, there was water from the pump there, a fireplace to cook by—"and the lavatory still works," he finished with steely finality. If Mistress Tremorne would supply a camp bed and a few cooking utensils, that would be all he would be needing.

But Mistress Tremorne could not countenance such a one-sided arrangement. They set to, hammer and tongs, into an argument closely followed by the worried ears and eyes of Bel Ria. At the height of it he suddenly yawned, rose, stretched and departed downstairs to Janet.

Unexpectedly, Alice Tremorne was seized with laughter. "He's right," she managed to say at last. "We *are* being very boring indeed—I give in! Now will you give in over your idea of crouching over a grate with a frying pan and do me one more favour—accept our hospitality for meals?"

MacLean could make concessions too. He accepted gracefully, managing to restore Mrs. Tremorne to the position of benefactor.

"It's the grand holiday you will be giving me," he said. "Board and lodging and recreation—what more could I want? I had nowhere else to go anyway—except perhaps to Scotland, to sort things out with Donald Sinclair—"

The words hung between them. Alice Tremorne interpreted correctly. "That can wait," she said flatly. "It will wait for ever as far as I am concerned. But the coach-house needs sorting out before the winter, doesn't it? And, after all, I am a very old lady with no one to turn to for help with it, aren't I?"

"Aye," said MacLean, enigmatically as ever. He patted Bel Ria, something she had never seen him do before, and nodded cheerfully enough as he departed, but his eyes looked troubled.

Mrs. Tremorne watched him go with the stirrings of real affection. Already she was planning to feed him like a fighting cock during his stay. He was too thin, and often seemed tired and strained. Perhaps it was because of that terrible scar on his head.

He came with an ecstatically returning Bel Ria, and settled into the tackroom—finding that Janet had determinedly added her own touches of carpet and reading light—and as he took off his uniform in exchange for working rig, he shed the outside world of 1943 for the little self-contained one of The Cedars.

Bel Ria was plainly very put out at first when his separate lives were brought together virtually under the same roof. But, although he slept in Alice Tremorne's bedroom, walked with MacLean across the fields in the evening, and sat between them at meals, during the rest of the day he soon felt free to pursue his own ends, spending more time with the donkey and with Janet— their company undoubtedly restful and undemanding. He spent many hours too on his garden wall vigil, his eyes distant, yet his ears flicking to all movement up and down the road.

"It's as though he were watching for someone to come up that road. I used to think it was whoever he belonged to before, but you're here now—and he still waits," said Mrs. Tremorne one morning. She was sitting in a garden chair in the garage, pressed into dating and listing the intact wine bottles which MacLean had excavated from the debris. Now he paused in his hammering and emptied his mouth of nails.

"He would lie like that for hours on board too," he said. "Staring at nothing, as though sleeping with his eyes open. . . ."

NEIL MACLEAN sawed and hammered and painted the days away, completely absorbed in his work. The first two days, palms blistered, back aching and head throbbing, he had fallen into his camp bed in the harness room almost immediately after supper. Now, brown and fit, free for the first time in months of the headaches which had plagued him since they had removed the fragment of metal from his head in the hospital at Alexandria, he did full justice to Mrs. Tremorne's carefully plotted meals.

Neil, as she and Janet always called him now, had developed an easy relationship with Mrs. Tremorne. Both loved an argument, and they had much to argue about, but disagreement always discomforted Bel Ria, and his initial nervous yawnings, heralding his departure from the scene, were usually enough to make them agree to differ on the subject.

Janet had blossomed, and her refreshing down-to-earth viewpoint, her often hilarious gossiping anecdotes were the perfect

82

foil to his taciturnity. He found time to refurbish an old bicycle discovered rusting in the toolshed for her shopping expeditions, and he found too that she made an excellent carpenter's mate, with a good head for heights. Followed up the ladder by delighted Bel Ria, they spent many hours working companionably on the roof.

In the evenings sometimes they read or listened to the wireless; sometimes all three sat knitting or sewing, Bel Ria asleep in their contented midst. But Mrs. Tremorne liked it best when she could persuade Neil to talk about the Ark.

One evening he brought over a few photographs to show her. The first was of a fair haired young man, standing by a ship's rail, wearing a duffle coat, a small monkey muffled up in a rollnecked jersey in his arms. By his feet, looking up at the monkey, was Ria of the Ark, far sturdier then in his thick, almost shaggy coat but still recognizably her Bel.

"Atlantic convoy," said MacLean. "That was the doctor. He wasn't long qualified, but I served under none better. He sent me these pictures after I got back here."

The next was of a thick-set bearded man in tropical uniform, newly stepped off a gangway, at his heels a massive bull terrier looking towards the camera with a shark-like smile.

"The captain coming aboard at Gib. with Barkis. Himself was the fine gentleman," said MacLean with such finite simplicity that Alice Tremorne passed swiftly on to the last picture.

This was of a very tall young seaman with the same little monkey perched on his shoulder, this time wearing a shoulder harness and lead over a white singlet and pair of absurd white shorts.

"Lessing and Louis in the Mediterranean," said MacLean.

Mrs. Tremorne looked at the photograph with a magnifying glass. "So tiny and delicate," she marvelled. "Such a little scrap of a thing to have gone through so much—"

"He was a thrawn wee beast," said MacLean with some vehemence. "At least with me," he added with sudden honest insight, "as if he knew I couldn't abide his capers. But the men were daft about him, and so was Ria for that matter. When Ria

83

didn't come back after Plymouth, he was aye searching for him on board. For a while he wouldn't eat, and he was all huddled up and listless, the way sick monkeys are, but it was warm in the Med, and there was plenty of fruit and nuts and the like, and after a while he seemed to forget and settled down."

"And where is he now?" asked Mrs. Tremorne.

"He went down with the Ark," said MacLean, his face expressionless.

Mrs. Tremorne had not heard properly. "*Where* did you say?" she repeated.

MacLean looked across at her. Ria watched him, his eyes uneasy. "He went with Lessing and the others—" he said gently, "and he's still with them."

"What a happy ending," said Mrs. Tremorne with relief.

"Aye," said MacLean.

He thought of Louis again that night, lying awake in the harness room that now looked as neat and snug and ship-shape as he could have wished. In those desperate moments after the Ark had been hit by two JU 88s swooping out of the rising sun, there had naturally been no time to think of Louis. Helplessly out of commission, the Ark was a sitting target. The decision was taken to abandon ship. MacLean was one of the last to leave and, scrambling over the wreckage, he saw a flicker of movement and Louis leaped onto the rail ahead. He grabbed as he passed but Louis struggled and bit and fought free to swarm up a stay out of reach. He was last seen high on the wireless mast that still remained miraculously straight and intact, clinging to a stay, his yellow duster trailing from one paw. . . .

For weeks afterwards, when twisting restlessly in the hot, long hospital nights in Alexandria, there had been plenty of time to think, to try and equate his obsession over the manner of death of one Capuchin monkey with the deaths of so many fine men.

Thinking back to that time, it was as though now he saw it in perspective for the first time and was able to understand at last. Loss of life was an accepted gamble that men took when they went to war. But no animal went to war.

He suddenly recalled Sinclair's ravings about bears and horses and rabbits—the "innocents" he had called them. The innocents? Fanciful talk he would have said then—ravings indeed. But now? All he knew now was that nothing could ever be the same again; he could never return to the laboratory after the war—there would be too many Rias and Louis there to remind him.

He slept, the little ghost of Louis laid to rest at last, along with all the other animals that had passed through his hands, as innocent now as then.

Early in the morning he wrote a long letter to Donald Sinclair, ending it:

> . . . so that you must tell me what you would like done for I am not easy in my mind to bide this way when it is your right. I should have written long before. Mind you I do not speak for Mrs. Tremorne for after all this time she thinks of the dog as hers—she has been willing enough to let him be with me this half-and-half way, but only because she would do anything for him and it seemed to be his own decision. He is a strange dog.
>
> I will hope to hear from you soon. In the meantime I will try and make him stay here when my leave is up, for finding his own way between D'port and here is too risky with the traffic. And too long, for I am thinking now he must be nearer eleven than ten.

He addressed and sealed the envelope, then stamped it resolutely. He would post it now, before breakfast. There was a faint scratch at the door; Bel Ria had arrived, unusually early, in time to accompany him. He limped more noticeably than usual on their way to the postbox, sometimes going on three legs.

Later he told Mrs. Tremorne of his decision to leave Bel Ria when his leave ended. The news was not received with the pleasure he had expected.

"Does that mean that . . . that you're going away, going back to sea?" she said at last, sounding almost fearful.

"Nothing of the kind," he said. "I'll be at Devonport for a while yet, I hope. It just seemed that with the winter coming on it would be easier for *him.*" He saw to his embarrassment that she had tears in her eyes. "Mind you, Mistress Tremorne," he went on severely, "that doesn't mean any fancy work with the clippers and ribbons and the like the moment I've gone—there's plenty to be done yet outside so I'll be backwards and forwards to keep an eye on him."

"But perhaps he won't stay once you've gone through that gate," said Mrs. Tremorne worriedly. Then, with sudden Machiavellian cunning, she went on: "Why don't you take Janet to the pictures this afternoon for a start? To get him used to the idea that you *will* come back?"

"The *pictures?* In the *afternoon?*" he said, so obviously horrified at such decadence that she laughed.

"*Goodbye, Mr. Chips* is hardly an orgy. Bel and I will have a nice afternoon pampering ourselves in front of the fire. Why don't you go?"

"Why not? Why not indeed?" he said, suddenly reckless.

Mrs. Tremorne watched them go. Bel Ria made no attempt to follow. "How *nice*," she said as she settled down for a cosy chat with him on her lap. "How nice it would be—I could bring my bedroom downstairs, which would be much easier for us, wouldn't it?—and they could have the whole of the upstairs, and then we could all be together! Wouldn't that be lovely, my darling?" Bel Ria regarded her with enthusiastic interest. After a while they both had a little nap.

When she woke up she confided another thought: "The coach-house would make a wonderful surgery, wouldn't it?" Bel Ria looked at her inquiringly. "I mean if he went back and finished his veterinary degree one day—did you know he only had a year to go?"

The dog stirred his tail agreeably. The rain drummed on the window. It was very peaceful. They had another little nap.

On the day of Neil's departure, Bel Ria seemed reassured when he saw that his work clothes remained in the tackroom. Janet held him at the gate, subdued but unprotesting as she waved his paw cheerfully in farewell. Then he followed her quite happily to find Fred and the morning's egg harvest.

Donald Sinclair's reply, awaiting him at the barracks, was movingly warm and percipient:

. . . besides, I have no "right" as you said in your letter—it is between you and Mrs. Tremorne, for the dog has belonged to both of you over these years, and he was with me for less than twenty-four hours. His real owner risked everything for me, and in the end the only way I could repay her at all was to see that her dog was cared for—and that was where you came in.

I hope that one day we will meet and have a good yarn about those days—perhaps next year when I expect to come south for a week or so . . .

Neil handed the letter to Mrs. Tremorne on his next visit without comment. When she had finished reading she was silent for a long time.

"So it was a woman," she said slowly at last. "The one he really belonged to, I mean—I think I always knew he never really belonged to either of us." She looked at the letter again, then handed it back. "Strange—how he *found* people, first Sinclair and then me. But not you—"

He put the letter back in his pocket with an air of finality. "You make him sound like a failed St. Bernard," he said briskly. "Perhaps he found me *out* instead! And now, I've only got until nine, so there's just time to get another coat of paint on before the light goes." Clearly the matter was closed.

THE QUESTION OF POSSESSION was never to be revived. Bel Ria was left to himself as the humans became increasingly possessed by their own intertwining lives, but so gradually did this detachment come about over the following year that it went unremarked.

Only occasionally now did he search their faces to interpret some shadow of expression, or sit alertly with his head turning from one to another as they spoke. The impulse to bestow his dance seldom overtook him now, for he was no longer rewarded with Mrs. Tremorne's pleasure, only frustrated by her concern. It had seemed to her that he had become over-intense and anxious then, and sometimes he even panted as though the performances exacted too great an effort, and because of this, sympathetically

87

attributing it to rheumatism in his injured paw, she tried to avoid them altogether.

Neil, returning in the spring of 1944 after a long period of absence, noticed no change other than a whitening muzzle. But that day he was occupied with more pressing affairs. He had been posted to a Combined Operations base in Sussex and had come back on an unexpected forty-eight hour leave.

Bel Ria had shadowed him from the moment he had turned in at the gate, but after the first greeting it was Janet who received all the attention from then on, for within ten minutes of his arrival she and Neil had become engaged.

Janet made only one proviso: that Alice Tremorne should always be their responsibility, no matter what. Neil seemed only surprised that she would bother to mention this.

"But I've never thought other than that I'd be taking on the pair of you," he said. "Do you want me to propose to her as well?"

"It won't always be easy," Janet warned. "Bel Ria can't live for ever, and when he's gone she'll be lost for something to lavish her love and attention on. You're *sure* you want to take it on? And please, no 'aye' for an answer this time."

At his feet by the garden wall, Bel Ria looked up.

"There will be bairns to take his place one day," he said. "And yes, I was never surer of anything."

He bent down to pat Bel Ria, and then, to Janet's amazement, picked him up and held him in his arms. Bel Ria managed to look so awkward and embarrassed by this departure from custom that he put him down after a moment.

"I've never seen you do that before," she said.

"I was just seeing what it felt like," he said sheepishly.

Everything would go on just the same, they agreed as they walked back to the house, until Neil was demobbed and would get his gratuity—perhaps even a grant as well—to finish off the year for a veterinary degree. And in the meantime, as Mrs. Tremorne's bedroom had by now been moved downstairs to the dining room, perhaps they would be able to use part of the upstairs as their own quarters. And . . .

From the window Alice Tremorne saw them coming, Bel Ria running ahead, the three beings who filled her life. She sat back in her chair with a deep sigh of content. Bel Ria arrived now, well ahead of the others, and displaced *The Times* on her lap. She hugged him tightly, and then in her excitement dabbed her eyes with one of his ears instead of her handkerchief. "At *last*—I was beginning to think we'd have to do it for him!" she said.

A few minutes later, she received the news with every appearance of overjoyed astonishment. Not long afterwards she had a sudden inspiration for the conversion of the upstairs part of the house. They received this with equal pleasure and surprise.

In June, immediately following D-Day, Janet took on a part-time post with the ARP in addition to the railway canteen, so Mrs. Tremorne and Bel Ria were alone for most of the day now. But far from being lonely they were very contented and occupied. Wine-making now impossible with rationed sugar, they had taken up the challenge of cooking. Planting stools in strategic resting places around the kitchen and scullery, Mrs. Tremorne moved from one to another, talking to her enthusiastic chief tester ensconced on a nearby chair, as she put her full ingenuity into making something delicious out of war-time substitutes and those rewarding eggs.

The months slipped by most satisfyingly. In August the fall of Paris was celebrated with *Oeufs parisiens*, in September a land-mine exploding in a field half a mile away rocked the house and flattened a magnificent *Soufflé Arnhem*. October brought the British occupation of Athens and exotic (curried) *Oeufs à la grecque*. Even the hens themselves did their bit. Her triumph was the wedding feast in December with one of them in aspic.

After this excitement, Neil returned to Sussex, Janet to her jobs, and Bel Ria and Mrs. Tremorne settled down again. It was not until months later that Mrs. Tremorne was forced to admit that Bel Ria was slowing up. On the day that the long-silenced bells pealed out across the land again, he failed to make the low jump onto the wall. "Perhaps we're not *quite* as young as we were, my darling," she admitted, "but let's rejoice anyway!" And she arranged to have a garden seat moved under the wall.

But in truth, she herself seemed rejuvenated in the last year, for there was so much to look forward to. Now that the war was at last over she no longer felt bound to supply His Majesty's forces with knitted comforts, but could ply her needles instead in an endless stream of matinée jackets, bootees and bonnets for the baby that was on the way. And the assurance that she would be the child's godmother and proxy grandmother all rolled into one gave her *carte blanche* to order the best in furniture and equipment for the nursery in the same manner as she had years before ordered the best for a nameless little dog.

There was another more immediate excitement to be realized too, the long-awaited visit from Donald Sinclair. She could think of little else the week before. Bel Ria was shampooed, trimmed and brushed to perfection, and she thought that he must know that there was something unusual in the wind, for he became very restless and questioning the day before the visit.

She was alone in the house on the day itself, a day that had become unexpectedly even more momentous: early in the morning Neil had taken Janet to the hospital—some three weeks earlier than anticipated.

The charged atmosphere since that dawn awakening had affected Bel Ria too. He became increasingly restless, importuning, roaming from room to room, up and down the stairs, then back to her. He whined at the door to be let out, then minutes later scratched at it to be let in. She watched him settle on the sanctuary of the wall in the early afternoon almost with relief.

He was there when his soldier came walking up the road. Minutes before he came into view Bel Ria half rose, ears pricked, tensed and ready. For the first time, he jumped down off the wall onto the road. He waited, crouched low and quivering.

Donald Sinclair did not recognize him at first glance, so neatly unobtrusive against a peaceful suburban background; then, as he drew nearer, the unmistakable eyes drew him back down the years to that road in France and the dusty desolate little figure with its rider clinging tightly around its neck. Then the eyes had been filled with wary entreaty: now they were bright and somehow calmly expectant. He waited until that soldier who had once tried to drive him off picked him up and held him close in his arms. He buried his head in the man's jacket, as though seeking once more the reassurance of a bandage torn from familiar clothing.

Sinclair could feel the heart beating fast beneath his hands. He stood for a long minute, for he was deeply moved, then he walked slowly towards the house.

Alice Tremorne came to the door, realizing at once who this stranger must be.

"I'm Donald Sinclair," he said, and put Bel Ria down. They shook hands.

She shuffled into the kitchen on his arm and sank into the nearest chair. "I think this is an occasion that calls for something a little special," she said, and directed him to the cupboard with the Sloe Gin, '36.

"My best vintage," she said as she poured two glasses. "I never drink it without thinking of Bel—Bel Ria, I mean, he saved my life, you know, he found me—"

She broke off and looked across to where he sat now with his muzzle laid on the man's knee, whining softly. She had never seen him like this before, wholly concentrated on the man, excluding her even when she spoke his name. Strangely the exclusion did not rankle. She had warmed immediately to this tall gentle-faced man with the same soft accent as Neil, the same dark blue eyes. "Oh, there is so much to tell you, so much to ask—let's begin at the beginning and go on to the end."

The sloe gin reminded Donald Sinclair of the old gypsy man's fire-coursing brew. It might not be the beginning, but he spoke of this now. . . . He was a natural story-teller. Drawn on by Mrs. Tremorne's rapt attention he recreated in vivid detail the close security, the excitement, the tragedy and courage of those eventful hours in Bel Ria's life that he had shared.

She spoke only once, when he described the perfection of communication between the dark woman and her dog in the performance on the road. "So that was what he was trying to tell me," she said sadly. "Oh, Bel, if only I had known—"

But Bel Ria had ears only for this voice that stirred memory, that reached back to the rolling open roads of the caravan world.

It was dusk when the story ended. The kitchen was very still and peaceful. Mrs. Tremorne roused herself after a long silence. "I wonder what his real name was," she said, and told of John Peel's hounds and how Bel had picked out his name.

"I don't think I heard the gypsy speak directly to him once," said Donald Sinclair. "She would nod, or use her hands, or just look his way and that was all. But it is curious that he picked on an English word like 'Bell'." He drew out of his pocket a white pillbox and handed it over. "It was around his neck," he explained. "I brought it for good luck—for the bairn that's coming."

Mrs. Tremorne opened the box and took out a tiny silver bell, the handle threaded by a narrow metallic strip. She shook it gently, smiling at the unexpectedly clear sweet tone.

Bel Ria's head turned as though electrified by the sound, his ears pricked, then for the first time since Sinclair's arrival he came to her. His tail moved faster and faster, he cocked his head from one side to the other as she tinkled the bell again. She slipped the ribbon around his neck. He tossed his head, shook it, then moved it from side to side in a deliberate rhythmic control that kept the clapper chiming continuously. Enchanted, Mrs. Tremorne clapped her hands in time.

"He had bells around his paws too when he danced on the road," said Sinclair. He clicked his fingers and Bel Ria came running to him, his whole bearing jaunty and confident.

He offered his forepaws, insistently, one at a time. Donald Sinclair took each one in turn, encircling it with his fingers, smiling down regretfully, but Bel Ria seemed satisfied with the action. He stood stockstill between them for a moment, then with head erect he straightened his back and extended his forepaws in the ritual that had always preceded the tantalizing fragment of the dance bestowed from time to time on Mrs. Tremorne.

He took the opening step—and at the same moment the front door slammed, footsteps ran across the hall, then the kitchen door burst open.

"Janet's fine!" Neil MacLean shouted. "And it's a boy—Janet's got a fine wee boy for us!"

He rushed at Mrs. Tremorne and hugged her, then he turned to Donald Sinclair and an incomprehensible flood of Gaelic goodwill followed, accompanied by much handshaking and backslapping.

Bel Ria was overtaken by the sense of rejoicing too. He raced around the kitchen like a two-year-old, scattering the rugs on the linoleum. He skidded to a halt and barked excitedly, but such was the jubilation that no one heard this demand for notice. In an attempt to be more closely involved, he jumped onto a chair, but abandoned it when Mrs. Tremorne unknowingly dropped her fur wrap over his head when she went to find the hoarded whisky to wet the new Scot's head. His exuberance died away and he sat, pressed close against the soldier's leg.

They sat around the table after the initial toast to the new life. They grew ever more mellow as reminiscences and plans flowed back and forth. They drank a toast to Janet, and in due course to one another.

"And to Bel Ria," remembered Mrs. Tremorne at last, looking around for him, remorseful at her oversight. "To my darling Bel— for if it were not for him, the three of us would not be celebrating now."

He emerged from under the table and sat before them. "Bel— Ria—Bel Ria—" he heard at last, and the hand that lay on his neck threaded fingers through the ribbon there to set the bell tinkling clearly in the sudden silence.

He had his audience's full attention now. He rose stiffly to his hindquarters, then straight and steady, his eyes fixed ahead, he pirouetted before them.

Mrs. Tremorne had been privileged to see these opening movements of his inexplicable little dance. Neil MacLean had never seen nor even known about it. Long ago, Donald Sinclair had been one of a spellbound audience that had watched it to the conclusion. But now in the gathering dusk of a silent room, the little dog did not dance for him, or for her, nor did he even look apprehensively in Neil MacLean's direction. He danced for the one who had taught him. But her bidding never came, there were no signalling fingers or tapping foot, no guiding flute to accompany him, and he became confused and uncertain. Panting hard now, shaking his head for the reassurance of the bell, he circled slowly and faltered, half-lowering himself to the floor.

Helpless, his audience watched. He rose again unsteadily, repeated the circle, and tried to follow on into a tight spin.

"Oh, no—no, Bel," pleaded one; "Let him be," said another; and the third who alone could set his *pas seul* against its proper background, looked on silently.

But suddenly Bel Ria seemed to receive confidence. His head went back and his eyes looked forward with a steady eagerness, as though long custom had recalled the closing movements and there was no longer any need for direction. There was nothing to disquiet now in the certain dignity and perfection of his finale.

He circled, slower and slower towards the finale, his forepaws lowering and his head drooping to the proper spaced intervals, once more the perfectly controlled clockwork toy running down. But this time when he sank to the ground he did not rise again to take his applause. The act was over. His timing faultless as always, he had gone.

Sheila Burnford

Mrs. Burnford is a friendly, thoroughly down-to-earth person, a grandmother now with three grown-up daughters. We were fortunate enough to meet her during her recent visit to Britain in connection with the publication of this, her latest book. For, although she was born in the Scottish Highlands, and later went to school in France, she is now proud to be a Canadian citizen—her husband was a paediatrician there—and has a house on the shores of Lake Superior, near to Thunder Bay.

She is a woman of many enthusiasms, mostly connected with the natural world about her. After writing her international bestseller, *The Incredible Journey*, which was made by Walt Disney into an immensely successful film, she took two years off from civilization to go and live in an Indian village in the far Canadian north. She has written fascinatingly about her experiences during that time, in *One Woman's Arctic*.

She believes passionately in getting her facts right. Much of *Bel Ria*, for example, comes directly from her own personal experiences. From her childhood in Provence come vivid memories of gypsy caravans and of the performing animals that often accompanied them. She was in Plymouth throughout the blitz on that city. More recently she has visited St. Nazaire and personally spoken to survivors of the ill-fated *Lancastria*. Her husband served in destroyers during the war, and himself brought back a dog of somewhat doubtful parentage from Crete.

Animals, she believes, have an innate dignity we humans rarely afford them. Her intention in writing *Bel Ria* was to portray a dog that clung indomitably to its own identity while seeming to bend to the whims of its various human owners. She has no time at all for the usual run of sentimental animal stories. "The moment I read that 'Rover thought . . .' I close the book," she says.

Without a doubt it is this attitude of informed and affectionate commonsense that has endeared her books to such a vast public. The story Mrs. Burnford is writing at the moment remains something of a secret. She wisely doesn't want to talk about it until she's certain it's going to work. But whatever it is, she may be assured that it will be awaited eagerly by countless readers throughout the world.

THE NAKED COUNTRY

a condensation of the book by

MORRIS WEST

Illustrated by Gordon Crabb
Published by William Heinemann

To the aborigines the valley was a precious, holy place. To Lance Dillon, however, it was simply a fertile oasis in the midst of the surrounding desert, ideal pasture for his herd of prize cattle.

In such a head-on clash of cultures, stone-age and modern, violence was inevitable. With ritualized death as its merciless outcome.

Twenty miles away, at the Dillon homestead, his wife Mary rode determinedly out in the company of the tough policeman Adams, to try to save her husband's life. Already their marriage was in ruins. She hated the outback, and everything it stood for. And gradually, as the gruelling search dragged on, she began to face the possibility that they would be too late, that Lance Dillon would never be found alive. . . .

HE HAD BEEN RIDING SINCE DAWN, away from the homestead towards the climbing sun. The river was at his left, a torpid snake sliding through the swamps and the lily ponds and the flood plains, green with wild rice. On his right was the paper-bark forest and ahead the gaunt heave of the escarpments of the Stone Country.

He sat loose in the saddle, long in the stirrup, head bent against the glare, his rangy body rolling to the gait of the pony. Dust rose in grey eddies. Heat beat down from a steel-blue sky, parching his lips, bleaching the moisture out of his leathery skin; but he rode on, tireless and patient, towards the red ridges where spinifex and wollybutts thrust their roots into crannies of the sandstone.

His name was Lance Dillon, and he held title, along with a pastoral mortgage company, to Minardoo, newest and smallest station on the southern fringe of Arnhem Land. He was thirty-seven, which is late for a man to come into the cattle business in competition with the big syndicates and the old families who are the kings of the Australian Northwest.

Twenty miles behind him the aboriginal stockboys were fanning out to begin the muster, yearly prelude to the long trek to the railhead. They would brand the new stock, cull out the scrub bulls —stringy crossblooded sires who might taint the breeds—then begin herding back to the homestead. Lance Dillon was the bossman of this wide-flung operation, but today he was riding away from it, intent on private business.

To a newcomer, the cattle country promised little but debt and disillusion. The syndicates held most of the land, and the best of it. They kept priorities over trucking and shipping space, they had first call on experience and manpower, and above all they had capital for pasture improvement, water conservation, transport, slaughter yards and freezing plants. They could kill their own beef, chill it and fly it straight to the ships, while the small man must drive his steers a hundred and fifty miles and watch his profits decrease with every pound they lost on the trek.

It was a gambler's business and the winnings went to the man who could sit longest on his cards. Lance Dillon knew it, yet he had mortgaged himself to the neck to buy into the game. He had reasoned that the answer for the small man was better bloodlines: hardy stock bred to the monsoon summer and the parching dry season, resistant to ticks, growing meat instead of sinew.

This was why he now rode to the edge of the Stone Country. Behind the first escarpment was a valley, watered by a perennial spring. There were shade trees and sweet grass, where a new and noble sire could breed his wives free from the raids of scrub bulls and dingoes, untouched by the parasites that bred in swamp pastures. Here were three thousand pounds' worth of blood bull and fifty first-class cows with their calves. If Dillon's judgment had been right it was the first smell of success, and he could soon spit in the eye of the financiers who kept him close to strangling point.

He reined in the pony, dismounted and unhooked the canvas waterbag from his saddle. He half filled his hat with water and held it under the pony's muzzle until the last drop was gone. Afterwards, he held the bag to his own lips and took a long, grateful swallow.

It was then that he saw the column of smoke over the hill. He cursed quietly, jammed the stopper back into the waterbag, hoisted himself into the saddle and set off at a canter.

The smoke had only one meaning: the myalls were in the valley. All this land was blackfellow country and the myalls—nomads who lived resolutely apart from the white settlements—had ranged it for centuries. They were the world's most primitive people, who had never built a house, made a wheel, nor learned the use of clothing. Their weapons were spears and clubs and boomerangs. They ate kangaroo and buffalo, reptiles and grubs, yams and lily roots, and honey plundered from the wild bees. They ranged free as animals within their tribal areas, and the only signs of their passing were the ashes of campfires or a body, wrapped in bark, in the fork of a tree. Sometimes, if game were scarce, they might kill a steer from the white man's herds, but this was a convention of survival, with no hostility on either side.

Lance Dillon understood the primitive rights of the nomads and respected them; but the valley was his domain. His word had gone out to the tribal elders and until this moment they had respected it. The smoke was a kind of defiance which puzzled him. More, a campfire might grow to a grass fire which would destroy his pasture in a night. The myalls saw no difference between bloodstock and bush buffalo, and this herd was for breeding, not for blackfellow meat.

The thought was painful to him, and he urged the pony in a lathering gallop to a narrow gorge which marked the entrance to the valley. Here he saw that the log barrier had been torn down and the thornbush palisade pushed to one side. His face clouded, he walked the pony towards the basin, where the gorge opened out. When he reached it, he reined in and looked across the valley floor, gape-mouthed with shock and fury.

There was a hunting party of eight or ten myalls, husky, naked bucks, armed with spears, clubs and throwing sticks. Three of them had worked the cows and calves into a blind corner of the valley. The others were circling the bull, which watched them with hostile eyes. Before Dillon had time to utter a word, there were three spears in the great animal, and two men with clubs were battering its hindquarters to bring it down.

Dillon sat paralysed by the sight of the senseless slaughter. Then, with a wild howl of anger, he clapped spurs into the pony and raced towards the myalls, whirling the long lash of his stockwhip, trying to cut them down. They scattered and his momentum carried him beyond them, while the dying bull bellowed and tried to raise itself on its forelegs. Dillon wheeled sharply and charged again, but before he had gone twenty yards a spear caught him in the back, high up on the right shoulder, so that he almost toppled from the saddle. Another flew over his head, a third carried away his hat. He knew they would kill him if he stayed.

Gasping with pain, he galloped back towards the defile, the spearhaft dangling from his shoulder. The myalls followed him to the mouth of the defile, then turned back to the slaughter of the great bull for which Dillon had paid three thousand pounds.

For the first wild minutes, anger, pain, and blind self-preservation drove Dillon headlong. He was a mile from the valley among paper-bark trees before he slackened rein and tried to take command of himself.

The wound in his shoulder was deep and bleeding profusely. The barb had torn through the muscles and the drag of the hanging haft was agony. He could not ride twenty miles like this under the noon sun—yet to rid himself of the spear would call for surgery more brutal than the wound itself. The mere contemplation of it made him sick. The haft must be broken off and the head forced through his body until it could be drawn out in front. He closed his eyes and bent his head until the faintness passed.

Then anger pumped new strength into his body. The slaughter of the bull made a monstrous mockery of all his hopes. He was finished, ready for the bailiffs, because a bunch of meat-hungry myalls wanted to show their maleness by cutting down the master of the herd.

Then a new thought struck him. They weren't meat-hungry at all. The grass flats were full of kangaroo and wallaby and stray steers. There were geese on the billabongs and fish in the river. This was deliberate trespass—against the tribal elders and himself.

He remembered that all the bucks had been young. The old ones knew the power of the Northwest police. Tribal killings were one thing, but violence against the white man was another, and the old men wanted no part in it. The young ones resented the authority of the elders and the presence of strangers on their tribal preserves. They must prove to themselves and to their women that they were men and would one day rule in the councils of the tribe. But when the first heat had subsided they would see

102

how the vengeance of the white man would fall on the whole tribe. So they would try to conceal their trespass.

They would try to kill him and hide his body. Fear took hold of Dillon again, a constriction round his heart. He looked towards the ridge to see silhouetted against the skyline a solitary figure trailing a bundle of throwing spears.

Soon they would track him like a bush animal, by hoof pad and broken twig and the ants clustered over his blood drops. They would circle between him and the homestead, cutting off his retreat. The river was his one hope. It would break his tracks and water his pony and cleanse his wound. Its shore-growth would shelter him while he rested and, with luck, he could work his way downstream back to the homestead.

He took a long drink from the waterbag, tightened the reins in his left hand and, with the spear still jolting pitilessly in his back, set off towards the distant water.

MUNDARU squatted on a limestone ledge and watched the white man's progress, marked by the shift of a shadow among the tree boles, the rise of a flock of parrots, the panic leap of a grey wallaby. The slow progress towards the river was clear. Mundaru noted these things, calculating how long it would take his quarry to work his way downstream to where Mundaru planned to intercept and kill him.

Dillon had been wrong in his judgment of Mundaru and his associates. Their entry into the valley had not been a trespass but a ritual return to an old, sacred place where the spirit people lived. An order to stay away from it was meaningless. The ridges which Dillon saw as a pen for his stud were a honeycomb of caves whose walls were covered with totem drawings, the great snake, the kangaroo, the turtle, the crocodile and the giant buffalo, Anaburu, which was Mundaru's own totem, the symbol of his personal and tribal relationship.

The slaughter of the bull was an act of religious significance. In Mundaru's tribe, the totem must be killed and eaten, for from this mystical merging flowed strength—and a promise of fertility. The intrusion of the white man was a dangerous interruption of a life-giving ritual, which must be avenged if Mundaru and his totem brothers were not to suffer in their own bodies.

So Mundaru, the Anaburu man, planned his killing. First he would eat the flesh of the bull which the others were now roasting. When he had eaten, he would paint his body with totemic patterns, in ochre and charcoal and the blood of the bull. The others would go with him to flush the quarry but he, Mundaru, must be the one to kill him. They would hide the body in a spirit place, where the policeman would never find it.

Beyond this point there was doubt and a small darkness of fear. By attacking the white man, Mundaru had taken the first step outside the tribe. He had killed before, in blood-feud, directed by the elders. They had given him a spear made potent by magic. But this time there would be no magic to help him, because Willinja, the sorcerer, hated Mundaru. He knew Mundaru coveted his latest wife.

Far away Mundaru saw a white egret rise and knew the white man had entered the high grass of the swamp lands. He walked back to the campfire.

LANCE DILLON groped his way through darkness and fiery pain, then lay still, trying to remember. He had cleared the timber and the pony was thrusting towards the river flats. Suddenly, scared by a snake, it had reared and thrown him with a sickening impact. After that, nothing.

Cautiously, he stretched one leg, then the other; the bones were unbroken. Groping upwards to his right shoulder his fingers encountered a sticky mass of blood, scurrying ants and the serrated edge of the spearhead. He understood that the fall had snapped off the haft and driven the head out over his breast.

He closed his eyes and lay back sweating until the agony subsided. Then he groped for the broken-off haft of the spear and, using it as a stave, tried to hoist himself to his feet. Twice he collapsed, gasping and retching, but the third time he made it and, leaning on the staff like an old man, began to stumble towards the river, half a mile away. It took him more than two hours to reach it.

At the water's edge he drank greedily from his cupped palm. When he felt a small strength seeping back, he worked his way out of his shirt, rinsed it in the stream and tore parts of it with his teeth and his left hand into strips.

Steeling himself for the brutal surgery, summoning all his strength, he closed his fingers round the spearhead and wrenched it forward. To his surprise, it came free, with a rush of blood and a pain that stabbed through him like a knife. He laid the jagged head beside him, and using the strips of shirt, began to cleanse the wound. Every movement sent a leaping pain through the torn muscles. He thought of bathing his shoulder in the river, but remembered that this was crocodile water and that the blood might bring them in search of him. Suddenly there was a new fear: blood-poisoning. A native weapon must be crawling with infection.

Chewing on the bitter thought, he remembered a thing out of a lost time. He had seen the homestead aborigines plastering cuts with spider-webs, and someone had remarked that there was a relation between the web and penicillin. He looked around and saw, strung on a pandanus, a web with a huge black spider in the centre of it.

He inched his way up the bank, struck at the web with the spearhaft, then rolled the sticky threads into a ball and packed them into the wound. After many failures he succeeded in fixing a bandage over his shoulder and under his right armpit and tightening it with a tourniquet.

When it was done he felt weary, hungry and desperately alone. He was faced with the simplest problem of all—survival. All this land belonged to him, but he could starve amid its primal plenty. Desperately he tried to reassemble the scraps of knowledge he had picked up from aboriginal stockboys and old bushmen who had lived blackfellow-fashion in the outback. There were edible grubs in the tree boles, lily roots in the lagoons, yams and ground nuts on the river flats. The flesh of a snake was white and sweet-tasting, but a lizard was oily and hard to digest. The aborigine did not hunt at night. He was afraid of spirit men. Dillon, light-headed, caught at this last scrap of memory.

If he could gather a little food and find himself a hole for the daytime, he might build enough strength to move at night, while the myalls were huddled over their campfires. The river could be his road, the darkness his friend. But time was against him. Any moment now, the hunters might come: black, naked men, with flat faces and knotted hair and killing spears wrapped in bundles of paper-bark.

WHEN MUNDARU and his myalls came out of the valley, the first thing they saw was Dillon's riderless horse. Two of the bucks moved towards it but Mundaru called them back. The horse would make its way to the homestead, or be picked up by the stockboys. Its discovery would lend the colour of an accident to the white man's death. Acknowledging his cleverness, they followed him as he walked in a wide arc until they came to the clearing where Dillon had lain after his fall. Mundaru knelt to examine the signs.

Here the white man had stood a long time. There he had begun to walk. The track was as plain as that of a wounded animal and they followed it swiftly to the water's edge. Then they halted, momentarily puzzled, until Mundaru saw a patch of sand whose surface was still soft while the surrounding area was set in a dry crust. He frowned with displeasure. The white man knew he was being hunted. He had begun to cover his tracks.

Twenty feet from the spot where Dillon had entered the water, Mundaru found a flat stone, kicked out of its mooring. The quarry was heading downstream. They had only to follow him, beating the banks as they went. Mundaru waited until three of the bucks had waded across to the opposite bank; then they set off, walking fast, eyes alert, like hounds closing in for the kill.

MARY DILLON stood on the homestead veranda, watching the shadows lengthen across the brown land, the ridges turn from ochre to deep purple, the sun lapse slowly out of a dust-red sky.

The days were a blistering heat when the thermometer on the doorpost read a hundred and fifteen and the willy-willies— whirling pillars of wind and sandstone grit—raced across the home paddocks. The nights were a chill loneliness, with the dingoes howling from the timber and the myalls chanting down by the river, and Lance snoring, oblivious of her terror. But in this short hour, which was neither dusk nor twilight, the alien, primeval land became gentle and Mary came nearest to peace.

It would never be truly home to her. After three years of marriage to Lance Dillon and two visits to her family in Sydney, she knew it for a certainty. She was a city girl. She needed a husband home at seven, pulling out of the driveway at eight thirty in the morning, and a comforting presence in between—not this brown leathery man with his bleak ambition, gone for days at a time.

Other women lived a hundred miles from their nearest neighbour yet made happiness for themselves in the outback. When she heard them talking on the daily gossip session over the pedal radio and heard the contentment in their voices, she wondered why she had never been able to attain it. "Give it time and patience, sweetheart," Lance had told her, in his calm, positive fashion, "and you'll grow to love it. Isn't it worth a little waiting and a little courage?"

But the land was still a stranger, and Lance was becoming one too. He was as gentle as ever, considerate in his casual fashion; but he seemed not to need her any more. Soon she must face the question: what to do about it? This land demanded a wholeness. One could not love it with a divided heart, nor fight it with a defective relationship. A man with a discontented wife was beaten before he began. Her choice, therefore, was simple: make good the marriage promise or go away, leaving the man and the land to work out their own harmony.

Three years ago, when Lance had come striding into her life, she had had no doubts at all. Lance was a country giant in suburbia, a land-tamer. Now he looked disappointingly different. The immensity of the land dwarfed him and its harshness had honed the humour out of him. She still loved him. But enough . . . ? That was a question she could not wait too long to answer.

She shivered and walked into the house where the soft-footed lubra servants were bustling about the kitchen. Tonight was an occasion, it was her wedding anniversary and Lance had promised to be home by sunset.

Normally, he paid little attention to punctuality, explaining patiently at first, later with irritation, that in the territory a man could travel only as fast as his tired horse. It was big country, the herds were scattered. She must learn not to nag—a nagging woman was worse than saddle galls to a bushman. More importantly, the stockboys had scant respect for a hen-pecked boss.

But tonight—his eyes had brightened as he said it—was different. He would not go to the muster, but out to the valley, where the breeders were, and would be home by dark. He had kissed her, and the memory of the kiss was the one small light in the gathering darkness of doubt and disillusion. Perhaps tonight it would flare up into a renewal of passion, of hope for both of them.

In the dining room, Big Sally was laying the silver. She was married to one of the stockboys and her heavy body was shapeless with child-bearing. She was dressed in a black cotton frock and starched apron, but her feet were bare and her broad, flat face looked incongruous under the maid's white cap. She looked up as Mary entered and said in her husky voice: "Boss come soon, eh, Missus? Catch 'im bath, clean clothes. Eat good, drink good. Maybe this time make 'im piccaninny longa you?" She went into gurgles of laughter and, in spite of herself, Mary laughed too.

"Maybe, Sal. Who knows?"

"You dream 'im right, he come. . . ."

The aborigines believed that, in the making of a child, spirit must be dreamed into the womb. Lance and she wanted a child desperately but so far, it seemed, they had not dreamed right.

She walked to the sideboard and almost without thinking, poured a Scotch and drank it slowly. It was cocktail-time in the city and this was her commemoration of the life she had left behind.

Once, in their first year of marriage, Lance had come home late to find her sitting by the fire with a drink at her elbow. He had chided her, smiling: "Never drink with the flies, sweetheart. I've seen too many station wives hit the bottle because they'd slipped into the habit when they were lonely. If you want to drink, let's drink together."

The insinuation angered her and she blazed out at him. "If you can't trust me in a little thing like this, how can you trust me in the big ones?"

He was instantly contrite. "Mary, I understand this country better than you do. I know these first years aren't going to be easy. So I try to warn you. That's all."

His gentleness charmed the anger out of her, but she could not bring herself to surrender; each night at the same time she took one drink in futile affirmation of her right to be herself.

She walked into the living room, sat down, and began leafing through an old newspaper. Presently the paper slipped to the floor and she dozed.

Suddenly Big Sally was shaking her; the clock read 9.45. "You eat now, Missus. Boss no come. Dinner all burn up finish!"

Anger took hold of her. "Put the boss's dinner in the oven. Give the rest to the girls. I'm going to bed!"

She hurried into the bedroom and threw herself on the bed, sobbing in bitterness and defeat. Lance had failed her, the country had defeated her. It was time to be quit of it all.

DILLON looked out across thirty yards of moonlit water to the myalls' campfires on the beach. They were roasting meat from the bull, and the smell of burnt hair drifted across the water. Their weapons lay on the sand and they seemed absorbed in their meal and talk, but at every sound—the cry of a night-bird, the leap of a fish—they became watchful. Dillon cautiously daubed more mud on his face, lest a chance gleam of moonlight betray his presence.

He had found this place five minutes before the hunters had come stalking him down the banks, and he had been here six hours already, waist deep in the stream and hidden in a tangled barricade of pandanus roots and driftwood. He was in "croc water" but he had to choose between the certainty of a myall spear, and the chance of a big saurian sleeping in the mud.

Leeches were battening on him, the water was bleaching his skin, and clouds of insects were buzzing about him. As the cold crept into his blood, his wound throbbed painfully and he forced a thick twig between his teeth to stop their chattering. Suddenly,

110

desperately, he knew that he could not stay conscious much longer. Yet if he lapsed into sleep, he would slide into the water and drown.

Painfully, he turned his head, searching for a projection that might hold him. Finding none, he undid his belt and slid it from his trouser-top. Then he looped the belt high round his chest and buckled himself to one of the palm roots, so that he hung suspended under the armpits. He let his body go limp, while his mind surrendered itself to the illusion of rest. It was no more than an illusion, pain-haunted and full of terror. He was burning in a dark sea, drowning in a cold fire.

When he woke the upper part of his body was cramped and from the waist down there was no sensation. With infinite care he eased himself out of the belt until he was standing again. Soon, after the myalls had gorged themselves with meat, they would sleep till sunrise. Then he must move, find food and warmth; but how and where?

MUNDARU was puzzled. Squatting on the sand, with the meat of the totem warm inside him, he thought over each step of the trail from its beginning in the high grasses to its end in the river shallows. He was convinced the white man could not have out-distanced them. In the morning, he would cross the river and look again.

He sat a little apart from the others and did not speak to them, nor they to him, but their thought was clear. He was diminished in their sight by his failure to come up with the white man. They watched him with sidelong, speculative glances. In the morning they might well go back to the tribe. Mundaru could not—not without shame. He must follow to the kill or to his own death.

Now he was ready for sleep. He stretched his body on the sand and closed his eyes. But sleep would not come. His thoughts flew back, like a green parrot, to the camp, where Menyan would be sleeping by the side of her husband, Willinja, the sorcerer. She was named for the new moon, slim and young. When she was still a child her father had promised her to Willinja. From that moment she was lost to Mundaru.

111

Menyan's eyes told him he was pleasing to her, but she was afraid of her husband, as Mundaru was afraid. Willinja's cold eyes could look into a man's brain and Willinja's spirit travelled abroad out of his body, seeing what was done in the most secret places.

Mundaru must not fight him—yet. But with the white man dead, and the white man's strength absorbed into himself, he might be ready to enter into open conflict. A cold tremor of anticipation shook him.

INCH BY INCH Dillon slewed himself round until he could see a narrow opening between the upper pandanus roots and the mud bank. It was, perhaps, three feet above his head. If he could pass through it, he might scale the high bank and head across the grass flats away from the sleeping myalls. He was very weak and this effort might well prove too much for him.

He began to scoop footholds in the bank, lowering each handful in the water, letting it float soundlessly away from his palm. It was child's labour, but before it was done, he was trembling and the sweat was running down his face. A new risk presented itself: his clothing was full of water. The moment he climbed upwards, it would spill out noisily.

He rested many times before he was free of his boots. Trousers and tattered shirt came next, and as he worked his way out of them he could feel bloated leeches clinging to his flesh. He crouched naked in the stream, debating whether to try to salvage his clothing against the heat of the day. Finally, he let the garments sink to the bottom. Then with wracking effort he hoisted himself into the first foothold. Behind him, in the water, was the spearhead which had slipped unnoticed from his grasp.

FOR SERGEANT NEIL ADAMS, Northern Territory Mounted Police, the dog days were coming. He knew the symptoms: the day-long depression, the restless nights, the itch in the blood for whisky or a woman or an honest-to-God brawl—anything to break the crushing monotony of life in the outback.

No one who lived long in the territory escaped the disease. They called it "gone troppo". The cattlemen hit the outback

112

settlements and launched themselves into a week of drinking and fighting. The stockboys and the station aborigines grew sullen and disobedient and went walkabout into the bush. Women became tearful and shrewish. Some of them lapsed into brief love affairs with the nearest available man.

For Sergeant Adams, the treatment was work, and more work. His headquarters were at Ochre Bluffs, a small huddle of clapboard buildings under the lee of a range of red hills. His territory extended a hundred miles in every direction and included a population of cattlemen, publicans, storekeepers, two doctors, four bush nurses, transient pilots, stock inspectors, well-sinkers, drifters and whites gone native. He took the census, sobered drunks, tracked down tribal killers, settled disputes on brands and boundaries, registered births, marriages and deaths.

Much of it was paperwork; the rest meant days in the saddle, nights by a campfire, with Billy-Jo, the aboriginal tracker, for company. In the inchoate life of the territory, Adams was a symbol of ultimate order. He could not afford to be a drunk or a lecher. At the first lapse, his authority would be destroyed completely.

So, when the black mood began he and Billy-Jo would pick up the tracks of a nomad group and follow them to a water-hole. Adams would talk with the elders, pick up hints of feuds and medicine killings. After a while he would emerge renewed and ready for a new effort.

He had one inflexible rule. At such times, he never went near a homestead unless called to an emergency. He was thirty-five years of age, six feet tall, handsome in a rugged fashion. He knew himself too well to trust himself in the company of a lonely woman whose husband might be absent for days at a time.

A few minutes before nine on this raw, hot morning he sat in his office waiting for the radio circuit to open. Soon the monitor station at Jamieson's Creek would come on the air, calling in the homesteads and the mission stations and the police offices over three thousand square miles of territory. They would report their needs and their problems. Adams would detail his own movements.

Dead on the hour, the voice of the monitor came crackling:

113

"LXR . . . Jamieson's Creek calling in Network One. Check in everybody, please . . . no traffic until everyone has reported!" Then roll-call began.

"This is Coolangi. We're in."

"This is Boolala . . ."

"Hilda Springs in and waiting . . ."

Behind each voice was a face, a family, a community, and Adams knew them all. Each station answered briskly and briefly. But when the monitor called Minardoo homestead there was a change. A woman's voice, high and urgent, answered.

"Hold it, please! This is an emergency! I'm Mary Dillon. My husband didn't come home last night. The stockboys found his horse near the homestead this morning . . . There was blood on the saddle. They're out looking for him, but I'm dreadfully worried."

Fifty listeners heard her and felt for her, but only the monitor answered. "Hold it, Mrs. Dillon. Did you get that, Sergeant Adams?"

"Adams here. I've got it. Mrs. Dillon, just sit tight. I'll talk to you in a moment. . . . Does anybody know if there's a plane near Ochre Bluffs?"

Out of the static a thick Scots burr answered. "This is Jock Campbell, laddie. Tommy Gilligan's due in with the mail in twenty minutes. Do you want me to send him over for you?"

"Yes, please, Jock. Tell him two passengers with packs. Me and Billy-Jo."

"Will do, laddie. Expect him in about an hour and a half."

"Mrs. Dillon? Sergeant Adams again. I'm coming over with Gilligan. With luck I'll be there in three hours. I'm bringing a tracker. I want two saddle horses and a pack pony. Also, make me up a medical kit. Bandages, antiseptic, sulpha-powder and whisky. Is that clear?"

"Quite clear. I'll be waiting."

"Jamieson's Creek? Pass the word to the doctor. I may have to get in touch with him in a hurry."

Adams flipped off the power. Mary Dillon's report troubled him—for more reasons than one. Blood on a man's saddle meant blackfellow trouble. Tribal violence against the whites had died out long ago. Single incidents were now so rare as to be sensational; and they were generally connected with women, smuggled liquor or the intrusion of shady characters into tribal preserves. But, whatever their cause, they were a headache to the local police authority. Native affairs were a tender political issue in the federal capital, as in the territory itself.

All this was only half of Adams's problem. The other half was Mary Dillon herself. Of all the women in his territory, this was the one to whom he felt himself the most vulnerable. He had met her at a dance on Coolangi Station, a slim, dark woman in a modish bouffant frock. He remembered the smile she gave him when he asked her to dance, the feel of her body as she relaxed in his arms, her relief when he was able to talk about things that interested her. He understood how she felt. Lance Dillon was a driving man, with neither the time nor the wit to give this woman what she needed.

Adams had time, passion and a practised bachelor's way with the ladies. Since then he had occasionally seen her at the homestead with Dillon and they had both welcomed him with the offhand friendliness of the bush. But the memory of that first night still clung to him.

Now they must meet again, alone. He frowned and ran his fingers through his hair in a gesture of indecision; then he walked to the door and shouted for Billy-Jo, the black tracker.

WILLINJA, the sorcerer, sat cross-legged in the shadow of a high rock and waited for the men of the tribe to come to him. He was tall, strong but ageing, the skin of his body puckered over long decorative scars on his chest and belly. His wide mouth was full of yellow teeth and his broad, flat nose receded into craggy brows. His grey hair and beard were powdered with ochre dust, so that against the dark skin of his face they stood out like fire.

On the ground he had drawn the totems of the tribe: the great snake, the buffalo, the crocodile and the barramundi fish. Behind the drawings were the instruments of his magic: a round river stone marked with ochre; a long sliver of quartzite pointed at one end, and at the other trailing long strands of human hair; a small bark dilly-bag containing human bones.

To the ignorant, Willinja was a primitive, squatting in the dust toying with childish trifles. To his people he was a man of power, a keeper of ancient knowledge, an initiate of the spirit-folk who, at the time of his induction, had killed him, dismembered him and then made him whole again, gluing his parts together with magical substances. When life was disturbed by malignant influences, he alone had the formulas for the restoration of order.

Now the men came towards him in three groups, the first carrying spears and clubs, the second bearing sticks and the long, deep-voiced instrument of music, the didjeridoo. Behind them, unarmed, shamefaced, walked the buffalo men who had been Mundaru's companions at the bull killing and who had returned without him.

The first two groups settled themselves to the right and the left of Willinja, the musicians on one side, the spearmen on the other. The buffalo men sat facing Willinja so that between them all was a hollow square of sacred ground. The buffalo men told of the wounding of the white man and Mundaru's pursuit of him. Willinja closed his eyes and sat rock-rigid. After a long while, he spoke in the spirit voice.

"We have lived in peace. We have slept safe with full bellies. Our spirit places are untouched because the white man and his people pass by like wind and the blown leaf. Until now. . . !"

His voice rose to a wailing pitch and he leaned forward and pointed to the drawing of the buffalo in the dust.

"This is Anaburu, which is the sign of Mundaru. This he may kill and eat, and no one would refuse him. But this . . ." He outlined in the dust a big Brahman bull. "This is not Anaburu. This is a white man's animal. If Mundaru kills it there is death for all of us, the men of the Gimbi. The white men will move us to a strange country where our spirits will forget us."

Willinja waited, then dropped his voice to a low key. "But I have talked with the spirit men. They say there is a hope for us, if the death that threatens us is sung into the body of Mundaru!"

Immediately the fear went out of the buffalo men, in a long

116

audible exhalation. Willinja stood up, picked up the stone with ochre markings and laid it in the centre of the square where all could see it. They knew it was the symbol of Mundaru.

Willinja next picked up the quartzite blade with its pennon of hair. He pointed it at the stone which bore the name Mundaru. The others watched, tense. The blade was a spirit spear, pointed at the victim. Then, abruptly, the singing began, the melody counterpointed by the throbbing notes of the didjeridoo. Every line was a death wish, directed against the man-stone in the dust.

"May the spear strike straight to his heart. . . ."

"May the fire burn his entrails. . . ."

"May the Great Serpent eat his liver. . . ."

When the chanting stopped, Willinja put down the spirit spear, and the spearmen and the musicians walked slowly round the death stone then headed back to the camp. Only the buffalo men waited, submissive, until Willinja showed them how they must kill Mundaru.

NAKED, DILLON lay on a patch of warm mud and looked up at the sky through a meshwork of reeds and swamp grass. He had slept a long time, and he was still lapped in the languor of rest and warmth. He felt no pain, no fear, only the detachment of a ghost looking down on its discarded body.

It wasn't much of a body any more—streaked with mud, scored by brambles and the bites of swamp insects. One shoulder was a pulpy red mass, from which the tracks of infection spread out. But life was still pulsing sluggishly under the welted skin, and somewhere pain and panic were beginning to wake again. However unwillingly, the ghost must enter into his battered habitation.

But not yet, not just yet. This small suspension of pain was too precious to surrender. He must use it to take hold of reason before it slipped away for ever. He had left the river. He remembered that. He had climbed the bank from the dark pool while the myalls slept. Then he had crawled across the grass country to this billabong covered with lily pads, whose bulbous roots would give him food. He had dragged a small dead branch to sweep away his tracks. With luck, the myalls might miss him.

117

The first mouthfuls of lily roots were watery and bitter and he had retched painfully. But he managed to hold some down; then he lay on the wet mud and slept till the sun was high.

Now the lily flowers were open, the green slime in the shallows shone with a sickly brilliance and ripples spread out from a brood of cruising ducklings. A pair of egrets waited for an unwary fish. The lagoon was full of life and food but he was too weak to hunt it, and he dared not raise his head above the high grasses for fear the myalls might be watching.

Suddenly, out of the blank sky, he heard the aircraft. . . .

MUNDARU heard it, too. He leaned on his spear and looked up. Before his companions had left him they had warned him that the white men had the power to call each other over great distances. Then the big bird always came, sometimes with the policeman, Adamidji, sometimes with another, who carried a powerful magic in a little black bag. For this reason they would not stay with Mundaru any longer. Mundaru had not argued. By his own act he had set himself outside the tribe. He could not turn back.

As the big bird banked high over the swamplands, he saw in the distance the head and shoulders of a man and one arm waving frantically. Mundaru stood waiting to see what the bird would do. It swung round slowly and headed towards the homestead. Mundaru, silent as a snake, began thrusting through the waving grasses towards the lily pond.

IT IS ONE OF the ironies of existence that a man's life may hang on the humour of his surgeon's wife, or the state of a taxi-driver's liver, or the angle of sight from an aircraft. At the precise moment when Adams might have seen Dillon waving from the grass his attention was caught by Billy-Jo, shouting and pointing.

"Look, boss! Kirrkie come up! Bird belong dead thing."

Sighting along the black tracker's hand Adams saw the flight of hundreds of kite-hawks, sure sign to the bushman of a carrion kill. He tapped Gilligan, the pilot, on the shoulder and shouted in his ear. "Over to the right—behind the ridges!"

As the aircraft came in low, Adams looked down to the green

valley, the brood cows cropping with their calves at heel, and, in the centre, the mangled carcass on which the kites had been feeding.

Billy-Jo turned to Adams. "Boss! I know this place! Spirit caves for Gimbi tribe! White man's cows in spirit place. Maybe Gimbi men make trouble, eh?"

Adams nodded thoughtfully. Half the trouble in the territory began with the clash between the pragmatic philosophy of the whites and the dream-time* thinking of the aborigines. The small aircraft rocked as Gilligan lifted it over the ridge. Gilligan shouted, "Where to now?"

"Head for the homestead."

Billy-Jo called again. "Stockboys, boss!"

They were riding in line abreast, strung out. They would be the riders from Minardoo, and they had still not found Dillon.

Mary Dillon was waiting for them on the runway. She came running, face flushed, hair wind-blown, slim in a mannish shirt and jodhpurs. At the last step she stumbled and almost fell into his arms. He held her for a moment longer than was necessary, feeling her need and relief.

"Did you see anything?"

The eagerness in her voice gave him an odd pang of regret. He shook his head. "Only your stockmen. We flew over the valley behind the sandstone bluffs. One of the herd there is dead. It looked like the bull."

"Oh no!" Her terror seemed disproportionate.

"Is it so important, Mrs Dillon?"

"Important! We mortgaged ourselves to the neck to buy it. Lance said it was our only hope."

"I'm sorry. As soon as we're ready, we'll ride out there. Can you give us a quick lunch?"

"It's ready for you now. The horses are saddled and the packs are made up."

Luncheon was a hurried, dismal meal. When they had finished,

*To the aborigines the dream-time represents not only their past history, with its sacred myths, but also the on-going spiritual or religious life of all aborigines in the present.

Adams sent Mary outside to check the supplies on the pack ponies, while he had a conference with the pilot.

"This looks bad, Gilligan. Dillon could be dead already."

The pilot nodded. "What do you want me to do, Neil?"

"Can you make another flight over the valley tomorrow morning? I could get the stockboys to clear a strip."

"How will I know where you are?"

"We'll build a smoke fire."

Gilligan made his farewells and Adams went with him to watch the takeoff. When he came back, he saw that there were three saddle horses instead of two, and that the pack ponies also carried blanket rolls and ground sheets and waterbags for three.

"I'm coming with you, Neil," Mary told him in a rush of words. "I think I'd go mad if I had to wait here for news."

He was tempted to refuse violently. All his experience—of the country, of women, and of himself—told him that this was a dangerous folly. Instead, he said: "Better bring something warm. Pack some liniment too—you'll have saddle sores before you're much older."

THE MOMENT Dillon had tried to signal the aircraft, he knew he had made a fatal mistake. No pilot would have attempted a landing in the swamplands and now, for a certainty, his pursuers would be on his track. He was trapped between the grass and the lily pond, a pale frog on a mud path waiting for the urchins to scoop him up in a bottle. A sob of weariness shook him, and the first tears since childhood forced themselves from his eyes. He buried his face in his muddy arms and wept.

After a while he began to take note of the swamp noises: the shrilling of the cicadas, the susurration of the grass, the occasional boom of a frog, and the chitter of a reed-hen. There was a rhythm to it, as if the giant land were wheezing in its noonday doze.

Suddenly the rhythm was broken. Far away to his left there was a squawking, and a few seconds later a big jabiru flapped its ungainly way over his head. The hunters had flushed the bird as, soon, they must flush the man. There was no way of escape and there was no weapon to his hand but the swaying reeds.

120

"The reeds. . . !"

From somewhere out of a forgotten storybook a vivid picture presented itself: a prisoner, hunted by his gaolers, hiding in a stream and breathing through a reed. His reaction was immediate. He tried to tear out a handful of reeds but the tough fibres resisted him. He knelt and bit off a pair of stalks close to the root. Then he bit off the tops, tested them by suction, and found that the air flowed freely.

He slid into the water at a spot where the green scum had parted. When he found it deep enough he exhaled, so that his body sank to the bottom, and then he worked his way under the lily roots, feeling for a snag that might hold his body submerged. His rib cage was almost bursting before he found it, but he hooked his toes under it and let his body lie diagonally, face upwards, so that the reed projected through the lily pads. He had to blow desperately to clear it of scum but finally he was able to breathe in short, regular gasps.

MUNDARU had moved fast and now was standing on the spot where his quarry had lain. The marks of him were everywhere: the shape of his body in the mud, the crushed and torn reed stalks, the place where he had slid into the lagoon. Yet, the surface of the pond was unbroken. Ducks were swimming placidly, the ripples fanning out in their wake. Egrets stood in elderly contemplation round the verge. A blue kingfisher dipped like a flash of lightning over the pink flowers.

Mundaru squatted on his heels and waited a long time, but no alien sound disturbed the familiar harmony. The white man had disappeared completely.

A chill fear crept in on the buffalo man. Perhaps the white man was already dead, and his restless emanation was walking abroad, mocking Mundaru and leading him on to destruction. Perhaps he was still alive, but using a more potent magic than Mundaru had expected. Perhaps this was not white man's magic at all, but the malignant working of Willinja.

Abruptly his thoughts turned to Menyan, Willinja's wife. Inside the tribe she was denied to him, but now, an outlaw, he might take her if he could, whether she consented or refused. Afterwards they could flee to the fringe of the white settlement, where other detribalized men and women lived a new kind of life. The thought gave him a new goal. But first he must find the white man. . . .

Mundaru picked up his spears and killing club and headed off through the reed fringes.

When, a long time later, Dillon broke despairingly out from the lily beds, the myall had disappeared and there was nothing to show which way he had gone.

MARY DILLON and Neil Adams were riding stirrup to stirrup, with Billy-Jo behind them, leading the pack ponies. For long stretches Adams rode in silence, but, just when it seemed to Mary that he had forgotten her, he would point out a new thing—a strange bird, a distorted bottle tree, a pile of fertility stones raised by the aborigines. He had a care for her, and she was grateful. But there was still something that needed to be said.

"Neil," she said soberly, "you think this is blackfellow trouble, don't you? Lance could be dead . . . killed."

"He could be. He probably isn't."

"It might be better if he were."

The bleakness of the statement staggered him but he had been long drilled to composure. After a moment he said quietly: "Do you want to explain that?"

"There's not much to explain. We're head over heels in debt to the pastoral company and they told us last month they wouldn't advance us any more. Now the bull is dead, we're ruined and I don't think Lance could stand that."

"Do you really think Lance would crack?"

She nodded emphatically. "Yes. He has great courage, but he's single-minded. He's gambled everything on this breeding project and he's told me more than once it was his last throw."

"And you?"

She caught the undertone of irony in his question. "I'm one of those who survive by walking away and cutting their losses."

"You'd walk away from Lance? Don't you love him?"

"Not enough to stay and let this blasted country wear out

122

everything that was good between us. Does that shock you, Neil?"

"Nothing ever shocks a policeman. Besides, it's a pleasure to meet an honest witness." He gave her a sardonic sidelong grin.

"One question. What are the odds on Lance being alive?"

He answered flatly: "At this moment, even money. But the odds might be better on the course. . . . Come on, let's ride."

But the longer they rode, the more the question nagged at him: which way did she want the odds—longer or shorter? And which way did he want them himself?

WILLINJA, the sorcerer, was waiting for the buffalo men to complete their ritual preparations and present themselves to him, ready for the kill. Like all the initiates of the animistic cults, he was a man of singular intelligence and imagination. In any society he would have risen to eminence. He was pharmacist, physician, psychologist—and good in each capacity. He was priest and augur, diplomat and judge. Behind his broad receding forehead he carried relatively more knowledge than any four men in a twentieth-century society. More than most men he understood social responsibility.

This, in effect, was his problem now. He had ordered what was, in the tribal code, a legal killing. But the legal process would fail if Mundaru killed the white man first. Tribal killings were forbidden by the white man's law, and the white policeman, Adamidji, would see two crimes instead of one. Willinja could not explain, in any intelligible fashion, his efforts at prevention and punishment. There were things the white man would never understand, and this lack of understanding impeded the course of age-old justice.

From the shadowy recesses of a cave the buffalo men came out, limping from their recent ordeal. They were in pain, but the pain was an ever-present reminder of the sacred character of their mission. It was more: their burnt and dislocated toes had become magical eyes to guide them towards their quarry. Their feet were shod with kadaitja boots, made of emu feathers and kangaroo fur and daubed with blood from their own arms. They would not leave footprints like ordinary men, because until the act was done, they were not ordinary men. Even their spears were special. . . .

They stood before Willinja, heads bowed, awaiting his crisp, clear commands. Time was important. If possible Mundaru must be killed before he killed the white man. He must be speared—in the middle of the back. The spear must be withdrawn and a flake of sharp quartz, representing the spirit snake, must be inserted to eat the liver fat. The wound must be cauterized, and Mundaru, with the spirit snake eating his entrails, must be driven until he died in his tracks. The man who threw the spear must never be named, because this was a communal act, absolved from revenge.

Willinja dismissed them curtly and stood watching their swift, limping run towards the river. Then he strode back to the encampment. The women were beginning to straggle in, loaded with yams and lily bulbs and wooden dishes full of wild honey, but Menyan was not among them, and Willinja waited, uneasy, for the arrival of his youngest wife.

IT WAS LATE afternoon when they pushed their tired horses into the valley. The kites wheeling round the carcass of the bull rose in screaming clouds as the riders approached. The air was heavy with carrion smell, and Mary reined in while Adams and Billy-Jo rode forward. She saw them dismount and begin casting the ground for tracks.

Curiously, the black man was now in command. All the way from the homestead, she had hardly noticed him. He had that attitude of faintly-smiling acquiescence, which the aboriginal affects in the presence of the white man. His hair was grey and his face deeply lined. He wore riding boots, denims and a patched shirt of check cotton. His shoulders stooped as if he were ashamed of being seen in the white man's cast-offs. But here he seemed to take on new authority.

In spite of her fatigue she edged her horse closer to follow their talk. Adams yelled at her: "Stay where you are! We're having enough trouble. The stockboys have walked all over the ground."

This male brusqueness was the last straw. She propped the pony hard on his hindquarters and yelled back: "It's my husband you're looking for! Just remember I'm interested!"

124

He did not answer, but threw her an ironic salute and bent again to talk to Billy-Jo, who, crouched like a scenting dog, was moving towards the far end of the valley.

Her irritation subsided as quickly as it had risen. She felt foolish, a nuisance to others and a disappointment to herself.

Twenty minutes later Adams and Billy-Jo finished their circuit of the valley, remounted and rode back to join her. Adams's face was clouded with concern and his voice was gentle.

"Sorry to keep you standing about, Mary. We had some trouble picking up the tracks."

"But you did find what you wanted?"

He nodded gravely. "Lance came in at a gallop. He must have caught the myalls killing the bull. It looks as though he was wounded by a spear, because he wasn't thrown or pulled out of the saddle."

A sharp fear took hold of her. Her voice trembled as she asked, "What happened then?"

"We don't know. The stockboys may have found something, but the way they've been blundering round here, I doubt it. We'll pick up his tracks at the mouth of the gorge and follow from there. He can't be far away."

The answer seemed to satisfy her and he was content to leave it. There was no point in telling her the other things that he and Billy-Jo had found: the ochre dust and charcoal sticks and the animal fur, with which one of the myalls had daubed himself in preparation for a new killing.

WHEN DILLON crawled out of the water he was in an extremity of weakness; one shoulder and breast were throbbing with pain and his limbs were shaken with uncontrollable tremors.

He knew now that unaided he could never reach the homestead alive. The infection in his shoulder was spreading and fever mists, prelude to delirium, rocked his mind. The appearance of the aircraft meant that Mary had understood that he was in trouble and had summoned help. He must get out of the high grasses and head back to the river, where he might have a chance of meeting the searchers. Here in the swamp reaches he was buried as if in a

green tomb. He began to drag himself sluglike along the ground
before the insidious luxury of dozing daydreams could rob him
of will.

ALONE ON the river-flat Menyan was digging for yams. Except for
a small pubic tassel of kangaroo fur, she was naked, and she
squatted on her haunches prising up the long brown tubers with a
pointed stick. By the white man's measure she was fifteen years of
age, and she had been married to Willinja from the time of her
first period, but so far she was childless.

This was the reason for her working alone. The older women
had made fun of her as barren and useless, until she had wandered
off to escape their taunts. She knew as well as they did that it was
not her fault, that old men did not make so many children as
young ones. Yet she was still child enough to throw off cares
quickly, and still woman enough to hope that one day a young
man might buy her from Willinja.

If she could choose she would prefer Mundaru. There was a
vitality about him that set him apart from the other bucks. He
wanted her badly. Given the opportunity, he would try to take her.
But she knew she could not surrender to him now. Mundaru had
been cut off for ever from the tribal communion. To mate with
him would be like mating with a dead man. The thought chilled
her.

Suddenly there was a rustle in the grasses behind her and a
shadow fell across her naked back. She looked up and her mouth
opened in a soundless scream as Mundaru, painted and armed for
the kill, advanced towards her.

WHEN THEY reached the gorge, Billy-Jo dismounted and walked
ahead, casting about for Dillon's tracks among the newer prints
made by the stockboys. Adams and Mary sat watching him while
the ponies cropped the sparse tussocks at their feet.

"A thing to notice, Mary. Billy-Jo has kept his primitive skills.
The stockboys have lost theirs. They don't have to depend on
them any more to stay alive. I'm thinking of Lance. If he escaped,
his survival depends in part on his physical condition and in part

126

on his knowledge of the country. There's lots of food—if you know where to find it."

"I—I think he knows."

A hundred yards away Billy-Jo pointed towards some paperbarks. As Adams and Mary trotted towards the trees, the stockboys rode out. Adams swore softly when he saw that they had not yet found Dillon, then he reined in and waited for them. Mary gasped with fear, for Jimmy, the head boy, had Dillon's hat hung on his pommel. He handed it to Adams then made his report in tumbling, liquid pidgin.

Adams listened, then explained it quickly to Mary. "They picked up Lance's hat in the timber, where they found his tracks. They followed them into the grasses and came to a spot where he must have been thrown, then they came back to meet us."

"What are you going to do now?"

"Get Jimmy to take us there. The other boys can clear a landing strip. Gilligan's flying back this way tomorrow morning."

He rode off with the stockboys towards the open plain at the foot of the ridges, leaving her alone with Billy-Jo. The old man watched her with shrewd, sidelong eyes, then said tentatively: "Sergeant good man, Missus. See much, say little, trustim sure."

"I know, Billy-Jo. But I'm worried about my husband."

The old man shrugged. "Missus young. Catchim new husband, makim piccaninny longtime yet."

She flushed. It was no new thought to her, but uttered by a stranger in a bastard tongue, it had a new and shocking impact. She turned and stared across the plain to where Adams was pacing off the rough strip. It was easy to admit she was drawn to him. He was a man in equilibrium, stable and content, whereas Lance, for all his driving power, seemed always in conflict.

When she saw Adams galloping back with Jimmy, she dismissed the thought abruptly lest he read it in her eyes.

The shadows were lengthening as they came to the grass patch where Dillon had been thrown. Jimmy held the horses while Billy-Jo and Adams made their examination, with Mary behind them, watching intently. As the tracker read the signs, Adams translated them.

"This is where he was thrown. You see how the grass was broken and the ground hollowed a little by the impact. He lay some time, bleeding, then apparently got up and walked away, using a stick. From here he headed down to the river—it's a good sign because it shows he's thinking straight."

He broke off as Billy-Jo called his attention to new signs: a wisp of fur, a smear on a grass stalk, a depression in the swampy earth. She saw him frown, questioned him sharply:

"Something new? What is it?"

His eyes were hard, but his voice was controlled. "The myalls came this way, too. It must have been afterwards, because there's no sign of a struggle."

"That means Lance is dead, doesn't it?"

He could not tell whether a wish or a fear prompted the question. He shook his head.

"Not yet. It means that the odds on his survival have shortened. Jimmy, head back and join the others. Keep them working on the strip till dark, and start again at sunrise. We'll push on."

FIVE MILES away, the kadaitja men, limping in their feather boots, had reached the river and were fanning out over the flats to begin the hunt for Mundaru. They walked in two worlds, infused with supernatural power, but applying the simple rules of the hunter: stealth, concealment, calculation.

There was no doubt in their minds that Mundaru knew of the sentence promulgated against him. This was the virtue of projective magic, that the victim sensed it long before the moment of execution. More than this, they knew that the white men were out. They had seen the plane and the dust kicked up by horses.

The spearmen were hidden from each other and spread over a mile of country, but they moved in perfect co-ordination. Their communication was a cryptic mimicry of animal noises: the raucous cry of a cockatoo, the honk of a swamp goose, the thudding resonant beat which a kangaroo makes with his tail on the ground, the high-rising whistle of a whip-bird.

Towards the end, Mundaru would hear and understand, but it would be too late. The kadaitja men would be circling and closing

128

in on him. There would be a silence, long and terrible; and out of the silence would come the throbbing note of the bull-roarer—the tjuringa, the sacred wood or stone, which is pierced with holes so that when it is twirled in the air, it roars deeply in the voice of the dream-time people. To Mundaru it would be a death chant, and before its echoes died he would fall to the sacred spear thrust.

THEY CAME to the shade-dappled river on foot, leaving the horses tethered on the high bank. Adams and Mary waited while Billy-Jo began scouting.

The weariness of the long ride was in their bones and Mary felt her courage thinning out with the decline of the day. Her face was drawn and dustmarked. Adams, too, was tired; she saw it in the droop of his shoulders. Yet he was as alert as ever.

Billy-Jo came hurrying along the sandy bank, his dark weathered face set in a frown of puzzlement. He pointed upstream. "Blackfellow tracks all about. Walkim up and down. Makeim fire, eat and sleep. No tracks for white boss. No clothes, no blood, nothing."

A gleam of admiration brightened Adams's eyes. More to himself than to Mary, he muttered: "Clever boy. He used the river to break his tracks."

"Loseim light fast, Boss. Maybe we cross river and look around, eh?" Billy-Jo spoke quietly, but with complete authority.

Adams turned to Mary. "We'll have to leave you for a while. Bring the horses down here, water and tether them. Then collect wood for a fire. There's a rifle in my saddle-bucket. There's no danger, but if you want us in a hurry, fire two shots. We'll be back by dark."

The words were on her tongue to tell him that she knew nothing about handling horses, that she had never fired a rifle in her life, and that the terror of emptiness haunted her like the beginning of madness. But she said only, "You go ahead. I'll have a meal ready when you come back."

For the first time in their day-long company, Adams smiled approval. He patted her shoulder and said gently, "Good girl! We won't be gone long."

She unsaddled the tired horses awkwardly, yet with satisfaction in the simple labour. She resented Adams, but she was eager to please him. She hitched the horses to a palm bole and began to gather driftwood along the river bank. By the time she had finished she was hot, filthy and uncomfortable. She found a clear rockpool, stripped off her clothes, and stepped into the water until it covered her breasts and lapped the hollow of her throat.

The touch of it was like silk on her parched skin. The tree shadows lengthened across her body, the sky darkened slowly to crimson, but she lay there until from far across the river she heard Billy-Jo calling: ". . . Dillon . . . Boss Dillon. . . !"

And then, more distant, the long despairing ululation of Adams's voice: "Dillon! . . . Answer me!"

MUNDARU heard, too—so close that he could see the shouting man through the grass. A single leap and a spear thrust would silence the shout for ever, but Mundaru squatted, motionless as a rabbit, until the man had passed far beyond him. This was not his victim. Besides, he was tired now from the day's stalking, from hunger, and from the long, violent ravishing of Menyan.

He had not counted on her terror, her cowering rejection of him as if he were unclean or a spirit man. A token flight, an ultimate surrender—this was the ritual of a tribal abduction when a young wife was "pulled" from an ageing husband. But Menyan's reaction had been quite different, so that in the end he had to beat her savagely before he took her. Only afterwards did he understand the reason: Menyan knew what he himself had merely suspected. The tribe had pointed the bone at him and sung him to death.

Now he crouched, listening for the sounds that would herald the coming of the kadaitja men and clinging to his last hope: that he might find his own victim, eat his liver fat and so arm himself against the magic of the tribal avengers.

THE KADAITJA men heard the voices too, and they froze, their painted faces pointing like the muzzles of hounds towards the sound. They did not understand the words, but the import was

130

clear: the white men were looking for their lost brother. The white men were a possible impediment to a ritual act necessary for the safety of the tribe. If they came across Mundaru first, they would take him away, beyond the reach of the sacred spears.

So they waited, alert for the signal from their leader which would tell them what to do. The cries stopped. Out of the silence they heard the signal—the cry of a whip-bird, once, twice, and again. They moved forward slowly, parting the grasses as the wind might part them.

Distant but clear, the shouting began again but this time on a new note, sharp and urgent: "Billy-Jo! Over here! Hurry!"

DILLON heard it, as he had heard all the others, through the whirling confusion of fever. It meant nothing to him but a new nightmare against which his tired brain struggled as he made his reptilian progress through the grass roots.

In these dragging hours he had learned many lessons: that time is relative; that there is a climax to pain and, after that, a numbness; that once a man topples off into darkness there is only the blind compulsion of the will urging him forward.

It was the will that drove the tired heart and kept the sick blood pumping. It was the will that kept the hands clawing, trailing the body after them like a bloated bladder. The will gave sight to eyes glued with suppuration; it stifled the agony of sunburn and insect poison; it shouted down the siren voices that urged him to sleep or to stand up and dare the spears.

Dillon was beyond reason but his last logical thought was etched in his brain. He must keep moving. All else was illusion—a swamp fire luring him to destruction. So he paid no heed to the voices calling his name, and kept dragging himself forward. But being part-blind he did not see that every movement was taking him farther from the river and his rescuers.

DARKNESS came down at a single stride, and Mary piled more wood on the fire, so that the flames leaped up. She could not begin to cook until the blaze had died into coals but she needed the warmth and the radiance to hold at bay the terrors of the night.

131

To divert herself she began laying out the food and the utensils. Suddenly, the tin plates fell from her hands with a clatter. The startled horses whinnied and over her head a bird squawked and flapped away. She threw herself on the sand and covered her face with her hands.

Then she heard the sound of men splashing through the water. Sick with relief and shame, she began to make a show of preparing the meal. But when Adams and Billy-Jo stepped into the light she gasped with shock. Billy-Jo was carrying over his shoulders the limp body of a native girl.

Adams's face was drawn, his mouth tight as a trap. He said curtly, "We found her over by the swamp; she's in a bad way."

The tracker laid the dark, childish body down on the sand and Mary looked at Adams with startled eyes when she saw the extent of the injuries. The face had been battered, the breasts and the narrow flanks were covered with blood. She was alive but her breathing was irregular.

"Who is she? What happened to her?"

"Beaten and raped. She's married, the pubic covering shows that. Whoever did it must have surprised her. She fought, and this happened."

"It's horrible." Mary turned away as nausea gripped her. Adams examined the small body with clinical care.

"Bring me a water bottle and the whisky." He forced a few drops into the broken mouth. "She'll die tonight. I'd like to get a word or two out of her before she goes. See if you can clean her up a little, then cover her with blankets and bathe her face."

Mary turned away to get blankets and a towel from the saddle-packs. Adams followed her and laid a tentative hand on her shoulder. He said wearily: "I'm sorry, Mary, I haven't anything to tell you about Lance. It might take us half a day to pick up his tracks in the grass over there."

He ran his hand through his thick hair in a gesture of puzzlement. "The girl's tied in with this somewhere but I can't see how just yet. It's possible that the man who raped her is the man who is hunting your husband. Billy-Jo seems to think it's only one man now, judging by the tracks. At this stage, it's just a guess. If

132

we could bring the girl round. . . ." He patted her shoulder. "It's a messy business, but see what you can do for her."

She felt a surge of pride in his reliance on her. "Give me ten minutes and then I'll get your supper ready."

He stretched out on the sand, leaned his head on one of the saddles, lit a cigarette and lay staring up at the velvet sky in which the stars hung low as lanterns.

The rape puzzled him. It was out of character with what he knew of aboriginal custom, an uncommon crime because there was generally no need to resort to it. Infidelity was less important in tribal code than the preservation of public order and the saving of face for the husband. Why was the girl prepared to risk violence and death rather than satisfy her attacker?

He got stiffly to his feet and walked over to watch Mary bathing the girl's face with a damp towel, while Billy-Jo squatted on his heels. After a while the girl's body began to shake, her eyelids fluttered and her head rolled. A babbling issued from her swollen lips. Adams took the towel from Mary and handed it to Billy-Jo. "Keep bathing her. If she makes any kind of sense, talk to her."

The tracker bent over the girl, crooning in his tribal language.

Adams took Mary's hand and walked down to the edge of the river. "If she woke and saw you she would be afraid. She would probably say nothing. Besides, Billy-Jo understands her language."

"You really know your job, don't you?" she said admiringly.

"I know the country. I like my job . . . most of the time."

"What do you mean by that?"

He made an eloquent gesture of deprecation. "Nothing of importance. Except that the work is easier without personal involvement."

She looked at him sharply but he was staring down the dark reaches of the river. "Meaning you're involved now?"

"In a way, yes."

"D'you want to talk about it?"

"No. Not yet, anyway."

They walked down the beach. For the first time since they had met they seemed to be in harmony, a current of communication running between them.

"Neil . . . the girl back there . . . the thing that happened to her . . . how can even primitive people live such brutal lives?"

"The answer is, my dear, that they don't. They live differently, but not brutally. They love their children. They love their wives. They are tender to them, though they never kiss as we do. Walk through a camp and you'll see a man tending a sick woman, stroking her hair, fanning her with a leaf. The fellow who raped that girl is as much a criminal inside the tribe as he is to us."

"Lance used to tell me the same thing. I was never interested before."

"You never had to be interested. Your husband was prepared to think for you." There was no malice in his tone.

They came to a large rock that thrust out into the river, and sat on top of it; Adams lit cigarettes. After a while she asked him, hesitantly, "Neil, can you explain something to me?"

"There are lots of things I can't explain to myself just now," he told her with rueful irony. "What's bothering you?"

"Myself . . . Lance, too. How can two people begin in love, live together for a few years and end . . . the way we are? Lance loves me, but he's hurt and disappointed. For myself. . . ." She flicked her cigarette stub into the water and watched it float away in the blackness. "Somewhere out there, Lance is lying, wounded or dead. I'm going through all the motions of a good and faithful wife, but deep down inside me I don't care." Her voice rose to an hysterical pitch.

"You've had a rough day," said Adams with cool good-humour. "You're tired and so am I. Neither of us wants to eat our indiscretions for breakfast. Let's get back and start supper."

When they reached the campfire they found the tracker squatting beside the coals, smoking placidly. The girl had lapsed again into unconsciousness. While Mary busied herself with the meal, Adams turned to Billy-Jo.

"Did you get anything out of her?"

The tracker nodded, his eyes bright with triumph. "Name Menyan, Boss. Wife of Willinja, man of big magic. Man who beat her want her long-time."

"Why didn't she take him?"

134

"Willinja pointim bone, singim dead. Send kadaitja men killim. Woman no want dead man."

"Why did they point the bone?"

"Killum bull. Try killum white man. Blackfella want no trouble with you, Boss."

"What's the name of this fellow?"

"Mundaru, buffalo man."

"So that's it!" Adams's face brightened as understanding dawned. Then the full import of the situation struck him. "They're all out there—kadaitja men, Mundaru, Dillon."

The tracker shook his head and shot a significant glance at Mary. His voice dropped to a whisper. "Dillon dead, Boss."

"Why do you say that?"

"Easy, Boss. Blackfellow way . . . Make killing first, eat liver fat, make strong. Take woman after."

Adams frowned. It fitted perfectly, the cyclic psychology of the primitive. A sudden sound cut across the path of his thoughts, a slithering, a long splash, a gurgle of water. "Crocodile, Boss!" said Billy-Jo.

Adams already had the rifle in his hands.

"Over there, Boss, by driftwood."

Three seconds later Adams fired, and the next instant the big saurian was heaving in the water, his tail clouting some piled driftwood and sending it flying. After a while the crocodile rolled over, exposing the pale underbelly, and drifted into a backwater.

Billy-Jo began wading across the stream. Crocodile skins were worth money and, since a policeman could not engage in private trade, this was his perquisite. Before he reached the crocodile they saw him fish something out of the water. Then he headed away from the dead beast and back to the pile of driftwood.

Five minutes later, he was at the campfire, holding Lance Dillon's shirt and trousers and the head of Mundaru's spear.

MARY STARED in horror at the rent, bloodstained shirt. But Adams examined it with professional care and after a few moments his eyes gleamed with admiration. Item by item, he pieced out his deductions for her. "Your husband's quite a man, Mary. He was

135

wounded in the shoulder. He got the spearhead out and tore strips from his shirt to bandage himself. He knew that he had no hope in open country by day, so he settled himself behind that driftwood over there and waited for darkness. He probably made a break during the middle of the night."

"But why without his clothes?"

Adams rubbed a reflective hand over his stubbled chin. "I don't know. What would you say, Billy-Jo?"

The tracker shrugged. "Maybe clothes snag on roots. Maybe wet and heavy for sick man. Anyway, big mistake. Night-time, no clothes, fine. Daytime, hot sun, white man burn up, finish."

Adams frowned. The thought had occurred to him, but he would have preferred to leave it unspoken. He turned to Mary. "Now, can we eat, please?"

His casualness was disarming, even though she knew he was using it to gain thinking time. She began ladling tinned stew, thick slices of damper, pannikins of coffee laced with condensed milk. While they ate, Menyan stirred and muttered in delirium. Adams got up to force more water and whisky into her mouth and draw the blankets closer around her.

When the meal was over, they washed the dishes in the river, spread out the blanket rolls and lay back, heads pillowed on their saddles. Mary said, her voice shaky. "Don't judge me too harshly. I'm mixed up, lost. I—I've learnt a lot today."

"You're doing fine, Mary." His voice was gentle. "Go to sleep now. Everything will look different in the morning."

She rolled over on her side and soon the rhythm of her breathing told him she was asleep.

Now he was free to try to fit the jig-saw pieces into a coherent pattern.

If Dillon were dead the kites would be circling over his remains, but in the last hour of sunlight they had seen no carrion birds. Alive then. But what would be his condition after twelve hours naked in the sun, two nights of wounds and possible poison? Let him survive that. Then ask could he survive the shock of financial ruin and the loss of his wife?

Think about his wife, resentful, discontented, afraid—yet with a core of honesty and courage. She attracts you; galls you like a pebble in your shoe. You've never asked more of a woman than a happy tumble in the hay and a goodbye without any tears. Why should you care what goes on behind the brooding eyes of this one? If Dillon is dead, will you want to take over his wife?

Push this untimely thought away. Turn a policeman's eye on the drama. There is a rapist-killer out there. By law he belongs to you. If the kadaitja men kill him you must visit vengeance on them and the tribe—even though you know this will be a legality and not justice.

Suddenly he heard the cry of a whip-bird, twice repeated. He sat up, every sense alert. The black tracker sat up, too, and pointed out across the water.

"Kadaitja men, Boss. No fear night spirits."

"I wonder if they've found him yet?"

"Not yet. When find him, hear tjuringa—bull-roarer. Tjuringa make spirit-song for death."

"We'll move in when we hear it. We sleep in turns, an hour at a time. You sleep first. I'll wake you."

The whip-bird called again, and this time it was answered by the squawk of a cockatoo. The cockatoo cry was close—downstream and near the river. Adams picked up his rifle and began to work his way down towards the bank.

Near the river fringe he waited, his heart thumping. Time passed with agonizing slowness, then the kadaitja man came into view.

He was a tall buck, daubed from forehead to knee with ceremonial patterns. He moved with a swift, shuffling gait, favouring the right foot, and when he came closer Adams saw that his shins and his feet were covered with parrot feathers and kangaroo fur. In his right hand he carried three spears and a throwing stick, in his left a short club, carved in totem patterns.

Adams was not a superstitious man, but the sight woke in him the old atavistic terror of the unknown. Death had many faces and this was one of them. He held his breath as the kadaitja man came abreast of him and passed on, his feathered feet soundless in the powdery dust. Twenty yards ahead he turned aside, parted the tall grass stalks and disappeared. Adams eased himself out of his cramped position.

Halfway back to camp he heard Mary scream in terror and went running to her.

MUNDARU also heard the scream and the marrow clotted in his bones. He was lost now, without recourse. He knew it was the spirit essence of Menyan, haunting the place where he had killed her, because there was no one to perform the ceremonies of singing her to rest. She would be looking for him now, ranging over the swamp. The wingmalung would be with her—the malignant ones who strike illness into the bodies of those who neglect their debts to the departed. There was no escape from the dead, no remedy against the wingmalung except tribal magic and from this he was for ever cut off. He had heard the calls of the kadaitja men, but he had counted on time to find the white man before they came to kill him at sunrise. Now even this hope was gone.

He picked up his spears and bending double, began to work through the grass, slowly, as though he were hauling against a heavy load. Magical influences were at work on him, draining his life fluid, dragging him back.

Eastward the moon rose higher and its radiance lit up his course. But even this held no joy for Mundaru. Menyan was named for the moon. The moon was an eye spying out his movements, reading them back to the spirit essence and the wingmalung.

He dropped and began to crawl, as Lance Dillon had done. A faint hope sprang up inside him when after an hour, he found that he was crawling in a set of tracks made by another man—a man who, resting every few yards, had left blood on the razor edges of the grass leaves.

ADAMS CRADLED Mary in his arms, soothing her like a child after a nightmare. Her shirt was stained with blood. She clung to him, shaking, the words tumbling out of her.

"I seemed to hear a cry. When I woke up, she was lying across

138

me . . . her face on mine. She must have died just at that moment. . . ."

"Easy. I won't leave you, girl. It's over now. I know . . . I know. . . . It's over now. . . . Did you bring any clean clothes?"

"There's a shirt in my saddle-bag."

"Get out of those things. I'll rinse them in the river."

But when she tried to take them off her hands would not obey. Adams knelt and undressed her to the waist. She shivered as the cold air struck her and he drew her against him for warmth while he buttoned on the clean shirt and drew on his own heavy cardigan over her shoulders. She surrendered like a child to the small intimate service. If love were anything but a fiction, he was close to it in this rare moment of tenderness and pity.

Adams tried to get her to sleep again, but she held to him desperately, and after a while he lay down beside her on the blanket with her head pillowed on his arm. He stroked her hair, and talked to her softly. Little by little the panic drained out of her and her body relaxed in sleep. For a long time he lay wakeful, her hair brushing his lips, her breast rising and falling against his own.

DURING THE NIGHT the bitter cold of the desert crept across the swampland. The cold was a trial to the kadaitja men. They were accustomed to going naked, but at night they slept with fires at their bellies and their backs, with the camp dogs curled beside them and their womenfolk lending them the warmth of their bodies.

When the moon was high the man with the whip-bird voice called them together and had them hoist him on their shoulders. For a long time he stood there, scanning the land with eyes made keener by the aura of power within which he moved. The country was wrapped in a silver dream. The swamp was flat as ice; the grass was an unbroken carpet. No bird sang; no animal stirred. Only the frogs and the crickets made a mystic chorus, punctuated by the distant howl of a dingo and the haunting cry of a mopoke.

Finally, the kadaitja man saw the thing he had been expecting. Half a mile away, the grass was stirring as if an animal were

139

running through it. He knew that the animal was Mundaru. He knew that Willinja's magic was drawing Mundaru towards a sacred place, a deep cave at the roots of a bottle tree.

Before he reached it, they would take him. And when the spirit snake had been planted in his body they would drive him towards it, so that he would die in the shadow of the power he had flouted.

It was time to go. They lowered him and he told them where they must walk to come up with Mundaru at first light.

IN THE SMALL hours Dillon woke, lucid for the first time in many hours. The place in which he found himself was strange to him and in the bleak radiance of the moon he saw how far he had strayed from the river. Now his last hope of rescue had dwindled to nothing. It surprised him that he was not more afraid—that he was even relieved to be absolved from further agony.

But one more effort was demanded of him—summoning all his strength he began to drag himself towards a large bottle tree. Once in its shade, he could compose himself and wait for death. Every few yards he had to rest. He would lie flattened on the pebbles, weak, gasping, feeling the fever rise; then he would go on, heedless of the sharp stones that raked his belly and his chest into running wounds.

As he came closer to the bottle tree he saw, ranged in a circle around it, painted poles, some flattened like palm leaves, some tall as maypoles. Between them the ground was thick with fallen leaves. Dillon knew the poles indicated a sacred place: sometimes a burial ground where the dead were stored in hollow palm trunks, sometimes a repository of sacred objects.

The bottle tree would give him a back-rest, and he wanted to sit upright to watch the dawn and the coming of his killers. A bushman's caution told him that the carpet of leaves might hide venomous snakes, but a second reflection urged him forward. A snake bite might finish him quickly, cut short the final agony.

He crawled into the dusty aromatic leaves. There was a kind of pleasure in their touch on his scarred and naked skin. The tree was only ten feet away when without warning the ground gave way beneath him and he felt himself rolling over into blackness.

140

MARY WOKE to moonlight and the comforting warmth of Adams's body. His free arm held her to him like a bond. She had slept three years in the marriage bed with Lance, but it was longer than she cared to remember since she had lain with him like this, relaxed, with passion a whisper away.

A day's ride and ten minutes of terror had brought her to this point with Neil Adams. What drew her to him was hard to define, harder to deny. Where did she go from here?

Carefully she eased herself up to a sitting position and looked about. The moonlit river flowed placidly and, fifty yards away, Billy-Jo stood, a black sentinel, staring towards the hidden chorus of the bull-frogs.

As if for the first time she saw the other face of the hated land— not hostile, but passive, hungry for the touch to transfigure it to fruitfulness. What she was seeing now was what Lance had tried vainly to communicate to her. In the first flush of this revelation, it seemed she could get up and walk alone through the vastness without fear.

Then from the west there came the mourning howl of a dingo. Another answered, then another, until the night was filled with a graveyard chant. She shivered and slid back under the blanket. At the same moment, Neil opened his eyes. Their faces brushed. His arms went round her and the wasteland howling was hushed by his first whispered words.

IT IS NOT given to every man to approve the interior of his own tomb before he occupies it, and Lance Dillon was vaguely grateful for the privilege. As his eyes grew accustomed to the twilight, he saw that he had rolled down a ramp onto the sandy floor of an underground cave.

The air was dry and warm, tinged with a fusty odour which he could not identify until he caught the outline of bats hanging from the fretted limestone above him. One or two of them were dipping about in the darkness with faint mouselike squeaking.

Slowly the vague shapes of his surroundings solidified: the groining of the rock roof, the points of stalactites, the niches in the walls, stacked with bundles wrapped in tree bark. He guessed that these last were the weapons and bones of long-dead warriors cached by the myalls in their sacred place. Suddenly the stillness was broken by a single clear note as if someone had flipped a fingernail against a crystal goblet. For a minute Dillon lay listening but the sound was not repeated. His thoughts drifted. . . .

The drover's son who wanted to be a cattle king . . . the stripling stockrider, plugging his first thousand head of beef over five hundred miles of drought-stricken country to the railhead . . . the leather-faced gunner in the Japanese war, trading his cigarette and beer rations for a few extra pounds in his paybook . . . the day his number came up in the repatriation ballot for a lease of Crown Land in the territory. All the years of penny-pinching, of meagre cheques and lean credit, until he could build his first house and pay off his first mortgage and buy decent stock. So long as he was small and struggling, the big combines were prepared to leave him alone. But from the day he made his leap into the breeding they began to put pressure on him—always on the same tender spot: credit. But the greater the pressure the more determined he became.

Now he saw it as a monstrous folly. Other men had laughed and got drunk and laid their last shillings on a filly; he had lived as disciplined as a monk while his marriage had gone from bad to worse. Who now was in profit—he or they?

Again the crystalline sound rang out. This time he understood what it was: the fall of a drop of water into a pool. He began to drag himself towards it. Finally his hands touched a pillar of limestone and the sound of water seemed to come from directly above his head. With a last convulsive effort he hauled himself upward to a ledge. He threw his body across it and dipped his face into a shallow basin of icy water. The touch of it was like knife-blades on his torn skin but he lapped at it greedily.

Around the basin lay shards of limestone, long as daggers and almost as sharp. His fingers closed on one and a coal of anger began to glow inside him. He had suffered enough. He had run to the edge of the last dark leap. Why should he wait tamely till they thrust him over it? From here, stone dagger in hand, he could make a final leap at the first of his attackers.

IT WAS THE last hour of the dark when Adams got up, settled the blanket around Mary and went to take over the watch from Billy-Jo. The black tracker had nothing to report. The kadaitja men would probably remain silent until the first light of day.

Adams sat on a rock ledge while his body relaxed into the sad sweet contentment that follows the act of love. But there was a bitter dreg to poison the after-taste of possession. He was a man who had taken another's wife, a policeman who had betrayed his trust. Well . . . it was done. And for the first time in his life he had come close to love—the pain, the power and the mystery of it —when possession seemed more like a surrender than a conquest. Would it look the same when the sun came up?

He stared across the water at the driftwood pile behind which Dillon had hidden only twenty-four hours ago. Again Adams was touched with admiration for the endurance of the man, naked, wounded and alone, pitting himself against the myalls to whom the bush was an open thoroughfare.

At the sound of a footfall he turned to find Mary standing over him, her face pale in the moonlight. He took her in his arms and they held to each other. Then they sat down, hands locked.

"There's something I want to tell you, Neil." Her voice was soft and solicitous. "I'm glad it happened and I'll always remember. But if you don't want to remember, I'll never remind you."

"Is that a dismissal?"

She shook her head slowly. "It's an act of love. It's the only way I can tell you you're as free now as you were before. If Lance is dead, I'm free. If he's alive and well, I was going to leave him, anyway. And I love you, Neil. Now what do *you* want to do about it?"

His eyes dropped away from hers. "I—I think we should both wait and see."

"That's all I was trying to say, Neil," she told him coolly. "I love you enough to leave you free. Now kiss me, and let's not talk any more."

But even in the kiss there was still the sour taste of regret, the comfortless revelation that guilt is a lonely burden—and that a man needs a special kind of courage to carry it in silence.

WHEN THE FALSE dawn crept into the sky, Mundaru halted. He was cold, weary, hungry and confused. All night he had been creeping in the tracks of the white man. At every moment he had expected to come up with him, living or dead: but still he had not found him.

Ahead the grassland faded out into a wide empty area limited by the limestone ridge where painted poles were grouped around the sacred bottle tree. Mundaru lapsed into the despairing conviction that the white man had died long since and that what he had followed was a spirit-shape, luring him to destruction.

With the conviction came calm. The kadaitja men would find him waiting, a passive participant in the ritual of propitiation. Stiffly he got to his feet. The light was spreading now, the stars receding to pin-points. The first bird of the morning rose. It was a kite, and soon there would be many more of them, wheeling above, waiting for him to die.

Halfway to the ridge he laid down his spears, unwrapped his fire-sticks and squatted to coax flame into a handful of spiny grass. The motion of twirling the stick between his palms, spinning its point against the hard wood of its mate, blowing the first spark into a tiny flame, brought some satisfaction. He could not challenge the sacred spears, but at least he could go through the last motions of manhood, with the first gift of the dream-people flowering into flame under his hands.

A long shadow fell across the ground in front of Mundaru, and he looked up to see six men, painted and motionless as rocks. In their upraised arms they carried throwing-spears, and the barbed heads were pointed at his breast. Between bars of yellow ochre their eyes looked down at him, cold as granite.

From behind him the bull-roarer began, a thin howling, growing to a drumming roar. The ground vibrated to it. It hammered at his skull and crept into the hollows of his bones and filled his entrails.

The kadaitja men listened immobile. The roaring went on for nearly twenty minutes, then stopped abruptly. There was a sound like a rush of bird-wings at Mundaru's back and he pitched forward with the sacred spear in his kidneys.

LONG BEFORE the bull-roarer began, Billy-Jo had the horses saddled and the pack ponies loaded. Mary and Adams were standing by the fire drinking scalding coffee. The tension between them had eased and they talked companionably of the day ahead.

"I'd like you to understand my reasoning, Mary. I'm working on the assumption that your husband is dead. All the signs point that way. The only man who can give us any information is the man who's been tracking him—Mundaru. The kadaitja men are after him and they'll get him. In a kadaitja killing, the victim lives for some hours. That's the point of it. He dies by a magical power, not by a man's hand. If I can find him before he dies, I may be able to get something out of him. If we fail there, then Billy-Jo and I will beat the swamp for the rest of the day."

"You're a good policeman, Neil. Believe it always." There was tenderness and a curious touch of pity in her voice.

He kissed her lightly, tossed the dregs of his coffee into the fire and turned away towards the horses just as the first booming of the bull-roarer sounded across the swamp.

Billy-Jo flung out his hand. "Over there, Boss. Long way. Outside swamp."

"We'll try to skirt the billabong. No point trying to hack our way through." Adams turned to Mary. "You ride between Billy-Jo and me. No matter what happens, do exactly as I tell you."

They splashed across the ford, and had gone perhaps a mile, when the bull-roarer stopped. Adams stood in his stirrups and scanned the grassland. Then he set off at a canter with the others trailing him.

For the next mile Mary felt everything, saw everything, yet her thoughts were bent backwards: to the homestead, to the slow death of her love for Lance, to the swift passion that had driven her into the arms of Neil. She was still a wife, but not the same wife. The wholeness of herself had been broken and parcelled out, valueless to one man, worth how much to the other? Was Neil's hesitation dictated by fear for himself, or concern for her?

Ahead of her Adams reined in and pointed to a thin column of brown smoke. "What do you make of it, Billy-Jo?"

"Kadaitja men. Takeum man. Burnem spirit snake in back."

145

Adams turned to Mary. "This is it. Close in."

"I'm scared."

His hand closed over her own. "Don't worry. We'll be together from here on."

As they urged their horses through the high, rank grasses, she wondered what meaning she should read into those eight simple words.

MUNDARU was lying spreadeagled in the dust. The kadaitja men were squatting round him, holding his twitching body, while their leader extracted the spearhead from his back. In the fire beside them lay the sacred stone, like a heart absorbing heat from a fiery body.

There was a rush of blood, and a kadaitja man held the lips of the wound together while he rummaged in a bark bag. He brought out a finger-length sliver of white quartz and inserted it deep in the wound, covering it with a plug of gum resin. Mundaru heaved convulsively but the kadaitja men held him down and forced his mouth into the dust.

Without a moment's hesitation the leader plunged his hand into the coals and grasped the white-hot stone. Then he laid it over the wound in Mundaru's back to cauterize the flesh and resin. When the operation was over, he put the stone on the ground, filled his mouth with water and squirted it on the stone to wash off any evil that might have clung to it.

There remained only the death walk. At the first step Mundaru collapsed but they dragged him up, set his face to the sacred place and prodded him forward with their spears. Miraculously, he stayed on his feet and with one hand clamped to his back, he began to shamble ahead.

A foot outside the circle of painted poles they laid hands on him again, turning his head this way and that so that he might see the symbol of the power he had outraged. Then with one concerted heave they tossed him into the leaves and watched the ground swallow him up. The echoes of his despairing scream were still in the air when the shot rang out, and they wheeled to face the riders pounding over the plain.

146

THE SCREAM woke Dillon out of a doze filled with feverish phantasms. Sunlight was slanting down from the entrance to the cave. It was morning, then. He eased himself carefully on the rock ledge, focusing on the spot where the sunbeam struck the sandy floor.

Terror flooded through him. There, crouched on all fours, was a myall black. As the myall raised his head, Dillon could see the bulging eyeballs and the mouth drawn back from the white teeth. This was the man who had wounded him in the valley and who had found him at last, cornered and ready for the kill.

Every nerve in Dillon's body was alive with the instinct of survival. With a huge effort he forced himself upright, his fingers tight round the stone dagger. He blinked away the sweat that bleared his eyes. The myall was a pace away from the foot of the platform, on his knees, snuffling at the sand, breathing in short savage gasps as he moved closer.

It was now or never. Holding the dagger in both hands Dillon plunged downward onto the body of the myall. He felt the point dig deep into flesh, heard the sound as the limestone snapped, then darkness swept over him like a wave, tainted with the smell of death.

JUST OUTSIDE spear range Adams halted his little troop and sat watching the painted men drawn up in line across the entrance to the sacred place. Their spears were notched to their throwing-sticks and a single untimely gesture would bring them running to outflank the riders and cut them down. He might hold them off with gunfire; but this would mean killing, and in the code of the territory policeman this was a destruction of twenty years' work in the management of the nomads.

He turned to Mary and said quietly: "I'm going with Billy-Jo to talk to them. If there's trouble, ride like hell for the river and get the stockboys. Billy-Jo! We'll go on foot."

The tracker dismounted. Adams ostentatiously shoved his rifle back into the saddle-bucket, then he too dismounted, and the two walked slowly towards the painted men, holding out their hands, palms upturned to show that they came without weapons.

148

Twenty yards from the poles they halted. The hostility in front of them was like a wall. Adams moistened his dry lips and said to the tracker, "Tell them we come in peace. Tell them we know what has been done to Mundaru and that we know what they do not—that he raped and killed the wife of Willinja. Tell them where the body is and that they should take it back to their camp."

The tracker raised his husky voice in the manner of the tribal orator. It rang in the emptiness, now high and dramatic, now rolling in resonant periods. When he had finished speaking, the men muttered, then one of them laid his spears on the ground, stepped forward and began to speak. Billy-Jo translated.

"Mundaru dead. Eaten by spirit snake. Leaveim in spirit place. Blackfella business. White man no touch."

"Tell them we understand blackfella business. Boss Dillon is lost and we think Mundaru killed him. This makes it white man's business. I want to go down into the spirit place and talk with the spirit of Mundaru. Say that we have done service for Willinja and helped his wife. He has a debt to us."

Billy-Jo took up the theme again, and Adams knew enough of the language to understand that the tracker was drawing heavily on the personal credit of the policeman with the tribes. He was emphasizing that Adams had always paid his debts, had never infringed tribal custom, had never spoken with the forked tongue of the liar, had defended the blacks against the predatory drifters, and that his friendship was strong and his vengeance terrible.

The answer of the kadaitja man was emphatic. The life of Mundaru was forfeited to the spirits, and the white man must not enter the spirit place.

Adams found himself in a dilemma. The myalls knew the white men tried to save the victims of tribal vengeance and bring them to trial in their own fashion. They knew, too, the unwritten law that their secret places must be respected. Defiance of this law would destroy his credit and earn him nothing but a spear-thrust in the ribs. He decided to play for time.

"Billy-Jo, do they know what has happened to Boss Dillon?"

No. They did not know. But if he were dead this debt was paid by the death of Mundaru.

149

Adams took a deep breath. He was gambling now. "Then tell them this: I believe that Mundaru tracked the white man to this place and either drove him into the spirit cave or killed him and hid his body there. If this is true, his spirit will not rest but will haunt the place for ever and destroy the magic of the tribe."

Billy-Jo shot him a dubious glance and spoke again. This time the myall's answer was more bargaining.

"He say you go down, maybe come up with Boss Dillon, maybe not. But you no take Mundaru. Mundaru belong spirit snake."

For all the danger of the situation Adams felt a flicker of sardonic amusement at the neat way they had trapped him. They wanted Mundaru at all costs. They were the official executioners. To get what he wanted he had to wrench the law in their favour, but he had no choice. He turned to Billy-Jo.

"Tell them I agree. Tell them to go and pick up the girl, Menyan. I will leave Mundaru in the spirit cave."

"They want to stay, Boss. Watchim go down. Watchim come up."

Adams's face clouded with dramatic anger. "I have never spoken a lie. If they do not believe me, let them kill me now!"

He advanced, ripping open his shirt and baring his breast. It was the kind of theatrical gesture the primitives understood: man asserting his maleness by boasting and provocation. Three feet from the kadaitja spokesman he halted, and they faced each other, the painted man, the policeman, their faces stony with mutual defiance. Then the spokesman grunted assent and turned away.

The kadaitja moved off to the grasslands. Adams and Billy-Jo walked back to the horses and Mary. As they cantered towards the big bottle tree, she said shakily: "I was afraid for you. When I saw you walking out towards the spears, I—I thought, if anything happened to you, I couldn't bear it."

Her concern warmed him and restored a little of the confidence he had lost on the riverbank. A few yards from the painted poles Adams dismounted. "I'm going in alone, Billy-Jo," he said. "If Mundaru's alive, I'll send you down to talk to him. Wait here with Mrs. Dillon." He rummaged in the saddle-bag and brought out a torch. He stood a moment shining it into the gaping vault, then stepped down the ramp and was lost to view.

HALFWAY DOWN Adams halted, listening and probing the darkness with his torch. There was no sound. The musty air was tinged with the acrid odour of blood.

The moving finger of light picked out the two motionless bodies, one flattened on the sand, the other flung over it like a sack. Adams edged his way carefully towards them, reached out a tentative hand and rolled the upper figure on its back. At the sight of it he turned away, retching.

The face was a swollen mass, the mouth frothy. One shoulder was a suppurating wound, streaked with infection. The trunk was scored with scratches, blistered raw from the sun. The joined hands clenched a stump of limestone.

Adams switched the torchbeam to the body of the myall and saw the limestone point projecting from the small of his back, near a cauterized spear wound. He reached out, then withdrew sharply from the cold contact. He slanted the torchbeam upward and saw the rock-platform where Dillon had lain. The picture was brutally clear to him. Dillon cornered in his last refuge. The dying aborigine blundering about the cave. The leap of the white man onto the body of the hunter. Now they were both dead.

He felt strangely elated. The slate was clean, the report could be written with truth and discretion. The obsequies could be arranged to spare Mary any of this grisly spectacle, and after a decent time they could begin to think about their own future.

Then the policeman's habit asserted itself and he bent to make an examination of the bodies. He raised the myall's arm and felt for the pulse. There was none. He jerked out the dagger and tossed it into a corner. No point in complicating the report. Cause of death—spear wound. A kadaitja killing. Period.

He bent to make a similar examination of Dillon. When he felt the pulse, his heart sank like a stone in a pool. It was still there, weak and uncertain. Lance Dillon was alive.

For the first time he understood the meaning of murder. The compulsion to sweep away an obstacle to happiness. Leave Dillon alone for a few hours and he would certainly die. He had only to tell Mary and Billy-Jo that he had found both men dead and then, to spare the widow the sight of the body, head back to join the stockboys, who would later carry the body back to the station for a postmortem. Inevitable finding: death from a spear wound, infection and exposure.

He could do it. Immunity was guaranteed. Here in the naked country, Neil Adams was the law. His word was beyond question.

The madness receded. He hoisted Dillon onto his shoulders and staggered up the steep incline.

MARY BENT over her husband, sponging his lips, holding his head up to take whisky and water. After the first cry of shock she had relapsed into silence and a fierce concentration, but her cheeks were bleached of colour.

After a while Adams said: "It's time we moved. Gilligan's coming back this morning. I want to make sure the strip's ready for him. We'll tie Lance on a pack pony."

"Will he last the distance?"

"God knows. We'll have Gilligan radio the doctor to stand by at the hospital. It's the best we can do."

Her next words shocked him like a blow. "If he dies, Neil, you mustn't blame yourself for anything. You could have left him in the cave and no one would have known. If I have to, I'll tell him that."

THE AIRCRAFT made two low circuits before it hit the strip. Gilligan climbed out and came towards them at a run. He gave a low whistle when he saw Dillon lying under the blankets.

Adams said: "You'll have to fly him straight to Ochre Bluffs. Radio the doctor and the hospital. Mrs. Dillon will go with you. Call for me at Minardoo homestead in the morning."

The stockboys carried Dillon to the aircraft while Mary and Adams stood watching. Adams said awkwardly: "I'm not running away, Mary. I've still got to clean up this job. There'll be time for us to talk later."

She did not look at him, but said quietly: "It's better this way. I need to be alone for a while."

Gilligan helped Mary into the cockpit, gunned the engine and headed back into the wind for the takeoff. When the Auster levelled off, Mary bent down to look at her husband, wedged against the wall of the fuselage, padded with packs and blankets. His eyes were still closed, his puffed distorted face lolled slackly and when she felt his pulse, it was still a hesitant beat.

She had spoken the truth when she told Adams that she needed to be alone. She felt the numbness of shock slipping away and reason beginning to take hold again. Her husband was alive. She could still feel for him and with him. The feeling was changed from what it had been, diminished, confused; but it was still alive. How long it would last was another matter.

There were so many questions—and the answer to all of them hung on the same slim filament by which Dillon clung to life. Even if he survived, how much of him would be left—how much of the tough, sinewy body, of the thrusting, disciplined spirit?

And Neil? What was he thinking now? What did he hope or fear from the brief encounter under the stars? How would he greet her twenty-fours hours from now? She let her head rest against the resonant hull of the aircraft, while the wide empty carpet of the land unrolled itself beneath her.

The land . . . ! She would never be afraid of it again. She had seen the worst of it—the pain, the blind cruelty, the blood drying in its dust. Yet she had heard its music, slept under its stars, surrendered to its harsh enchantment. It was her country now and she belonged to it; just as she belonged to each of two men.

WILLINJA watched the two horsemen take shape out of a mirage. He was not afraid of them, but he would be glad when they had come and gone. There were days when the care of his people was like a stone on his shoulders. He wished he could shed it, as a snake sheds his skin, and sit in the sun like other old men and let his young wives feed him and keep him warm at night.

He could not do it yet, because so far there was no young man fit to assume the burden of his power. Perhaps there never would be. The young bucks were drifting away to the towns, to the homesteads and to the prospectors' camps, aping the white man's manners, his dress and custom, rejecting the old knowledge.

The kadaitja men had come back to report the death of

153

Mundaru, the murder of Menyan, their bargaining with Adamidji. Menyan's body was now buried on the riverbank. Casual burial was good enough for a woman, provided that she were sung to rest in the proper fashion. In the camp they were making the preparations: gathering every article she had worn or touched, piling them in a hole in the ground to be burned when the sun went down. If they were not burned, the wingmalungs would cling to them and bring sickness to the tribe.

Willinja would not grieve for her. He was too old for anything but regret. His anger was directed against Mundaru, whose folly had destroyed a breeding woman and brought the tribe in jeopardy.

When the riders dismounted, he gave no sign that he had seen them. Adams sat in front of him and waited. It was perhaps three minutes before the sorcerer raised his head. It was longer still before they began to talk, Billy-Jo acting as interpreter.

"There has been a killing," said Adams. "Mundaru, the Anaburu man. The white man is still alive. You sent out the men in feather boots. This is forbidden. You know that."

Willinja stared at him with brooding eyes. "Would the white man be still alive if the spirit snake had not killed Mundaru? You say we are under white man's law. Is the white man here to hold my bucks in check? Is he here to protect my wife? He comes and goes, and when he is not here who is afraid of him? But they are always afraid of the kadaitja boots."

Adams nodded gravely, considering the logic of this. After a while he said, "Who killed Mundaru? The kadaitja men, or the spirit snake?"

"The spirit snake."

"If it had been the kadaitja men you would understand that I must take them to Ochre Bluffs for punishment. But a spirit snake is different and I cannot touch such a one."

A gleam of approval brightened the eyes of the sorcerer. This was a man who understood the subtleties of rule. He said gravely: "Today, Mundaru is eaten by the spirit snake. Tonight, we sing the wingmalung out of . . . that girl. Tomorrow, the white man's cattle will be safe."

154

AS THEY rode towards the homestead, Adams felt a glow of satisfaction. He had conceded a point but kept a principle. He had lubricated a little the rasping contact between twentieth-century man and his stone-age brother. It helped him to feel a whit more at ease with himself. So long as a man stuck with situations he could control, he could maintain respect. In the argot of the cattle-country, Adams had been a "clean skin with no brands on his hide". But tomorrow, back at Ochre Bluffs, would he brand himself—lover to Lance Dillon's widow, or co-respondent in his divorce?

He loved this woman. If love meant anything it meant honesty, courage, a high head and a challenge to the world to wreck it if it dared. Why then was he skulking away?

Then in one stride he came up with the truth. It was not the love that was in question, hers or his. It was the cost—his own willingness to surrender the whole or a part of himself to any woman. To be a lover was one thing—no care and no responsibility. To be a husband was quite another—all care, all responsibility and the wedding ring worn like a hobble chain.

The ponies ambled homeward through the heat haze, while Adams lolled in his saddle and thought of Mary.

LANCE WAS CLIMBING out of a spiral pit of darkness. The climb was slow and painful, full of checks and reverses. Then a light began to show, and he found himself looking into Mary's face. He tried to reach for her, but made no contact. He tried to call but no sound came. Finally he drifted out of limbo and into sleep; and when he opened his eyes, he saw bending over him a black-haired fellow with a wide grin and a dangling stethoscope.

"So you're awake, eh? They breed 'em tough on Minardoo."

Dillon's voice issued in a husky squawk. "Black Bellamy! The mad doctor! How am I doing? How did I get here?"

Robert Bellamy sat on the bed, chuckling. "By rights you should be dead. Neil Adams found you, and your wife brought you in three days ago."

"Mary . . . where is she?"

"Resting. She's been with you night and day since you came.

155

You're going to rest yourself now." He felt the prick of a hypodermic in his arm.

Bellamy frowned and wiped the sweat from his forehead. He'd had a rough week, and for the last three days Dillon had been fighting with death while they pumped penicillin into him. It seemed Dillon had won his battle, but it was a partial victory at best. His heart had taken one round of punishment too many. He could lead a normal, temperate life, but he had ridden to his last muster, thrown his last steer.

The doctor walked across the dusty little compound of the hospital to the nurses' quarters. He pushed open the door of the cool dim lounge with its rattan furniture, piles of old magazines and pots of struggling cactus. Mary stood up to greet him.

"Sit down, Doctor. I'll pour you a drink."

Bellamy watched her as she stood pouring from a bottle of beer. In the last three days, she had grown visibly older—no, more mature. The skin was still young, the figure firm, the walk confident. But the skin had tightened over the bones of her face, the mouth had thinned a little, there was an air of deliberation and control about her.

She questioned him calmly. "How is Lance?"

"Pretty well, considering what he's been through. The infection's under control. The broken rib will mend in time. The burns are clearing up. But there's a certain amount of damage to the heart. He'll have to slow down. No heavy work, no violent exercise. On a careful regimen, he could outlast both of us."

"Can he still run Minardoo?"

Bellamy shook his head. "Not the way he's been doing it. With a good manager, maybe yes. But I understand you've been having a rough time lately. And now you've lost the bull. I suggest you cut your losses. Get Lance a desk job with the pastoral company handling other people's mortgages."

"That would kill him quicker than anything. Have you told him?"

"Not yet. I'd like to wait till he's stronger. It'll give you some time to think things out, too."

"I've already done that. We're going to carry on Minardoo. I'll

156

run it myself until Lance is well. Then we'll share it. I called the pastoral company and they'll see us through."

For a moment he stared at her in amazement, then threw back his dark tousled head and laughed: "You of all people! The city chick chirping up to the crows and the bush-hawks. Lord love you, girl, I didn't think you had it in you!"

ALONE AGAIN in the dim room, Mary lay back on the settee. The future stretched before her, bleak as the Stone Country. Why had she done it? Not for guilt and penance. It takes a tougher woman than Mary Dillon to sit with a man for three days and two nights and watch him battling for breath, to hear him call your name while poison is clotting in his heart muscles, to hold his hand and feel it grip yours as if it were the life-strand, to watch death take hold of him and see him fight his way free—and then take your own tableknife and cut his throat.

Another lesson she had learned too. You live with a man for breakfast and dinner and the Sunday roast. For eight hours of bedtime you love him or loathe him. But the only one you live with twenty-four hours of the day is yourself. And for so much of living you need so much of self-respect.

She had seen Adams briefly on his return from Minardoo. He had come to the hospital, made solicitous inquiries, held her hand for a few moments. Then he had gone, too quickly, with too little regret. She did not blame him. Yet there had been moments when heart and body cried out for the comfort of his arms. Had he acted differently she might have decided differently about her future with Lance; but he had not spoken. Soon it would be her turn to go to him: but not yet.

WHILE THE afternoon shadows lengthened across the dusty town, Adams sat in his office writing his report on Lance Dillon and the kadaitja killing. It was a neat piece of work. It would read well in Darwin and on the minister's file in Canberra. These things were important to an ambitious policeman.

Then he looked up to see Mary, pale but composed, a little smile breaking on her lips. He stood up and took her in his arms.

157

"I'm sorry we couldn't get together before," he said gently. "But it didn't seem wise. People talk."

"I understand that." There was no rancour in the level tone. "But we have to talk sooner or later, don't we?"

"Of course. How is your husband?"

"Bellamy says he's out of danger now."

"I'm glad for him—and sorry for us."

"Why sorry? If we love each other, we can still arrange things—one way or another."

"It's not as easy as that. Don't you see . . . ?" His eyes fell away from hers.

Her heart went out to him in his humiliation and perplexity. "Neil, answer me one question. Do you love me?"

"You know I love you, Mary. But . . ." He could not complete the sentence. The single word hung between them like a suspended chord of music. She knew it was no use hurting him or herself any more.

She took his face between her hands and kissed him full on the lips. There were tears in her eyes but her voice was steady.

"I love you, Neil. Not as much as I did. Not as much as I could. But wherever I am, whatever happens, there'll still be a corner of my heart that belongs to you."

She turned away and he sat like a stone man, watching her go. With her hand on the doorknob, she said, "I almost forgot to tell you—I decided before I came—I'm staying with Lance. I'll be running Minardoo from now on."

Before he had time to think, the words were on his lips: "Are you going to tell him about us?"

She stared at him, silent, then walked out into the sunlight. Adams sat down, buried his face in his hands, and for the first time in his life found grace to be ashamed of himself.

THREE DAYS later, Dillon lay wrestling with despair. Bellamy had given him the verdict. His first reaction had been to reject it. A fellow was halfway into the grave when he could not sit a horse and plug round the herds and hold a yearling under the iron. Then cold reason told him that if Bellamy said it, it was true. The

158

whole hideous irony broke on him. He had survived so much—to be reduced to a young-old man, nursing his heart in the shade. He was a cripple for life, and this was a cruel country for the maimed. Tears forced themselves out from his shut lids.

Then Mary came in, an unfamiliar figure in jodhpurs and a starched shirt, her hair wind-blown, her face tinged brown from the afternoon sun. She kissed him on the forehead, wiped the tears from his cheeks and sat down beside the bed. She said gently: "So Bellamy told you."

"Yes . . . It's too much. I can't . . . I can't . . . !"

"Listen to me! We're going to run Minardoo together."

"Together? You don't know anything about the cattle business, and besides, we're flat broke."

"No Lance, we're in business. I told the pastoral company they could foreclose any day they wanted. And I'd plaster the story all over the country that they put a returned serviceman off his land because the blacks had killed his bull and damn near killed him. So they've given us a three-year extension and some extra working capital to get us going again. I've already been down at the stockyards to watch an auction."

"My God, Mary!" Panic made him seem for a moment like his old self. "You didn't buy anything?"

"No." She patted his hand in maternal assurance. "But I learned a lot."

He stared at her unbelieving. "You've changed, Mary."

Her face clouded. "Yes. I'm going to tell you how and why. I want you to listen and try to understand. Afterwards, you will tell me what you want to do. Before all this happened, I was going to leave you, for good."

He closed his eyes and grappled with the thought. When he opened them again, she saw that he understood. He said gravely: "I know I didn't give you much of a life."

"It wasn't the life, Lance. It was you I wanted."

"I know that now. In the cave everything seemed futile except you. Did I make you very unhappy?"

"You made me want someone else."

She was sparing him nothing.

"Did you find him?"

"Yes."

"Did you . . . ?"

"Yes."

"Oh!" A long whisper of weariness. He closed his eyes and lay back on the pillow. Then he asked dully: "Do I know him?"

"It was Neil Adams."

"Why are you telling me now?"

"Because I've learnt something important to both of us. You can't live in this country with a lie. When you've heard me through you may not want me any more. Then I'll go away and start a new life of my own. If you do want me, just as I am, I'll stay and try to make you a good wife, and help you build a good property. But not with a lie, Lance. I'm sorry, deeply sorry. But I'm not going on being sorry all my life. If we come together again I want to try to have a child. If we can't make one of our own, I want to adopt one and rebuild our love around it. That's all, Lance. . . . If you'd like some time to think, I'll go away and . . ."

"No!" He caught at her wrist. His eyes were grave and hurt, but not bitter. He said soberly, "I don't know if it will work any more than you do. I'm hurt, shamed too. If I weren't tied to this bed, I'd take you out and thrash you . . . and Mister bloody Adams too. But even while I was doing it, I'd know I need you, girl, more than I ever did."

A ghost of a grin brightened his eyes. He lay back on the pillows, the strength drained out of him. There was no gesture of reunion except the slight tightening of his grasp on her wrist before he released her. Already he was on the border of sleep and she was glad for him. Tomorrow would be time enough to care.

She walked out onto the veranda and watched the sun go down, a glory of gold and purple and crimson behind the ramparts of the naked country.

Morris West

Morris West was born in Melbourne, Australia, in 1916, of Roman Catholic parents. The oldest of six children, he studied for the priesthood, and spent eight years as a teaching monk. In 1941, however, just before taking his final vows, he left the priesthood. He joined the army, becoming a cipher expert and serving three years in the Pacific.

After the war he began writing plays and serials for Australian radio and formed his own production unit, creating in one year as many as two thousand fifteen-minute episodes. Ten prosperous years later Morris West, now married, sold out his interest in the company and turned to writing books. It was during a visit to Italy that he met Don Mario Borrelli, who was running an orphanage in Sorrento, and the book he wrote about Don Borrelli's work, *Children of the Sun*, became his first bestseller.

He moved to England then, working for the BBC and for a time joining the "Panorama" team. The *Daily Mail* commissioned from him a series of articles on the Vatican, and out of these grew his most successful novel, *The Devil's Advocate*. Bestseller after bestseller followed: *The Shoes of the Fisherman*, *Summer of the Red Wolf*, *The Salamander*, *Harlequin*. . . .

Always, perhaps as a result of his early training, it has been man's moral dilemmas that have interested him most. "I find myself going back more and more to the great religious books," he says. "The most painful process—and I have to do this when I write a book—is to take time to contemplate. Our civilization is all against this, and you don't have time to think."

Fortunately Morris West's great success has bought him the time he needs, and he uses it well. He and his family were living in Austria, freezing in the Alps, when he decided to draw upon his intimate knowledge of the Australian desert to write *The Naked Country*. In this he presents a moral dilemma again, and an affirmation of his profound belief in the dignity and timeless value of the many ancient cultures still to be found upon this earth—telling at the same time the unique brand of vivid and exciting story that is his hallmark, and that he seems able to weave as easily as he breathes.

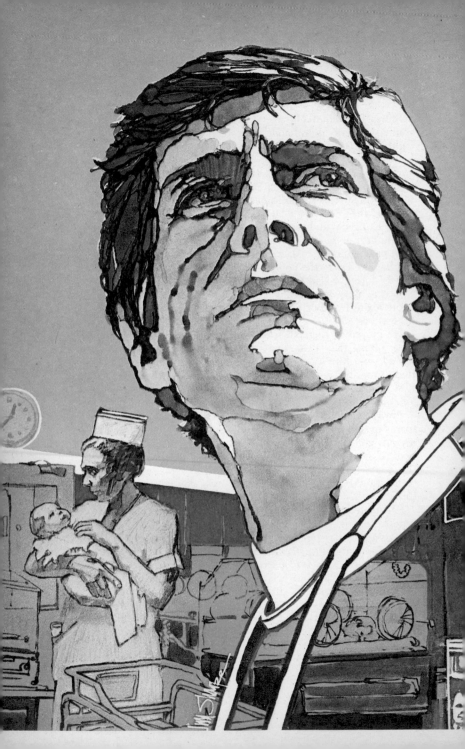

THE PHYSICIANS

a condensation of the book by

HENRY DENKER

Illustrated by Jim Sharpe
Published by W. H. Allen

Dr. Grant, young, idealistic, and totally dedicated to the care of the newborn, is involved in the treatment of the infant grandson of John Stewart Reynolds, powerful business tycoon and generous patron of the hospital where Grant is a staff member. When postnatal complications cause the baby to be brain-damaged, it is Grant whom the enraged old man blames.

Grant's only hope of refuting the serious charge of malpractice rests on the talents of his brilliant young lawyer, Laura Winters, and on her belief in his innocence—a belief that is soon re-inforced by their mutual love.

Together, in a compulsively dramatic story set against the two worlds of medicine and law, they fight for his career.

CHAPTER ONE

HE WAS never conscious of how intense he appeared as he bent over his microscope to adjust it precisely. Now, as he reached for his scalpel, he glanced involuntarily at the wall clock. He ran his fingers through his hair, a sign he felt under pressure. He was urgently aware that he had promised to lecture the mothers of another low-income housing project later in the day. Time. There was never enough time.

He applied his scalpel to the sliver of tissue on the slide under his microscope and began to examine the cells. His handsome face was grave as he discovered the outrageous degree of damage that might have been avoided, if only the mother had understood proper prenatal nutrition. Here was yet another infant who, but for fetal malnutrition, might have been born normal. And who would have survived.

Suddenly the squawk box sounded over his head. "Dr. Christopher Grant!"

Laying aside the scalpel, he reached for the phone.

"Dr. Sobol wants you, sir."

"Of course." Mike Sobol never intruded unless it was urgent. "Ring him."

In a moment he heard Sobol's voice—old, tired, and a bit apologetic. "Chris, do you mind coming up to ICU? Right away?"

165

"Be right there."

Why are hospital elevators always so slow? Grant thought as he started racing up four flights of stairs to the neonatal intensive care unit. But with a full load of tiny patients in the neonate—newborn—nursery, and teaching part of each morning, added to his first love, research, there was little he did not do on the run.

Even as he rounded the last landing, his mind went back to his current paper on brain-damaged infants, those malnourished patients that he had labeled "Reynolds babies" after Reynolds Houses, one of the major low-income developments in the city. He was constantly aware of the ironic fact that his laboratory, his research, the very halls he was striding through, were made possible by the benefactions of the same man who had built the development—John Stewart Reynolds.

Dr. Sobol was waiting just outside the glass wall of the intensive care nursery. With him was a tall man, gray-haired and distinguished. He looked familiar. When Sobol spied Chris he started toward him alone, intercepting him halfway down the corridor. A small man, Dr. Michael Sobol looked even smaller in the stiff white lab coat he wore on his rounds and during his lectures in the medical school. He had a flushed face that seemed perpetually troubled. Behind his glasses, his eyes always seemed tearful. His hair was thinning, and mostly gray. He did not seem impressive enough to be chief of the entire pediatric service of a university-affiliated hospital as large and important as Metropolitan General.

"Chris," the little man addressed him softly, "we have a neonate just referred from Parkside Polyclinic. Two to three weeks less than full term, but twenty-six hundred grams, so it's not a preemie. Obviously jaundiced, though not dangerously. Still, I want you to take this on yourself."

Grant's quizzical expression made Sobol explain. "The infant's name is Simpson. But it might as well be Reynolds." Sobol made a half-turn in the direction of the tall stranger who waited at the door of the intensive care nursery. Now Chris Grant made the connection. The distinguished face had the same profile that appeared on the bronze donor's plaque in the research wing. The man was John Stewart Reynolds.

"So Reynolds' daughter is the mother," said Grant.

"Chris, you know that no infant on my service is more important than any other," Sobol defended himself. "But in this case—"

To ease his discomfort, Grant said quickly, "Don't worry, Mike, I'll give it all the time it takes."

"Good . . . good." Sobol was gratified. "And I'll see to it we make up for interrupting your research."

At the intensive care nursery Chris eased the door open, allowing Sobol to enter first. When Reynolds started in after him, Chris gently blocked the man's access. "There's nothing you can do in there," he explained.

Reynolds' face flushed. He was not used to being forbidden anything. "That's my grandson. I have a right to know what's wrong with him—what's being done for him."

"Mr. Reynolds, right now I don't know what you could do except get in the way of people who are trying to help your grandson." Grant slipped into the room, closing the door behind him.

Reynolds made no secret of his resentment. He stared through the huge glass window at every move Chris Grant made.

At first glance Neonatal Intensive Care had the look of an efficient private aquarium. Transparent plastic tanks called Isolettes were ranged against the walls. In each enclosure a sick or premature infant struggled for life. Some were so few hours old that they still assumed the fetal position, crouching so that their tiny protruding ribcages emphasized each spasmodic breath. Many had intravenous (IV) tubes strapped to arm splints designed to keep the IVs safely and securely fixed.

Taped to almost every fragile body were electrodes. These were connected in turn to the equipment behind each Isolette which monitored the vital signs. Other sensors helped to regulate the surrounding temperature and humidity.

In one such plastic enclosure Baby Simpson, not quite forty-eight hours old, was breathing fairly normally, though his bronze skin color gave disturbing evidence of his jaundiced condition.

Chris Grant stared at him for a moment. Heir to a great fortune and much power, this five-and-a-half-pound infant looked no different from all the others that passed through his hands. Tiny, squirming, his red face wrinkled, his eyes clenched tight, he was a small and pathetic bit of humanity, facing life with all its uncertainties. Not the least of which was his present condition.

Chris Grant inserted his hands through the access portholes of the Isolette to make a superficial examination, mainly to palpate the baby's liver.

"Liver doesn't seem unusually firm," Sobol commented. Then he urged, "Take a look at the transcript that came over from Parkside."

Chris reached for the record, which the head nurse had ready for him. He began to scan it, till his eye hit the important fact.

"An Rh-negative mother?" he asked suspiciously.

"But read on." Sobol's tone warned him not to judge hastily.

"No previous pregnancy. No previous transfusion. No titer level for antibodies on an early pregnancy Coombs' test," Chris read off, thinking that, given these facts, the mother's being Rh negative would not seem to be the key to the infant's jaundiced condition.

"The transcript says they tested for infection and found no sign of any. But you know Parkside . . ." Sobol cautioned.

That comment reflected the eternal war between university hospitals and private ones—the research institutions never quite trusting the work done at the private hospitals, and they in turn always accusing the teaching hospitals of being too wedded to theory, research and experimentation.

"What was the last reported bilirubin?" Chris asked.

"There's only been one," Sobol said. "They got fourteen."

"Only one bilirubin? In an infant as obviously jaundiced as this? And with an Rh-negative mother, besides?"

"You think that's something?" Mike Sobol said. "Take a look at the report on the infant's Coombs'."

Chris glanced at the record again, then looked up, startled. "Rh incompatibility! How is that possible?"

168

"At this stage of the game, what does it matter?" Mike asked. "If that result is correct, this baby is going to require very special attention."

"Did they get signed consent for an exchange transfusion?"

"Not according to the transcript," Sobol said.

"Damn, they should have! In case it's necessary," Chris snapped. He had seen enough to know that swift action was necessary. He was about to demand equipment to draw a blood sample, but the head nurse, anticipating him, handed it to him. Passing his hands through the portholes again, he gently and carefully extracted some blood from the heel of the tiny patient. He transferred it to the test tube, sealed it and handed it to the nurse. "I want a bilirubin. Another Coombs'. And have them do a blood smear for infection. Stat!"

As the nurse left for the lab, Chris turned to an intern. "Dispatch a messenger to Parkside. I want a sample of the mother's blood. Should have been sent over with the transcript! I don't trust any lab results but our own!"

"Chris, you'll check with me every few hours?" Sobol asked. Grant nodded, and then the older man left for his class in the medical school. Mike Sobol knew that he could resume his teaching and administrative duties without concern. An angry, determined Chris Grant was Sobol's insurance that the infant would be cared for to the very best of any doctor's ability.

On the way out Sobol stopped to exchange a few words with John Stewart Reynolds, who stood glaring at Grant through the glass wall. He was obviously a man who trusted no one. Not even experts in fields about which he himself knew nothing.

Grant examined the infant again. The liver definitely felt normal. "Let's get this little one into a phototherapy unit," he said.

The head nurse moved the baby, with his electrodes and IV, to another Isolette. Then Chris closed the infant's eyes and carefully applied squares of gauze, held in place with tape. When he was positive that the gauze was so firmly in place that no light could penetrate and damage the retina, he brought a stainless lid down over the Isolette. Its underside held a battery of twelve short

169

fluorescent tubes. When Chris threw the switch, a blue-white light bore down on the tiny bronze patient. Chris withdrew his hands through the portholes and watched for a few moments.

When he finally turned away, he noticed that Reynolds still was glaring at him through the window, his doubt and anger even more apparent now than before.

"I'll be in my office," Chris said to the nurse. "Call me the second any word comes back from the lab."

Before he had fully opened the door, Reynolds confronted him. "Well, Doctor?"

"If you'll come to my office—" Grant said.

"Let's go!" Reynolds said impatiently. There was no further conversation till Chris closed the door of his small cluttered office and pointed to a seat. Reynolds remained standing, preferring, it seemed, to use his height to give him superior position. In the days that were to come, Chris Grant would discover that it was one of Reynolds' favorite tactics.

Reynolds was tall, and in good condition for a man probably in his sixties. His skin was tightly drawn over a strong jaw. His hair was white and short-cropped in military fashion. His voice had a gritty quality which served notice that he could be dangerous if enraged. Many employees and competitors had learned that over the years.

Chris was aware of some of the legends that had grown up around John Stewart Reynolds. But when it came to medicine, particularly in his specialty of neonatology, Chris was not one to yield to most professionals, let alone a layman, no matter how important the man might be.

Once the door was closed, Reynolds demanded, "I want to know what that child has! And what you intend to do about it!"

"A case of jaundice. And I'm already treating it. Till those tests come back from the lab, I have to proceed cautiously," Grant explained.

"I didn't see you treat him with anything! You took blood and you've got an intravenous on him. Or is there something special in that intravenous? If so, I demand to know what!"

170

"Mr. Reynolds, if you want to help, you're going to have to do two things."

"If it involves money, or flying in specialists or equipment . . ." Reynolds seemed ready to pull out his checkbook.

"First, sit down," Chris Grant said in a flat voice. "Second, if we can discuss this quietly, I'll tell you everything you want to know."

"Does it look serious?" Reynolds asked more temperately, finally slipping into a chair.

"Not so far," Chris said. "But we'll know more when we get a confirmation from our own lab on the cause of the jaundice. That's the reason for that blood sample. And those monitoring devices. It's essential to keep testing for some hours to see whether his jaundice grows better or worse. Most newborns have it to a slight degree. That is what we call physiologic jaundice."

"If it's so common, why did Coleman get upset?" Reynolds asked suspiciously.

"Coleman?" Chris had not heard the name before.

"The young fellow covering for Dr. Mitchell, my daughter's doctor. Mitchell's got the flu and doesn't want to expose any infants. Good man, Mitchell. Most meticulous."

"I've heard," Chris agreed.

Reynolds reverted to his original question. "If physiologic jaundice is so common, why did Coleman have the boy sent here?"

"As a simple precaution." Chris defended Coleman, even though he had never met him. Laymen had a way of blaming doctors, not nature, for illness. "Jaundice can be serious. It is caused by a number of things. An infection of some kind. Or an ABO incompatibility, where the blood of the mother and child are not compatible. In this particular case an Rh incompatibility is likely. Or where an infant is premature—"

Reynolds interrupted. "He's not premature! He's only preterm, by two weeks. Three at the most, according to Dr. Mitchell. And since he's more than a full twenty-five hundred grams, he can't be classified as premature."

Chris was surprised at Reynolds' knowledge. "I didn't say your son was premature. . . ." Chris began, realizing that he had used

171

the designation son instead of grandson. "But preterms tend more to jaundice than full-terms. The reasons have to do with complicated blood chemistry."

"You can explain them to me. I'm not one of your ignorant charity parents!" Reynolds stood up, towering over Chris Grant.

Chris stared up calmly. "We don't have this much trouble explaining anything to our 'ignorant charity parents.' They listen. And they understand we're doing all we can to save their kids."

"You're an insolent young bastard," Reynolds exploded. "I'm going to order Sobol to have you taken off this case!"

"Frankly, I wish you would."

"Don't think he won't do it. Do you know that *I* was the one who insisted on bringing Sobol here from Mt. Sinai? When the rest of the board said they were uncertain about bringing in a Jew to head up the department, I said, 'When it comes to medicine, get the best. And if the best is a Jew, get him!' "

"That was very sound," Chris said, refraining from making any more obvious comment. "Sobol *is* the best."

"That isn't the point! Right now the point is that a man who can affect your medical future is asking you for information relating to his only grandson. And you can't even be civil enough to give it to him!"

"I've given you all the information we have at this time," Chris said, seeking to bring the interview to an end.

"I want to know what the possible dangers are, and what can be done to overcome them," Reynolds insisted. "I have a right!"

Softly but quite firmly Chris said, "I should think his mother would 'have a right.' Or his father—"

"His mother's recovering from a difficult delivery. And his father is out of town. I had to send him to St. Louis on a business deal."

Chris decided that he might as well inform the older man completely. "Mr. Reynolds, since you arranged things so that you're in charge, I will give you all the relevant facts. Jaundice occurs when a disease destroys the infant's blood supply—his red blood cells begin to break down. That releases a yellow substance—bilirubin—into the bloodstream. That yellow substance

172

is what gives the jaundiced patient that bronze cast. The seriousness of the problem depends on the amount of bilirubin in the
blood. If it is kept low enough and its effects wear off, the bilirubin
is excreted and no harm is done."

"But if it isn't kept low enough?" Reynolds pressed.

"If the bilirubin in an infant goes as high as twenty, then it can
be dangerous. I like to start worrying at fifteen. Sometimes even
less. Depending on the patient."

"You said dangerous. How?" Reynolds demanded.

"If it's concentrated enough, the bilirubin reaching the brain can
create a condition we term kernicterus."

"Which is?"

"It has adverse effects on the brain. Affecting sight. Or speech.
Control of limbs. Or general brain function."

"You mean my grandson could be brain-damaged? Look, I don't
give a damn what it costs! Fly in whatever specialists you need.
I want that child to have the best of everything!"

"He's getting the best of everything."

"What's he getting, an intravenous to give him nourishment?"

"There's an antibiotic in that intravenous. If there's the slightest
chance of infection in his bloodstream, I like to medicate instantly,
even before the lab reports get back. That's part of the immediate
treatment."

"Part?" said Reynolds dubiously. "I didn't see him get anything
else."

"You saw me lower that lid over his Isolette. That was for what
we call phototherapy. It's the process of treating jaundice by the
application of intense blue light."

"Those were nothing but ordinary fluorescent lights! What the
hell kind of quack medicine do you practice here? Get Sobol on
the phone!"

"He's teaching a class right now."

"When my grandson is involved I don't care who's doing what!"

"Mr. Reynolds, it wouldn't help your grandson one bit to
interrupt Sobol's class. Right now no one, not even Sobol, can tell
you any more than I can."

"You get him out of that class—" Reynolds suddenly realized he was shouting, and his loss of control made him pause. When he continued, it was in a softer voice. "Look, you have to understand. This is my grandson, my only male heir. That young man in that plastic box can be anything he wants! Including President of the United States! He's got to be whole, strong." It was more a plea than an argument.

"Mr. Reynolds, if our reports confirm those in the transcript from Parkside, I don't foresee any serious trouble. The percentages are greatly in his favor."

"You didn't seem to think so before," said Reynolds. "Watching you through the glass, I could see you were upset."

"Yes," Chris admitted, "I was. On the transcript your grandson's bilirubin was fourteen. That's why I applied phototherapy at once. That helps to bring down the bilirubin."

Reynolds seemed somewhat relieved. "How does it work?"

"Well," Chris began cautiously, fearful that at this juncture any explanation was worse than none at all, "when we bombard the infant's body with the light rays in blue fluorescent tubing, the bilirubin breaks down and is more easily excreted in the urine."

Reynolds was not convinced. "Doesn't make sense," he muttered, "to depend on such a cure for a sick boy."

"Why not?" Chris asked. "It was an old wives' cure for a hundred years to put the babies with jaundice near the window. They recovered faster. Till one day a doctor decided to investigate. Was it sunlight that had the strange power to heal? Or any light? It turned out to be just light. And blue light worked best of all. It's become a fairly common treatment in the last few years. And it's certainly the safest step to take while we're waiting for the lab results to tell us if your grandson's condition is growing better or worse. But till we know, we do not take rash or extreme measures."

"What if his condition *is* getting worse?" Reynolds demanded. "What do we do then?"

If Chris had been less irritated, he might have been amused at Reynolds' use of the word we.

174

"If his condition becomes markedly worse, we will then resort to what we call an exchange transfusion."

"Exchange transfusion?" Reynolds asked.

"We slowly exchange the damaged blood of the infant with healthy blood of the right type, until we have given him a fresh blood supply twice over."

Reynolds was about to ask more questions when the phone mercifully interrupted. "This is probably the lab," Chris said as he lifted the receiver. "Bilirubin, sixteen. Under the circumstances, not too bad. Infection? Negative? Good. What about the Coombs'?" He sat up a bit more erectly. "So it *is* an Rh incompatibility? Are you sure? Run that test again. Why? Because according to the transcript, even though the mother is Rh negative there was no prior sensitization. Run it again! And I'll want to repeat the bilirubin in two hours."

Chris hung up. Reynolds asked dourly, "Bad, h'm?"

"No. Overall, I'd say it looks favorable."

"What about the Rh incompatibility? You seemed upset."

"Not upset. Just surprised," Chris said, wondering how it could have happened. But he had no time to dwell on that. Reynolds was pressing him.

"Isn't a bilirubin of sixteen close to the danger zone?"

"Not too close. Eight hours ago it was fourteen, but the test was done in another hospital. Part of the small difference—and the rise to sixteen *is* a small one—may just be what one has to expect with different technicians and equipment. I'd say a change of only two in eight hours is a damn good sign."

Chris picked up the phone, asked for Neonatal Intensive Care and spoke to the head nurse. "In two hours have a sample of the Simpson baby's blood drawn, and send it down to the lab. I'll be back by then. And you might as well get ready for an exchange transfusion. We'll make a decision after the next bilirubin."

Reynolds did not even wait till Chris hung up. "What did you mean, Doctor, you'll 'be back by then'?"

"I'm due down at Rixie Square to deliver a lecture to a group of underprivileged mothers on prenatal and postnatal care," Chris said, taking off his lab coat and slipping into his dark blue blazer.

"Do you mean that while my grandson is in dangerous condition you're going out to deliver a lecture?"

"Mr. Reynolds, there's nothing I can do for your grandson without another bilirubin. That won't be taken for two hours. Meantime, all we can do is keep him under phototherapy, and wait. I can be more useful lecturing than simply standing around."

"Look!" Reynolds said abruptly. "I'll pay you any fee! Stay here. Send someone else to give that damned lecture!"

"If I could accept a fee, which I can't, being a full-time employee of this hospital, it would be taking money under false pretenses. There is absolutely nothing I can do for your grandson right now," Chris said patiently. "But if you want to do something for him"—he pulled a paper out of his desk drawer—"have this consent form signed by his father or mother. It will allow us to do an exchange transfusion if necessary."

"Why do you need a consent form?" Reynolds asked.

"Because exchange transfusions entail risk. There's a three percent incidence of complications," said Chris. "And an almost one percent incidence of mortality."

"Mortality?" Reynolds said, surprised. "You mean an infant who gets an exchange transfusion has a chance of dying?"

"Only one chance in a hundred. But that's the reason we try to check a rising bilirubin with phototherapy before resorting to transfusion."

Reynolds nodded, fearful and not so insistently angry as before. Then he reached out for the paper. "Can't I sign that? I don't want to alarm my daughter."

"Hospital regulations say the mother or father," Chris replied, not unsympathetic to Reynolds' concern about his daughter.

"All right," Reynolds finally agreed, "but I'll be right back. Make sure you are, Doctor."

Chris charged the command to Reynolds' longtime habit of giving orders, and decided not to let it bother him. "See you in about two hours."

Reynolds stopped in the doorway. Chris noticed for the first time how steely blue the old man's eyes were. "Doctor, you bring that boy through in . . . in good condition . . . and I promise you anything you want. A new lab. A new wing. New equipment. Any appointment you have your heart set on."·

"We'll do the best we can," Chris said. "We always do."

The old man did not move. "Think of it as treating a future President of the United States. I want you to give him that much care!" The old man turned, and started down the corridor. Chris watched him go, thinking, He means it, he really means it.

On his way out, Chris stopped at the intensive care unit to have another look at his patient. There was no noticeable change. But in two hours Chris would know.

CHAPTER TWO

THE meeting was held in Public School 146 in Rixie Square. Here was the city's most devastated slum area. Amid some of the oldest and worst of the city's tenements rose some of the newest and tallest of the city's low-income housing developments. Several of them were Reynolds-built projects. Public School 146 had been opened three years ago to accommodate the added population.

As Chris Grant sat on the platform of the school auditorium with the principal, a buxom black woman, he watched the mothers enter and fill the hall. Some were extremely young, obviously pregnant for the first time; some surprisingly old to be bearing children. *El Medico*—as many of them called Chris—had a reputation in Rixie Square, and these women, mainly black and Hispanic, came to see the handsome young man who talked to them in words they understood. He told them everything they wanted to know. He was not impatient with their halting accents, as were some doctors in the clinics where they'd sought help. And he did not ask for anything—not their votes or their support for racial causes.

The sounds of voices died as the principal called the meeting to order and introduced Chris.

"*Tú eres una madre antes de tener tu bebé*," Chris began. "You are a mother *before* you have your baby."

177

They laughed at his mispronunciations, some of which he committed intentionally, so they'd laugh and relax.

Then he launched into the serious discussion in which the word milk—*leche*—was most prominent. In addition he stressed the importance of prenatal examinations and the absolute necessity for mother and child to have a substantial, balanced diet. He added that this country had raised whole generations of boys and girls who rose from poverty to become successful and respected citizens. But only by force of their brainpower. He explained that the secret of brainpower lay in proper nutrition in those early months before and after birth.

As he came to the end of his talk there was a burst of eager questions. He answered as many as he had time for, being careful not to seem to be in a hurry. When he had to leave to make it back to the hospital, he promised to return and speak again. They rose to give him an ovation, their cries of "Doctor" and *"El Medico"* following him out.

JOHN Stewart Reynolds was waiting outside the intensive care unit, peering through the glass at the Isolette in which his tiny grandson lay under the bright blue light of the fluorescent tubes. As Chris came down the hall Reynolds turned to confront him, but before he could speak, Chris said, "We should have an answer from the lab by now. I'll let you know."

He slipped into the room and went to the Isolette. He thought he could detect a slight lessening of the bronze color. The night nurse came to his side. "They take that blood sample?" he asked.

"More than five minutes ago," she informed him. "The results should come in any minute."

"I'll wait here till they do," Chris said, concerned.

He had actually been very conservative in setting forth the case to old man Reynolds. A bilirubin that would not be disturbing in an infant three or four days old might be very alarming in the first twenty-four hours of life.

As long as he had to wait for lab results, he decided to call Coleman, the referring doctor, at Parkside Polyclinic. Chris wanted

178

to find out what drugs had been administered to Mrs. Simpson during pregnancy. Laymen know about the much publicized effects of thalidomide. But other drugs have disastrous effects as well—even aspirin, if taken in large or continued doses.

Coleman verified from Mitchell's records that no damaging drug had been administered to Reynolds' daughter. He also assured Chris that the membrane had not ruptured too early, which greatly reduced the chances of the infant's having received a complicating infection during birth.

The transcript from Parkside clearly stated that the two Apgar tests—evaluations of circulatory, respiratory and neurological conditions—had been made in the delivery room in accordance with standard practice—the first, one minute after birth, and the repeat, five minutes later. The infant had a normal score both times. But on the main fact Chris wanted to ascertain, the transcript was sketchy, and Coleman was not much more informative.

"When did you first notice the jaundice?" Chris pressed.

Coleman paused a moment before answering. "Actually, I wasn't the one who noticed it. With my own patients to handle, and suddenly having to cover for Mitchell, I wasn't able to get back to any patient as frequently as I usually like. The first I knew was early this morning, when the nurse called me. . . ."

"This morning," said Chris, not concealing his surprise.

"I told you I was busy as hell!" Coleman answered sharply. "In fact, I was the one who suggested to the family that we refer the infant to your department."

"Fine, but does anyone know if that infant showed signs of jaundice in the first twenty-four hours or not? I have to know!"

"I'm afraid I couldn't answer that. When I saw the infant, after the nurse called me, it was almost thirty-six hours after birth," Coleman finally admitted.

Chris's further pursuit of that vital fact led him back to the infant's chart, which indicated that the first time anyone noted a change in the infant's color was some thirty-two hours after birth. Thus no one could accurately tell Chris Grant when the first signs of jaundice had appeared.

The telephone in Intensive Care did not ring. It flashed. Chris took the phone from the nurse. "Dr. Grant here. Yes? What did you come up with on the Simpson baby?"

"Bilirubin, still sixteen."

Secretly, Chris had expected it might even rise somewhat. But it seemed the phototherapy was holding the situation in check. That was encouraging. Not conclusive, just encouraging.

"Thanks. We'll be repeating the bilirubin again in two hours. Make sure there's someone there to run it through."

He decided to wait out the night, or most of it, till some marked trend established itself. Either the bilirubin would climb, or else the phototherapy would bring it down.

When Chris came out John Reynolds was waiting for the report. In the normal course of things the bilirubin should now begin to drop. He would stay around to make sure that it did, or to take countermeasures if it didn't, meaning an exchange transfusion. Had Reynolds secured that written consent from his daughter?

The old man handed it over. "What do we do now?"

"I'll run the test again in two hours. Till then we just wait."

"If you haven't had dinner yet, would you like to join me?"

"I'd prefer to eat in the cafeteria here. It's easier for them to reach me."

"Mind if I join you?" Reynolds asked.

"You'll have to carry your own tray," Chris warned.

"You young bastards are all alike!" Reynolds exploded. "When I started out as a kid, I carried a lunch bucket. I'll bet you don't even know what one of those is! I wasn't born into wealth. I earned it. The hard way. I've eaten in places you wouldn't stoop to enter. So don't give me that about having to carry my own tray!" Then he suddenly said, "If you'd like a drink, I have a bar out in my car. My chauffeur could bring in a bottle."

"No, thanks. Not when I'm on duty."

"Mind if I have one?" Reynolds asked.

"The day when someone named Grant can tell someone named Reynolds what he can or can't have will be a mighty cold day."

Instead of irritating Reynolds, the reply made him smile.

180

"You're cocky," he said. "But I like that. I was the same at your age."

Though John Reynolds loaded his tray with roast beef, potatoes, salad, dessert and coffee, he ate virtually nothing. Chris came to the conclusion that the old man was hungry only for company. When they had finished, there was still almost an hour to wait, and Chris invited Reynolds on a trip around Babies' Pavilion.

"You might enjoy an unofficial look at how your money's being utilized," Chris said, smiling.

Reynolds nodded and drained his mug of coffee, and they set out. Chris showed him through the operating rooms, the nurseries, the therapy rooms. In the neurological testing room he saw the older man flinch, thinking of his grandson, and Chris continued quickly through to his own laboratory, where he explained his current research, careful not to use the designation Reynolds babies, which for the first time he related to a man, not a group of buildings.

The two hours had elapsed. They went back to Intensive Care. While Reynolds waited outside, Chris examined the infant, took another blood sample and decided to take it down to the lab himself.

The bilirubin test did not take longer than five minutes. This time when he saw Reynolds in the corridor, he was able to approach him with a big smile. "I think we're out of the woods," Chris said. "This bilirubin was fourteen point five."

"Down!" Reynolds was smiling too, obviously relieved.

"The phototherapy did it," Chris said, kidding the old man by adding, "Those ordinary fluorescent lights. Quack medicine!"

"I guess it did!" Reynolds exulted.

Chris held open the door to Intensive Care. "Come on in if you'd like." He tossed the old man a sterile gown.

They approached the Isolette where Baby Simpson lay under the battery of lights. The infant breathed shallowly, but regularly, undisturbed by the IV and electrodes fastened to his body.

Reynolds stared at the infant and his eyes misted up. Suddenly it became strikingly clear to Chris Grant that all that John

181

Stewart Reynolds had ever worked for was wrapped up in this baby. Chris wondered whether there had ever been a Reynolds son. Or had he been forced to settle for a daughter?

"Can you tell yet?" the older man asked suddenly. "I mean about damage . . . brain damage."

"We'll test him in a day or two, and make a judgment. That doesn't mean that new evidence can't show up four or five months later. But I'd say we caught it in plenty of time."

"Okay, okay," Reynolds finally whispered. Then he asked, "Can I put my hands through those things and touch him?"

"If you scrub, it couldn't do any harm," Chris agreed.

Reynolds washed his hands as if the life of his grandson depended on it. Chris showed him how to slip his hands gently through the flexible plastic portholes. Gingerly, the old man let his fingers run over the tiny body. Then he withdrew his hands carefully, allowing the portholes to close again.

Out in the deserted hallway Reynolds said, "I want to thank you, Doctor. You certainly do know your business. Stay with him for the next forty-eight hours, till you're sure, and I will be in your debt forever. You'll find that I am one man who not only feels gratitude, but knows how to show it."

"Nothing I did was done with that in mind," Chris said.

"Grant, the day will surely come when John Stewart Reynolds can do something for you. When it does, whatever you want will be as near to you as your telephone."

Knowing that one does not put off a man like Reynolds with protests, Chris Grant contented himself with a simple thank-you.

Reassured, Reynolds once more walked with the vigor of a young man as he started down the corridor toward the elevator. Chris Grant watched him turn the corner, thinking, John Stewart Reynolds must be a great friend to acquire, or a powerful enemy to avoid. But Chris realized he had come to accept the old man, even to like him, because of his intense devotion to his grandson.

On his way to his apartment in the dorm opposite the hospital, he picked up an early edition of the morning paper. Dominating the front page was a glaring headline: RIOT IN RIXIE SQUARE!

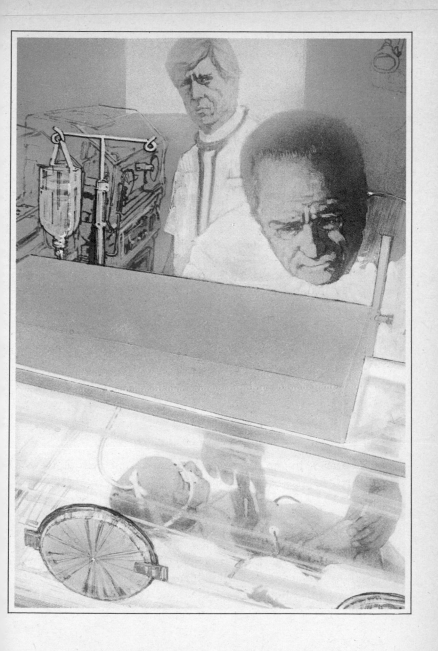

"Damn," he said to himself, and began reading the details. Due to some as yet undetermined cause, a riot had erupted in front of Public School 146 shortly after his lecture there. Rioters had invaded the business district, smashing windows, stealing liquor, groceries, television sets and transistor radios.

Chris dropped into bed exhausted, pursued by images of those friendly, eager women he had lectured that afternoon. His last conscious thought was that he hoped none of them had been involved or hurt in that damned riot.

THE Simpson infant recovered nicely. Its bilirubin went down sharply in the seventy-two hours after its exposure to phototherapy. Insofar as it was possible for a neonatologist to check out so young an infant, Chris Grant had assured himself that there were no aftereffects. The pediatric neurologist confirmed Chris's findings. Judging from all tests and reactions possible at this early stage, the infant's development seemed fine. At the end of eight days Chris released the infant to his mother.

Mike Sobol was particularly grateful to Chris, since he had plans for a new laboratory specifically for neurological research on neonates. The tightening of federal monies meant that Sobol would have to go hat in hand to a few wealthy men, prime of whom was John Stewart Reynolds. Chris had made his task much easier now. Or so it seemed, for a time.

CHAPTER THREE

FOUR months had gone by. Dr. Christopher Grant was delivering his research paper on his Reynolds babies to the Neonatological Society of the United States. The grave and silent manner in which the audience listened encouraged Chris. He was about to present informal comments after reading his paper when he noticed a man enter through the side door of the auditorium. The intruder whispered something to one of the doctors, who then pointed at Chris. The intruder seemed distressed, but sat down to wait.

Chris forced his attention back to his address.

184

"The special importance of these infants whom I have chosen to designate as Reynolds babies is not medical alone. These children are the product of a so-called enlightened society. Their families were moved out of the slums into new housing projects. They are presumed to exist above the poverty level. Yet there has been very little improvement in the unfortunate children."

Chris noticed the man, sitting near the door, becoming restless and fingering a slip of paper. But he continued, for this was the substance of his talk.

"Billions of dollars are used in an effort to help these children *after* the damage has been done. With far less money they could have been born normal, productive human beings, if their mothers had been taught the importance of proper prenatal nutrition. A generation ago the stereotyped Negro in our most popular forms of entertainment was lazy and shiftless. People laughed at him, never considering that the two most notable characteristics produced by severe malnutrition in children are *apathy* and *lethargy!* What some of us have been taking to be a racial characteristic or a genetic inferiority is really something that by deprivation *we* have bred into a substantial portion of our black population.

"I say a reordering of priorities is demanded. We must use our medical knowledge to make sure that our nation's social and economic programs are not based on theory but on hard medical fact. If we don't, one deprived generation will breed another, and another and another. I will ask, before this meeting is adjourned, that we pass a resolution urging the government to consider and act on these findings."

The applause that greeted his conclusion was strong, except from the area immediately in front of him, where the older and more conservative doctors sat. Chris was neither surprised nor disappointed. At the moment he was most anxious to discover the identity of the man who was pushing his way through the crowd, reaching over the heads of the doctors and waving the slip of paper, saying, "Dr. Grant! This is urgent!"

Chris took the note and glanced at the brief message. "Call your hospital at once."

"Excuse me—excuse me—" he said abruptly to the doctors who were trying to talk to him, and left the auditorium to find a phone. A number of disturbing thoughts were flashing through his mind. The main one was that Mike Sobol might have had a heart attack; he'd already had a massive coronary, and with teaching duties, research, administrative chores and his desperate effort to secure enough money to launch the new neurological lab, Mike had been overworking.

Chris made the long-distance call to the hospital, and the switchboard put him right through. When he heard Sobol's voice he was greatly relieved, but it sounded tired and almost breathless. "I hated to interrupt you, but this couldn't wait. This morning John Stewart Reynolds called me. He said the Simpson baby shows evidences of being retarded. Brain-damaged!"

"I won't believe that till I examine that infant myself!"

"That may not be easy. Reynolds is blaming you for the whole thing." Before Chris could recover sufficiently to answer, Sobol went on. "Chris, get on a plane! Come right home!"

Chris went straight to his room to start packing. But even before he had put his few shirts into the bag, there was a knock on the door. Jeremy Bingham, of Children's Hospital in Boston, and Carl Ehrenz, head of Pediatrics at UCLA's hospital, were there.

Bingham was smiling as he said, "We're not here as a committee but as competitors. We caught each other in the same elevator, each in the act of sub-rosa head-hunting. What it comes to, Grant, is that we both want you. And at optimum terms. The choice is up to you. Do you want to practice in a civilized community like Boston? Or would you prefer to do covered-wagon pediatrics out in frontier country?"

Both men laughed, but Chris, thinking of Reynolds' implacable anger, was tempted for a moment to accept any offer that would take him away from a confrontation with the Reynolds empire. If it hadn't been for Mike Sobol's troubled voice, Chris might have discussed the proposals. Instead he said, "Doctors, I thank you both. But I've just been called back for an emergency. Please don't think I'm rude. But I do have to pack and get to the airport."

186

Bingham dropped his casual façade to say very soberly, "Grant, if you find that you're interested, let me know. Immediately!"

On the flight back Chris considered all the possibilities. Could the Simpson infant have been turned over to him too late? In preterm babies with an early onset of jaundice, damage could be swift. Still, the bilirubin had never reached dangerous levels, and phototherapy had worked. Yet here it was four months later and there were signs of brain damage. Impossible, he decided.

Most likely the child was not retarded at all. An overanxious, overambitious grandparent like John Stewart Reynolds probably just expected too much of the infant. Come to think of it, hadn't he mentioned to Reynolds that signs of brain damage were most likely to appear at four to five months? Well, the old buzzard must have been waiting and now was diagnosing any sign that displeased or disappointed him as brain damage.

Chris refused to be alarmed.

"The man is unreasonable, I know," said Mike Sobol. "But because he is, we have to be careful. Extremely careful."

"Who examined the infant?" Chris asked.

"Mitchell. True, he likes money, but I still respect him as a practitioner. If he says that child shows evidence of brain damage, I have to believe him."

Chris was stunned. "I'm sorry about what this might do to your plans for a neurological lab, Mike."

"We live at the mercy of royal largesse, no matter what laymen think. But I'll work it out."

Yet Chris could tell by the way Mike's wispy hair was matted to his damp scalp that this was a severe blow to his plans.

"Before I accept Mitchell's diagnosis, I want to examine that baby," Chris said. "I'd also like to examine the mother. And question the father."

"I can't promise anything, Chris. After all, we have no legal right to demand an examination. I can only ask it as a courtesy."

"Our examination and a complete history are important in making any diagnosis," Chris persisted.

"I'll try to explain that," Sobol said. He pushed aside some papers on his desk and found the phone. They were both silent during the moments it took to put through the call.

"John, this is Mike Sobol," he began softly.

"Yes?"

"Grant is back from that meeting. He is greatly distressed. And he thinks that perhaps there's been a misdiagnosis. He'd like to examine the child himself—"

Reynolds cut in. "Mitchell is our doctor. And I trust him!"

"With all due respect to Mitchell, no doctor in this world is infallible. Another opinion can't hurt. John, please. We are very concerned about that child and we're only trying to help."

There was a long pause before Reynolds said, "If you could do the examination at my home, and if Mitchell would be in attendance, then I think it might be arranged."

"Good, good," Sobol said, gratified. He tried to make it sound like a casual afterthought when he added, "And, John, there might be some questions that only your daughter could answer. Could she be there?"

"Grant may examine the child in Mitchell's presence, if he wishes. But my daughter will not be there!" Reynolds spoke so loudly that Sobol didn't have to repeat the statement for Chris.

"All right, John. Would this afternoon be too soon?" Sobol asked.

"This afternoon. Four o'clock," Reynolds said with crisp impatience, and hung up.

THE Reynolds home rose up from the highest point in the exclusive Walnut Hill section of the city. After Chris Grant and Mike Sobol entered the grounds of the estate, it took some minutes to arrive at the house. There was already another car with MD plates parked in the circular driveway. Mitchell had obviously arrived before them.

They were admitted to the house by a butler, led up the broad staircase and shown into the room where the baby rested. Chris was surprised to find that it was a completely equipped nursery, the sort that well-to-do parents, rather than grandparents, would

188

furnish. It reinforced his initial feeling that John Reynolds regarded the infant as his son rather than his grandson.

Reynolds greeted them with grim reserve. He introduced them to Hugh Mitchell, whom Sobol knew fairly well but whom Chris Grant had never met before. Mrs. Reynolds, a tiny, fragile woman, waited near the bassinet. She attempted to smile, but did not quite succeed. Evidently she was under great tension, as if in some way she, too, were on trial. When she extended her hand, Chris found it icy cold.

He stared down at the child, a fine-looking infant. Blond, red-cheeked, with a small delicate nose. But Chris Grant knew that sometimes the most terrible of mental deficiencies afflict the most beautiful infants, as if by some perversity of nature.

As he looked at the child, waiting to see what its reaction to him would be, he asked Mitchell, "He eat well?"

"Moderately," Mitchell said.

"Sleep?"

"Not too badly," Mitchell admitted.

"Weight gain?" Chris asked.

"Below normal," Mitchell replied, his manner making a comment as well.

Chris reached into the bassinet to run his fingers lightly over the infant's head. There were no signs of pronounced cranial deformity. But when he used his tape, he confirmed for himself his first serious suspicion: the infant's head was slightly less than normal size. He reached into his pocket for his flashlight and passed the lighted end before the infant's eyes. No tracking reaction. He tried again. The eyes remained aimless and unfixed, not at all stimulated by the light.

He picked up the tiny patient. The boy was almost completely limp in his hands—dishraggy, in the terminology of his specialty. Chris felt the first strong pang of fear. Aware that John Reynolds was glaring at him, Chris returned the infant to the bassinet and placed him face down, hoping that he would respond by raising, or at least trying to raise, his head. He lay there, inert. Chris gently lifted the head. But he could tell that the tonic quality of

189

the neck muscles, which should have evidenced itself by three months at the latest, was lacking. His hands ran the length of the tiny body, confirming that it was underdeveloped.

He brought the infant to a sitting position, but the baby could not maintain himself and slumped out of control. He placed him on his back. As he turned to find a diaper, he could see Mrs. Reynolds, trembling with the tension which had accumulated in the room since Chris began his examination. Mike Sobol was perspiring profusely. Mitchell remained silent, vindictive.

Chris placed the diaper lightly over the child's face; an infant four months old should make some effort to move it away. This infant did not. He was clearly abnormal, probably brain-damaged.

Chris finally dared to meet Mike Sobol's eyes. Their worst fears had been confirmed. Chris knew the evidence was overwhelming. An electroencephalogram—or brain scan—would only confirm findings already too apparent.

Reynolds broke the silence, asking in a tone of suppressed hostility, "Well, Doctor, what now?"

Chris turned to him. "I would have to concur in Dr. Mitchell's diagnosis." Then he added suddenly, "I want to talk to the mother!"

"Young man, you will talk to *me!*" Reynolds answered sharply. "Come along!" He opened the door, waited till Grant and Sobol preceded him, and pointed the way down the broad stairs to a paneled library.

On a huge antique walnut desk there was a battery of phones that connected John Stewart Reynolds to his various nationwide enterprises. On one corner of the desk was an electronic computer screen on which Reynolds could summon up the price of any stock or commodity on any exchange. It seemed to Chris that the man might run the whole world from this room, surrounded by antiques, costly paintings and whole walls of old books.

Reynolds took his place behind the desk, but did not sit down. "My grandson is brain-damaged!" he said fiercely to Chris. "All the evidence we have shows he was perfectly normal at birth!"

"When he was turned over to us, he was not perfectly normal," Chris replied. "There was clear evidence of jaundice. That's why

190

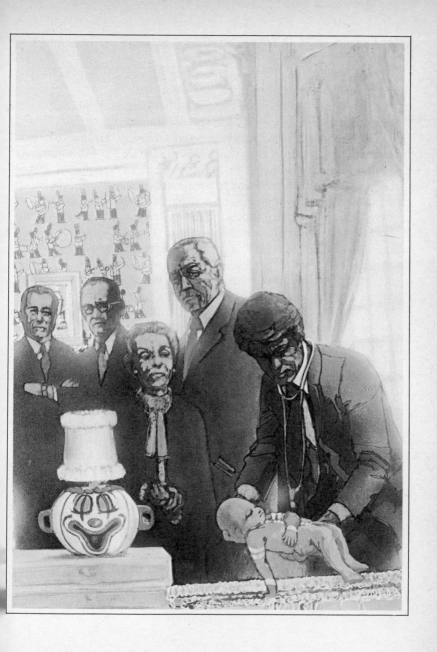

Dr. Coleman sent him to us. Mr. Reynolds, I still say I want to talk to your daughter!"

"You'll talk to me! Truthfully. Something you did not do before, young man! Why didn't you tell me everything?"

"Everything?" Chris asked, puzzled, looking to Mike Sobol for some explanation. But Sobol was equally confused.

"Yes, everything!" Reynolds accused viciously. He moved from behind his desk. "You damn doctors think you have a monopoly on understanding. Once the symptoms began to appear, *I* was the first to spot them! I went to the medical library and looked up all the signs and symptoms of neurologic deficiencies in infants from birth to age four months. Those tests you did upstairs—*I* did them myself. *I* was the one who called it to the attention of my daughter. To Dr. Mitchell's attention. Where my grandson is concerned, I no longer trust anybody!"

"Mr. Reynolds," said Chris, "you were there. You watched every step of the treatment for the first twenty-four hours after the infant was turned over to us. You saw the jaundice diminish within twelve hours. Don't you remember?"

"Oh, yes, I remember!" Reynolds began to shout. "But what I didn't know at the time, and what you deliberately concealed from me, were the aftereffects."

"What aftereffects?" Chris demanded.

"I found out a number of interesting things in that medical library, young man! All about your precious phototherapy! Why didn't you tell me about the risks? It upsets their tiny stomachs. It gives those poor little things rashes. It can cause eye damage."

"The first two effects are transitory," Chris said. "And I guarded against eye damage. You saw that yourself. Any doctor will tell you that that child is not suffering from retinal damage."

"What about his head size? One doctor wrote that in some infants phototherapy results in inhibited head growth!"

"And recent papers dispute that altogether," said Chris. "Including one by that same doctor."

"What good does it do me to hear that, when upstairs my grandson is lying there, his head smaller than normal? You never should

192

have done it. Never! That little boy will spend the rest of his life—and *my* life—a benign idiot. Forty years I've waited for a male heir. If not my son, then my grandson. And when he finally did come along, he was destroyed, destroyed! By men who are supposed to know. By men who lie. Who conceal. Who tell you all about the benefits of treatment without telling you about the risks. Don't you think you're going to get away with it! Before I'm through with you, you'll regret the day you ever decided to go into medicine. I'll destroy you. I'll sue you for malpractice. Five million dollars! I don't give a damn if I don't collect a dime as long as I destroy you. Then try to get an appointment at any other hospital. You are finished as far as medicine is concerned in this country."

"John, if you have no regard for anything else, think of what you'll be doing to our hospital, a hospital you helped to build and maintain," Mike pleaded.

"And the one time in my life when I really needed it, what happened?" Reynolds demanded hoarsely. "I don't give a damn about that hospital from now on." The degree to which he wanted his vengeance became apparent when he added, "It won't just be Reynolds' money you'll be missing from now on. It'll be state money and federal money. I have power I haven't begun to use! But you, Chris Grant, I'll break you if it's the last thing I do."

JOHN REYNOLDS SIMPSON an Infant, by his father,
  LAWRENCE SIMPSON and LAWRENCE SIMPSON
                                            Plaintiffs,
              —against—
METROPOLITAN GENERAL HOSPITAL, CHRISTOPHER GRANT,
    M.D., and MICHAEL EDWARD SOBOL, M.D.
                                      Defendants
    Plaintiffs, above named, complaining of the
  Defendants by their attorneys, PARKINS, SEARS
  and WADLEIGH, respectfully allege:

Chris Grant stared at the heading on the legal document, the first that had ever been served on him during his lifetime. Then he read through the rest. He was charged with having been guilty

193

of malpractice in the treatment of the infant, John Reynolds Simpson, resulting in serious and permanent injury. The amount of damages sought was five million dollars. Ridiculous, he knew. But he could still remember Reynolds' threat, though Reynolds' name did not appear in the papers.

Mike Sobol was also served with a copy, as was the administrator of the hospital. Since Reynolds' attorneys—Parkins, Sears and Wadleigh—were counsel to Metropolitan General as well, they asked to be relieved of that duty because of the obvious conflict of interest.

The real defense, therefore, fell to any law firm to be selected by Medical Underwriters, the insurance company that covered the hospital and its employees for malpractice suits.

As soon as the suit was filed it received extensive coverage in the press, because the name Reynolds was involved and because of the huge amount of damages at stake. During the next ten days Chris Grant received two letters. One was from Boston, from Jeremy Bingham, informing him, "Due to the urgent need to fill the position, we have had to settle on another physician as assistant professor." The second letter came from Carl Ehrenz at UCLA. Though the wording was different, the effect was the same.

The medical mark of Cain was on Christopher Grant, practically at the outset of his successful career.

CHAPTER FOUR

CHRIS stared through the transparent wall of the Isolette at the full-term but pitifully undersized infant struggling to catch its breath. The high-pitched crying was interrupted only when the tortured body convulsed in a spasm and a greenish vomit erupted from its twisted mouth.

"Where's the mother?" Chris asked the intensive care nurse.

"Ward C, Maternity. Name's Grove."

"Anyone ask her?"

"She admitted she had a fix on the way to the hospital."

194

Staring down at the struggling infant, Chris whispered angrily, "She say how much of a habit she has?"

"Ten bags a day."

"Get me a kit and some chlorpromazine," said Chris.

As she turned away to fetch the injection kit and medication—an antiemetic tranquilizer—the light on the phone flashed. A young nurse in training held the phone out to him.

Chris took the receiver. It was Sobol. "Chris, aren't you supposed to be in my office?" It was a command, phrased in the form of a question. That wasn't Mike Sobol's way.

"I've got a neonate addict at a highly dangerous stage."

"The investigator is here from the insurance company."

"He'll have to wait!" Chris said brusquely. He resented the threat to himself and to his patients, whose welfare from now on might be subordinated to the demands of the lawsuit. But he was immediately sorry that he was letting Sobol bear the thrust of his anger. More gently, he added, "Be there as soon as possible."

Reaching through the portholes of the Isolette, Chris sterilized an area of the infant's thin buttocks. He swiftly inserted the needle and delivered the drug. The infant struggled slightly, then seemed to surrender to the procedure.

Chris waited till the sedative began to take effect. "He'll sleep now," he said to the nurse. "Every time he wakes, feed him. Get as much food into him as he'll take. Whatever he can retain is to the good. I'll be in Dr. Sobol's office. Watch this infant closely. If he evidences tremors, or shows uncontrolled vomiting after being fed, call me immediately."

Chris strode down the corridor wondering. Even if he could save the infant's life, though chances were against it, to what purpose? Were there studies of the later life of such children, of the eventual effects of having an addicted mother? Perhaps this infant already had a predisposition to addiction that would in the end destroy it anyhow. This was one of those rare days when all pediatrics seemed futile.

He reached Sobol's office. "Go right in," Sobol's secretary said, without any of her usual warmth. Her manner was only a hint of what awaited him inside. He knew it the moment he saw Mike's red, tense face.

"Chris, I want you to meet Mr. Colwell. He's the investigator from the insurance company that covers us."

Charles Colwell was a tall middle-aged man. Chris estimated him to be at least twenty-five pounds overweight and dangerously flabby. Colwell held out his hand, allowing Chris to shake it. It, too, was soft and limp, and the man's florid complexion bespoke many lunchtime martinis. His voice was soft and ingratiating. He had an annoying tendency to smile as he spoke. It was an unnerving smile, which Chris took to mean, "Do you realize the danger of your position?" Before even a few minutes had passed, Chris Grant formed a distinct dislike of Charles Colwell.

"We've had some preliminary conversations with Reynolds' counsel," Colwell said. "After all, none of us has anything to gain from long litigation, do we? We'd like to avoid a trial, for all our sakes. Especially yours, Dr. Grant."

"I'll do what I can to cooperate," Chris said, more to reassure Mike Sobol than for any other reason.

"Cooperation, that's the key to success in lawsuits," Colwell said, smiling. "We'll all be better off in the long run if we're frank and honest with each other."

"Mr. Colwell," said Sobol, his temper showing, "what gives you the feeling that Dr. Grant is going to be less than completely honest and frank?"

"I didn't say that. I merely like to state the ground rules so everybody understands. We have a right to complete access to the hospital records, to the doctor's private records, even to the doctor's thoughts at the time of this alleged malpractice. What he thought is possibly as important as what he did, in such a case."

Colwell put aside his yellow legal pad and got up from his chair. "For example, sometimes a doctor puts a note into the patient's chart that, on reconsideration, he regrets. In fact, sometimes it's possible that the doctor might want to change his notes, to make the record a clearer, more honest presentation of what actually happened. . . ." Colwell let his statement hang in midair.

196

"Are you suggesting that a hospital chart should be subject to tampering?" asked Sobol.

"Who said anything about tampering?" Colwell defended himself. "Corrected to reflect an accurate picture of what happened."

"There's nothing in that record that I would want to amend," Chris stated flatly.

"Doctor, perhaps if you realized what you're up against, you wouldn't be so damned noble. It's a dirty business, malpractice. Plaintiffs will resort to almost anything. Especially a man like John Reynolds. And you're the one he's after, Doctor."

Colwell drew a cigar out of his breast pocket, removed the cellophane wrap and bit off the end. "I'm only saying, if you're going to make any changes in that record, this is the time to do so. Before he gets his hands on it. Because he will. He will."

"I know that record and the chart," Chris said. "There is nothing I want to change. And even if there were, I wouldn't alter it."

Colwell nodded sadly. "I wish I could be that cavalier about my career." He sucked at the end of his cigar before observing, "There's going to be a letter from the insurance company in a few days."

"Letter?" Sobol sensed a new danger. "To whom?"

"To the hospital. You. And to Dr. Grant. You see, where the amount of the suit exceeds the three-million-dollar coverage in your policy, then the individual doctors and the hospital can be liable. So you have a right to call in your own counsel, even though they can have no official standing in the case."

Chris made a mental note to check on Colwell's statement. It might be a threat, or it might be true.

"Doctor, I don't think you fully appreciate the significance of what I just said," Colwell continued. "It's proof that this is a personal vendetta. Reynolds doesn't need the money. He knows, and his lawyers know, that five million is an outrageous sum. But it keeps you from hiding behind the hospital's insurance company. He wants your head. So I'd think seriously about what's *in* that record. And then about what you'd *like* to have in it. It's your last chance for the benefit of hindsight."

"That record stands!" Chris said firmly.

197

"Okay." Colwell seemed to resign himself to the worst. "Now, there are some questions I have to ask." He lit his cigar. "This phototherapy is fairly new, isn't it?"

"It's been used very effectively for almost ten years," Mike Sobol declared protectively.

"How firmly established is it, really? I mean, do you know of any reputable hospitals where it *isn't* in use?"

"There are some. What about it?" Chris asked angrily.

Colwell smiled. "Grant, as an old hand at this law game, let me give you some good advice. When you answer questions in a legal case, give straightforward answers without emotion. No one, especially no judge, is interested in how you *feel*. He wants facts.

"Now then, Dr. Sobol," Colwell continued. "You never presented this therapy to the hospital's review board on experimental procedures, did you?"

"We didn't, because by the time we adopted the therapy it was no longer in the experimental stage. In fact," said Sobol, "that was one of the reasons I tried so hard to get Grant to join our staff."

"What was?"

"Phototherapy. He had experience with it in his previous post and I wanted such a unit set up here. I have never regretted it."

Colwell nodded soberly. Then the small unsettling smile flicked across his face. "I merely asked whether you put this procedure to a hospital committee. And you gave me a lot of information I never asked for. Information that would invalidate your testifying with any effectiveness on behalf of Dr. Grant. You admit he's your protégé; you brought him here to practice phototherapy; you're prejudiced in his favor. You'd make one hell of a lousy witness."

Colwell bit off the wet end of his cigar. "Remember, both of you. Only answer what you've been asked. Don't explain. Don't apologize. Don't argue. Just answer."

"Look," Sobol fought back. "We're doctors, not professional witnesses. Not actors who learn a part and repeat it as directed!"

Colwell smiled. "I'm your friend. I'm on your side. Wait till you meet the opposition. You'll wish you *were* an actor."

The phone rang just then. Sobol answered, and handed the phone

198

to Chris. It was the neonate intensive care nurse. The Grove infant was vomiting again, and had developed respiratory trouble.

"I'll be right there!" Chris said, hanging up.

"One minute, Doctor!" Colwell said. Chris had started for the door, but turned to face Colwell. "I have to warn you, Dr. Grant. Normally the plaintiff is the one who has to scrounge for doctors to testify to the malpractice of another doctor. But Reynolds has muscle. There'll be a long line of very good doctors who'll testify against you!"

"I'm sorry about that. Now, I have a patient. . . ."

Once the door closed behind Chris, Colwell said, "You'd better warn that young man—he's in bigger trouble than he suspects. It could ruin . . ." Colwell paused, as if·debating whether to reveal the information. Finally he said, "There's been talk down at the company of settling. For a very fancy figure. But in malpractice suits you generally have to get the insured's permission to settle."

"Yes, I can see that," said Sobol. "After all, the hospital's reputation, the doctor's reputation are involved. And a settlement is an admission of guilt. Things like that are never quite forgotten."

"Some doctors see it that way. Others settle because they are glad to have the whole mess finished."

"Dr. Grant is not likely to agree to do that," Sobol said. "And I'll tell you something, Mr. Colwell, I'm not likely to agree either. Your company is haggling over money. I am fighting for the future of a brilliant young man. Hotheaded, yes. But devoted. That infant upstairs is probably going to die, but it's still more important to him than your whole damn company."

The Grove baby did die that night. Chris watched its struggle to the last. It had been a losing battle from the start.

THE board of trustees of Metropolitan General was composed, as most hospital boards are, of lawyers, successful businessmen and, recently, two women—wives of wealthy men—who had the time as well as the personal drive to offer themselves to public service. Each of the sixteen members of the board was proud of the outstanding reputation of Metropolitan General.

Thomas Brady, chairman of the board and a respected banker, had had the unpleasant duty of calling the meeting to discuss the grave matter of *Simpson* vs. *Metropolitan General, Christopher Grant, M.D., and Michael Sobol, M.D.* This was the first time in its long history that every single member of the board of trustees was in attendance. Once they were settled, Brady began. "We must all agree that this is a sad and distressing lawsuit. Our counsel, Mr. Waller, is here to give us an assessment of our position."

Avery Waller was a senior partner in the law firm which would act as legal adviser to the hospital. Short, plump, rosy-cheeked, Waller was toying with the Phi Beta Kappa key on his gold vest chain. Now he leaned back and cleared his throat.

"I've had our men go into this thoroughly, and I must warn you at the outset that, since Dr. Grant is a full-time employee of the hospital, there is no legal basis on which we can escape liability if his malpractice is proven. If a judgment is found for the plaintiffs over and above the amount of our policy coverage, then this hospital as well as Drs. Grant and Sobol will be financially responsible.

"Now, my office has examined the hospital records and all lab findings. It is our considered recommendation that this board should try to reach a settlement. The insurance company agrees. Especially since their investigator reports that our Dr. Grant's tendency to be combative would make him very vulnerable on the stand." The distressed faces of the board members made it clear they understood all the implications involved.

Then Waller added, "Nor does it enhance our case that behind the plaintiffs stands John Reynolds. Any jury will know that he is not motivated by money, but by a desire for justice. Which presents us with another ugly aspect of this case—public reaction."

Mrs. Elliot Forster was quick to volunteer. "I can imagine! People will say, 'If that's the treatment Reynolds' grandchild got, imagine what our own children can expect from Metropolitan.'"

Cyrus Rosenstiel, a department store owner, said, "And I wouldn't blame them. I say, let's get it over with. The longer this drags on, the worse it will look! Do we have any indication from the insurance company as to Reynolds' disposition to settle?"

200

Waller said grimly, "One of our lawyers plays golf with two partners in the law firm which is representing him. He tried to feel them out on the issue of settlement and ran up against a stone wall."

Chairman Brady leaned forward. "Whoever here is on the best terms with John Reynolds should visit him to say how sorry we are and that we are willing to assume the blame. But also tell him what damage can be done to this hospital if he persists in taking this matter into court. We might also," Brady lowered his voice somewhat, "promise him that Dr. Grant will be dropped from our staff as soon as possible."

Cy Rosenstiel said, "I would suggest a committee to visit him— Tom Brady, Ellis Jackson and Ed Clarke."

Brady waited to see if there were any other suggestions, then said, "If Ed and Ellis are willing, I would undertake to head the committee."

Brady was about to adjourn the meeting when there was a sharp knock on the door. Mike Sobol came in, wearing a dark suit instead of his lab coat. "So, it's still going on," he said. "Good!"

"Actually, the meeting has just . . . " Brady looked about the table. Most of the trustees would have preferred to leave the issue closed, but they were reluctant to offend one of their most revered staff chiefs. Brady finally gave the floor to Sobol with a brisk gesture. The doctor spoke with an unaccustomed determination.

"Tonight, because of what's at stake, I felt I had to come before you. I can guess what went on here before I arrived. Of course, save the hospital! Save our reputation! Silence all the bad publicity! I can understand that." From the trustees' reaction, Sobol had no need to be told. "Yes, I can imagine you've already made your decision. John Reynolds must be appeased. And since he already has a surfeit of material things, payment must be made in blood. Specifically that of a young doctor. A doctor who in good faith pursued a proper course of treatment. Something went wrong, but precisely what, no one knows. How will it help Reynolds or his grandson to destroy the career of Christopher Grant?"

There was a considerable amount of throat clearing before anyone chose to answer. Chairman Brady assumed the burden of the argument. "Mike, with government monies becoming harder and harder to come by, we can't be too zealous in protecting the reputation of this hospital. When we apply for funds for one of your own projects, for example, we can't have this unsavory lawsuit hanging over us. It is our considered judgment that our duty is to protect the hospital, not any single individual."

"So you're determined to settle," Sobol said sadly. "You want to trade away the future of a brilliant young doctor to soothe the angry vanity of a man, because he has great power?"

"He's done a great deal for you, Mike," Brady said.

"No one knows it better than I," Sobol admitted. "But that doesn't mean that I have to stand by while he deliberately destroys a man. No one has proven Dr. Grant guilty of malpractice and I doubt anyone will. Not to my satisfaction."

"Unfortunately, Doctor, they only have to prove it to a jury's satisfaction," said Waller.

"Till they do, I maintain Chris Grant is innocent. But it isn't even his innocence that is paramount in my mind. What I am thinking about is what happens if we don't stand up for Grant. How does this hospital, this medical school, attract the best men, if we get a reputation for ruthlessly abandoning young doctors at the first sign of trouble? If you try to settle this case, every young man we want from now on will ask himself, 'If I go to Metropolitan General and get into any kind of trouble, will they crucify me?' And most of them simply will not come."

"Exactly what would you have us do?" Waller demanded.

"First, you must not settle this case!" Sobol declared. "That's the same as admitting that Grant is guilty of malpractice. Second, we have to fight, and give him the best defense we can."

Brady decided it was time to close the discussion. "Mike, we understand your position. But we, the trustees, are responsible for this institution. We have decided on a course of action we think temperate, wise and expedient in very difficult circumstances. I'm afraid you'll have to abide by our decision."

"Gentlemen," Sobol said, "you seem to have overlooked one point. Where malpractice is involved, a company generally can't settle without the consent of the insured. I can tell you right now that Grant won't give his consent. Nor will I."

"You're right. Up to a point," Waller replied. "If this were Grant's policy, or yours, you could prevent a settlement. But this is the *hospital's* policy. . . ."

Mike hesitated. Finally he spoke softly. "Then I'm afraid I have to tender my resignation." He turned and walked out of the room.

Brady thought for a few moments before speaking. "Twenty-one years. The man made that statement after twenty-one years in this hospital. I don't think anyone would do that out of loyalty to one young doctor. No, I believe that Mike Sobol does see this as a blow to the medical school and our hospital. He is not a man to indulge in whims. He has said he would rather resign than watch us damage Metropolitan. The question no longer is, Do we let one young doctor stand in our way? It is, Do we sacrifice Mike Sobol or do we fight? On this issue, I think we have to reconsider our stand. . . ."

After more than two hours of debate, the board of trustees of Metropolitan General decided that at this time they would not give permission to the insurance company to settle.

CHAPTER FIVE

"TWENTY thousand dollars?" Chris Grant repeated, stunned.

Mike Sobol said glumly, "He's one of the best litigation lawyers in the city. He said he had to consider the time-consuming paperwork, the examination before trial, and of course the trial itself. All together, it would be twenty thousand dollars, or higher."

"That's almost as much as I make in a year," Chris said. "Do we have to have an attorney of our own?"

Mike nodded. "If Colwell could suggest that you falsify records, who knows what they'll come up with next?" Sobol had not told Chris about his meeting with the trustees, but he knew he might not prevail with them the next time. This was really why he had begun to investigate personal legal counsel. But the fees did seem out of the question; a man like Mike, who had devoted his life to academic medicine, did not accumulate large amounts. Twenty thousand dollars would represent a sizable part of his savings.

"Colwell says our own lawyer wouldn't even have any official status in the case. Would merely be advisory," Chris said.

"The lawyer I consulted agrees," said Mike. "But he feels it's essential we know how well we're being protected by the insurance company. We need someone we can trust, someone who is working only for us."

"Still, twenty thousand dollars," said Chris.

Mike reached for the dry pipe which he merely sucked on since his heart attack. He placed it between his teeth and then broached his real purpose. "Chris, suppose there were someone young. Not in the same league as a lawyer with a twenty-thousand-dollar retainer but a good, thorough counsel with an excellent law-school record who has been working with a solid firm for several years and whose fee would be nominal. Say anything *we* set."

"Why would one lawyer ask twenty thousand, and another be willing to do the same job for whatever we can afford?"

"Because she happens to owe me a favor," Mike said.

"*She?*" Chris asked.

"Yes, *she*," Mike Sobol repeated. "She's been waiting for the chance to pay me back. This is it."

"A favor?"

"Her life," Mike said gently. "She was born a preemie. It was highly doubtful she'd make it. The family was so grateful that Rose and I were asked to be her godparents. We've known her all her life. She calls us Aunt Rose and Uncle Mike." Then he added sadly, "Or used to when Rose was alive."

"A girl," Chris observed again.

"A bright girl. A thoroughly good and nice person. I don't think she'd ask you to falsify records or commit perjury. She'd give us the best advice she could. Advice we could follow."

"At least the price is right," Chris said, permitting himself his first smile during this discouraging discussion.

"Before you agree, I want you to talk to her. It's essential that we only retain someone in whom we both have confidence."

"Sure. Okay," said Chris.

204

Mike had his secretary place the call to Miss Laura Winters. "Laura? Uncle Mike," Sobol began. "I'm sitting here with my associate. Or do I say my codefendant? I think it might be a good idea if you two met and discussed the matter. . . . Wait, I'll ask." He said to Chris, "What would be a good time?"

"I'll be finished in the lab at about eight this evening. How about eight thirty?"

Mike relayed the information, then turned to Chris. "There is an excellent Italian restaurant called La Scala, where I'd like you two to be my guests for dinner. Just mention my name to Guido, the owner. He'll put it on my bill, which he rarely lets me pay." Mike spoke into the phone again. "La Scala, at eight thirty? Right, where Rose and I took you when you graduated from high school."

CHRIS tried to concentrate on his research, but found his mind grappling with legal problems instead. When he had first learned of the malpractice suit, his reaction had been combative and defiant. But after his confrontation with Colwell, he had begun to appreciate the grim, tiring process of the law. Why did Mike want another lawyer? Did he suspect they might not get all the protection they were entitled to from the hospital?

And a woman lawyer. A mere girl. He left his work with considerable reservation and started downtown to La Scala.

As soon as Chris entered the restaurant Guido seemed to recognize him. "The lady," Chris was told, "is already waiting." He glanced at the table Guido indicated, and felt uneasy. She looked barely twenty, and from this distance she seemed tiny as well. If lawyers went by the pound, this was one he could afford. As he followed Guido among the tables, he kept staring at her. She was a blonde, her hair neat and feminine in its arrangement. She was dressed in a dark silk outfit with a touch of color at the throat. Close up she was a bit more mature than he had first thought and not so small.

When they shook hands he looked down at her from his six-feet-one and found her to be an extremely attractive young woman. For some reason, that also made him doubt her qualifications as a lawyer. If she suspected, she didn't give any hint. She simply said, "Sit down, Doctor," putting their relationship on a straight professional basis.

She kept it that way throughout dinner. She talked about Mike, the close ties they had, possibly because Rose and Mike had had no children. She asked Chris about his research, his teaching, his hospital practice. Gradually she had him talking about himself. Something he did not like to do. He even told her about the addicted Grove baby and its vain struggle.

Laura stared across the table, studying Chris's face. He noticed that she had very blue, extremely warm eyes. They made him self-conscious and he started picking at his food again.

When they finished dinner they still had a great deal of talking to do, and she suggested they go to her apartment. There was no doubt the invitation was for a purely business meeting.

Her apartment was a reflection of herself. Small, neatly arranged, warm and yet efficient. She put some coffee on to brew, then settled down in a large comfortable chair, drawing her legs up under her. Chris sat opposite her on the sofa.

"Do you have any idea," she asked suddenly, "how long a lawsuit like this takes? If one side or the other wants to stall, it can drag on for years." She lit a cigarette. Her eleventh, Chris noted with disapproval. "There'll be constant interruptions of your work," she continued. "They'll make your life hell. The insurance company lawyers will be after you to tell your story over and over to experts they intend to hire to testify for you during the trial. They'll come up with bright ideas from their dirty-tricks department, and don't think Colwell's suggestion was an exception. Of course, if a lawyer made such a suggestion to you directly, he would be subject to disbarment. That's why they sent Colwell. He's only an investigator. But the significant thing is that they felt impelled to suggest you falsify your records. That means your case isn't too strong. That they have doubts about the judgment you exercised in treating the infant. Insurance companies will throw anyone to the wolves to avoid a big settlement. That's why Mike had to battle so hard at the trustees' meeting—" The look of surprise on his face stopped

206

her. "I guess you weren't supposed to know about that," she said apologetically.

"I don't want Mike taking risks for me," Chris protested.

"He did. And he will," Laura said simply. "You know Uncle Mike." Chris nodded. "I'm not sorry I told you," she said. "I don't believe in concealing anything from a client. We have to be honest with each other; that's why I'm taking the time tonight to explain things. When I'm finished, you may not want me for your lawyer. And I may not want you for a client."

Later, they were working on the second pot of coffee, sitting together on the sofa, and she had led him through his entire treatment of Reynolds' grandchild. When she mentioned the possibility of many experts testifying for the plaintiffs, he protested.

"Nobody, certainly no honest doctor, can testify that what I did was malpractice!"

"Dr. Grant, a firm like Parkins, Sears and Wadleigh doesn't go serving a summons and complaint without having the word of some respected doctors that they *will* so testify!"

Laura lapsed into thought for a moment. "One other thing I know. Parkins, Sears and Wadleigh do not usually handle malpractice suits. Before very long we're going to see some eminent counsel pop up to take over at the trial."

"What does that mean?" Chris asked.

"You have specialties in medicine. Well, we do in the law. Men who do one thing so expertly that they are virtually invincible. John Reynolds must have said, 'Get me the best and the most expensive negligence trial lawyer!' And my guess is, that means only one man."

"Who?"

"Harry Franklyn," Laura said. "We'll know how far they're willing to go if we hear that name, because I can tell you now, Harry Franklyn doesn't take any case he even suspects he might lose. And in a courtroom he's the most disarming and effective lawyer I've ever seen."

"Harry Franklyn." Chris repeated the name he'd never heard before, but which suddenly embodied the enemy.

208

Laura Winters was silent for a time. Then she announced, "Yes, I'm going to be your lawyer. Even merely as a consultant, it'll be fun to watch little Harry Franklyn at work." She smiled. "Yes, little. Franklyn's no taller than I am. And never speaks above a whisper if he can help it. But then a cobra doesn't make much noise either."

She reached for another cigarette. He glanced at her reprovingly, and at the ashtray laden with stubs.

She noticed and said crisply, "Let's get two things straight, Doctor. First, I don't intend to listen to any lectures from you about my smoking. I smoke too much. I know it and it won't help if you keep reminding me of the fact. Second, this can only work out if it remains a purely professional relationship."

"Okay," he agreed.

"Good night, Doctor," she said, ending the evening.

On his way home he had to admit that he had been greatly impressed by her professional attitude and probing questions. Yet he couldn't help regretting that he had met her under such impersonal circumstances.

THE infant breathed spasmodically. Its rib cage, a tortured structure, seemed fragile as eggshells. Chris Grant examined the infant swiftly, while Frank Walp, the pediatric surgeon, stood by, ready to carry out his own examination. It didn't take long for him to confirm Chris's findings. The stethoscope clearly revealed the existence of a defective valve which rendered the infant's heart incapable of forcing enough blood through its system to carry vital oxygen to all parts of its body.

"Keep it on a respirator," said the surgeon. "So I have time to prepare. See you in the operating room."

The surgeon left. Chris lifted the little patient, whose frantic heart fought so to overcompensate for its defect that he could feel it thrusting against the flexible ribs. The urge to live was as strong, as desperate, in a day-old infant as in older, stronger patients Chris used to see on the wards during his days as an intern.

Chris—scrubbed, gloved and masked—entered the operating room. The patient had seemed tiny in its Isolette; now it appeared almost insignificant in the midst of the massive equipment. The anesthesia was completed, and Walp made his first incision.

Engrossed, Chris followed every move of Walp's hands. Chris, too, had considered becoming a surgeon. Open-heart surgery was reaching prominence when he was a medical student, and it fascinated many doctors who were deciding on a specialty.

Consciously, Chris had finally opted for neonatology, out of concern for those children who confronted danger in their earliest hours of life, but subconsciously his choice had its roots in events which took place when he himself was only four years old.

His mother had been a conscientious woman who worked hard to make up for the fact that Chris's father, Phil Grant, was one of those men destined always to be a marginal worker. His job as a bus driver did not pay well, but it was enough for a family of three to live on. When Chris's mother became pregnant again, she continued to take in laundering until her last weeks of pregnancy. Chris would play under her ironing board while she talked to him happily about the baby that was soon to arrive.

The trouble came when she was very big with child. One afternoon the phone rang, and from her first few words Chris knew, even as a four-year-old, that something terrible had happened. He remembered she had hung up, reached swiftly for her coat and said, "You'll have to stay with Mrs. Molloy. But I'll be back as soon as I can—"

She didn't finish that sentence. Or her next one. Which was more a sound of pain than a word. Then she made her way to the door and cried out, "Edna!"

Fortunately their neighbor, Edna Molloy, was home and quick to call an ambulance. They wrapped Chris's mother in a blanket, put her on a stretcher and carried her out of the apartment. They loaded her into the ambulance and slammed the doors. It pulled away sounding its siren.

His father came home later that afternoon, his hand bandaged. From the way he carried it, Chris knew it hurt very badly. But as soon as Phil Grant discovered what had happened he rushed to the hospital. That night Chris slept at the Molloys'.

In the days that followed, especially after his mother came home from the hospital without the long-promised baby, Chris discovered from the little that was said that his father had had an accident with the bus. Although he was not legally at fault, he did not get his job back again.

From that time on, his mother did all the work, going out to do laundry in other people's homes. His father occasionally found odd jobs, but nothing steady. Nights when Chris was supposed to be asleep in his small bed he could hear his mother sometimes, weeping. His father slept, or pretended to. She would slip quietly out to sit in the kitchen, even when they had no heat.

Once Chris dared to open the kitchen door and stand watching her. She did not seem to notice him, yet she said, very softly, "Come, darling. Come."

He went to her and she reached out to draw him close. Cold as he was, she felt colder. Her face was damp.

"Mama, are you crying for the baby?" he asked.

She didn't answer.

"Did it . . . die?"

Again she didn't answer, only held him tighter.

"Why did it die, Mama? Will I die, too?"

"Oh, no, no!" she said, lifting him into her lap. "It died . . . it died because it couldn't breathe. Babies born before their time, their lungs are too small, or their hearts, for them to breathe."

"Where do they go when they die?" he asked.

"Little babies always go to heaven."

"Will I go to heaven when I die?" Chris had asked.

She pressed him closer. "You won't die," she protested, rocking him till he fell asleep, but not before his face was wet with her tears. When he woke the next morning he was in his own bed.

He never asked her about the baby again. But she never stopped weeping for it. Chris would be aware of his mother leaving her bed and going out to the kitchen to cry. She never said that it was his father's accident that caused her premature delivery. But his father apologized to her for it for the rest of their dismal lives. Neither of them ever recovered from the loss.

Chris recovered, but it left a mark. The events that began that terrible day contributed to his electing the field of pediatrics, and the subspecialty of neonatology, so that tiny infants, born defective, or stricken in their early hours, would have a chance. So that mothers would not have to sit and weep for what could not be properly mourned or retrieved.

And now, as he stared down at the small field of operation under the surgeon's hand, Chris Grant found himself wondering, as he often did during neonate surgery, what the defect was that had robbed him of his little brother.

Today's operation was going well. Walp was through the soft bones of the rib cage and into the chest cavity. With skillful fingers he found and corrected the defective valve. In a short time he began the final suturing, which he insisted on doing himself.

As Walp turned from the table, leaving the infant in the care of a pediatric nurse, he said to Chris, "I'll be up on the ward about three o'clock, right before my rounds. See you then."

"I won't be there," Chris was forced to say. "Lawyers. There's a pretrial examination today."

"Oh," was all Walp said. Chris did not know if that was meant to express solicitude or disapproval.

Ten minutes later he left the hospital for Laura Winters' office. She had insisted they meet to go over strategy before his first confrontation with Parkins, Sears and Wadleigh.

Laura was employed by a substantial and well-regarded law firm whose offices overlooked Courthouse Square. When Chris caught sight of her at her desk, blond hair in slight disarray, giving instructions to a secretary about some papers, he was impressed. This small but very nicely proportioned young woman had a surgeon's approach to her profession. That she was attractive besides, in some way amused him. Attractive women had no right to be so efficient and businesslike.

She dispatched the secretary, turned to Chris and said crisply, "Oh, yes," as if he were just another order of business on her crowded calendar. Then she relaxed a bit and said, "Sorry, Chris, but it's been one of those days. Do sit down."

212

When he was in the leather desk chair she rose and stared out the window, her back to him. "It's going to be very difficult to explain this to a layman," she said suddenly. He was unused to having himself referred to as a layman, but on reflection, insofar as the law was concerned, that was what he was.

"In medical malpractice," Laura continued, "the defendant is questioned in an area of his life that is most precious to him—his profession." She turned, her blue eyes carefully focused on him. "If the jury decides that you are guilty, your view of your life and your profession will be affected. A man facing such an accusation can become highly emotional. That's why this talk, before we go across the square to the Parkins office. You cannot, you must not, under any provocation, give vent to anger during this preliminary examination. No matter what charges are made, what snide inferences are drawn, you must steel yourself to answer the questions as directly as you can. Do not volunteer. Do not argue. You are only a witness. Do I make myself clear?"

He could not resist smiling and saying, "Yes, Mother, it's perfectly clear."

Angered, Laura said, "This case cannot be treated as a source of amusement! Even when we are alone. It endangers you. It belittles me. I will not have it!"

It seemed to Chris that in that brief moment she had become a bit emotional herself. She felt it, too. For she regained her composure and said, "Now we're ready to go."

THE offices of Reynolds' attorneys were impressive. On the walnut-paneled waiting-room doors were gold-leafed the names of fourteen senior partners.

Paul Crabtree, representing the insurance company, was waiting for Chris and Laura. Crabtree, a tall, rangy man with an easy smile and a warm, deep voice, pretended to be delighted to meet them. Actually he was as concerned as Laura about what impression their key witness would make. His real purpose was to evaluate Chris's worth to the defense. Later he would report back to the insurance company his opinion of their chances.

Present also was James Spalding, a partner in Waller's law firm, here to protect the interests of the hospital. He seemed reserved and noncommittal. But then, Chris reminded himself, Spalding, like Laura, could only advise. Crabtree was the only lawyer legally empowered to act for the defendants.

The four of them were shown into a conference room. In a moment two lawyers in the Parkins firm entered—Arthur Cross, a tall, gray-haired man with a measured smile, and William Heinfelden, who carried the file and a yellow pad filled with questions. Heinfelden was of medium height, with broad shoulders testifying to his days as a university football player.

The stenotypist appeared, and while she was setting up her machine, Cross joked, "These days it's even harder to get a doctor to make an office call than a house call."

Chris was not amused. "I was in surgery until forty-five minutes ago!" he answered crisply.

Laura could tell that Heinfelden now realized how edgy the doctor was. Chris knew he had already done the one thing Laura had warned him against. He assured himself that once they got into the questioning he would be in complete control.

They lined up at the table like two teams in combat. Cross gestured to the stenotypist, who administered the oath. That done, Heinfelden took over. Cross, like Crabtree, had come only to evaluate the strengths and weaknesses of the case. Laura sat alongside Chris, praying that he would keep his temper in check.

Heinfelden's first questions were routine, harmless—Chris's full name, residence, his schools and medical training. The lawyer also elicited the information that Chris had worked his way through high school and college. Medical school was easier. He had been awarded scholarships.

Finally, Heinfelden got to the subject of Chris's research and his published papers. "Tell me, Dr. Grant, could it have been your own past—coming from a poor background—that first interested you in the arrested brain development of malnourished children?"

"I don't know. Perhaps."

At that point Laura leaned forward and glanced sharply at Paul

Crabtree. Crabtree cleared his throat and said, "I don't see what bearing any of Dr. Grant's research papers have on this litigation. We object to his answering any further questions of this nature."

Heinfelden smiled and turned back to Chris. "Doctor, the treatment involved in this lawsuit—would you say it was a matter of a doctor's discretion?"

"Every treatment is a matter of the doctor's discretion. One doctor has success with a certain form of therapy or a certain drug and has confidence in it. Another doctor's experience might be slightly different, and he might favor another drug or another therapy." From Laura's movement at his side he knew he had answered more fully than he had need to.

"Dr. Grant, was there any other course of treatment open to you when you decided on phototherapy for the Simpson infant?"

"Yes." Chris had determined not to use any extraneous words.

"Such as?" Heinfelden asked.

"An exchange transfusion would have been possible."

"But you didn't choose to do that?"

"No. It is a time-consuming procedure. In my judgment the infant could benefit more from exposure to phototherapy. Certainly, until the tests came back from the lab, telling us what was causing the jaundice. It could have been sepsis. In this case, we found that it was an Rh difficulty."

"And meanwhile you merely put the infant into a plastic box and let the fluorescent light shine down on it?" Heinfelden asked.

"No," said Chris, growing resentful. "I started an intravenous, to nourish the infant and to administer an antibiotic. If there was infection, I wanted to treat it at once."

"Doctor, is it possible that the use of phototherapy can inhibit the proper growth of an infant's head?"

"That was reported in earlier papers, but has since been disproved," Chris said flatly.

"Is that why you never told John Reynolds about it?"

"I told him everything that was valid and pertinent," Chris said. "Once I'd taken the immediately indicated steps, we went to my office and I gave him a full explanation of the therapy. I wanted to set his mind at ease. He was quite concerned, and naturally so. After all, this infant was his only male heir."

"He made a point of that, did he?"

"He made a point of almost nothing else!" Chris retorted.

"Tell me, Doctor," Heinfelden continued. "Did you explain any of the therapy to John Reynolds *before* you took those steps?"

"There was no time. The infant was obviously jaundiced. Treatment had to be started immediately," Chris said, his impatience no longer in check.

Laura touched his arm to calm him down. The gesture did not escape Heinfelden's notice. "Dr. Grant," he said, "earlier in this examination you told us that it was possible for two doctors to differ on what course of treatment to follow in a given case."

"Yes," Chris agreed gingerly.

"Did it ever occur to you to call in another doctor for an opinion in the Simpson infant's case?" Heinfelden asked suddenly.

Chris hesitated, then answered, "No, no it did not."

"Is it possible, say, that Dr. Sobol might have prescribed an exchange transfusion in this case?"

"I would doubt it," Chris said.

"In other words, Doctor, you assumed Dr. Sobol would agree that phototherapy was the sole and proper treatment in this case?"

"It wasn't up to Dr. Sobol to decide. The patient had been turned over to me. It was my responsibility."

"You didn't want to be overruled, is that it?"

"There was no reason to expect that I would be overruled!" Chris shouted.

"If that is really so, Doctor, wouldn't it have been more professional to check with Dr. Sobol before making such a momentous decision on your own?" Heinfelden asked pointedly. "Or would that have been asking too much of a vain young man who is so sure he is always right that he wouldn't deign to ask for a more experienced opinion?"

"Object!" said Crabtree.

"Object, hell!" Chris shouted, standing up. "I want to answer that question!" Before anyone could stop him, he said, "Vanity

216

had nothing to do with it! If you've had experience and know your business, you don't go checking your opinion every time you are faced with a choice. If you do, you're a poor excuse for a doctor!"

Laura blanched. Crabtree exhaled in impatient defeat. "Doctor," Heinfelden concluded gently, "you should know that failure to consult with other doctors in certain circumstances can be deemed malpractice."

WHEN they reached the street Laura delayed Crabtree and Spalding by saying, "Gentlemen, I think we ought to discuss this *together*."

Crabtree was about to plead another engagement, but Spalding said, "Yes, I think we should meet. Come to my office."

In Spalding's office Chris indicted himself. "I did it. Despite all the advice, I lost my temper, gave away information."

"Fortunately"—Spalding tried to find a bright side—"they didn't dig too deep or in the right places."

Laura said gravely, "Gentlemen, I think from *their* point of view the examination was eminently successful. They found out what kind of witness Grant is." Chris felt a surge of resentment as Laura continued. "And I think before long we're going to be presented with a new and additional cause of action."

"Such as?" Spalding asked.

"Failure to obtain informed consent."

"For using phototherapy? Ridiculous!" Crabtree scoffed.

A bit morosely Chris admitted, "You know there are hospitals, not many, but some, in which such consent is standard practice."

"Why the hell didn't you tell us that before?" Crabtree asked.

"It's so unusual . . ." Chris tried to explain.

Laura was not cowed by Crabtree. "How did a thing like their strategy escape you today?" she asked him. "Maybe they didn't probe too deeply because they didn't want to expose their line of future cross-examination. Maybe whoever is making the moves behind the scenes wanted today's examination conducted in just this way."

"Whoever is making what moves?" said Spalding.

217

"Take one guess," Laura invited.

Crabtree and Spalding spoke in unison: "Harry Franklyn."

By the end of the week Laura Winters' first prediction came true. Parkins, Sears and Wadleigh applied for leave to amend their complaint to include a new cause of action, failure to secure informed consent. Judge Bannon, into whose hands the case had passed, granted their motion. Laura accompanied Mike Sobol to a pretrial examination much like Chris's. Heinfelden dwelt on the fact that Chris was doing research when Mike first called him.

The question now remained: Would Laura's second prediction turn out to be correct? Would Harry Franklyn appear in the case as trial counsel for the plaintiffs?

CHAPTER SIX

THE annual conference of pediatricians had been scheduled at Metropolitan General long before *Simpson* vs. *Metropolitan General, Grant and Sobol* became a fact. To transfer the meeting to another university hospital would have entailed enormous disruption of travel and hotel reservations. It would also be construed as a prejudgment of the case. But the conference placed an additional burden on Mike and Chris, who were forced to endure countless, though well-meant, references to the trial.

Because Laura had attended some of the lectures, Chris invited her to the final banquet. They were just leaving the ballroom when Chris was intercepted by an old classmate. Harvey Bellamy was a well-established pediatrician now, and Laura could imagine how safe new mothers must feel in entrusting their infants to this blond, tanned man who exuded magnetic confidence. His wife, Claire, was not only beautiful, but beautifully dressed.

"Chris, it's been so long," said Bellamy, "and we haven't had a minute alone this week. Let's all have a drink."

In the cocktail lounge Harvey Bellamy first made small talk about medical practice in southern California, stressing the easy living there for families with young children. But once the waiter had brought their drinks, Bellamy became quite direct.

218

"Remember the week we finished internship, I begged you to come into practice with me? Well, now I'm making that offer again. Leave this mess. Even if you lose this case, no jury will ever vote a five-million-dollar judgment. Financially, you won't be touched. The insurance company will take the whole loss."

"The insurance company is willing to settle," Laura volunteered.

"Let 'em! *Make* 'em!" Bellamy urged. "For your own good, Chris, get it over with."

"You just don't understand, Harv."

"Don't I? Don't forget that in medical school we ranked one, two. And sometimes two, one. I could have taken your route, but I didn't. Was I wrong? You tell me. I have a twelve-room house. From the living room we see the California desert. It's everlastingly lovely. And a climate you won't believe. My children go to the best private school. More important, I don't have to depend on federal funding, financial donors, a boss or a board of trustees. There are eight doctors in my medical group. We have the latest and best equipment. And don't overlook the advantages of a professional corporation under the new tax law. You'll be fixed for life in only five years!"

He glanced at Laura to enlist her help, and she realized that Bellamy was presuming a relationship that did not exist. When she didn't answer, Bellamy continued. "Chris, we need a well-trained pediatrician. You can't just sit back and let them ruin you. Out where I practice, nobody gives a damn about a legal suit."

"Well, right here where I live, people *do* give a damn. *I* give a damn!" Chris said sharply.

Bellamy would not be put off. He went on with obvious and complete sincerity. "I'll hold it open as long as I can. And remember, I want you, because you're the best pediatrician I know." To Laura, Bellamy said, "Talk to him. He owes it to you if not to himself. That's what you both want, isn't it? A good life together, kids, everything..."

Laura smiled and said simply, "If we had any kids together, it would be embarrassing to say the least. Chris is my client, not my fiancé."

"Well, I'll be!" Bellamy said. "Watching you two, I could have sworn . . . Chris, promise me you'll think about it!"

"Okay, Harv, I'll think about it."

ON THE way home, Chris drove Laura's car. They talked little. Finally the silence goaded him into making an explanation.

"Harv is a first-rate physician. The rest of it—the money, his life-style, his business setup—don't let that fool you. He wouldn't be that successful if he weren't good. It's just two different ways of approaching medicine. I don't fault him. But I don't have to choose the same way. Do I?"

When she didn't respond he asked frustratedly, "Don't you have an opinion?"

"As a woman? Or as a lawyer?"

"Both," Chris said.

"As a woman I say to myself, 'It does sound like a great way to live.' Did you see her sable coat and that dress? It was in *Harper's Bazaar* two months ago."

"Do you read *Harper's Bazaar?*" Chris asked, surprised.

She answered a bit testily, "I wasn't born wearing a gray flannel suit." He realized she was joking, yet underneath there was a solid protest against his having obliterated her femininity.

"Look, that was your idea for this relationship from the start. Remember?" They were silent until they reached her apartment house, where he insisted on seeing her to the door.

Hoping to end the evening on a lighter note, he said, "Come to think of it, Harv isn't as good a diagnostician as I used to think."

"Because he misinterpreted our relationship?" she said defensively. Then she added, "Well, he isn't the only one."

Chris stared down into her mischievous blue eyes. "What does that mean?"

"The other day Mike asked me the same question."

"Mike," Chris repeated. He reached out for her. "You mean everyone can see it except us?"

He was about to kiss her when she made one last protest. "It'll be wrong. . . ."

220

He kissed her anyhow and could feel her small body press against him. Feelings they had both suppressed so scrupulously erupted. She made no pretense at sending him away. With the swiftness that only mutual desire can mobilize, they were lovers. He wondered if her severity as a lawyer was necessary for the very reason that she was, really, an unusually passionate woman.

It was very quiet in the room, and he could feel the beating of her heart. His fingers traced the outline of her profile in the dark, until he felt the dampness of her cheeks.

He whispered, "It's not something to cry about." He raised up on his elbow, stared down at her. Her eyes were closed, but she could not stop the flow of tears.

"What's wrong? That silly notion that lawyers and clients have to keep each other at arm's length?" He tried to draw her close.

"No," she protested, "I have to say this. So we both know what can happen. Men who have been through lawsuits—libel, malpractice—where their character was in question, where they've been forced to justify past lives or professional conduct, suffer quite terrible consequences."

"Even if they win?" Chris asked, disbelieving.

"Even if they win. Somehow their marriages dissolve. Wives who stuck with them loyally through the entire fight leave them when it's over. And their careers are never the same either."

"Why?" Chris asked.

"Maybe it's because people never can forget the charges that were made against them. Somehow the charges endure, and maybe wives begin to believe some of the lies, too. But whatever the reason, the relationships are never the same."

"It won't happen to us!" he protested fervently, but she was not reassured.

"This isn't even an ordinary malpractice suit. Reynolds isn't out to win. He's out to destroy you. And because I love you, he'll destroy us both. It would have been better if we hadn't fallen in love."

"Now that *is* something to cry about," Chris said softly. He drew her close to him, holding her head against his chest.

In a while he said, "Of course, there's Harv's offer. If we did decide to settle."

"Yes," Laura agreed. "The house. The view . . ."

"Look, I don't want an inventory. I want an answer!"

"If you can't even talk about it without getting angry, then the answer is obvious," she replied very gently. "And Chris, darling, what makes it all a perfectly nice, delightful way for Claire Bellamy to live is that her *husband* thinks it's a perfectly nice, delightful way to live. But give those same things to a woman whose husband hates them, and in a very short time every convenience, every luxury, even the everlastingly lovely desert would become a rebuke. You couldn't live with it. So neither could I. I'm afraid we have no choice but to see the case through."

"Despite what it might do to us?"

"Nobody ever said there was a good answer to every question," she said sadly. "At least, for the time being, we have each other."

CHRIS Grant was in the neonate nursery, staring through the plastic top of an Isolette at a bronze-skinned infant which was gasping for breath. Chris inserted his sterilized hands through the portholes to palpate the infant's liver. He didn't like what he felt. "Get me a transfusion setup," he ordered his resident.

Chris lifted the chart that hung from the Isolette. LOPEZ, BABY. *Premature.* GESTATION: *Thirty-four weeks.* GENERAL APPEARANCE: *Eyes, conjunctiva yellow. Skin, generalized jaundice.* Notes made three hours ago.

Chris could see now that those signs had become even more ominous. When the nurse came in Chris said, "We're going to do an exchange."

"On this one?" the nurse asked softly.

Irritated that his judgment was being questioned, Chris ordered in a brusque whisper, "Damn it, search that chart and let me know if there's consent for a transfusion! I have to prepare."

"Yes, Doctor," the nurse said quietly, though it was obvious her feelings were hurt.

As Chris scrubbed, the nurse located the consent in the chart.

The resident returned with a supply of the proper blood, the catheters, needles and dosages of protamine.

Chris checked the infant's heartbeat, observed its respiration, then began the exchange. Slowly he inserted one catheter into the infant's umbilical vein. Using an empty hypodermic, he withdrew a small amount of the infant's damaged blood. Then, as cautiously, he injected a like amount of the new blood into the umbilical artery. He stopped to check the infant's heartbeat. For this unfortunate baby only an exchange transfusion would be effective, but its chances of surviving this procedure, which entailed many slow repetitions of withdrawal and injection of blood, without complication were small.

The light on the telephone began blinking with monotonous persistence. The nurse answered. Holding her hand over the mouthpiece, she said, "It's Dr. Sobol. He says it's important."

Chris completed injecting the portion of fresh blood before answering. "Tell him I'm doing an exchange. But I'll be there as soon as I can." When he had finished the transfusion, he said, "Keep close watch on this one. Frankly, I think the prognosis is bad. If there's any radical change, call me in Sobol's office."

The minute Mike saw Chris, he asked, "Have you forgotten the meeting with the board and the attorney?"

"Oh." Chris was dismayed. He glanced at his watch. It was past three o'clock, the time set for the meeting.

Chris noted that the old man was paler, thinner. Perhaps the only decent thing for Chris to do was go along with a settlement. A man with a massive coronary behind him was not a good subject for this kind of stress. Before Chris could say anything, though, Mike started off for the boardroom.

The members of the board, the insurance company attorney and Avery Waller were all in attendance. As soon as Mike and Chris were seated, Waller leaned forward in his chair and said, "Crabtree has what we feel is good news."

Crabtree steepled his fingers and drummed them nervously. "Yesterday we were officially notified that Harry Franklyn has been retained to handle the case if it proceeds to trial."

Chris remembered all of Laura's forebodings.

Crabtree smiled. "Well, Harry and I are old antagonists. So I called to welcome him aboard. It doesn't hurt to be on friendly terms with the adversary. He let me know that he's been masterminding this case from the beginning."

"Is that supposed to make us feel good?" Chris demanded.

Crabtree turned on the young doctor with an impatient stare. "Harry Franklyn is too shrewd a man to be that informative without having some motive. I'm certain he was hinting, 'If you've got an offer that makes sense, I have Reynolds' ear.'"

Mike exploded. "Were we brought here to go into the matter of settlement again?"

"Mike, please!" Cyrus Rosenstiel begged, acting as spokesman for the board. "All we're asking is that you listen to what Mr. Crabtree has to say."

"I guess the least we can do is listen," Mike said finally, but he could not bring himself to glance at Chris.

Chris wished that Laura were present. She'd know if Crabtree were misstating the situation for some purpose of his own. He studied Crabtree, who continued. "I thought as long as I had Franklyn in such a cooperative mood, I'd make a stab at settling. He fended it off, but not too strongly, so I immediately called the insurance company. They surprised me with the biggest offer of settlement I've ever heard them make. Half a million dollars. I relayed it to Franklyn, who called me early this morning."

Crabtree glanced at Chairman Brady. "Franklyn's answer was that the *figure* would be acceptable. He said his clients were not primarily interested in financial compensation. Their chief concern was to protect other families using Metropolitan."

Chris felt an angry rush of blood to his face, but Crabtree did not pause. "Franklyn said that they wanted a complete admission from the defendants that the treatment was undertaken in error and that there was a willful failure to disclose its inherent risks at the time the therapy was applied."

Before Chris could reply, the phone rang. Brady answered it with great impatience. "Dr. Grant? Yes, yes, I suppose so."

224

Brady held out the instrument to Chris, who listened a minute, then said, "Oh? I see. Well, complete your notes. I'll add mine when I get back." Chris hung up, turned to Mike. "The Lopez baby didn't make it."

"I expected that," Sobol said. To the others he observed, "Exchange transfusions aren't successful every time either."

Chris remained standing. "Gentlemen, I've been told you can settle this matter over my head. But when it comes to my own culpability, then I do have rights. What John Reynolds wants is my professional death warrant, signed by my own hand. Any psychiatrist would tell you that this is highly suspicious conduct. But one doesn't dare have such suspicions about John Reynolds, does one? Well, I am not about to give in to his outrageous demand. You gentlemen can negotiate with the enemy; I do not wish to be part of it. Mike?"

Sobol rose and preceded Chris out of the room.

LAURA Winters was some minutes early for her appointment at Parkside Polyclinic, an imposing private hospital. Some of the most expensive and reputable doctors in the city were its chief stockholders, and no doctor was invited to join the staff without the proper social as well as professional recommendation.

Laura glanced at her watch. It was time. For days she had been discreetly trying to establish contact with someone in the Parkside records office. Finally it turned out that one of her clients, Judson Dahn, for whom Laura had handled several delicate private matters, knew someone who was happy to help.

Now Laura Winters went up to the information desk, asked for the woman whom Dahn had recommended. She was directed to an office on the floor below, where Ethel Grayson was waiting. She greeted Laura with a smile and fixed the door so that it would lock when she shut it. "I'm going to go up to the admitting office on the main floor. I'll leave you here alone. For about fifteen minutes. The file is in the bottom drawer of that green metal file cabinet. Whatever notes you can make in fifteen minutes will be okay with me. Just remember, I never showed you anything."

"Yes, of course."

As soon as the door was closed, Laura pulled out the bottom drawer of the cabinet. There lay a thin file, labeled SIMPSON, BABY. In parentheses appeared c/o JOHN STEWART REYNOLDS.

Laura scanned the hospital chart, which had been kept during the forty-odd hours that the infant had been a patient at Parkside. Dr. Coleman's report indicated the infant was the result of a somewhat difficult but not abnormal delivery, weighed very slightly over the required 2500 grams, and was thus not labeled premature. From all other indications the child appeared normal. Both Apgars, the first overall examinations at the time of birth, presented no evidence of any defect. Although Laura did not understand the lab report, which Chris would have to evaluate, the file seemed to reinforce the claims made by Parkins, Sears and Wadleigh. The infant, with a somewhat higher than average though not dangerous bilirubin, had been referred to Metropolitan General for treatment.

Laura laid out the papers under the desk lamp and trusted that her camera would pick up clean, legible copies. After returning the file to the drawer, she left, and took her film to the photo shop in her office building. Within the day, the prints were ready, and she called Chris at the hospital and invited him to her apartment for dinner. From the sound of her voice he knew it was to be strictly a business meeting.

She had prepared a simple meal. Before she cleared the table she said, "You look at this while I do the dishes."

Chris settled down in the easy chair and took the copies of the file from their envelope. "Laurie, where did you ever get these?" he asked, shocked.

"Never mind," she called as she loaded the dishes into the washer, "just read them."

As he returned the copies, she asked anxiously, "Well, does the file answer any questions? Is there any information that might reveal any other cause of that infant's damage?"

"No. Frankly, the records don't even contain enough vital information to make them particularly useful to a doctor. They're

226

very sloppy. Hardly worth the effort to get them. But now, tell me. How did you do it?"

She told him. When she finished, he came to her and took her in his arms. "Was there anything illegal in what you did?"

"No. But Miss Grayson's breach of hospital confidentiality was illegal. However, the records might just prove to be more useful than you think. If they're changed in any way, and then introduced during the trial, it will be hard for Franklyn's witness to explain why they don't match the set we have. We have to be prepared, even though they may not be changed at all."

"Look," he said, holding her tightly, "I don't want you to take any risks because of me. You're doing enough already." He kissed her. "No risks. Promise?"

"Okay. Promise," she said. She pulled away from him to look for her cigarettes. The flaring match illuminated her face, which seemed very tired. "Chris, the trial will start soon. In the days we have left I want you to keep asking yourself if there was any possible way that infant could have been damaged that was unrelated to your treatment."

"Anything *could* have happened," Chris said impatiently.

"Chris," she cautioned, "in a case where we don't have any idea what did happen, we have to line up as many *could have happeneds* as we can. Just continue to think about what might have damaged that infant aside from the phototherapy."

"Damn it, why do you keep thinking it was the phototherapy?"

"Because you can't tell me that it wasn't," she answered coolly. "And eventually we'll have to come up with an answer, if we expect to have any chance of winning."

CHAPTER SEVEN

CHRISTOPHER Grant, M.D., stood at the foot of the wide steps and stared up. He had seen photographs of the old courthouse many times, usually as a background for a politician making some pronouncement. But Chris Grant had never before had reason to ascend those broad, worn stone steps.

Now he started up with Laura at his side. Behind them were Paul Crabtree and Avery Waller. Though Waller had no more official standing in the case than Laura Winters, he and Crabtree functioned like partners, representing the interests of the hospital. They had held many meetings from which Laura was excluded, and they had agreed on their strategy.

The corridor of the courthouse reeked of millions of cigars and cigarettes consumed over the years by nervous witnesses. They found Courtroom 405. Outside the leather-covered doors a neat plaque announced that Justice Timothy Bannon was presiding. They entered.

There were few spectators in the courtroom when the opposing parties took their places—Chris and Laura at their counsel's table, William Heinfelden and a junior partner at the plaintiff's table. Only minutes after the court attendant had led in the first thirty potential jurors, a sound of excitement was heard outside the courtroom. Chris and Laura turned to look. When the doors were thrust open John Stewart Reynolds entered, calling behind him, "Gentlemen, it is far too early for me to make any statement. But when the proper time comes, you may be sure I will not remain silent!"

Having disposed of the press, Reynolds started briskly down the aisle, followed by a smallish man dressed in a conservatively cut suit, white shirt and solid blue tie. The man wore glasses that added to his undistinguished look. He shook hands with Heinfelden, and with equal pleasantness approached the defense table and shook hands with Crabtree and Waller. "Dr. Grant, Miss Winters," said Crabtree, "this is Harry Franklyn."

Chris shook the little man's hand. It was soft, limp. Surely this was not the grip he expected after all the warnings he'd heard about Harry Franklyn. But this was exactly the effect Harry Franklyn intended to produce. He had spent years cultivating his courtroom appearance so that it was inoffensive, disarming, almost nondescript. He liked jurors to become his friends, to feel sorry for him if possible, to sympathize with his client certainly. Above all, he did not wish his impression to betray to any juror that he was such a successful trial lawyer that for each of the past

228

seventeen years his fees never totaled less than a million dollars.

Franklyn retired to his own table. John Reynolds was already ensconced in an armchair, gazing about the courtroom. When his eyes swept over Chris Grant, there was not the faintest glimmer of recognition. It was as if in John Stewart Reynolds' mind Chris Grant had already been wiped out.

Suddenly the clerk called for silence. At the command, "All rise!" the door from the judges' robing room opened. The Honorable Justice Timothy Bannon entered. He was a tall man, thin, and his face exuded character.

Bannon took his place in his high-backed chair and ordered the clerk to commence the jury selection. The clerk spun the drum and began to draw names out of it. When fourteen men and women had been named and seated, the clerk arranged the cards on the jury board and handed it to Harry Franklyn. One by one he questioned them and dismissed those jurors who, for one reason or another, seemed prejudiced or unwilling to serve. Franklyn seemed particularly interested in eliminating anyone who had been involved in a medical case or who had relatives or close friends who were in the medical profession.

As some jurors were excused, others took their places. The procedure droned on, and Chris began to lose interest. By the time the lunch recess was declared, he was relieved to rise and stretch. "Franklyn must get paid by the day," he observed.

Laura said in a curt whisper, "Did you notice he was slowly but surely stripping that jury of black people? One thing is clear. He doesn't want any blacks on the jury."

"Why?" Chris asked.

"That's what I'd like to know," Laura said. "But we'll see. We'll see. Let's go get some lunch."

The afternoon seemed equally dull. When Laura tried to point out to Crabtree the fact that Franklyn was eliminating all the blacks, he shrugged it off with a kind of amused boredom.

Then Crabtree's turn came. As an insurance company lawyer, he tried to eliminate all who had been involved in litigation, and he favored people who were self-employed, on the theory that they had a greater respect for money and so would favor a smaller award.

By the end of the following day Franklyn and Crabtree had arrived at twelve jurors and two alternates whom they both deemed acceptable. The sole black, a woman, was one of the alternate jurors. Whatever Harry Franklyn's motive, he had succeeded in securing his twelve white jurors.

Justice Bannon swore in the fourteen persons selected and ordered Franklyn to be ready to begin the plaintiffs' case as soon as court convened the next day.

PROMPTLY at ten o'clock Harry Franklyn made his opening statement. He approached the jury box, rested his arm on the rail and spoke in a tone so intimate that even Bannon had to lean forward and cup his ear to catch the words.

"Ladies and gentlemen, I don't know about you, but to me, if you deprive a man of his arm or his leg, that is horrible enough. But what about an infant who in the very first hours of its life has been doomed by a doctor's negligence to be brain-damaged?"

He paused as though the gravity of the case he must present had already overtaxed him.

"That is the case we are involved in. We know that a normal, perfectly healthy child was born to Mr. Lawrence Simpson and his wife. After birth a condition developed in that child that called for further treatment. Two eminent doctors will testify to what sort of treatment was needed. And because it was deemed advisable for its safety, the child was turned over to Metropolitan General Hospital, specifically to Dr. Michael Sobol, who in turn referred that helpless infant to Dr. Christopher Grant, another defendant in this case." Franklyn turned slightly to direct the jury's gaze toward Chris, who instinctively withdrew.

Franklyn continued. "The child was then subjected to a treatment that resulted in brain damage. We will introduce physicians, the best in their specialty, to give testimony to that effect. As we will introduce physicians who will, unfortunately, testify to the present sad condition of that infant.

"While we take the position that no amount of money can

230

repay either the child or its family for the damage that has been done to it, a large award may teach other hospitals and doctors to exercise more care in the future."

Franklyn hesitated a moment, as if to seal a bargain with the jurors. Then he started back to the table.

"Mr. Crabtree?" Judge Bannon invited the defense to make its opening statement.

Where Franklyn had been small, almost timid, Crabtree was large, and made no attempt to restrain his booming voice. The jurors sat up and listened intently.

Crabtree began by expressing great regret for the unfortunate child, but he assured the jury that neither the hospital nor the doctors were responsible. He cautioned the jury that the occurrence of brain damage did not mean that anyone was at fault. Sometimes such tragedies were unfortunate accidents of nature. He would prove, through the testimony of eminent and respected doctors, that the steps taken in relation to the unfortunate child were good and accepted practice, carefully carried out. Thus neither the hospital nor the doctors were either legally or morally culpable.

Since the burden of proof was on the plaintiffs, Crabtree did not commit himself to proving more than he had to. Even Laura felt that it was a perfectly effective opening.

Franklyn took up the burden of establishing the plaintiffs' case. In a methodical manner he began with Hugh Mitchell, the doctor who had the first contact with Mrs. Simpson when she suspected she might be pregnant. Silver-haired and distinguished, Mitchell answered every question in a benign and helpful way. Franklyn led Dr. Mitchell through his initial examination of Arlene Simpson, including the blood tests.

"Please tell the jury, if you will, Doctor, about the results of the tests."

"Normal in all respects. Except for one thing. Mrs. Simpson's blood was Rh negative."

"Is that bad, Doctor?"

"Not in this instance," said Mitchell. "The fact that a potential mother has Rh-negative blood is not important in the bearing of

232

her first child, though it can have dire consequences for succeeding children. Or, I should say, it *used* to have dire consequences. Now, with the advent of a substance called RhoGAM, we are able to prevent damage to future children by treating the mother after the birth of the first child."

"Please, Doctor, would you explain further? I'm sure the men and women on this jury are highly intelligent and will understand." Having flattered the jury, as well as prepared them for a complicated medical discussion, Franklyn gave Mitchell free rein.

"First, everyone in this world has either Rh-negative or Rh-positive blood. All negative means is that a certain protein substance is not found in the red blood cells. It only becomes important when a woman is pregnant, and it only presents a problem when the baby is Rh positive.

"At the end of a first pregnancy there is a chance that some of the baby's Rh-positive blood will cross over into the mother's bloodstream. The mother's body will treat Rh-positive blood as a foreign substance, and manufacture antibodies against it. This does not affect the child that is already out of the mother's body, but if that woman has any future babies that are Rh-positive, then her blood, which now has antibodies, will fight the blood cells of the unborn baby, slowly destroying it, either while it is in the uterus or after it is born."

Mitchell continued his explanation. "There is the possibility of another problem connected with an Rh-negative mother. If she had at any time been given a blood transfusion of Rh-positive blood, she would then be sensitized and her body would manufacture antibodies that could affect even a first child."

"And did you check Mrs. Simpson?" Franklyn asked.

"Yes. She said she had never had a transfusion. I also had the lab run a Coombs' test to determine the titer level of her blood. That tells us the level of the antibodies in her blood, if in fact there are any."

"And the Coombs' test showed that Mrs. Simpson had no antibody problem in her blood that would affect the birth of her first child?" Franklyn nailed down his point.

"Correct. It did appear that there was no antibody problem."

"Now, at the time of delivery," Franklyn began, "are there tests done on every baby right in the delivery room?"

"Yes. The Apgar tests. They evaluate the infant's color, respiration, heart rate, spontaneous movements and reflexes one minute after birth, and again five minutes after birth, to determine if the infant has been born in normal condition," Mitchell responded.

"And were the Apgar tests made on the Simpson baby?"

"I wasn't there, Mr. Franklyn," Mitchell responded simply, as he had been instructed to do. "When it came time for Mrs. Simpson to give birth I was ill with the flu. I'm afraid you'll have to ask Dr. Coleman about the actual details of the delivery."

"I see," Franklyn said. "So your last contact with the Simpson family was just before the delivery?"

"Oh, no," Mitchell corrected. "About a day and a half after the delivery I received a call from Dr. Coleman. The infant was beginning to evidence not only a disturbing bilirubin, but a Coombs' that showed an Rh problem. Coleman wanted to refer the boy to Metropolitan General, where he could benefit from more intensive care, but wished my approval."

"And did you concur?" Franklyn asked.

"Unfortunately, yes," Mitchell replied.

Crabtree rose at once to object to the word unfortunately. Bannon ordered it struck.

"Doctor, when you agreed with Dr. Coleman that the infant should be turned over to Metropolitan, did you have any idea what sort of treatment was going to be administered?"

"I expected there would be an exchange blood—"

Crabtree's objection was strenuous, and Bannon ruled in his favor.

Franklyn did not intend to press his luck. Later, experts would testify as to the desirability of a transfusion over phototherapy. He turned the witness over for cross-examination.

Crabtree shifted the focus from the method of treatment followed by Chris Grant. "Dr. Mitchell, you testified that to make sure there were no antibodies present in Mrs. Simpson's blood, you had a

234

Coombs' test done. Would you consider that test totally reliable?" he asked.

Mitchell smiled. "No medical test is infallible, Mr. Crabtree. But a doctor doesn't rely on the test alone. Taken together—a negative Coombs', a woman having her first child, with no history of a transfusion, no serious illness—one doesn't have to pursue the matter further."

"Despite the fact that you admit a Coombs' isn't infallible? And it now appears that that Coombs' was indeed incorrect. Wouldn't taking a second Coombs' have been advisable?"

"To what end? All of the information we had indicated that it was not necessary."

Since pressing Mitchell further might elicit his opinion on Grant's treatment, Crabtree finished with the witness.

Dr. Robert Coleman was next.

Franklyn established the handsome young doctor's experience and expertise, then brought him to the day of the infant's delivery. "Doctor, were you present when the Apgar tests were done?"

"Of course," Coleman replied. "In fact, even though it is customary for the delivery-room nurse to do both Apgars, I did the first myself. I wanted to be absolutely sure, in view of Dr. Mitchell's close relationship with the grandfather of the child."

"And what did you find?" Franklyn pursued.

"The one-minute Apgar was seven. Certainly in the normal range," Coleman said.

"And the five-minute Apgar?"

"Done by the nurse. With a score of nine. The infant was in excellent condition," Coleman reported.

"Did that condition continue, Doctor?" asked Franklyn.

"Unfortunately, no. The next morning a nurse informed me that the infant was exhibiting slight jaundiced coloring."

"And what did you do?"

"I immediately ordered a bilirubin and a Coombs' test and left instructions to be called the minute those reports came back from the lab," Coleman stated righteously. "Even if I was in surgery—I had two patients scheduled for that afternoon. When the results came back I *was* paged in the operating room. And when I came down to the nursery I examined the lab reports."

"What did you find?" Franklyn asked.

"The infant had a bilirubin of fourteen, and the Coombs' test revealed that he was suffering from an Rh incompatibility. I ordered an immediate follow-up bilirubin and waited right there for the result. I didn't want to waste time."

"And what was the result of that second test, Dr. Coleman?" Franklyn asked.

"Before the results came down from the lab I called Dr. Mitchell at his home and told him what I'd found. He agreed with the suggestion that I refer the Simpson baby to Metropolitan General at once. There the infant could have the constant observation he needed. Frankly, I would have preferred to keep the baby at Parkside, but with my own practice, plus Dr. Mitchell's, I felt it in the infant's best interest to refer him."

"Having decided that, what did you do?"

"I called Mr. Reynolds. Then I received a call from Dr. Sobol at Metropolitan General. An ambulance was coming to pick up the Simpson baby. He asked me to have a transcript of the infant's hospital record ready, which I did."

Franklyn turned away, indicating that he had completed his direct examination. Coleman had been a good solid witness.

"Ask him about the phone call!" Chris whispered fiercely to Crabtree.

"What phone call?"

"I called him to get more information than was on the Parkside transcript. He couldn't even tell me exactly when the first signs of jaundice appeared," Chris declared.

"Is that important?"

"You're damn right! An infant who exhibits jaundice in the first twenty-four hours is at greater risk. And what happened to that second bilirubin test? It never showed up on the transcript."

Crabtree rose to undertake the cross-examination. "Dr. Coleman,

236

did you at any time have any conversation with Dr. Grant about the Simpson infant?"

"Yes. He called me. He wanted to know who first noticed the jaundice. I told him, as I told Mr. Franklyn, it was the nurse."

"Doctor, why wasn't the time those signs first appeared recorded on that hospital transcript?"

"I couldn't answer that," Coleman said.

"Do you think it would have been desirable for the other doctor to have that information?"

"Yes, I think so."

"Doctor, isn't it a fact that it is *crucial* for a doctor to know the exact time, since a child who evidences signs of jaundice in the first twenty-four hours is at greater risk than one who evidences it two or three days later?"

"Yes, that's true. And I told him that the nurse did not notice the signs till the end of the first twenty-four hours," Coleman said.

Chris signaled to Crabtree, but the lawyer shrugged him off. He referred to his notes and, while still looking down, asked suddenly, "Dr. Coleman, you said you ordered a second bilirubin test. Can you tell us what it disclosed?"

"I'm afraid I can't," said Coleman. "Once the infant had been referred, that report became academic, since I knew that they would do their own tests at Metropolitan."

"You were not curious about what that second test showed?"

"Mr. Crabtree, in the press of daily practice a doctor doesn't have time to indulge his curiosity. That was especially true when I was covering for Dr. Mitchell."

"Did you ever follow up by calling Dr. Grant to inquire about the progress of the Simpson baby?"

"Since I assumed the infant was in good hands, I also assumed it would receive proper care," Coleman said. "Frankly, I have had enormous regrets since that time. If I had had any idea of the kind of therapy Dr. Grant was using—"

Crabtree interrupted. "Doctor—"

But Coleman overrode him to conclude, "I would have gone down there myself and taken that infant back!"

Bannon banged his gavel to cut off Coleman's answer, but it was futile. As was his order to the jury to ignore Coleman's last words. Crabtree decided not to pursue his cross-examination any further. He felt that he had at least raised some cloud over Coleman's testimony, though he knew that Franklyn was delighted to have had the question of phototherapy raised in such a provocative way. The jury's appetite had been whetted.

Crabtree retired to the table, where Chris exploded in a burst of angry whispers. "Damn it, why did you let him get away with it? How could he *not* care about that second bilirubin?"

Crabtree turned on him. "Look here, Doctor, you stick to medicine! Let me take care of the law. There's a basic rule in cross-examination: never ask any question to which you don't know the answer. How do we know what that second test showed?"

IN LINE with his original strategy, in the afternoon Harry Franklyn recalled Dr. Mitchell to the stand. Franklyn moved to the far end of the jury box, forcing Mitchell to turn and face the jury as well. Laura nudged Chris gently. It was clear that Franklyn was depending heavily on Mitchell's forthcoming testimony. Both Laura and Chris edged closer, ready to make notes.

"Dr. Mitchell, after the Simpson infant was released from Metropolitan General, what was your relationship to it?"

"By that time I was over the flu and able to examine the infant. It was apparently in good health, but I studied the transcript and all the lab reports from Metropolitan General anyway."

"Were you favorably impressed by what you found, sir?"

"I was favorably impressed by the *apparent* result. The lab reports showed a decreasing bilirubin. The charts indicated the infant's vital signs were all good. But I was not pleased by the method chosen to treat the infant at Metropolitan General."

"Dr. Mitchell, exactly what treatment are you referring to?"

"The phototherapy that was used."

"Doctor, could you explain for the jury precisely what phototherapy is?" Franklyn asked.

"It is a treatment for jaundice which consists of placing the sick

238

infant under a battery of fluorescent lights for from a few hours to a few days. To my mind, the eventual aftereffects of phototherapy are still too uncertain, and it is not nearly so satisfactory a treatment as an exchange blood transfusion."

"Despite the fact that it is used in some very fine hospitals?" Franklyn asked, pretending to impeach his own witness.

"That's the trouble with institutions which practice academic medicine! Academicians tend to forsake the tried and true for the new and experimental, just to see the results," Mitchell declared.

"Using the patient as a guinea pig, so to speak?" Franklyn suggested.

Crabtree was up and out of his chair, and Bannon sustained his objection. Franklyn withdrew the remark, then asked, "Doctor, in your expert opinion, what caused brain damage in this child?"

"Based on a study of the laboratory tests, the records, the treatments prescribed, the only possible cause could have been the phototherapy applied by Dr. Grant," Mitchell stated.

"How can you pinpoint the cause so exactly?"

"Because at no time was there a bilirubin recorded that exceeded sixteen milligrams per one hundred milliliters of blood. An infant born only two weeks preterm is not likely to suffer brain damage from a bilirubin that does not climb up to twenty."

"In your opinion, then, Dr. Mitchell, did the use of phototherapy constitute a departure from good medical practice?"

Chris felt Laura stiffen. She had warned him that the key factor in any malpractice case was whether the defendant had departed from good medical practice. Once that question was introduced and answered in the affirmative, Chris's chances with the jury were not favorable. He waited for Mitchell's answer.

"In my opinion, in this case the use of phototherapy was definitely a departure from good medical practice," Mitchell stated firmly.

"One more question, Doctor. With phototherapy in its present state of development, would you consider it necessary for a doctor to receive informed consent from the parents or the guardian of the infant about to be so treated?"

"The relative responsible for any patient should be informed of all the dangers before consenting to any therapy," Mitchell declared. "I understand it was not done in this case."

"Move to strike that last!" said Crabtree.

"Strike it," Bannon ruled.

"That is all, Doctor," Franklyn said quietly, and moved to the counsel table. There was no disguising the fact that he felt he had laid a solid foundation for his case on two grounds, malpractice and failure to secure informed consent.

Crabtree rose to cross-examine. "Dr. Mitchell, would it surprise you if I said there are as many as a thousand hospitals using phototherapy?"

"It wouldn't surprise me. Nor would it impress me. A mistake does not gain medical credence by the number of times it is repeated," said Mitchell.

"Do you always tend to be conservative in your adoption of new methods, new drugs?"

Mitchell smiled for the first time. "Among experienced practitioners we have a rule. Use any new medicine on strangers first. Then on patients. And finally on your own family, if the other two groups survive."

Even the jury enjoyed that, laughing aloud. Bannon made no effort to silence them, though he glared at the spectators. Rather than go against the tide of feeling, Crabtree permitted himself a broad grin. "And you feel that way about phototherapy?"

"Most decidedly!" Mitchell said.

Suddenly, Crabtree changed course. "Doctor, do you know that an exchange blood transfusion can produce serious complications?"

"Of course," Mitchell said.

"Can you explain some of them to the jury?"

"If you wish," Mitchell said grudgingly. "In some cases an exchange can lead to infection or shock, but the mortality rate is very low."

"Doctor," Crabtree began, "do you, of your own knowledge, know any doctor who used phototherapy and induced an infection in an infant?"

240

"Infection? No, I do not."

"Do you know of any case where phototherapy has induced convulsions or an irregular heartbeat?"

"No."

"Yet those are complications that can result from an exchange transfusion, are they not?"

"Not if it's done correctly!" said Mitchell.

"Doctor, is it accurate to say that the alternative treatment available to Dr. Grant was not without risk? In fact, it might have turned out to be far *more* risky than the phototherapy which was used?"

"Not at all!" Mitchell declared. "At least with an exchange transfusion the results are immediate and can be dealt with. But with phototherapy you never know. The effects can show up weeks later or, as in this case, months later!"

"Move to strike that!" said Crabtree. "There is still no proof that phototherapy had anything to do with the present condition of this infant."

Judge Bannon leaned forward thoughtfully. "The doctor's answer will be allowed to stand."

It was too late in the day to put a new witness on the stand. Bannon excused the jury with a warning not to discuss the case.

CHAPTER EIGHT

THE second day of the trial Harry Franklyn introduced a distinguished expert in pediatric neurology, Dr. Walter Lawler, and launched into his examination of the Simpson infant. "Doctor, based on the tests you've made, would you give us your estimate of the degree of functioning power that the child has now, or will have?"

"Probably he will never exceed the mental age of about six."

"And why, in your opinion, is that?"

"Tests indicate that the cause of brain damage was kernicterus, a condition that results from an excess of bilirubin in the blood. As a general rule, a bilirubin twenty milligrams or higher per one

241

hundred milliliters will seriously affect the brain stem and cells."

"Doctor, is it significant to you that there is no laboratory report on record which shows that infant to have had a bilirubin of over twenty?"

"Not particularly. We've had evidence of brain damage in cases where the bilirubin never quite reached twenty. When a bilirubin exceeds fifteen, I am inclined to urge an exchange transfusion at once," Lawler stated flatly.

The distinguished Dr. Lawler's testimony was the most injurious yet. He was making a direct connection between Chris Grant's treatment and the damage done to the child.

Crabtree rose quickly for cross-examination. "Dr. Lawler, you never saw the Simpson child until some days ago, did you?"

"No, I did not," Lawler admitted.

"Would you say that a doctor who has examined a patient at the time is in a better position to make a decision as to treatment than a doctor who is relying solely on a file?"

"As a general rule, yes," Lawler conceded. "But not in this case. Because we know the result. And it was disastrous."

Whatever Crabtree had achieved by his first questions was swept away with that explanation. Yet he had to continue. "Doctor, isn't it true that a doctor may make a mistake without being guilty of malpractice?"

Before Lawler could answer, Chris Grant stood up, thrusting aside Laura's restraining hand. "No matter what this lawyer says, I do not admit to having made a mistake! He's not my lawyer. He was hired by an insurance company and I don't want him making any admission for me!"

Judge Bannon banged his gavel and glared down from the bench. "Young man, you will refrain from any further outbursts. As it is, we will now have to consider the effect of your interruption on this trial. Counsel will approach the bench!"

Crabtree, Waller, Franklyn and Heinfelden came forward, and an intense whispered discussion followed. Mere disclosure that an insurance company was involved could be grounds for a mistrial, since juries were known to react with great antipathy toward large

242

companies. On the other hand, Crabtree decided, there was nothing to be gained by a new trial.

Displaying some false reluctance, Franklyn agreed. For Chris Grant had revealed himself to be emotional, dedicated and hence, as a witness, extremely vulnerable. Whatever else happened, Franklyn knew he could win his case during his cross-examination of Chris Grant. No, Harry Franklyn wanted no mistrial.

Crabtree resumed his cross-examination, but the session was soon over. At the plaintiffs' table there was an air of satisfied confidence, as Reynolds exchanged some words with Franklyn. Chris knew that before the trial was over he would have to face that small ferret of a man. And he had already come to fear him.

The desultory way Crabtree and Waller gathered up their papers revealed how badly the day had gone. Chris and Laura were left standing alone at the foot of the courthouse steps.

"I'd better get back to the hospital," he said. "There are two cases I've got to look at. But we could have a late dinner."

"No, I have some work to do, too," she said.

"Okay." He leaned over to kiss her good-by. She seized him suddenly, held him tight, but avoided his lips.

"Laurie?" he asked, apprehensive.

"I don't know why I did that," she admitted. She kissed him on the lips with her usual intensity. He watched her as she ran down the stairs briskly and got into a cab. Something had changed, but whether it was in her or in him he wasn't sure.

THE moment he reached his office, Paul Crabtree phoned Tom Brady, chairman of the board of trustees of Metropolitan General. Three hours later Crabtree, Brady and a majority of the trustees were assembled in the paneled boardroom. Crabtree recited the unhappy events of the day. It was just past midnight when the board voted to empower Paul Crabtree and Avery Waller to engage in discussions which might lead to early settlement of the case.

Before court opened the next morning, Crabtree met in chambers with Judge Bannon and informed him that it might be possible to discuss settlement. Bannon said he would bring his good offices to bear.

By the time Harry Franklyn was introducing his first witness, a folded note was placed on Crabtree's table. It invited him and Waller to a luncheon meeting with Reynolds and Franklyn at the Downtown Athletic Club.

Though they left the courtroom at noon recess as seeming adversaries, Franklyn, Reynolds, Crabtree and Waller were all soon gathered in a private dining room at Reynolds' club. Lunch was served.

"Gentlemen," Reynolds said, "in the final analysis any settlement will depend on the plaintiff, my son-in-law. But I have no doubt that he will be guided by my advice."

Nor did anyone else in the room. "Now, we can save a lot of haggling," Reynolds said, "if we acknowledge one thing. We will not accept any settlement of this case insofar as defendant Grant is concerned. Is that clear?"

Both Waller and Crabtree ceased eating. Reynolds glanced at Harry Franklyn, who wiped his lips with the large napkin and cleared his throat slightly. Now, when he talked, he used his full voice and not his soft courtroom tones.

"I've studied that insurance policy very carefully," he said. "Under its terms, if the company wants to settle, it needs the hospital's agreement. Grant is *not* bound by that insurance contract. Once he separates himself from the hospital's stand, he is no longer a beneficiary. If the hospital agrees to settle and Grant does not, you gentlemen are completely off the hook."

Waller answered first. "Yes, but what if Grant chooses to settle rather than go it alone?"

"I've made my fortune," Franklyn said, "by being a student of human nature. That arrogant young man won't settle!"

Crabtree attempted to clarify the options. "I would like to confirm this. You are willing to settle whether or not Dr. Grant chooses to carry on this defense alone. We want any settlement we reach to be final. I mean, not to be upset if Grant decides to give up, after all."

Reynolds smiled grimly. "I'm willing to take that gamble. I want that young man alone in court."

"What about Sobol?" Waller asked.

"I'm sorry about Sobol," Reynolds said, "but he can make his own decision."

It took two days to arrive at the exact terms of the settlement. During that time the trial continued, but at a low level of excitement. Franklyn introduced several medical experts, whose testimony served to support that of the neurologist, Dr. Lawler. Crabtree only went through the motions of cross-examining them.

During a midmorning break on the third day Grant led Laura to a corner outside the courtroom. "What the hell's going on? Nobody is actually doing anything!"

"I know," Laura said, not daring to vent her own fears.

At the end of the day, as Crabtree gathered up his papers, he observed to Laura, "I think you, Grant, Waller and I better have a little meeting."

"I think so, too," she agreed swiftly.

As soon as they were all comfortably seated in Crabtree's office he began summing up the trial, but it was merely a prologue to his final statement. "So we, all of us, came to the conclusion that the only intelligent course is to settle. We're at the point now where we've just agreed on the figure."

"Without telling us?" Laura demanded angrily.

"Since you have no official standing in this case, we were within our rights to proceed on our own. Now, I should think this is your chance to bury the whole sad affair," Crabtree advised, but Chris interrupted by rising violently from his chair.

"I'll let you know." He burst from the room, slamming the door.

Laura paused only long enough to say, "You bastards!" Then she raced after Chris.

Crabtree and Waller sat back, undisturbed.

"I hope Grant doesn't do anything foolish," Waller said.

"He will," Crabtree said. "He will. Franklyn was right—he's headstrong. And with a knack for putting his neck in a noose."

THEY WERE COMING to dinner, Chris Grant and Laura. Mike Sobol was having company for the third time since Rose had died. So it was an occasion, and Mike had determined that it would be the kind of dinner that Rose used to prepare. He would serve mushroom and barley soup, a healthy green salad, veal chops with fried potatoes, and then nut cake from the Viennese bakery near the hospital. It went off extremely well. Mike had set a presentable-looking table, using the best of Rose's linens and her holiday silver.

After dinner Mike said, "I've done a good deal of thinking since Brady told me about the settlement yesterday. There's the principle involved, but there's the practical side as well. What do we do for a defense? Without the insurance company footing the bills, do you mortgage your whole future to defend yourself against a madman with unlimited money?"

Laura spoke up very firmly. "I'm qualified to carry on this case alone."

"One girl against Reynolds' whole law firm?"

She smiled. "Only one lawyer at a time can examine any witness, so it doesn't matter to me how many men they have. Frankly, all the while I've sat in court I've been saying to myself, 'I could do ten times the job that Crabtree's doing.'"

Mike smiled. "But Laura, my dear, can you objectively appraise this case when what it comes down to is whether Chris made the right decision or not? Could you ever believe that he *didn't* follow good practice? Could you admit to yourself, as a lawyer, that this is a bad case?"

"It isn't the best I've seen, but I think it's defensible."

"There's one other factor to consider," Chris said. "I'm determined to go on with this case, but I want you to settle, Mike. I've been doing *my* share of thinking, too. You built the department. You can hold it together no matter what happens to me. You're an institution, Mike."

"So I'm an institution, am I? You very nice idiot! I'm yesterday. You're tomorrow. You count. We both settle or neither of us—"

"Mike, you have to be practical!"

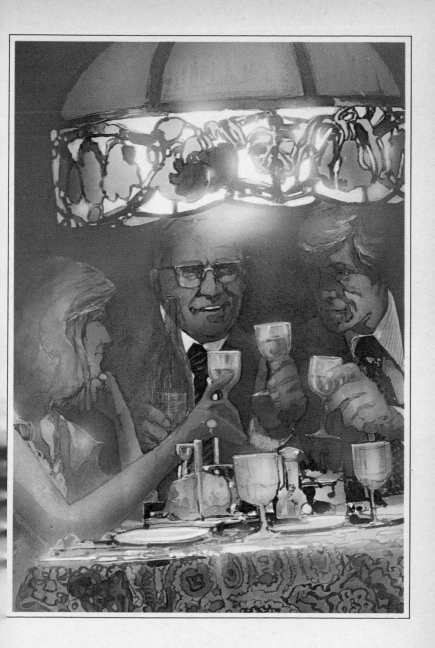

"Oh, I'm practical. I've thought it all out very clearly. At sixty-four I don't have much time left. No university wants a man that old to head up anything as rapidly changing as pediatrics. And no drug or chemical firm needs a man that old to head up research. I know. I've been making inquiries. You should see the stack of beautifully phrased letters that all say no without ever using that one-syllable word."

"All the more reason why *you* have to settle," Chris insisted.

"Reasons! All our lives when we have a tough decision to make, we set down all the reasons *for* and *against*. Then we decide . . . on the basis of emotions! Just as I'm doing now. Earlier this evening, when I was in the kitchen cooking, I kept thinking of Rose. I know what she would be saying now: 'Mike, that young man needs all the help he can get. If you're there alongside him, that'll count. And if there are consequences, so what? We were going to retire to Florida one day anyhow. . . .'"

"Mike," Laura said, "tell me honestly, you don't mind putting your fate in the hands of a woman?"

He smiled. "Never tell an old Jew about what a woman, even a small woman, can accomplish. After all, where do you think the legend of the Jewish mother started?" Suddenly his eyes, which had been sad, sparkled. "Let's have a toast." He went to the kitchen and came out with a bottle of wine.

"The last bottle Rose and I bought for Passover."

He poured three glasses, held up his own. "To all the foolish people of this world, who can't reason themselves into doing the wrong thing."

CHAPTER NINE

"John Stewart Reynolds!" The court clerk summoned the next witness to the stand. The trial was continuing against Dr. Grant and Dr. Sobol.

A muffled tremor of excited anticipation erupted in the crowded courtroom. No one felt the shock more than Laura Winters, unless it was Chris Grant, who sat beside her. They had no prep-

248

aration, no hint that Harry Franklyn intended to allow John Reynolds to take the stand in this trial.

Franklyn had, in fact, gone out of his way to appear gracious and understanding when Laura took over the sole defense of Chris and Mike Sobol. He had readily agreed to the three-day recess she had requested to prepare herself.

Laura had expected several more days of Franklyn's expert witnesses, qualified doctor after qualified doctor who supported his case. Laura had long lists of questions ready, to force those experts into retreating from their strongly held positions and opinions. She had spent hours with Chris and Mike the past three nights to frame those questions. She was not at all prepared for the witness who now stood in the witness box, taking the oath.

Laura whispered to Chris, "Get on the phone! I want Mike here right away!"

By the time Chris returned, Harry Franklyn was already leading John Reynolds through his early background. Reynolds revealed that he had come from a large, poor family. He had risen from a hod-carrying construction worker to a contractor with one truck. When the Great Depression struck and most large contractors had huge overheads, his small business expanded.

During World War II, as a patriotic duty, he went into shipbuilding and airplane-parts production, laying the foundations of the huge Reynolds fortune, and in the wave of prosperity that followed, that fortune multiplied into millions.

There was not a sound from the audience throughout Reynolds' testimony. For all the jurors it was their first close look at a legend about whom they had been reading for a generation. Far from being the stern, forbidding giant they had believed, Reynolds was warm and compassionate. He had come from the same modest background they had. He was a grandfather rather than a nationally known industrialist.

Whatever impulse Laura might have had to attack or object, she knew she had to allow Franklyn to have his way, or run the risk of antagonizing the jury. Mike Sobol joined them just as Franklyn was ready to begin his real examination.

"Mr. Reynolds, I must apologize for asking you to recall the unhappy circumstances that led to this trial." With that preamble, Franklyn questioned him about the events surrounding the transfer of his grandson to Dr. Sobol at Metropolitan General. Finally he asked, "Mr. Reynolds, precisely what did Dr. Sobol do?"

"He looked over the transcript that had been sent along. He examined the baby. Then he had him moved into the intensive care nursery and said he had exactly the right man to take over. He called Dr. Grant."

"Mr. Reynolds," said Franklyn, "did you hear Dr. Sobol apologize to Dr. Grant for interrupting his research?"

"I did."

"Even though he was calling him to treat a sick infant, less than forty-eight hours old?"

"Yes," Reynolds declared, his indignation plain.

"Now, sir, will you tell us what Dr. Grant's attitude was when he arrived?"

"He seemed resentful—" Reynolds began.

"Object!" Laura called out.

Franklyn rephrased his question. "When you met Dr. Grant for the first time, what did he do?"

"He glanced at the transcript. Then Dr. Sobol went into the nursery and Grant started to follow. So did I. But Grant forcibly blocked my way at the door."

"Did you say anything?"

"I said, 'That's my grandson. I have a right to know what's being done for him,'" Reynolds said righteously. Several members of the jury unconsciously nodded in agreement.

"And what did Dr. Grant say?" Franklyn asked.

"I don't remember the words. But they were not polite."

"Object to the word polite!" said Laura.

"I had to stand outside the big glass window of the nursery and watch."

Now Harry Franklyn dropped his voice so low that all members of the jury were forced to strain forward to listen. "Can you in any way account for Dr. Grant's hostility?"

250

"I think he resented being taken away from his research—"

Laura came to her feet to object. "The question calls for sheer speculation on the part of the witness!"

Bannon allowed her objection. Franklyn smiled indulgently, then turned back.

"Mr. Reynolds, was anything said at that time that could account for Dr. Grant's attitude?"

"I was determined to wait all night if need be, to see how my grandson was progressing. So I accompanied Dr. Grant down to the staff cafeteria for a late supper. When I first asked if I could accompany him to the dining room, Dr. Grant said, 'But you'll have to carry your own tray.'"

"What did you understand that to mean?" Franklyn asked.

"It was an obvious reflection of his resentment of wealth. He struck me as just another one of those young radical activist doctors to whom medicine is not a science but a political tool."

Laura was on her feet again, calling out her objection. "That question is irrelevant and immaterial to the issues in this case. I demand that it be struck and that the jury be instructed to disregard the answer!"

As if wearied by constant interruptions, Franklyn turned to the bench. "If your Honor will permit, please withhold any ruling until my next few questions."

"Continue, Mr. Franklyn."

"Mr. Reynolds, aside from Dr. Grant's obviously prejudiced reflections on your wealth, did anything else happen that day to reveal his attitude?"

"Yes, sir. While my grandson lay terribly sick in that nursery, Dr. Grant left that hospital for two whole hours to go down to Rixie Square to deliver a lecture. His political leanings were so strong that they overcame his duty to his patient."

"Object!" Laura shouted, rising up out of her chair.

Franklyn turned to the bench swiftly. "Your Honor, I would assume that if the witness's statements are incorrect, the doctor can prove that to us when he takes the stand." Now that he had succeeded in challenging Laura to put Chris Grant on the stand,

251

Franklyn was quite prepared to accept any decision from the bench.

Bannon declared, "The Court will reserve its ruling. But it would urge Mr. Franklyn to get on with more factual testimony."

"Of course, your Honor," Franklyn agreed. "Mr. Reynolds, you were telling us how you were forced to stand outside the intensive care nursery and watch through the window as your grandson was being treated. What did you see, sir?"

"Dr. Grant examined my grandson. Then he did a very strange thing—"

"Object!" said Laura.

Bannon leaned forward. "The witness will leave out all qualifying adjectives and opinions."

"Dr. Grant moved an object into place so that the top would serve as a cover for the Isolette the baby was lying in. The underside of the lid was composed of fluorescent tubes."

"And then, sir?"

"He threw a switch and turned the lights on my grandson."

Franklyn shook his head ever so slightly, glancing at the jury from the corner of his eye. "Tell me, sir, before Dr. Grant turned those lights on your grandson, did he explain the procedure?"

"He did not."

"Did he tell you that that treatment involved risks?"

"He did not."

"At any time—before, during or after—did he ask *your permission* to use that treatment?" Franklyn asked.

"*He did not!*" Reynolds said, clipping each word.

Laura sat up stiffly, tense, as yet unable to prevent Franklyn and Reynolds from proving one vital cause of action in their complaint, that Chris Grant had not received informed consent from a close relative of the patient. Failure to do so in a case in which a potentially dangerous form of therapy was employed was clearly malpractice.

Franklyn continued. "Mr. Reynolds, if you had been informed as to the dangers—"

"Object to dangers!" Laura called out, seeing her chance.

252

With some annoyance Bannon suggested, "Mr. Franklyn, can't you ask your question without including phrases which counsel finds objectionable?"

Franklyn sighed wearily, letting the jury know that he felt hounded by a shrewish, interfering woman who made his work and theirs more difficult.

"Mr. Reynolds, since that day, have you learned more about the subject of phototherapy?"

"I have. The doctors, as well as the medical literature I consulted, both agreed on one thing. There is such a vast area of unknown aftereffects that phototherapy is a questionable form of treatment."

"I move to strike that answer in its entirety," said Laura.

Bannon, whose frustration was becoming more evident, turned to her. "And on what ground this time, young lady?"

"On the ground, old man, that—"

Before Laura could continue there was an outburst of laughter from the spectators. Red-faced, Bannon irately gaveled the courtroom to silence. Glaring down from the bench, he addressed Laura. "Counselor, I deem your remark to verge on contempt of court. Any similar manner of address will evoke prompt and proper action from this bench!"

The blood drained from Laura's face. She waited till the courtroom was completely silent. Then, her voice sure and strong, she said, "Counsel is quite willing to stipulate that all forms of address based on age or sex be eliminated from this trial."

Challenged, Bannon only replied dryly, "If counsel will state the basis for her objection, this Court will rule."

"Since Mr. Reynolds has not been qualified as an expert, any question which calls for an expression of his opinion on medical matters is highly improper," Laura stated.

Bannon glanced down at Franklyn before ruling. "Does counsel wish to rephrase his question?"

Franklyn turned to Reynolds. "If phototherapy had been explained to you by Dr. Grant, would you have given your permission to have it applied to your grandson?"

"I most definitely would not!"

Franklyn had succeeded in making his prima facie case on lack of informed consent. He continued. "Mr. Reynolds, can you describe for us the condition of your grandson?"

Reynolds turned toward the jury. "It was pitiful to watch the change . . ." he began.

Laura was furious at Franklyn's unashamed bid for the jury's sympathy. She knew only too well that to object now would aggravate the situation rather than diminish its effect.

Reynolds continued his emotional testimony, describing the frightening emergence of the child's symptoms, calling in first Dr. Mitchell and then the specialists, who all agreed that his grandson had suffered irreversible brain damage.

Reynolds was breathing rapidly now. "Despite all of Dr. Grant's promises"—he glared at Chris—"that child, born perfectly healthy, never will be well."

After Reynolds had finished, no one moved. Chris felt sorrier, perhaps, than anyone on the jury, for he knew better than they the dreams Reynolds had cherished for his grandson.

Laura saw how cleverly Harry Franklyn had overcome his chief obstacle. Despite wealth, position and power, he had made John Stewart Reynolds a figure worthy of sympathy. If Laura attempted now to break down any portion of Reynolds' testimony, the jury would resent her.

She had no choice but to rise and say, "If your Honor agrees, I would like not to cross-examine the witness at this time, retaining, however, my right to recall him later."

Bannon consulted the clock on the back wall and declared, "We will reconvene at ten tomorrow morning when the defense will be ready to present its case."

THEY finished their wine, but left most of their dinner. Chris paid the bill. "I'll get you home. You need your sleep," he offered.

"I need to get away even more," she replied. "I'd like to go for a drive."

He drove her car out onto the interstate highway, north of

the city, to where green fields and stands of trees smelled sweet in the late night air. He reached out his right arm, expecting that she would slide close as usual, but she remained on her side.

After some moments he asked softly, "Laurie?"

"Chris," she began tentatively, "can you remember how you actually *did* feel, the day you treated the baby?"

"What do you mean?" he demanded.

"First, I should tell you that the question of whether to put you on the stand isn't entirely in my hands. Even if I don't call you, Franklyn can. As a hostile witness. So we have to be prepared."

"What makes you think I'm not prepared to take the stand?" He paused. "Now, what were you trying to ask me?"

She said gingerly, "Chris, is it just possible that there is the slightest truth in Reynolds' statement that you had a long, deep, innate grudge against his family because of their wealth?"

"You don't believe that, do you?"

"What *I* believe doesn't matter. I have to know how you're going to respond if Franklyn puts that question to you."

"I have no doubts about what I did! If you do, then maybe you . . ."

He didn't complete his accusation. He had no need to. She knew. There was a long, oppressive silence in the car.

"Is that what you meant when you warned me how relationships are eroded during a trial?" he asked finally.

"Maybe."

After a while she said, "It's late. I think we should head back." They drove home in silence. When he brought her to her door he kissed her, but she barely returned the gesture.

"I'll see you in the morning," she said.

She locked her door, and had a forlorn feeling that it was an act as symbolic as it was practical. She had locked him out.

She went about her nightly routine, brushing her teeth, creaming her face before getting into bed, all the time thinking the confrontation tonight should have occurred weeks ago. If Chris had been just another client, that would have been the first thing she'd have asked for—a complete, honest recital of his feelings and thoughts during the fateful episode. Because she loved him, she had trusted him and then, still worse, revoked her trust.

She sat up in bed and found her cigarettes. She must make a cold appraisal of her situation.

If they lost, they could not afford an appeal. And if Chris had any future left in medicine, it would probably be in some remote place. So if they were to have a life together, she might have to give up her career or begin all over again somewhere else. She didn't know whether love could survive such uprooting.

She promised herself one thing. From now until the end of the case, she was going to be Chris Grant's lawyer, not his lover. And she realized she also had no choice but to put Chris on the stand. The crux of the case was Chris's judgment, and only he could justify that.

"Dr. Michael Sobol," announced the clerk.

Mike was sworn in, and seated in the witness chair. As Laura rose to question him, he thought that if the situation were not so grave he would have been amused. He kept remembering her as a blond-haired toddler, and here she was asking him questions about his schooling, his background, the long list of his professional accomplishments. Then she elicited from Mike the details of his first contact with the infant.

"Dr. Sobol, when you examined the infant, did it seem to you to be in extreme condition?"

"Not extreme. But anytime an infant has a positive Coombs' we take it seriously."

"In the situation you describe, Doctor, what would you as an experienced and expert pediatrician do?" Laura asked.

"Exactly what I did. I turned the infant over to a man in whom I had the highest confidence—Dr. Grant."

"In your opinion did Dr. Grant's treatment conform with good medical practice?" Laura asked the vital question.

"Without any doubt."

Thereupon Laura began to read back to him parts of the testimony from the plaintiffs' medical witnesses, asking him to agree or disagree. It was a time-consuming procedure, but it was necessary to dislodge from the jurors' minds many of the notions implanted by Franklyn. By the end of his direct testimony Mike Sobol had established some rapport with the jury. One felt that they believed him.

Harry Franklyn rose to the challenge. He advanced slowly toward Sobol, and said quietly, "Doctor, do you mean to tell us that, confronted with the same situation, you would have adopted the same treatment as Dr. Grant?"

"Precisely," Sobol replied.

"We have heard numerous experts testify that under like circumstances they would have done an exchange transfusion at once. Do you disagree with them?" Franklyn asked.

"I do not agree with your experts. For one reason. They were not there. I was. They did not examine the infant. I did. They are judging *after* the fact, and I am not. In my opinion, confronted by an infant with the signs presented, with a bilirubin of sixteen, one might *consider* a transfusion. But when the next lab report comes back showing that the bilirubin has stabilized, I don't think any doctor would urge an exchange transfusion. After all, it is a procedure not without risk, and if you will recall, the bilirubin then began to show a significant decline. Good medical practice does not indicate rushing into a transfusion."

The explanation was full and complete, more so than Franklyn would have liked. He decided to sharpen his attack.

"If your opinion is correct, then how do you explain the infant's current tragic condition?"

Laura watched the deep blush rise in Mike's face. "I'm afraid I can't answer that question," he said. "It is not always possible to ascribe brain damage to a specific cause."

"Do you know of any other cause besides improper treatment that could have resulted in such damage?"

"Cause? There are many causes. But in this case . . . no, I can't account for it," was his final sad admission.

"Thank you, Doctor." Franklyn did not pursue the matter. There was no need to.

Mike Sobol rose unsteadily, for the first time aware of how strongly his heart was pounding. He was simply not equipped to be a witness. He returned to the counsel table, avoiding Chris's eyes and Laura's. He felt that he had failed them both. Yet he had told the truth. A truth that could not be as conclusive as the law would like, but that was as much as medical science had to offer.

CHAPTER TEN

LAURA put several other expert witnesses on the stand. Competent doctors, of excellent reputation, they had volunteered to testify on behalf of the defense. Even though Laura knew that the only testimony that could sustain their defense was Chris Grant's, she knew, too, the danger involved in exposing him to Harry Franklyn's cross-examination. But it was a risk she had to take.

She called Chris to the stand. After establishing the excellence of his medical background and his work at Metropolitan General, Laura questioned him about his experience in phototherapy, the manner in which the treatment worked, its effects, its benefits.

Her strategy was to condition the jury to accept phototherapy as sound medical practice. She also wanted to give Chris as much time as possible to relax on the witness stand before facing the cross-examination.

Harry Franklyn made very few objections. After a while Laura became uneasily aware that he was going out of his way to give her an easy time.

By midafternoon she had led Chris Grant from the generalities of phototherapy and the known risks of exchange transfusions, through the specifics of the Simpson case, to the most delicate part of her examination—an attempt to disprove Reynolds' allegation that Chris had been motivated by prejudice in his handling of the case. Having established that Chris bore no hostility toward John Stewart Reynolds nor toward the rich in general, Laura asked, "Dr. Grant, was your decision to treat the Simpson infant in any way influenced by anything but your best professional judgment?"

"It was not."

258

"If you were confronted with the identical set of facts today, would you pursue the same course of treatment?"

"Given the same facts, yes, I would," Chris said with finality.

Laura stepped back from the witness box.

Instead of launching into his cross-examination, Harry Franklyn pointed out the lateness of the hour and asked for a delay until morning. Franklyn wanted to work on Christopher Grant when, with unlimited time, he could dissect this vulnerable young man.

THE next morning, when Laura, Chris and Mike Sobol took their places at the defense table, there was a stir at the door. The court attendants forced back eager spectators while John Stewart Reynolds, his wife and an unidentified young woman entered. Harry Franklyn led them down the aisle.

Puzzled, Laura whispered, "Who are they?"

Chris identified Mrs. Reynolds, but it was Mike who knew the younger woman. "Arlene Simpson, Reynolds' daughter."

"The infant's mother?" Laura reacted with great concern, wondering why Harry Franklyn would have elected to bring her into court at this particular stage of the trial.

Chris resumed the stand. While Franklyn was gathering his papers, Laura had a chance to glance at Mrs. Simpson. She was a slight girl, resembling her mother, with small, regular features. She appeared younger than she was, less able to cope with the burden of raising a brain-damaged child.

Laura could appreciate why Harry Franklyn had chosen to withhold her presence from the jury until now. Much as Laura resented the ploy, she had to concede its effectiveness. Already the jury was staring at the young woman, guessing who she was, instantly sympathetic.

Franklyn waited until he was sure all the jurors had noted Mrs. Simpson's presence, and then approached the witness. Affably, as if trying to be helpful to both Chris and the Court, Franklyn began. "Dr. Grant, perhaps we should resume with the last point raised by the defense. Would the court stenographer read back both the question and the answer?"

The stenographer found yesterday's stenotyping notes and read aloud, "'If you were confronted with the identical set of facts today, would you pursue the same course of treatment?'"

"And the doctor's answer?" asked Franklyn.

"'Given the same facts, yes, I would,'" the stenographer read.

"Dr. Grant, would you pursue the same treatment even though you have learned"—Franklyn turned to Arlene Simpson—"this unfortunate young mother's child is permanently brain-damaged?"

Laura and Mike exchanged angry glances. This was clearly another emotional appeal to the jury.

"Doctor?" Franklyn prodded.

"Based on the facts as they appeared at the time, I would still have to say yes. I would do the same, because it was the correct medical procedure."

Franklyn was delighted. His evaluation of Chris was correct. This was going to be a turkey shoot. For the benefit of the jury Franklyn shook his head in apparent distress. "Do I understand that you feel there was nothing to be learned from that drastic experience?" he asked.

"I mean," Chris said, beginning to evidence signs of irritation, "that my treatment was the only proper one in the circumstances."

Franklyn then decided on a sudden change of subject and attacked Chris on the basis of harboring, if not conscious, then unconscious, hostility toward John Stewart Reynolds. Chris's denials became increasingly exasperated.

Moving to his table to pick up some papers, Franklyn returned to the witness stand. Chris noted that the papers were reprints of medical articles.

"Doctor," asked Franklyn, "have you ever heard the term Reynolds babies?"

Chris flushed, then finally admitted, "Yes, I have."

"Could you explain to the jury who originated that term?"

Chris felt his mouth go dry. "I . . . It was a term I used for the brain-damaged children seen in the course of my recent research."

"Doctor," said Franklyn sharply, "did you create that term before or after you treated the Simpson baby?"

"I don't see what—" Chris started to protest.

"*Before* or *after* you treated the Simpson baby, Doctor?"

"Before," said Chris.

"Doctor, can you explain to the jury exactly why you alone among all doctors who have written on the subject use the term Reynolds babies?"

"It had nothing to do with John Reynolds!" Chris declared. "Most of the brain-damaged infants I see come from very poor homes. Their mothers live in tenements or in low-cost housing developments. By sheer coincidence my first few cases came from the development called Reynolds Houses. So for convenience I simply labeled them Reynolds babies."

"And thereafter you *simply* continued to use that name?" Franklyn remarked acidly. "You didn't think it was a matter of importance that you might be libeling a respectable citizen?"

"I didn't intend to libel anyone. I was dealing with a housing development that reflected a social problem of our times," Chris tried to explain.

"Wouldn't one of the other low-cost housing developments have reflected that social problem just as well?"

"I don't know," said Chris. "Maybe I used Reynolds because it was better known."

Franklyn seized on the admission. "So there *was* a reason. Your choice of that name *was* deliberate."

"It was deliberate, but not hostile. It reflected on a social problem, not an individual. In fact, the building in which I did my research was donated by Mr. Reynolds. Why would I try to libel or defame him?"

"Why indeed?" Franklyn said reproachfully.

Before Chris could recover, Franklyn turned to pick up a clipping. "Doctor, may I read you a letter that appeared in the September 3, 1970, issue of *The Journal of Medicine*? In fact, would you care to examine it first?" He extended a copy of the clipping to Chris, who glanced at it carefully. "Doctor, do you recognize the two names that appear at the end of this letter?"

"I've heard of Dr. Albert and of Dr. Rentler."

"Would you consider them doctors of excellent professional reputation?"

"Yes."

"Doctor, why don't you keep that copy so that you can check me as I read."

The letter which Franklyn read consisted mainly of a list of results of experiments in animals, showing in the opinion of the two doctors the possible hazards of phototherapy for human infants, including retarded growth. Franklyn turned to face the jury.

"Doctor, do you have any idea why those two doctors came to that conclusion?"

"There was a paper written some eight or ten years ago which reported cases in which phototherapy produced infants with smaller than normal heads. But that was disproved by later tests and observations. In fact, the doctor who wrote that original paper finally admitted his observations were wrong."

Chris was obviously about to lose his temper. Laura rose quickly. "Your Honor, may we have a recess now?"

But Franklyn was not about to give Chris time to relax. "Your Honor, I can understand the witness's discomfort. But the purpose of cross-examination is to elicit the truth. Not to serve the convenience or comfort of the witness, unless, of course, counsel wishes to state that he is ill."

Bannon leaned toward Laura. "Does counsel make such an assertion?" Laura shook her head. To Franklyn, Bannon said impatiently, "Continue, Counselor!"

Harry Franklyn, notes and exhibits in his hand, advanced toward the witness box.

"Doctor, a little earlier you made use of the phrase 'a social problem of our times.' Would you enlighten the jury as to the meaning of the phrase and its relevance to your work?"

Carefully, Chris tried to explain the vital necessity of educating the poor about proper prenatal and postnatal nutrition.

"Doctor, at what point do you think it a doctor's duty to become a political activist and use his medical practice to achieve sociological goals?"

262

"I am not a political activist!"

"Not even when you urge political action on a group of doctors at a large medical meeting?" Franklyn demanded.

"If a doctor observes that a certain set of conditions produces a dangerous and undesirable result, then it is his duty to speak out! And I don't give a damn what you label it!"

Chris saw Laura and Mike Sobol both react with dismay, and he shouted at them, "I'm a witness sworn to tell the truth. Well, that's the truth!"

Harry Franklyn remained sober, unsmiling. The witness was losing all restraint. Franklyn knew it was time to move toward his conclusion.

"Doctor," he asked with disarming gentleness, "isn't it true that you have a reputation in the community surrounding Metropolitan General for being the doctor to the poor? In fact, don't the Hispanic people there call you *El Medico?*"

"Yes," Chris conceded.

Franklyn prodded further. "Isn't it true, Doctor, that you also deliver lectures in the community?"

"Yes, of course."

"Isn't it a fact that you deem those lectures an important part of your political activism?" Franklyn demanded.

"If I can save an infant's life, or its brain, by giving a mother instruction in nutrition, I consider that a part of my work as a doctor. I do not call it political activism," Chris retorted.

"So, if we can take you at your word, Doctor, you examined the Simpson child for five to ten minutes, made some tests, put him under phototherapy, like a housewife puts a slow flame under a pot of stew so that it'll keep, and went off to give a lecture to women whose children were *not at that moment* in need of your services? Is that right, Doctor?"

"No!" Chris protested. "I did not use phototherapy as a holding action. It was the only thing to do till a trend developed."

"Doctor, would you care to amend your testimony about not giving preference to any patients?"

"It was true before. It's true now."

"Doctor, would you care to amend your previous denial of political activism?"

"No!"

"The talk you delivered the day the Simpson infant was referred, where was it given?" Franklyn asked.

"I don't recall," said Chris.

"Would it refresh your recollection if I said it was at Public School One Forty-six?" Franklyn asked.

"Oh, yes, that's where it was."

"Doctor, what part of the city is that school in?"

"What part? It's in Rixie Square. Everybody knows that."

"Indeed everybody does," Franklyn repeated. "Doctor, what was the date of your talk?"

"I don't know. The same day the Simpson infant was referred."

"And also the same day of the Rixie Square riot?" Franklyn asked, his voice soft.

"I guess so," said Chris.

"Dr. Grant, did you know that some of the women who had attended your lecture were in that mob?"

"No, I didn't know that," Chris said, searching for some help from Laura or Mike Sobol.

Franklyn waved a sheaf of newspaper clippings and said, "The news reports are here, if you care to examine them."

"I do not. They have no bearing on this case."

"I thought you might decide to withdraw your previous denials of political activism!" Franklyn said, raising his voice. "Or that you might finally admit that your time would have been better spent at the Simpson infant's side, instead of initiating a riot in Rixie Square."

Laura Winters was now painfully aware of why Harry Franklyn had fought so strongly to select a white middle-class jury. Short of a miracle, she did not see any chance left for a favorable verdict. But she could not permit Chris to leave the stand on that note. She came forward for redirect examination. After she elicited Chris's denials of Franklyn's accusations, she asked one final question. "Dr. Grant, at any time in the course of the treatment of John

264

Reynolds Simpson did you give thought to any other consideration than the welfare of that infant?"

"At no time," Chris responded simply, his face drained, his voice
barely audible to the jury. "A doctor . . . a pediatrician . . . is a
defender of the weakest and frailest of all patients. I consider myself their advocate, their protector. If I couldn't defend their right
to a healthy life to the best of my ability, I would leave the field
of medicine altogether. Call it political activism, call it anything
you want, I say it's a doctor's sworn duty!"

Five minutes later Laura stood beside Chris and Mike on the
courthouse steps. Reynolds and his family were just coming out.
Suddenly, Arlene Simpson turned slightly and her eyes made contact with Chris's. Staring back, Chris was startled. He had expected
to see hatred, but had instead found only pain. Then she got into
Reynolds' limousine.

CHAPTER ELEVEN

THEY were at lunch between sessions, Laura and Chris. They ate
little. During the morning Laura had put on the stand two doctors,
friends of Mike's, both of whom had testified that Chris's treatment
of the Simpson baby had been consistent with good medical practice. But she knew that they had had little impact on the jury. Now
she was frantically searching her mind for something that would
make those jurors a little less certain that Chris was responsible.

If there was any chance, it would be in Coleman's testimony.
She suggested it to Chris. After a moment's thought, he said, "That
second bilirubin. The one that's missing."

"If it came back from the lab after the baby was referred to your
care, what difference would it make?" she asked.

"Probably none," Chris agreed. "*If* it came back after the infant
was referred."

"If it came back before, the nurse would have entered it in the
hospital record, wouldn't she?"

"Not necessarily," Chris said. "In many hospitals the doctor must
see the lab report and initial it *before* it goes onto the chart. It could

work that way at Parkside. If a doctor found a disturbing report, instead of initialing it, he could simply slip it into his pocket, and it never would show up on the patient's chart."

"Chris, what could have been on the second lab report that would have disturbed Coleman so much?"

"Exactly the same thing that would have made him very anxious to refer the infant out of Parkside Polyclinic," Chris stated. "A bilirubin much higher than fourteen."

For the first time they felt a surge of optimism. Maybe the brain damage was not just an inexplicable accident of nature.

"I'm going after that report," Chris said abruptly. "If Coleman destroyed it, there's only one place to look—the laboratory log at Parkside Polyclinic. By law, every lab must keep a log of every test they do and every report they issue."

As HE strode down the corridor of the pediatrics wing at Metropolitan General, Chris was aware that he had now become the object of furtive stares. Before, most of the staff had a smile or quick hello. Now they were afraid of intruding, afraid an attempt at friendliness might be misconstrued as curiosity.

Mike Sobol was in his office, poring over some research results, when he looked up and saw Chris standing in his doorway. Mike could see that the long trial was taking its toll. Without even knowing it, Chris was becoming less aggressive, more withdrawn and self-protective. He had been badly hurt by this experience.

Chris closed the door and came directly to the point. "Mike, we must have access to the lab records at Parkside Polyclinic."

"Laura thinks it would help?"

"It would, if Coleman deliberately intended to lose that lab report on their second bilirubin."

Mike Sobol nodded. "There's Wellman," he said. "Fifteen years ago I got a desperate call from him. He had just had a most difficult delivery. He was a young man then, just starting out. Well, I took that infant on referral. Fortunately it turned out fine. He was most grateful and he told me if there was ever anything he could do . . ." Mike reached for his phone.

While the operator was trying to reach Wellman, Mike asked, "What date was the Simpson baby referred to us?"

"March sixteenth."

Mike waited till he heard Wellman's voice. "Mike?" Wellman sounded like a doctor on the run.

"Brad?" Mike asked. "Can you talk?"

"Depends." Mike could hear a voice in the background.

"Brad, it is a matter of vital importance to me to have a look at the lab log for March sixteenth."

"Oh?" was all that Wellman said, but Mike could tell that the younger man had jumped to the correct conclusion. There was a long silence.

Finally, Wellman said abruptly, "I never like to x-ray a patient simply to find out what sex the baby is going to be." He hung up.

Mike Sobol dropped the phone into its cradle.

"He guessed what it was about," said Chris.

"He guessed," Mike admitted. "I just hope he doesn't say anything to anybody else."

"Is there any other doctor you can contact?"

Mike started to count off the other men at Parkside who might be indebted to him. The phone rang. He picked it up.

"Mike?" It was Wellman. "Sorry I had to cut you off, but I thought it was better to handle this from a public phone. You want to know what lab work was done on the Simpson baby before it was referred?"

"Right. Brad, I don't want you to get into trouble, but we would appreciate any help we can get," Mike said quite frankly.

"It might take a day or two. But I'll get you the answer. I just hope it turns out the way you want."

"Time is running out," Laura warned. "We don't have much of our case left to present. And what we do have won't make it."

Neither Mike nor Chris had any suggestions.

Mike said, "I better check in with the hospital."

He reached the night nurse in charge. There were no emergencies, but there were several messages, all from a Mr. Bradford.

268

"He said to please call him at home. He was sure you would know the number."

A Mr. Bradford, Mike wondered. Then he realized it was Brad Wellman. He took out his little notebook, in which he had listed private numbers of doctors all over the country. It saved time during emergencies. Brad answered on the first ring.

"Well?" Mike asked anxiously.

"I found that second bilirubin report. It's in the lab log. I had them photocopy the page for that date."

"Yes, yes," Mike said. "What did it show?"

Chris and Laura both waited, not daring to breathe.

"I see," said Mike. "Could you drop it by the hospital? And thanks again. Believe me, anything you ever owed me is paid in full."

"That second bilirubin *was* higher, wasn't it?" Chris asked, after Mike hung up.

Before Chris could take too much comfort Mike said, "It was, but only eighteen point five."

"But who is to say that in the hours between the first and second tests the bilirubin might not have gone much higher?" Chris asked. "Maybe it was already on its way *down* when the lab caught it at eighteen point five."

"Exactly!" said Mike. "The worse the condition, the swifter the ascent and descent."

"We interpreted the bilirubin of sixteen as a rising trend, and started treatment. But that bilirubin might have exceeded twenty before the infant ever reached Metropolitan," Chris said grimly.

"And if it did . . ." Laura said, not daring to go on.

"The damage would have been done before Chris even saw the child," Mike concluded.

"I'm going to recall Coleman to the stand tomorrow!" Laura said with determination.

"Dr. Coleman," Laura began, "let's refresh our memory. As I recollect, you received a call from the nursery while you were in the operating room. And you learned then that the Simpson

269

baby was exhibiting signs of marked jaundice and had a bilirubin of fourteen—"

"Such information is not relayed over a squawk box," Coleman interrupted. "The doctor is simply asked to call the floor."

"Oh, I see," Laura said. "So it wasn't till you left surgery that you discovered what the bilirubin was?"

"Yes," Coleman replied.

"Doctor, how long after you received that message on the squawk box did you leave surgery?" Laura asked.

"I wouldn't remember a detail like that," Coleman said.

"Especially on a day when you were covering for Dr. Mitchell and had two patients scheduled for surgery? How long did it take to do each operation, Doctor?"

"Two to three hours at the most."

"So that if that call came in during your first operation, it would have been four or possibly five hours before you could go down to the nursery and see the Simpson baby's lab report."

Coleman hesitated, then replied, "I doubt it would have been that long."

"Doctor, how long does it usually take to do a normal routine lab test at Parkside?"

"About three hours."

"So that if the jury were to assume three hours for the test and add to that the four or five hours that elapsed while you were in surgery, that would mean that as much as eight hours could have gone by—"

"Eight hours did not go by!" Coleman interrupted. "Besides, this is all academic. The Simpson baby never had a bilirubin report higher than sixteen. And it started receding after that!"

"Doctor, would it surprise you to learn that the result on the second bilirubin you ordered was eighteen point five?"

Stunned, Coleman stared at her. Before he could speak, Laura turned to the bench and said, "I would like to offer into evidence a photocopy of the lab log of Parkside Polyclinic Hospital on the day in question."

At the plaintiffs' counsel table there was a hasty conference between Reynolds and Franklyn. Franklyn jumped up. "Your Honor, we demand the right to examine that document first!"

Laura held out the copy. "You may keep this, Mr. Franklyn, we have a number of them." As Franklyn took it, Laura advanced to the bench to offer a second copy to Judge Bannon. Bannon inspected it and looked at Franklyn.

"Your Honor," Harry Franklyn said, "I take an oath as an attorney and officer of this court that I have never seen this document before this moment!"

"We offer this report for identification," Laura said, "and when it is accepted we shall proceed with the examination."

It was Coleman rather than the judge who spoke. "Your Honor, if I can have a look at the report, I think I might be able to make the identification."

Laura studied him, suspecting some trick. Bannon granted the doctor's request. Coleman looked the document over carefully.

"Doctor, does that seem to be a true and genuine excerpt from the lab log at Parkside Polyclinic?" Laura waited, puzzled by his cooperation.

Finally, Coleman said, "Yes, this seems to be genuine."

Still suspicious, Laura offered it into evidence. Then she asked, "Doctor, would you be good enough to read us the result of the second bilirubin that appears alongside the name Simpson, Baby?"

Without changing expression Coleman read simply, "Eighteen point five."

"So that when the Simpson infant was referred to Dr. Grant its bilirubin was higher than the fourteen you first told us?"

"It would seem so," Coleman admitted.

"Doctor, did you or did you not see that bilirubin of eighteen point five before?"

"I did not."

"Is it the practice in Parkside Polyclinic that before a lab report is put on the patient's chart the attending physician initials it?"

"As a general rule, yes," said Coleman.

"Is there any reason to believe that the general rule was not followed in this case?" Laura demanded.

"Every reason," said Coleman. "Since I did not pay a visit to the nursery at Parkside after I had arranged to transfer the infant, that report was never seen by me, never initialed and therefore never entered in the patient's record."

"Doctor, let me ask the following hypothetical question: Assuming that an infant exhibits a bilirubin of fourteen, and is suffering from an Rh incompatibility, which tends to drive up the bilirubin at a fast rate, isn't it possible that the bilirubin might have peaked at twenty or higher? So that when the bilirubin was recorded at eighteen point five, it was on its way *down?*" Laura demanded. "And in fact, the infant might well have been damaged *before* it ever left Parkside Polyclinic!"

Her last words were shouted to override Harry Franklyn's objections. Bannon had to resort to his gavel to silence both lawyers. He glanced at Franklyn.

"Your Honor, it is sheer speculation that the bilirubin ever reached a figure higher than that recorded, and in any event the document in question had nothing to do with Dr. Grant's decision. I insist that the Court disallow this entire line of questioning," Franklyn argued.

Bannon considered the matter gravely, then ruled, "Taking into account the arguments of counsel, and being moved by the weight of the evidence actually submitted, this Court feels forced to rule out this line of testimony!"

"Exception!" said Laura, but she knew it was a futile protest.

"The record will show that counsel takes exception to the Court's ruling," Bannon said.

As Coleman left the stand, Bannon declared a recess till morning, at which time he hoped counsel for both sides would give him some idea of when they would be ready to sum up. It was a strong hint that he was expecting Laura to close her case so it could go to the jury by the weekend.

"Slippery as an eel," Chris exploded.

Mike Sobol, who had been deep in thought, suddenly said, "Maybe you're being too hard on Coleman."

272

"How?" Laura demanded.

"Let's reconstruct the pressures he was under that day. He's carrying a double load, Mitchell's practice and his own. He's busy in the OR. He gets a call from the nursery. But the only infant he's supervising there seemed healthy and should not be running into difficulty, according to its history. Why should he feel under any pressure of time?"

"He *was* dealing with a first baby," Chris conceded reluctantly. "And a mother who had no positive Coombs' during pregnancy, even though she was Rh negative. Statistically that about eliminates the problem. Okay, Mike, I can see where he could have been saying to himself during those operations, 'There's no emergency, it's a first baby.' "

"How do we know?" Laura asked.

"Because Mitchell, or any good doctor who examined a woman, could not have missed a previous delivery."

"Could Mitchell have known and been promised to secrecy?" Laura asked.

"No, my dear," Mike said. "An ethical doctor like Mitchell would still have told Coleman."

"Wait!" Chris interrupted. "There was another way Reynolds' daughter could have become sensitized, so that her antibodies would destroy her infant's blood. A previous pregnancy terminated by an abortion."

"Then a first pregnancy could end as an abortion, with no first *baby?*"

"Yes," Mike conceded.

"But if Reynolds' daughter had had an abortion . . ."

"I'd take an oath that she never told Mitchell," Mike said. "Otherwise he'd have taken precautions against Rh incompatibility."

"If she didn't tell her doctor, who *did* she tell?" Laura asked. "A roommate at college? She married shortly after she graduated. It could have happened while she was still in school. Someone would have had to know. A girl in that condition confides in someone. The man. She would have told the man involved. If we could find him."

As LAURA and Chris were leaving the courtroom the next day, one of the attendants handed her a note from her secretary. "Call me soon as you get home," she read.

On the way to her apartment Laura explained to Chris that she had had her office do a little checking into Arlene Reynolds' college days.

At the apartment, Laura placed the call. "We lucked out," her secretary said.

"What?" Laura demanded urgently.

"Arlene Reynolds attended Northfield, upstate, for four years, but she did *not* graduate. She dropped out two months before graduation."

Laura hung up and relayed the information to Chris. "One of us is going to have to drive up to the college immediately and make some inquiries."

"You have to be in court all day," Chris said.

"Exactly," said Laura. "You'll have to go yourself."

Chris Grant pulled into the town of Northfield so late that night that he had to wake the clerk at the old inn to find a room. The next morning a stinging cold shower made up for his lack of sleep. By nine o'clock he was crossing the broad Northfield campus, which was just recapturing its spring green after a long, snowy winter. The long-legged girls in jeans and boots seemed very young compared to his thirty-six years.

At the administration building Chris pretended that he was considering moving to Northfield and wanted a part-time appointment to the college clinic. He first spoke to Dean Emily Waterston. He was greatly relieved that she accepted him at face value. She even offered to call the doctor in charge of the infirmary to tell her that Chris was on his way over.

There were three students waiting when he entered the clinic. Finally, Dr. Florence Lumpkin was free. She was a tall woman, attractive, with coils of rich gleaming hair wound about her head.

274

Her face was strong, with a reassuring and wholesome look that inspired confidence.

She leaned back in her swivel chair as she listened to his story. Her bright brown eyes gave no hint of anything other than a keen interest in Chris's qualifications and his desire to take up practice in a small town.

"In these times the need for prenatal and postnatal care is much more necessary on the college campus than it used to be, Doctor," she observed when he finished.

It was the opening Chris had been seeking. "Have you been here long enough to observe the change?" he asked.

"Eight years."

Good, thought Chris. The time he was concerned with would fall well within that period.

"How did you handle things before the state legalized abortion?"

"In those days, if the girl decided not to have her baby, she had to go out of the country. Or else resort to illegal means. I always advised against that."

"Naturally," he agreed. "Most girls, when they get into trouble, do they come to you?"

"Most girls," she said, "but not necessarily all."

"Because they're afraid they'll be expelled?"

"No girl has been expelled for that reason in some years," Dr. Lumpkin said quickly.

"How many years has that liberal policy been in effect?"

"Long enough to include the period in which you're interested, Dr. Grant," she said, staring at him defiantly. "Did you think that I wouldn't recognize your name?" Then she became almost conciliatory. "You know that I can't help you, no matter how much I might want to. I have my professional obligations to this institution and to the patients I treat here."

"Doctor," said Chris, "that was the reason I had to resort to a ruse. I'm sorry I did, but at this point we're desperate. Unless we can prove otherwise, I will be unjustly convicted of malpractice."

Dr. Lumpkin did not relent, although she looked sympathetic.

"We're not entirely in the dark," he said, hoping to provoke her

275

curiosity. "We know, for instance, that if Arlene Reynolds did become pregnant, it happened during those last few months of her senior year. With her money, at that time—four years ago—she would probably have gone abroad, where she could have an abortion done safely. Then she either chose not to come back here, or her father wouldn't permit it. Is that a fair hypothesis?"

"I refuse to comment," she said.

"Well, I know one thing that I didn't know before," Chris said. "It *did* happen. And she came to see *you*."

"How can you know that?"

"If you didn't know anything about it then, there'd be no need for confidentiality now. You'd be perfectly free to speculate."

She didn't deny it. For the first time Chris felt that she was actually trying to help him. "I'm sorry to have put you in this position, Doctor," Chris said.

"If I were able to help, I would," she said.

"Do you have any advice at all?" he asked.

"Keep digging," was all she would say.

Chris stood outside the infirmary. The clock tower announced the end of one class and the beginning of the next. Students were crossing the campus from every direction. Chris tried to analyze what little he had gleaned from Dr. Lumpkin. She had said to keep digging, but how could he discover a close friend of Arlene Reynolds', four years after she had left? Unless, of course, the doctor was not referring to a student. Maybe some man on the faculty. By some means he had to secure Arlene Reynolds' scholastic file.

"I was referred here by Dean Waterston," Chris began, as glibly as he could. "I'm seeking some background information on a student who was in the class of '69—Arlene Reynolds."

Evidently the dean's name accomplished the purpose. The young girl in charge of the records room repeated efficiently, "Class of '69. Arlene Reynolds." She disappeared, and as time went by, Chris wondered uneasily if she had decided to check with the dean's office. Eventually, though, she returned with the file.

"Arlene Reynolds," she said as she handed it over. "But you

276

can't take it out of the office." She gestured toward a gray metal table in the corner. Anywhere, Chris thought, anywhere, as long as I can get a look at that file!

He scanned the index of papers. Background. First year. Sophomore year. Junior year. Senior year. Medical record. Activities. There was a list of the usual routine visits to the infirmary. Then the record ended abruptly. For the last few months of her senior year, mid-March through May, no record of any illness. No note of even a routine checkup.

It was understandable. The college was not likely to keep records on an illegitimate pregnancy.

Chris turned to Arlene's senior scholastic record. Alongside each of six courses was the name of the professor or instructor. Three were women, three men. Henry Wills, philosophy. Gregory Mayer, applied psychology. Arthur Ward, English literature.

As it turned out, Dr. Wills had retired two years previously. The secretary to the present chairman of the philosophy department offered to give Chris his address, but he saw no reason to visit anyone over sixty-five.

Dr. Gregory Mayer, professor of applied psychology, was also in his sixties. He was a tall man, wrinkled from the shrinking thinness of age. At Chris's mention of Arlene Reynolds, Mayer looked up thoughtfully. "Oh, yes. Nice girl. Unspectacular, but willing. She seemed like a timid girl. I often wondered if it was due to living in the shadow of such an important father."

There was no useful information to be obtained from Mayer, so Chris left as quickly as he gracefully could.

The registry just outside Croft Hall listed DR. WARD, ARTHUR, ENGLISH DEPARTMENT, ROOM 205. When Chris appeared in the doorway the secretary, middle-aged and plump, looked up, obviously annoyed at being interrupted.

"Did you have an appointment with Dr. Ward?" she asked.

"I was referred by Dean Waterston," Chris lied.

"Dr. Ward has a very busy schedule, but if you have time to wait, I'll see if he can accommodate you."

The woman pointed to a worn leather chair. Chris dropped into it, and after a few minutes the door to Ward's private office opened. A young woman, obviously a student, was leaving. The secretary went in, remained a few minutes, then came out and announced briskly, "Dr. Ward will see you now."

"Dr. Grant?" the tall black man asked, standing behind his cluttered desk.

Dr. Ward was in his thirties, lean, with alert and questioning eyes. His hair was worn in a slight Afro. His clothes were exceedingly conventional, a simple gray tweed jacket, dark flannel slacks and a blue knit tie. Chris either concealed his surprise very well or else Ward had become used to such a reaction during his years at the predominantly white college.

"Dr. Ward, I wanted to ask you—" Chris began.

Ward interrupted. "Dr. Grant, why did you find it necessary to lie? The dean sent you to Dr. Lumpkin. If you wanted to see me, you had no need to resort to the dean's name. A man on an honest mission would have no need of subterfuge."

"Sorry," Chris said. "But I hope that will reflect the urgency of my mission, not the integrity of it."

Ward gestured for Chris to be seated. "I'm listening," he said.

Ward was handsome and strong, his deep voice well modulated and gentle. It was apparent to Chris that he was a sensitive man with romantic appeal.

"Then, Dr. Ward, I will say right off that I am here to find out about Arlene Reynolds."

The involuntary concern in Ward's eyes confirmed what Chris had hoped to learn. "What would you like to know?"

"It's highly personal. But since my career depends on it, I have to ask. I am being sued for malpractice. If I lose the case, that will destroy everything I've worked for, the results of which might be of enormous help to your people in the years and the generations to come."

"Are you trying to bribe me with promises of what you're going to do for my people?" Ward asked. He turned away abruptly. "Why do you assume that unless you can do something for black people I will not tell you the truth?"

278

Chris waited silently. Ward stared out the window across the campus. Then he said over his shoulder, "What do you want to know?"

"Was she in love with you?"

"We were in love with each other," Ward corrected him gently. Chris realized now that the man was defensive because he was still deeply involved in the entire experience.

"I'm sorry," Chris began again. "I know it's painful, but we can't go forward with our defense until we know the truth. The entire issue of malpractice may come down to one fact alone. Had she ever been pregnant before she gave birth to her first child?"

Ward did not respond. The silence became heavy. "It's entirely possible that she could have been pregnant and I wouldn't have known about it," he finally said.

"That's true," Chris conceded.

"Look, it would have been bad enough if she had just been wealthy, but to be the daughter of a so-called self-made man was an overwhelming circumstance. I never met him, but I learned enough from her to know precisely the kind of man he is."

"I've met him," Chris observed. "She didn't exaggerate."

Ward continued as if he hadn't heard Chris's comment. "She was really very sweet. Terrified, in a way. That was what first called her to my attention, and I felt sorry for her. Yet she was a bright girl and quite attractive, too." He turned back from the window to find a cigarette. While the match was still flaring he looked at Chris. "I've had a long time to think about it. And I still don't know what the attraction really was." His burned fingers made him stop to flick out the match. "Unless it was a mutual awareness of our vulnerability. Hers in relation to her father. Mine in relation to my race. She helped me very much, because she loved me. And our colors did not matter.

"Then came the day when she felt sure she could tell her father that, with his permission or without, she was going to marry me. She seemed so strong suddenly. If I had suspected that she couldn't stand up to him, I wouldn't have allowed her to confront him. I loved her too much for that."

279

"She decided suddenly?" Chris asked.

"Quite suddenly," Ward admitted.

"Could that have been because she discovered she was pregnant?" Chris asked.

"I wouldn't know," Ward said quickly. Too quickly, it seemed. For he admitted, "And if I did know, I wouldn't tell you."

Ward turned back to the window. "The day she went home to tell him, I drove her down to the airport. She was so strong and full of conviction that I was certain she would be back. I watched her plane until it was out of sight." Ward was silent for a while. Then he said simply, "I never saw her again."

Chris could feel the depth of the man's pain. Ward had revealed the most intimate and scarring event of his life.

"She didn't call, didn't write?" he asked.

Ward shook his head slightly. "The news that she wasn't returning came to me through the college physician, Dr. Lumpkin."

"Dr. Ward, did you ever wonder why Dr. Lumpkin was the one to tell you, instead of the dean or Arlene's faculty adviser? Unless she *was* pregnant?" Chris asked, waiting confirmation. When Ward did not answer, Chris continued. "And being pregnant may have been the reason she felt strong enough to face her father. She had a weapon to use against him; only as it turned out, he used it against her. He forced her to fly to Sweden or Switzerland, where the thing could be done in utmost secrecy. You were never even told what happened to your child."

Chris paused. If Ward were going to make any admission, this was the time. He sank down into his chair, reached for another cigarette. Eventually it was clear he would say nothing.

Chris proceeded to tell him the facts involved in the lawsuit, from the moment when he had taken charge of the Simpson baby through the events of the trial.

Ward's only comment was, "It would be like Reynolds to think he could wipe out all memory of his daughter's pregnancy, especially by a black man."

"Do you think he would have gone so far as to forbid her to tell her own doctor?" Chris asked.

"Yes. And if he had reduced her again to being the girl I first met, she would have obeyed him."

"Do you understand the consequences of that?" Chris asked.

"Consequences?"

"By withholding that information she misled her doctors into believing they were dealing with a first pregnancy. They misdiagnosed the entire situation. Vital hours were allowed to pass, a delay that was probably responsible for what finally happened."

"The sins of the fathers . . ." Ward mused bitterly.

"The question now is, will *you* do something about it?"

"Do something? What?"

"Come to court. Testify. Let the truth be known finally."

Ward stared at him across the desk.

"I'm sorry," he said at last. "I . . . I couldn't do that to her. The child is damaged and that's enough for her to bear. I don't want to destroy what chance she has for making some sort of life. After all, she's married. What will happen if it comes out that before her husband there was a man, a black man? I simply cannot do that to her."

"No matter what it does to others?"

"I love *her*, not others," Ward said. "And when she does think of me, I want it to be with kindness, with love. I can only trust you to understand."

"I do," Chris said wearily. He could not bring himself to pursue the man any longer. But on his way to the plane he kept thinking that all his understanding wasn't going to do his case much good. Laura had wanted proof and he was coming home without it.

MIKE and Laura were as disappointed as Chris had expected, even though their theory was confirmed.

"A man like John Reynolds, whose pride is as important to him as his power," Mike said sadly. "Of course he would keep it secret."

"What an enormous difference it would have made," Chris replied, "if Mitchell had known beforehand."

Only Laura had not joined in the discussion. Her mind was working on the legal aspects of their predicament. When Chris looked at her she said, "Until someone testifies, we have only a theory. Not a fact. It has to be a witness whose knowledge is firsthand," Laura explained.

"What about Arlene Simpson herself?" Mike asked.

Laura shook her head. "Fear and guilt will keep her silent. Guilt about what she did. Fear of her father."

She was thoughtful for a moment, then said, "There's only one witness who knows the facts, and who is not afraid of Reynolds."

"Who is that?" Chris demanded.

"John Stewart Reynolds."

"I've known that man for twenty years," Mike Sobol said. "He'd never admit such a thing!"

"Pride can be a weakness—what doesn't bend has to break. It depends on how much pressure we can bring to bear on him."

"Laura, my dear, don't let us drive you into any foolish moves because of our impatience."

"Mike," she said soberly, "I'm fighting for more than a court victory. If I lose this case, I lose . . ."

She didn't finish. Tears welled up in her eyes. Mike looked at Chris, who stared back, his eyes admitting the true relationship that existed between them. If Mike had had reason to suspect before, they had now told him.

"There's nothing to be lost by going after Reynolds," Chris said, hoping to restore a shred of hopefulness.

"There's everything to lose," said Laura. "But it's either put Reynolds back on the stand—or sum up and go to the jury with an inadequate defense."

CHAPTER THIRTEEN

John Stewart Reynolds sat in his library, waiting for his wife to come down dressed and ready to leave for court. Today should bring the end of the trial. As far as Reynolds was concerned, the question of guilt had been clearly established. Now his interest was that the settlement be sufficient punishment to plague Christopher Grant for the rest of his career.

When he heard his wife's footsteps on the stairs, Reynolds started out quickly. He did not want to give her time to speak now. They had had several discussions, some tearful, about her earlier refusals to go to court. She could not understand that he had taken legal action as a duty, to protect the public from future experiments by young men like Grant.

Recently she had been weeping at night, and when he heard her, he assumed she was crying for their poor little grandson. Well, to-day would be the last sacrifice he would ask of her in relation to the trial. And only because Harry Franklyn had insisted on it. John Stewart Reynolds himself approached the day with an angry zeal.

Their daughter, Arlene, kissed young John as he lay in his crib. She stared down at him and smiled. The infant, more than a year old now, smiled back only tentatively. Then his face was clouded with its customary opaque stare.

Arlene turned to the governess. "Try to get him out more today," she suggested.

"Of course." The governess knew that Arlene was hoping the out-doors would serve to stimulate the child in some way. She also knew very well that it wouldn't.

Arlene went downstairs to find her husband, "Laddie" Simpson, waiting at the door, the car outside, the motor running.

"Come, honey, we can't be late," he urged. "It wouldn't look right, walking in after court is in session."

What Simpson meant was that his father-in-law wouldn't like it. Laddie would be relieved to have the case over and out of the news. Glad not to have to face the fact each time he met someone— I have a brain-damaged child. If he had had his way, there would never have been any trial. What was there to be gained, except some satisfaction for the old man? But as in all things since he had married Arlene, Laddie Simpson had bowed to her father's demands.

Well, after today he and Arlene could settle down with their own private grief and do what they could for little John.

Though they had talked about the possibility of an institution, they had reached no decision. But clearly Arlene could not take the daily confrontation with little John indefinitely. For some reason she blamed herself, though none of them should feel guilty, certainly not after the proof that had been adduced in the course of the trial. One thing was clear—somehow during the first hours of his life, John Reynolds Simpson had been damaged. Whether the fault was a dangerously elevated bilirubin or Grant's treatment, Laddie Simpson could not know for sure.

WORD has a way of spreading through courthouses. When an interesting case is reaching its climax, spectators gather like crowds in an ancient coliseum, ready to join in the process of observing and judging.

This was one such morning. The seats were filled a good hour before court was called into session. There was a stir of excitement when the Reynolds family filed into the room. In an attempt to deflate the impression they created, Laura made a conspicuous show of setting out several blue-backed memorandums. The clerk called for silence. Bannon entered, his black robe trailing, and took his place. Since the rules provided that the party who opened the case summed up last, Bannon turned to Laura. "Is the defense ready to sum up?"

"No, your Honor," Laura answered. "On reconsideration, the defense has decided to recall to the stand John Stewart Reynolds."

"What does counsel hope to establish that has not already been established?" demanded the judge.

"Certain matters to which Mr. Reynolds testified have, upon investigation, turned out to be subject to considerable doubt."

"Your Honor, we've already been through this performance," said Franklyn. "Her insistence on recalling Dr. Coleman to the stand served only to introduce a missing document which had nothing to do with Dr. Grant's decision. If this is another of Miss Winters' pointless ruses, I strenuously object."

Laura reached for one of the blue-backed legal papers. "Your Honor, there is no precedent that deprives an attorney of the right to cross-examine a hostile witness. If you were to so rule now, it would surely constitute reversible error."

Reluctantly, Bannon acceded. "The witness John Stewart Reynolds will take the stand."

Reynolds sat down in the witness chair, defiant and contemptuous. He welcomed the challenge.

Laura advanced toward the witness box, her carefully prepared list of questions in hand. "Mr. Reynolds, it has been some time since you testified, so may I refresh your recollection?"

"I have an excellent memory, but if it makes you feel better, go ahead," Reynolds said impatiently.

"At that time you testified that Dr. Grant failed to explain to you all the hazards involved in phototherapy?"

"That is true."

"Don't you really mean that he failed to disclose the *theoretical* dangers?" Laura corrected.

"I expect from a doctor what I expect from a businessman—full and honest disclosure!" Reynolds said, his voice beginning to rise.

Laura knew it was time for a diversionary attack.

"Mr. Reynolds, do you ever take aspirin? If you have a cold?"

He glared at her. "When I have a cold, yes. I have an aversion to medicine of any kind. I only take it when the doctor insists."

"Has any doctor ever told you that, in certain cases, aspirin can cause stomach bleeding, even hemorrhage?"

"No," Reynolds admitted.

Franklyn rose to interject. "Your Honor, I'd like to know, as I'm sure the jury would, too, where all this nonsense is leading."

Laura looked up at the bench. "I will make the connection very soon, your Honor."

"I think you'd better . . . " He was about to add "young woman," but Laura's challenging look made him bite back the words.

"Mr. Reynolds," she said, "if a physician did not instruct you as to these actual, not theoretical, dangers each time he prescribed aspirin, would you consider he was guilty of malpractice?"

"There is a vast difference between that and what happened to my grandson!" Reynolds exploded. "When you're dealing with an infant, nothing less than full disclosure is good practice," he insisted fiercely.

"Do you believe in full disclosure in *all* medical situations?" Laura asked.

"In all medical situations!" Reynolds affirmed.

"Full disclosure by the doctor, *and* full disclosure by the patient?" said Laura.

Laddie Simpson felt his wife sag against him. He assumed that the prolonged examination of her father was beginning to tell. He gripped her arm, but she pulled away.

"I don't know what you mean." Reynolds was a bit hesitant.

Now that she had made Reynolds uneasy, Laura knew it was the moment for another diversion.

"I mean, is it possible that your grandson's brain might have been damaged by some undisclosed genetic defect in the Reynolds bloodline?"

Franklyn leaped to his feet. "This exceeds the bounds of allowable cross-examination. My client will not be subjected to it!"

Laura turned to him and observed, "Well, at least we've been able to establish who is *really* your client, Mr. Franklyn."

The slip was not of great importance to the outcome, but she felt entitled to small satisfactions.

She addressed the bench. "Your Honor, since no real proof has been offered as to the cause of the brain damage to this unfortunate infant, I think we are entitled to dig into all the possible causes, even those that may have been deliberately withheld."

Before Bannon could rule, Reynolds himself shouted, "There isn't a damn thing wrong with the Reynolds bloodlines! I'll answer any question anyone wants to ask."

Having provoked Reynolds' challenge for her to continue, Laura asked, "Mr. Reynolds, how many children did your mother have?"

"Eight!" he replied crisply. "Five boys, three girls, all healthy!"

"Mr. Reynolds, how many children do you have?"

He glared at her. Finally he replied, "One."

"Only one? From a man who has just told us that his father sired eight healthy children? Only one, from the man who told us earlier how much he desired sons?"

Behind her she heard Franklyn object. Bannon was ready to

take up Franklyn's fight. "Young woman, this line of questioning is a profligate abuse of the right of cross-examination."

"Your Honor," said Laura, "if you want to hold me in contempt, do so! But I am going to ask every question I feel is necessary to discover every possible cause of brain damage that might play a part in this case."

"Young woman, approach this bench!" Bannon ordered, his face crimson with rage.

"Until I am addressed in accordance with my status at the bar, I do not intend to move."

Chris regarded her with a sudden sense of amusement. This woman, this girl, who could be so soft, so beguiling, had a streak of steel in her. Finally, Bannon was forced to say, "Counsel will approach the bench."

Franklyn quickly joined the conference and whispered fiercely, "Your Honor, unless counsel for the defense has specific information that she is trying to uncover with this line of questioning, I object to it."

Bannon glared at Laura. "Before the Court will allow you to continue, I demand some proof of such specific evidence."

Laura looked up at Bannon. "I promise the Court that before this witness leaves the stand I will make the connection between my line of questioning and the evidence."

"You refuse to reveal the nature of that evidence?"

Laura whispered back at Bannon, "*I damn well do!*"

"Young woman, I warn you now, unless you *do* make that connection, I will have you up on charges before the bar association for deliberately lying to this Court!"

Laura turned away, presuming she had permission to continue.

"Mr. Reynolds, I believe you were telling us that there is only one child of your marriage."

"It was my wife's fault—" He amended that at once. "My wife's condition." His eyes flicked slightly to his wife, as if apologizing for what he was about to reveal. "She had a difficult delivery, and they had to perform a cesarean. After that, the doctors explained it would be too dangerous. . . ."

288

"Did you ever feel that friends, associates, to whom you had made no secret of your desire for sons, wondered why you had none? Or did you tell them?"

"I do not discuss private family matters with associates or friends," Reynolds declared imperiously.

"Mr. Reynolds, are you a strong believer in personal privacy?"

"I may be considered old-fashioned by the likes of you, but, yes, I believe that a man's private life is just that!"

"How far does one go in an effort to achieve privacy?"

"How far?" Reynolds repeated, puzzled.

"Does one keep things secret only from one's friends?" Before Reynolds could answer, Laura continued. "Or also from one's lawyer? Possibly even from one's *doctor?*"

Reynolds' steel-blue eyes glared back. For the first time he suspected there was a pattern to these questions. Avoiding a direct answer, Reynolds asserted, "The trouble in these times is that too much has been made public. The press, the TV are always prying into things!"

Reynolds was breathing hard now, his face flushed.

Laura knew this was the time to close in. "Mr. Reynolds, I'm sure many citizens feel the way you do. Yet, how do you account for the enormous TV coverage of your daughter's marriage?"

"Well," Reynolds conceded, "there are times when you can't keep them out."

"And also times when you invited them in?"

Reynolds bristled. "It was a social event of great importance. The public was very curious."

"So you did invite the press in for that particular event. I wonder, Mr. Reynolds, if you would have been so quick to invite them in if, instead of marrying Mr. Simpson, your daughter had chosen to marry outside your social group? Say, if your daughter had chosen to marry a Jew? Or possibly a black?"

Reynolds tried to retain his look of impenetrability. But his tightening jaw muscles betrayed him. He decided finally that her question was an accidental thrust and said, "Since it never happened, I don't see any need to answer."

Laura did not press the point. It was sufficient that she had shaken him severely. She decided it was time to present the real case for the defense.

"Mr. Reynolds, you told us in your direct testimony that you went to the medical library to read up on phototherapy and other matters concerning your unfortunate grandson. Was that the only time you ever went to a medical library to do research?"

"Yes," he admitted in a hoarse voice.

"Did you know that your daughter has Rh-negative blood, Mr. Reynolds?"

"Yes. Yes, I did know."

"Yet knowing that, you didn't go to the library and look it up, did you?"

"There was no need. She was in the hands of a very capable doctor."

"Did you discuss the problem with him?" asked Laura.

"I was confident Dr. Mitchell would be able to take care of any problem that might arise."

"Even though he was not told all the facts?" Laura began to drive more sharply now.

Reynolds looked at her with new concern. Laura stared back. If he guessed by now that she knew everything, she didn't mind. It was Reynolds who finally turned his eyes away.

Now Laura demanded, "Mr. Reynolds, have you ever done any medical research on the subject of abortion?"

Chris Grant and Mike Sobol glanced at the plaintiffs' table, where Arlene Simpson sat stiff and breathless. Her delicate face was painfully white.

On the witness stand John Reynolds stared past Laura, past his wife and daughter. Laura called him to account. "Mr. Reynolds, have you or have you not ever done research on abortion?"

"I have never had need to do any reading on that subject."

"Then perhaps I should recall to the stand an expert to enlighten you," Laura suggested.

Though he was completely unaware of the course Laura intended to pursue, Harry Franklyn leaped up to object. But Laura

290

wheeled on him and said, "Mr. Franklyn, for the benefit of your own clients, I advise you to withdraw your objection!"

Franklyn felt a hand tug at his sleeve. He glanced down into Mrs. Reynolds' face. Her expression warned him not to pursue his objection. He slipped back into his chair.

With Bannon's approval, Laura recalled Dr. Grant to the stand. "Dr. Grant, will you explain the problems that face an Rh-negative woman, especially those that might affect her child?"

Chris faced the jury. He described how the mother's blood could be sensitized and produce antibodies, if she had either received a transfusion of positive blood or had a previous pregnancy. Once those antibodies were in her bloodstream, they could affect the health of any child she might bear. In fact, unless steps were taken, the infant might be severely damaged or even die.

When Laura was convinced that the jury had heard enough, she asked, "Dr. Grant, let us assume a woman has been sensitized by a transfusion of positive blood or by an earlier pregnancy. If her doctor knew that, would it modify his treatment?"

"It would make all the difference in the world. The doctor would have been alerted to an Rh incompatibility in the infant," Chris replied.

"And if he had been alerted?" Laura asked.

"He would watch for any sign of jaundice. He would be very careful to take a bilirubin every two hours, even if the child's color was good."

"Yet Dr. Coleman admitted he didn't do that?" said Laura.

"That was understandable. He *thought* he was dealing with a first baby."

"But, Doctor, the testimony of her doctor was clear—this *was* Mrs. Simpson's first baby, wasn't it?"

"Yes, it was," Chris answered. "But a woman does not have to give birth to become sensitized. She can be sensitized as a result of any previous pregnancy, however it was terminated."

John Reynolds turned white. His daughter, Arlene, pressed back in her chair.

"Doctor, if a woman had had an abortion and deliberately conspired to keep that fact from her doctor, would he be able to detect it on examination?" Laura asked.

"He would not," Chris answered.

"So that if a woman with Rh-negative blood had an abortion and was forced to conceal that fact from her doctor, he would not know that her blood had been sensitized?" Laura asked.

"He would not know." Chris stared at John Reynolds.

"Dr. Coleman testified that he was told by the nurse that the infant was jaundiced. He then ordered a bilirubin and a Coombs' test. Did he follow the proper procedure?"

"He did. Except that we know from his own testimony that it was many hours before he saw the results of those tests."

"Despite the fact that in dangerous cases a bilirubin should be done at least every two hours?" Laura asked.

"Dr. Coleman was misled into believing he was dealing with an unsensitized mother. So he felt that he had leeway as far as time was concerned," Chris explained.

"Then Dr. Coleman was working in the dark?"

"By the time he saw the infant, seven or eight hours later, the bilirubin probably had shot up past twenty. The brain damage undoubtedly occurred *before* that infant ever arrived at Metropolitan General."

"Therefore, Doctor, who would you say was responsible for the brain damage suffered by John Reynolds Simpson?"

Chris peered down at John Reynolds. "Whoever it was who made the decision to conceal Arlene Simpson's previous abortion from her doctor."

The blood drained from John Reynolds' face. Arlene turned and whispered an accusation only her father could hear.

His lips twitched. He breathed in shallow, almost imperceptible gasps. Then he muttered, "I . . . I need a doctor. . . ."

Laura turned to the bench. "Your Honor, Mr. Reynolds is obviously under great strain. I urge an immediate recess."

Harry Franklyn called across to Mike Sobol, "Please! Take a look!"

Mike moved to John Reynolds' side, reached for his pulse,

292

loosened his collar to ease his breathing. Reynolds did not respond. Under Mike's guidance, attendants raised Reynolds up and helped him out of the courtroom, through the judges' robing room, with Mrs. Reynolds following. Arlene Simpson rose and made her way up the aisle, her husband hurrying after her. Harry Franklyn remained at the counsel table alone.

AT TWO o'clock that afternoon Laura, Chris and Mike Sobol presented themselves in Judge Bannon's chambers. Harry Franklyn was fifteen minutes late. He explained that he had been meeting with his clients. With Laura's permission, Franklyn was permitted to make a statement without the presence of the court stenographer.

"On the instructions of my clients I am herewith terminating this action. I have also been authorized to give Dr. Grant and Dr. Sobol any public apology they consider acceptable. Mrs. Simpson is hopeful, however, that it will not entail disclosing events that might cause pain and damage to innocent persons."

Everyone in the room understood. "Mrs. Simpson has nothing to fear from us," Laura said. "We have no wish to embarrass or injure the man involved, either personally or professionally."

"Thank you," said the little lawyer, adding with bemused self-reproach, "I never thought, after all these years, that a client could fool me so completely."

Regretfully, Franklyn started for the door. His hand on the knob, he turned to face Laura. "Young lady—and I can call you that, because I have two daughters older than you are—young lady, you're one hell of a good lawyer. I'm not so unhappy at the thought of retiring when I see young ones like you coming along."

LAURA Winters, Chris Grant and Mike Sobol were having their celebration dinner at La Scala. Once the news of their victory was known, Guido had called Mike and insisted. He seated them at Mike's favorite corner table. Guido beamed and addressed him. "Tonight I do the ordering!" He smiled. "And the *vino*, a special bottle for a special night!"

Guido hurried off. Now Mike furtively drew a corked hospital flask of deep purple liquid out of his pocket.

"The last of Rose's last bottle of Passover wine," he revealed.

There was enough for three drinks. When he had poured them and admired the color, he raised his glass to Laura. "Chris, let's have a toast to our little girl. A very smart lawyer. A very nice human being. And, as an old hand at being married, I can tell you she'll make a wonderful wife."

All three touched glasses and drank.

"There's a lot of celebrating to do tonight," Mike announced. "For several years now they've been after me to take it easy. To step down, become professor emeritus. No small honor. This afternoon I notified them I would do just that—on condition that my succeeding chief is Christopher Grant."

"Mike, I owe you too much already," Chris protested.

"Idiot, I'm not doing this for you. I'm doing it for the hospital. Now, you say yes, and we'll drink to it. Okay?"

Chris nodded. They raised their glasses again. After they drank, Mike said, "Well, I am depending on you two to give me grandsons. And one granddaughter, too, just like her mother."

They started to raise their glasses. But Mike said, "No, please. This time, just Rose and I will drink."

THE next morning Christopher Grant, M.D., arrived at Metropolitan General Hospital to resume his work. He entered Babies' Pavilion, passing the huge bronze plaque that bore the strong profile of John Stewart Reynolds. As he pushed open the door to the hospital floor, he heard the squawk box calling, "Dr. Grant. Dr. Christopher Grant, call the intensive care nursery at once."

He went to the admissions desk and picked up the phone.

Henry Denker

Henry Denker's first professional piece of writing was a radio play produced when he was twenty-eight. Since when, as well as continuing his work for American radio, he has written plays for stage and television, film scripts, and many successful novels.

In *The Physicians*, this distinguished author brings together two of his principal life-long enthusiasms. As a young man he studied law at New York University and, before turning to authorship, worked for a time as a practising attorney. And he has been interested in the field of medicine for as long as he can remember. "Most of my friends are doctors," he says, "and I spend a lot of time visiting and researching in hospitals." In gathering material for *The Physicians* he found that the branch of medicine known as "neonatology" was so new that, as he says, "I ran across many doctors who had never even heard of it."

Born in New York City, he lives there still with his wife in an apartment near Central Park. A disciplined writer, he works every morning, seven days a week. When not writing or researching, he enjoys tennis and long walks through the busy, fascinating streets of Manhattan.

Captain Horatio Hornblower

a condensation of
THE HAPPY RETURN by C. S. FORESTER
Illustrated by James E. Bama

A
CLASSIC
OF OUR
TIME

Published by Michael Joseph

Of all fictional sea captains, Horatio Hornblower
is surely the most famous. In this, the first of his
many thrilling adventures, he is set a seemingly
impossible task. In his tiny, thirty-gun frigate *Lydia*,
alone on the stormy waters of the Pacific, he is to
destroy Spain's formidable power in the Americas. To
that end his secret Admiralty orders command an
unholy alliance—between a ship of His Majesty's
fleet and the evil forces of the colonial revolutionary
leader, El Supremo. However much Hornblower
may detest everything that El Supremo represents,
an order is an order. He clears for action and
stands in towards the coast of Nicaragua . . .
towards unimagined dangers, bewildering
changes of fortune, and the affections
of a remarkable Englishwoman,
sister to the future Duke of
Wellington himself.

We are proud to publish this modern classic of the sea, the
work of an internationally acknowledged master of his craft.

CHAPTER I

It was not long after dawn that Captain Hornblower came up on the quarterdeck of the *Lydia*. Bush, the first lieutenant, was officer of the watch, and touched his hat but did not speak to him; in a voyage which had by now lasted seven months without touching land, he had learned something of his captain's likes and dislikes. During this first hour of the day the captain was not to be spoken to, nor his train of thought interrupted.

In accordance with standing orders—hallowed by now with the tradition which is likely to accumulate during a voyage of such incredible length—Brown, the captain's coxswain, had seen to it that the weather side of the quarterdeck had been holystoned and sanded at the first peep of daylight. Bush and the midshipman with him withdrew to the lee side at Hornblower's first appearance, and Hornblower immediately began his daily hour's walk up and down, up and down the area of deck which had been sanded for him. On one hand his walk was limited by the slides of the quarterdeck guns, or carronades; on the other by the row of ringbolts in the deck for the attachment of the carronade train tackles; the space on which Captain Hornblower was accustomed to exercise himself each morning was thus five feet wide and twenty-one feet long.

Up and down, up and down, paced Captain Hornblower. Although he was entirely lost in thought, his subordinates knew by experience that his sailor's instinct was quite alert: subconsciously his mind took note of the shadow of the main rigging across the deck, and of the feel of the breeze on his cheek, so that the slightest inattention on the part of the quartermaster at the wheel called forth a bitter rebuke from the captain—the more bitter in that he had been disturbed in this, the most important hour of his day. In the same way he was aware, without having taken special note, of all the salient facts of the prevailing conditions. On his awakening in his cot he had seen (without willing it) from the telltale compass in the deck over his head that the course was northeast, as it had been for the last three days. At the moment of his arrival on deck he had subconsciously noted that the wind was from the west, and just strong enough to give the ship steerage way, with all sail set to the royals, that the sky was of its perennial blue, and that the sea was almost flat calm, with a long peaceful swell over which the *Lydia* soared and swooped with profound regularity.

The first thing Captain Hornblower was aware of thinking was that the Pacific in the morning, deep blue overside and changing to silver towards the horizon, was like some heraldic blazon of argent and azure—and then he almost smiled to himself because that simile had come up in his mind every morning for the last fortnight. With the thought and the smile his mind was instantly working smoothly and rapidly. He looked down the gangways at the men at work holystoning the main deck; as he came forward, he could see another party engaged on the same task. They were talking in ordinary tones. Twice he heard a laugh. That was well. Men who could talk and laugh in that fashion were not likely to be plotting mutiny—and Captain Hornblower had had that possibility much in mind lately. Seven months at sea had almost consumed the ship's stores. A week ago he had cut the daily ration of water to three pints a day—hardly sufficient for men living on salt meat and biscuit in ten degrees north latitude, especially as water seven months in cask was half solid with green living things.

A week ago, too, the very last of the lemon juice had been served out, and there would be scurvy to reckon with within a month and no surgeon on board. Hankey, the surgeon, had died of drink off the Horn. For a month now tobacco had been doled out

300

in half ounces weekly—Hornblower congratulated himself on having taken the tobacco under his sole charge before the whole store was used up. He knew that the men were more concerned about the shortage of tobacco than about the shortage of fuel for the galley, which caused them each day to be given their salt pork only just brought to the boil in seawater. The shortage of tobacco, of water and of wood was nothing nearly as important, however, as the imminent shortage of grog. Not the finest crew in the world could be relied on if deprived of their ration of rum.

Hornblower, pacing the deck, looked sharply once more at the crew. Seven months at sea had given an admirable opportunity for training the gang of jailbirds and pressed men into seamen, but it was too long without distraction. And there was no other King's ship within two thousand miles of them. The sooner now that he could reach the coast of Nicaragua, the better. Hornblower's mind began to run back through his recent calculations of the ship's position. He was certain about his latitude, and last night's lunar observations had seemed to confirm the chronometer's indication of the longitude. Probably less than one hundred miles ahead, at most three hundred, lay the Pacific Coast of Central America.

At once Hornblower's mind shifted to the problem of how to spend the next day or two. The men must be kept busy. There was nothing like long idle days to breed mutiny—Hornblower never feared mutiny during the wild ten weeks of beating around the Horn. In the forenoon watch he would clear for action and practise the men at the guns, five rounds from each. The concussion might kill the wind for a space, but that could not be helped. It would be the last opportunity, perhaps, before the guns would be in action in earnest.

Five rounds from the guns would consume over a ton weight of powder and shot. The *Lydia* was riding light already and it was time that he paid attention to the trim of the ship again. After dinner he would do the job properly and give Bush a free hand in exercising the crew aloft. Today they might beat their previous record of twenty-four minutes seven seconds for setting all sail.

Hornblower suddenly became aware that the wind had increased a tiny amount, sufficient to call forth a faint whispering from the rigging. From the feel of it upon his neck and cheek he deduced it must have shifted aft a point, or perhaps two, and even as he began to wonder how soon Bush would take notice of it, he heard the call for the watch. Clay, the midshipman on the quarterdeck, was bellowing like a bull for the afterguard. That boy's voice had broken since they left England; he was learning to use it properly now, instead of alternately squeaking and croaking. Still without taking visual notice of what was going on, Hornblower listened to the familiar sounds as the watch came tumbling aft to the braces. A crack and a yelp told him that Harrison the boatswain had landed with his cane on the stern of some laggardly or unlucky sailor. Harrison was a fine seaman, but with a weakness for using his cane. Any man who filled his trousers out tight was likely to get a welt across the seat of them solely for that reason, and Hornblower's meditations regarding this weakness occupied all the time necessary for the trimming of the sails. Ting-ting, ting-ting, ting-ting, *ting* went the bell. Seven bells in the morning watch. Hornblower had been walking for well over his covenanted hour, and he was aware of a gratifying trickle of sweat under his shirt. He walked over to where Bush was standing by the wheel.

"Good morning, Mr. Bush," said Captain Hornblower.

"Good morning, sir," said Bush, exactly as if Captain Hornblower had not been within four yards of him for the last hour.

Hornblower, looking at the slate which bore the rough log of the last twenty-four hours, was aware of a keen scrutiny from his first lieutenant, and he knew that internally the lieutenant seethed with questions. He had sailed with sealed orders, and when he had opened and read them, in accordance with his instructions, in 30° N. 20° W., he had not seen fit to tell even his second in command what they contained.

"Ha-h'm," said Hornblower, clearing his throat noncommittally. Without a word he hung up the slate and went down the companion and entered his sleeping cabin.

It was unlucky for Bush that he should be kept in the dark in this fashion, but Hornblower had refrained from discussing his orders with him not through any fear of Bush's garrulity, but through fear of his own. When he had first sailed as captain five years ago he had allowed his natural talkativeness full play, and his first lieutenant had come to presume upon the license allowed him until Hornblower had been unable to give an order without having it discussed. Last commission he had tried to limit discussion within the ordinary bounds of politeness—but he was always opening his mouth and letting fall one word too many, to his subsequent regret. This voyage he had started with the firm resolve (like a drinker who cannot trust himself to drink only in moderation) to say nothing whatever to his officers except what was necessitated by routine, and his resolution had been hardened by the stress which his orders laid upon the need for extreme secrecy.

His sleeping cabin, bulkheaded off from his main cabin, was half occupied by an eighteen-pounder; the remainder was almost filled by his cot, his desk and his chest. His steward, Polwheal, who had been putting out a razor and lather bowl, squeezed himself against the desk to allow his captain to enter; he said nothing, for Polwheal was a man of gratifyingly few words.

Hornblower stripped off his shirt and trousers and shaved standing naked before a mirror on the bulkhead. The face he regarded in the glass was neither handsome nor ugly, neither old nor young. There was a pair of melancholy brown eyes, a high forehead, a straight nose, a good mouth set with all the firmness acquired during twenty years at sea. The tousled curly brown hair was just beginning to recede and leave the forehead a little higher still, which was a source of irritation to Captain Hornblower. Noticing it, he was reminded of his other trouble and glanced down his naked body. He was slender and well muscled; quite a prepossessing figure when he drew himself to his full six feet. But down there where his ribs ended there was no denying the presence of a rounded belly. Hornblower hated the thought of growing fat as much as he hated the thought of growing bald; it was the reason why he, an individual who hated routine, forced himself to take that regular morning walk on the quarterdeck.

When he had finished shaving he stood while Polwheal hung a

ragged serge dressing gown over his shoulders. Polwheal followed him along the deck to the head-pump, removed the dressing gown, and then pumped up seawater from overside while his captain solemnly rotated under the stream. When the bath was finished Polwheal hung the dressing gown again over his dripping shoulders and followed him back to the cabin. A clean linen shirt —worn, but neatly mended—and white trousers were laid out on the cot. Hornblower dressed himself, and Polwheal helped him into the worn blue coat with its faded lace, and handed him his hat. As he stepped out again on the quarterdeck, eight bells rang.

"Hands to punishment, sir?" asked Bush, touching his hat.

Hornblower nodded. The pipes of the boatswain's mates began to twitter.

"All hands to witness punishment," roared Harrison on the main deck, and from all parts of the ship men began to pour up and toe their lines in their allotted positions.

Hornblower stood rigid by the quarterdeck rail, setting his face like stone. He hated ordering punishment and dreaded witnessing it. But there had been no avoiding the punishment of this morning's victim. He was a Welshman called Owen who could never refrain from spitting on the decks. Bush had sworn that he would have him flogged for every offence, and Hornblower had necessarily to back up his officer in the name of discipline, although Hornblower had the gravest doubts as to whether a man who was fool enough not to be deterred by the fear of a flogging would benefit by receiving it.

Happily the business was got over quickly. Owen howled as the cat-o'-nine-tails bit into his shoulders until, at the end of his two dozen, someone soused him with water and he was hustled below.

"Hands to breakfast, Mr. Bush," snapped Hornblower, hoping that the tan of the tropics saved him from looking as white as he felt. The row of officers on the quarterdeck broke up. Gerard, the second lieutenant, took over the deck from Bush. The ship was like a magic tessellated pavement. It presented a geometrical pattern; someone shook it up into confusion, and at once it settled itself into a new and orderly fashion. Hornblower went below to where Polwheal had his breakfast awaiting him.

"Coffee, sir," said Polwheal. "Burgoo."

Hornblower sat down at table. After seven months' voyage, the coffee was a black extract of burnt bread, and the burgoo was a mess of unspeakable appearance compounded of biscuit crumbs and minced salt beef. Hornblower ate absentmindedly, tapping a biscuit on the table with his left hand so that the weevils would all be induced to have left it by the time he had finished his burgoo.

There were ship noises all around him as he ate. Every time the *Lydia* rolled and pitched a trifle as she reached the crest of the swell which was lifting her, the woodwork all creaked gently in unison. From overhead came the sound of Gerard's shod feet as he paced the quarterdeck. From forward came a monotonous clanking as the pumps were put to the daily task of pumping out the ship's bilges. But these noises were all transient and interrupted; there was one sound which went on so steadily that the ear grew accustomed to it and only noticed it when the attention was specially directed to it—the sound of the breeze in the innumerable ropes of the rigging. It was just the faintest singing, a harmony of a thousand high-pitched tones and overtones, but it could be heard in every part of the ship, transmitted from the chains through the timbers along with the slow, periodic creaking.

Hornblower finished his burgoo, and was turning his attention to the biscuit when a wild cry from above caused him to sit still with the biscuit halfway to his mouth.

"Land ho!" he heard. "Deck there! Land two points on the larboard bow, sir."

That was the lookout in the foretop hailing the deck. Hornblower, as he sat with his biscuit in midair, heard the excited rush and bustle on deck. He wanted passionately to rush out on deck himself, but he wanted still more to appear in the eyes of his officers and crew to be a man of complete self-confidence and imperturbability. He forced himself into an attitude of composure, crossing his knees and sipping his coffee in entire unconcern as Mr. Midshipman Savage knocked at the door and came bouncing in.

"Mr. Gerard sent me to tell you land's in sight on the larboard bow, sir," said Savage, hardly able to stand still in the prevailing infection of excitement. Hornblower made himself take another sip of coffee before he spoke.

"Tell Mr. Gerard I shall come on deck when I have finished my breakfast," he said calmly.

"Aye aye, sir." Savage bolted out of the cabin; his large clumsy feet clattered on the companion.

"Mr. Savage! Mr. Savage!" yelled Hornblower. Savage's large moonlike face reappeared in the doorway. "You forgot to close the door," said Hornblower, coldly. "And please don't make so much noise on the companionway."

"Aye aye, sir," said the crestfallen Savage.

Hornblower sipped again at his coffee, but found himself quite unable to eat his biscuit. He drummed with his fingers on the table in an effort to make the time pass more rapidly.

He heard young Clay bellowing from the masthead, where presumably Gerard had sent him with a glass.

"Looks like two burning mountains, sir. Volcanoes, sir."

Instantly Hornblower called up before his mind's eye his memory of the chart which he had so often studied in the privacy of this cabin. There were volcanoes all along this coast. And yet—and yet—the entrance to the Gulf of Fonseca would undoubtedly be marked by two to larboard. It was quite possible that he had made a perfect landfall. Hornblower could sit still no longer. Remembering just in time to go slowly and with an air of complete unconcern, he walked up on deck.

CHAPTER II

The quarterdeck was thronged with officers—Bush, Gerard, Galbraith and Rayner, the four lieutenants, Crystal the master, Simmonds of the marines, Wood the purser, the midshipmen of the watch. The rigging swarmed with petty officers and ratings, and every glass in the ship appeared to be in use.

"What's all this?" Hornblower snapped. "Has no one anything to do? Get the royals and stun-sails off her, Mr. Gerard."

The ship burst into activity again with the orders which Gerard called from the quarterdeck.

For the next hour, the *Lydia* rolled smoothly over the quartering swell under plain sail.

"I think I can see the smoke from the deck, sir, now," said Gerard, apologetically raising the subject of land again to his captain. He proffered his glass and pointed forward. Low on the horizon, greyish under a wisp of white cloud, Hornblower could see something which might be smoke.

"Ha-h'm," said Hornblower, as he had trained himself to say instead of something more conversational. He went forward and began to climb the weather foremast shrouds. He was nothing of an athlete, and disliked this task, but it had to be done—every idle eye on board was turned on him.

The hand-over-hand climb tried him severely; breathing heavily, he reached the fore-topgallant masthead, and settled himself to point the telescope as steadily as his heaving chest, sudden nervousness and the corkscrew roll of the ship would allow. Clay was sitting nonchalantly astride the yardarm fifteen feet away, but Hornblower ignored him.

It was a strange landscape which the telescope revealed to him. There were the sharp peaks of several volcanoes; two very tall ones to larboard. As he looked he saw a puff of grey steam emerge from a vent in the side of one peak, and ascend lazily to join the strip of white cloud which hung over it. Besides these cones there was a long mountain range of which the peaks appeared to be spurs—a chain of old volcanoes, truncated and weathered down by the passage of centuries. The upper parts of the peaks and of the mountains were a warm grey.

"I thought I saw breakers just then, sir," said Clay. Hornblower changed the direction of his gaze to the feet of the mountains.

Here there was a solid belt of green, unbroken save where lesser volcanoes jutted out from it. Hornblower swept his glass along it, along the very edge of the horizon. He thought he saw a tiny flash of white, sought for the place again, experienced a moment of doubt, and then saw it again—a speck of white which appeared and disappeared as he watched.

"Quite right. Those are breakers sure enough," he said.

The *Lydia* held her course steadily towards the coast. Looking down, Hornblower could see, over a hundred feet below, a bow wave which told him the ship must be making nearly four knots. They would be up with the shore long before nightfall. He eased his cramped position and stared landward again. As time went on his belief that he had made a perfect landfall grew stronger. Between the two tall volcanoes he could now see a wide bay with an island in the middle of the entrance. That was exactly how the Gulf of Fonseca appeared in the chart, but Hornblower was aware that no very great error in his navigation would have brought them anything up to two hundred miles from where he thought he was, and that on a coast like this, one section would appear very like another.

But his doubts were gradually set at rest. The bay opening before him was enormous—there could be no other of that size which could have escaped even Spanish cartographers, on whose maps the Admiralty charts were based. Hornblower estimated the width of the entrance at something over ten miles including the islands. Farther up the bay was a big island of a shape typical of the landscape—a steep circular cone rising sheer from the water. There could be no possible doubt now that after eleven weeks without sighting land the *Lydia* was heading straight into the Gulf of Fonseca—a most notable feat of navigation.

"Mr. Clay," he said, "you can go down now. Give Mr. Gerard my compliments and ask him please to send all hands to dinner."

"Aye aye, sir," said Clay.

The ship would know now that something out of the ordinary was imminent, with dinner advanced by half an hour. In British ships the officers were always careful to see that the men had full bellies before being called upon to exert themselves more than usual. Hornblower shut his telescope, descended to the deck, and walked with self-conscious slowness aft to the quarterdeck.

Crystal and Gerard were talking animatedly beside the rail. Obviously, as indicated by the way in which they looked towards Hornblower as he approached, they were talking about him. And it was only natural that they should be excited. What the

309

captain intended to do next was of intense importance to them.

The *Lydia*, the first British ship of war to penetrate into the Pacific coast of Spanish America in sixty years, was in waters furrowed by the famous Acapulco galleon which carried a million sterling in treasure on each of her annual trips, and along this coast crept the coasting ships bearing the silver of Potosí to Panama. It seemed as if the fortune of every man on board might be assured if only those unknown orders of the captain permitted it.

"Send a reliable man with a good glass to the fore-t'gallant masthead, Mr. Gerard," said Hornblower as he went below.

TEN MINUTES LATER, POLWHEAL brought dinner to his cabin. Hornblower sat down and ate rapidly, forcing himself to gulp down the distasteful mouthfuls of fat salt pork. Under Polwheal's avid gaze he rose and walked through, stooping his head under the low deck, to his sleeping cabin and unlocked his desk.

"Polwheal!" he called. "Get out my best coat and put the new epaulettes on it. Clean white trousers—no, the breeches and the silk stockings. And the sword with the gold hilt."

"Aye aye, sir," answered Polwheal.

Back in the main cabin Hornblower stretched himself on the locker below the stern window and once more unfolded his secret Admiralty orders. He almost knew them by heart, but it was prudent to make certain that he understood every word of them. The first paragraphs covered the voyage up to the present: the need for acting with the utmost possible secrecy so that no hint could reach Spain of the approach of a British frigate to her Pacific possessions.

"You are therefore prohibited from coming within sight of land in the Pacific until the moment of your arrival at the Gulf of Fonseca." He had obeyed these orders to the letter; he had brought his ship here all the way from England without seeing any land save for a glimpse of Cape Horn.

Hornblower concentrated now on the orders that followed. He was "requested and required" to form an alliance with Don Julian Alvarado, a large landowner with estates along the western shore of the Gulf of Fonseca. Don Julian intended, with the help of the

310

British, to rise in rebellion against the Spanish king who had thrown in his lot with Bonaparte. Hornblower was to hand over to him the five hundred muskets and bayonets, and the million rounds of small-arms ammunition which had been provided at Portsmouth, and he was to do everything which his discretion dictated to ensure the success of the rebellion. He was to succour the rebels to the utmost of his power, even to the extent of recognizing Don Julian's sovereignty over any territory that he might conquer, provided that in return Don Julian would enter into commercial treaties with His Britannic Majesty. The next ten paragraphs dealt in high-flown detail with the pressing necessity for opening Spanish possessions to British commerce.

It was only after all this was accomplished that the orders went on to give Captain Hornblower permission to attack the treasure ships to be found in the Pacific, and moreover no shipping was to be interfered with if doing so should give offence to those inhabitants who might otherwise be favourable to the rebellion. It was also noted that the Spaniards were believed to maintain in these waters a two-decked ship of fifty guns, by the name the *Natividad*, for the enforcement of the royal authority. Captain Hornblower was required to "take, sink, burn or destroy" this ship at the first opportunity.

Lastly, as soon as might be convenient, Captain Hornblower was to communicate with the rear admiral commanding the Leeward Islands station for further orders.

Captain Hornblower folded up the crackling paper and fell into contemplation. Those orders were the usual combination of the barely possible and the quite quixotic, which a captain on detached service might expect to receive. Only a landsman would have given those opening orders to sail to the Gulf of Fonseca without sighting other land in the Pacific—only a succession of miracles (Hornblower gave himself no credit for sound judgment and good seamanship) had permitted of their being carried out. Starting a rebellion in the Spanish American colonies had long been a dream of the British government—several British officers ordered to make it a reality had, during the last three years, all lost in honour and reputation. And to crown it was the casual mention of the presence of a fifty-gun ship of the enemy. It was typical of Whitehall to send a thirty-six gun frigate so lightly to attack an enemy of nearly double that force. The British navy had been so successful in single-ship duels that by now victory was expected of its ships against any odds.

Indeed, failure to capture the *Natividad*, failure to start a successful rebellion, failure to negotiate the commercial treaties— any one of these quite probable failures would mean that his career would be wrecked. On his return he would have to face Maria, his wife, condemned as a man inferior to his fellows.

Having contemplated these gloomy possibilities, Hornblower heaved himself off the locker and strode back to his sleeping cabin.

Ten minutes later he stepped up on the quarterdeck; he noted with sardonic amusement how his officers tried without success to appear not to notice his splendid dress and his gold-hilted sword ("a sword of the value of fifty guineas," the gift of the Patriotic Fund for Lieutenant Hornblower's part in the capture of the *Castilla* six years ago). He cast a glance at the fast-nearing shore. "Beat to quarters, Mr. Bush," he said. "Clear for action."

The roll of the drum set the ship into a wild fury. Urged on by the cries and blows of the petty officers, the crew flung themselves into the business of getting the ship ready for action. The decks were soused with water and strewn with sand; the fire parties took their places at the pumps; the boys ran breathless with cartridges for the guns; down below, the purser's steward who had been appointed acting surgeon was dragging together the midshipmen's chests in the cockpit to make an operating table.

"Have the guns loaded and run out, Mr. Bush," said Hornblower. That was only a sensible precaution to take, seeing that the ship was about to sail straight into Spanish territory. The gun crews cast off the frappings of the breeches, tugged desperately at the train tackles to draw the guns inboard, rammed home the powder and the shot, and ran the guns out through the opened ports.

"Ship cleared for action, sir," said Bush as the last rumble died away.

"Very good, Mr. Bush. Send a good man with the lead into the main chains, and make ready to anchor." The breeze off the sea was strengthening every minute now, and the *Lydia*'s speed was steadily increasing. With his glass Hornblower could see every detail of the entrance to the bay and the broad westerly channel between Conchaqüita Island and the westerly mainland which the chart assured him afforded twenty fathoms for five miles inland. But there was no trusting these Spanish charts. "What have you in the chains, there?" called Hornblower.

"No ground, sir, within a hundred fathoms."

A dead hush descended on the ship, save for the eternal harping of the rigging and the chatter of the water under the stern. The shore must be very steep-to, then, because they were within two miles of land now. But there was no purpose in risking running aground under full sail.

"Get the courses in," said Hornblower. "Keep that lead going in the chains, there." Under topsails alone the *Lydia* crept in towards land. Soon a cry from the chains announced that bottom had been reached in a hundred fathoms, and the depth diminished steadily at every cast. Hornblower went halfway up the mizzen rigging to get a better view; everyone else in the ship save for the man in the chains was standing rigid in the blinding heat. They were almost in the entrance channel now. Hornblower sighted some driftwood afloat on the near side, and training his glass on it, he saw that it was floating in up the bay. The tide was making, then; better and better—if he was going aground at all it would be far better to do so on the flow than on the ebb.

"By the deep nine," chanted the leadsman.

So much for the Spanish chart which indicated ten fathoms.

"And a half eight."

The channel was shoaling fast. They would have to anchor soon in this case. Hornblower's eyes searched the channel in an attempt to determine the line of deepest water.

"By the mark seven."

An order from Hornblower edged the *Lydia* towards the farther side.

"By the deep nine."

That was better. The *Lydia* was well up the bay now, creeping over the glassy water, with the leadsman chanting monotonously, and the steep conical mountain in the middle of the bay drawing nearer.

"Quarter less eight. By the mark seven," called the leadsman.

No useful object could be served in going in farther. "Let go the anchor," ordered Hornblower.

The cable roared through the hawsehole while the watch sprang to furl the topsails, and the *Lydia* swung round to wind and tide while Hornblower descended to the quarterdeck.

Bush blinked at him as at a miracle worker. How much was fluke and how much was calculation Bush could not guess, but Hornblower had not only brought the *Lydia* straight to her destination; he had arrived in the afternoon with the sea breeze and a flowing tide to bring him in, and if there were danger for them here, nightfall would soon bring them the ebb tide and the land breeze to take them out again.

"Keep the watch at quarters, Mr. Bush," said Hornblower. "Dismiss the watch below." With the ship a mile from any possible danger and cleared for action there was no need to keep every man at his station. The ship broke into a cheerful buzz. Hornblower was puzzled for a moment, wondering what to do next, but his mind was made up for him by a hail from the lookout.

"Deck there! Boat putting out from shore. Two points abaft the starboard beam."

A double speck of white was creeping out towards them; Hornblower's glass resolved it into an open boat under two tiny lateen sails, and as she drew nearer he could see that she was manned by half a dozen swarthy men wearing wide straw hats. She hove to fifty yards away, and someone stood up in the stern sheets and shouted across the water in Spanish, "Is that an English ship?"

"Yes. Come on board," replied Hornblower. Two years as a prisoner of Spain had given him the opportunity of learning the language—he had long before decided that it was merely on account of this accomplishment that he had been selected for this special service.

314

The boat ran alongside and the man who had hailed scrambled lightly up the ladder to the deck. He wore a sleeveless black waistcoat aflame with gold embroidery, beneath it a dirty white shirt, and on his legs dirty white trousers terminating raggedly just below the knees. His feet were bare, and in a red sash round his waist he carried two pistols and a short heavy sword. He did not look like a Spaniard; the black hair which hung over his ears was lustreless and lank; there was a tinge of red in his brown complexion and a tinge of yellow in the whites of his eyes. A long thin moustache drooped from his upper lip. His eyes at once picked out the captain, gorgeous in his best coat and cocked hat, and he advanced towards him.

"You are the captain, sir?" asked the visitor.

"Yes. Captain Horatio Hornblower of His Britannic Majesty's frigate *Lydia*, at your service. And whom have I the pleasure of welcoming?"

"Manuel Hernandez, lieutenant general of El Supremo."

"El Supremo?" asked Hornblower, puzzled. The name was a little difficult to render in English. Perhaps "The Almighty" might be the nearest translation. "It is not to El Supremo that I am ordered to address myself," he temporized.

Hernandez made a gesture of impatience. "Our lord El Supremo was known to men until lately as His Excellency Don Julian Maria de Jesús de Alvarado y Moctezuma," he said. "You were expected here four months back."

"Ah!" said Hornblower. "It is Don Julian that I want to see."

Hernandez was clearly annoyed by this casual mention of Don Julian. "El Supremo," he said, laying grave accent on the name, "has sent me to bring you into his presence."

"And where is he?"

"Surely it is enough, Captain, that you should know that El Supremo requires your attendance."

"Do you think so? I would have you know, señor, that a captain of one of His Britannic Majesty's ships is not accustomed to being at anyone's beck and call. You can go, if you like, and tell Don Julian so."

Hornblower's attitude indicated that the interview was at an

315

end. Hernandez went through an internal struggle, but the prospect of returning to El Supremo without bringing the captain with him was not alluring. "His house is there," he said sullenly, at last, pointing across the bay. "On the side of the mountain, behind the point."

"Then I shall come. Pardon me for a moment, General." Hornblower turned to Bush, who was standing by with the half-puzzled, half-admiring expression on his face so frequently to be seen when a man is listening to a fellow countryman talking fluently in an unknown language. "Mr. Bush," he said, "I am going ashore. If I am not back by midnight, you are to read the government's secret orders to me, and to act on them as you think proper."

"Aye aye, sir," said Bush. There was anxiety in his face. "We'll bring you off, sir, safe and sound, if there is any hanky-panky."

"You'll see after the safety of the ship first," snapped Hornblower.

Then he turned to Hernandez. "I am at your service, señor."

CHAPTER III

The boat ran softly aground on a beach of golden sand round the point. The swarthy crew sprang out and hauled her up so that Hornblower and Hernández could step ashore dryshod. Hornblower looked keenly about him. A town, consisting of a few hundred houses of palmetto leaves, came down to the edge of the sand. Hernandez led the way towards it.

"*Agua, agua,*" croaked a voice as they approached. "Water, for the love of God, water."

A man was bound upright to a six-foot stake beside the path. His eyes were protruding from his head and it seemed as if his tongue were too big for his mouth. A circle of vultures crouched and fluttered round him.

"Who is that?" asked Hornblower, shocked.

"A man whom El Supremo has ordered to die for want of water," said Hernandez. "He is one of the unenlightened."

316

Hornblower resisted the temptation to ask what constituted enlightenment; from the fact that Alvarado had adopted the name of El Supremo he could fairly well guess.

Little miry lanes, filthy and stinking, wound between the palmetto huts. Vultures perched on the roof ridges and squabbled with the mongrel dogs in the lanes. The Indian population were all brown with a tinge of red, like Hernandez himself; the children ran naked, the women were dressed either in black or in dirty white; the few men to be seen wore only short white trousers and were naked from the waist up. Half the houses appeared to be shops, displaying for sale a few handfuls of fruits, or three or four eggs.

Tethered in the little square in the centre of the town some diminutive horses warred with the flies. Hernandez' escort made haste to untether two of them and stood at their heads for them to mount. Hornblower swung up into the saddle and trotted alongside Hernandez, bumping awkwardly. He was not a good horseman. The sweat ran down his face, and every few seconds he had to reach up hurriedly and adjust his cocked hat. A path wound steeply up the hillside out of the town, only wide enough for one horseman at a time, so that Hernandez, with a courteous gesture, preceded him. The escort clattered along fifty yards behind.

The narrow path was stifling hot, hemmed by trees and bush on either hand. Insects buzzed round them, biting viciously. Half a mile up the path some lounging sentries came awkwardly to attention, and beyond this point there were other men to be seen —men like the first one Hornblower had encountered, bound to stakes and dying of thirst. There were dead men, too—stinking masses of corruption with a cloud of flies which buzzed more wildly as the horses brushed by them.

At last the path rose over a shoulder of the mountain, and the forest at each side changed as if by magic into cultivated land with orange groves, and trees laden with fruit. The sun, sinking fast to the horizon, illuminated the golden fruit, and then, as they turned a corner, shone full on a vast white building, stretching low and wide before them.

"The house of El Supremo," said Hernandez.

In the patio servants came and took their horses, while Hornblower stiffly dismounted and contemplated the ruin which riding had caused to his best silk stockings. The superior servants who conducted them into the house were dressed in clothes similar in their blend of rags and finery to those Hernandez wore. The most gorgeous of all, whose features seemed to indicate a strong dash of Negro blood along with the Indian, came up with a worried look on his face. "El Supremo has been kept waiting," he said. "Please come this way as quickly as you can."

He almost ran before them down a corridor to a door studded with brass. On this he knocked loudly, waited a moment, and then threw open the door, bending himself double as he did so. Hornblower, at Hernandez' gesture, strode into the room, Hernandez behind him, and the majordomo closed the door. It was a long room, lime-washed to a glittering white, whose ceiling was supported by thick wooden beams, painted and carved. Towards the farther end stood a solitary treble dais, and in a canopied chair on the dais sat the man Hornblower had been sent half round the world to see. He was small and swarthy, restless and fidgety, with piercing black eyes and lank black hair turning grey. From his appearance one might have guessed at only a small admixture of Indian blood in his European ancestry, and he was dressed in European fashion, in a red coat laced with gold, a white stock, and white breeches and stockings; there were gold buckles on his shoes. He turned his piercing eyes upon Hornblower, who bowed stiffly.

"Captain Horatio Hornblower, of His Britannic Majesty's frigate *Lydia*, at your service, sir," Hornblower said.

"You have brought me arms and powder?" snapped Alvarado.

"They are in the ship."

"That is well. You will make arrangements with General Hernandez here for landing them."

Hornblower thought of his frigate's almost empty storerooms; and he had three hundred and eighty men to feed. Like every other ship's captain, he would be restless and uncomfortable until the *Lydia* was fully charged again with food and water and wood and every other necessary sufficient to take her back round the

Horn at least as far as the West Indies or St. Helena, if not home.

"I can hand nothing over, sir, until my ship's needs are satisfied," he said. He heard Hernandez drawing his breath sharply at this sacrilegious temporizing in the face of orders from El Supremo. But the latter realized the folly of quarrelling with his new ally.

"Certainly," he said. "Please make known to General Hernandez what you require."

Hornblower had had dealings with officers of the Spanish services, and knew what they could accomplish in the way of fair promises not carried out, and procrastination and double-dealing. He guessed that Spanish-American rebel officers would be even less trustworthy. He decided to make known his wants now, so that there might be a fair chance of seeing at least a part of his demands satisfied in the near future.

"My water casks must be refilled tomorrow," he said.

Hernandez nodded. "There is a spring close to where we landed. If you wish, I will have men to help you."

"Thank you, but that will not be necessary. My ship's crew will attend to it. Besides water I need—" and Hornblower proceeded to detail all the multifarious wants of a frigate seven months at sea.

Hernandez' face grew longer and longer during this formidable recital.

"Two hundred bullocks!" he said at last. "Five hundred pigs?"

"That is what I said," replied Hornblower, inexorably, the mildest of men except in matters regarding his ship. "Two hundred *fat* bullocks."

At this point El Supremo intervened. "See that the captain's wants are satisfied," he said, with an impatient wave of his hand. "Start now."

Hernandez promptly retired. The big brass-bound door closed silently behind him.

"That is the only way to deal with these people," said El Supremo, lightly. "They are no better than beasts. Doubtless you saw on your way here various criminals suffering punishment?"

"I did."

"They were incapable of absorbing even the simplest of conceptions. They could not understand the obvious principle that the blood of Alvarado and Moctezuma must be divine."

"Indeed?" said Hornblower.

"One of my earliest lieutenants could not shake himself free from the influence of early education. When I announced my divinity he was unable to realize that it was not a matter of opinion but a matter of fact. He was of course one of the first to die of thirst."

Hornblower was utterly bewildered by all this. But he clung to the fact that he had to ally himself to this madman. The revictualling of the *Lydia* depended upon it, and that was of primary importance.

"Your King George must have been delighted to hear that I had decided to act in concert with him," continued El Supremo.

"He charged me with messages to you assuring you of his friendship," said Hornblower cautiously.

"Of course," said El Supremo. His brows approached each other a trifle. "I suppose you are aware," he said, "of the history of the family of Alvarado? You know who was the first of that name to reach this country?"

"He was Cortez' lieutenant—" began Hornblower.

"Lieutenant? Nothing of the sort. I am surprised that you should believe such lies. He was the leader of the Conquistadores. Alvarado conquered Mexico, and all this coast as far as the Isthmus. He married the daughter of Moctezuma, the last of the divine emperors; and I am a direct descendant from that union. And now, Captain Hornblower, we had better discuss the plans for the extension of my Empire."

"As you please," said Hornblower.

"The King of Spain," said El Supremo, "maintains in this country an official who calls himself Captain General of Nicaragua. I sent to this gentleman some time ago a message ordering him to announce his fealty to me. He was misguided enough to hang my messenger publicly in Managua. Most of the men whom he subsequently sent to secure my divine person were killed, while a few were fortunate enough to see the light and are

320

now included in my army. The Captain General is now, I hear, at the head of an army of three hundred men in the city of San Salvador. When you have landed the weapons consigned to me I propose to burn this town, along with the Captain General and the unenlightened among his men. Perhaps, Captain, you will accompany me?"

"My ship must be revictualled first," said Hornblower.

"I have given the orders for that," replied El Supremo with a trace of impatience.

"And further," continued Hornblower, "it will be my duty first to ascertain the whereabouts of the Spanish ship of war *Natividad*. Before I can engage in any land operations I must either capture her or know for certain that she is too distant to interfere with my ship."

"Then you had better capture her, Captain. From information I have received she will be sailing into this bay at any moment."

"Then I must go back to my ship immediately," said Hornblower, all agitation. What would the lords of the Admiralty say if the *Lydia* were lost while her captain was on shore?

"There is food being brought in. Behold," said El Supremo. The door at the end of the hall was flung open as he spoke. Attendants began to walk slowly in, carrying a large table covered with silver dishes, and bearing four large silver candelabra.

"Your pardon, but I must not wait for food," said Hornblower.

"As you will," said El Supremo indifferently. "Alfonso!" The negroid majordomo came forward, bowing. "See that Captain Hornblower goes back to his ship."

El Supremo then relapsed into an attitude of contemplation. The bustle attendant upon the bringing in of the banquet he allowed to pass unheeded as he gazed blankly over Hornblower's head.

"This way, señor," said Alfonso, at Hornblower's elbow.

Hornblower followed the majordomo out to the patio, where two men and three horses awaited him. Without a word he swung himself up into the saddle. The escort clattered before him out through the gates, and down to the boat that waited by the shore. Night was now falling and the volcanoes flickered round the bay.

On board the *Lydia* the pipes of the boatswain's mates twittered in chorus; the marines brought their muskets to the present, and Bush was at the gangway to receive him with all the pomp and ceremony due to a captain returning on board.

Hornblower saw, by the lantern light, the relief in Bush's honest face. He glanced round the decks. Bush had very properly maintained all precautions for action.

"Very good, Mr. Bush," said Hornblower. Then he became conscious that not only were his best silk stockings in threads about his calves but his white breeches were stained by the dirty saddle. He felt ashamed that he had come back to his ship in this undignified fashion, and without, as far as he knew, having settled anything for the future. He took refuge, as ever, in uncommunicativeness. "Ha-h'm," he rasped. "Call me if there is anything unusual."

With that he turned and went below to his cabin.

CHAPTER IV

Hornblower felt a new strength running through his veins when he awoke the next day. He decided to fill the water casks and restock with galley fuel at once, and his first orders sent parties of men hurriedly to the tackles to hoist out the launch and lower the quarter boats. Soon they were off for the shore, manned by crews of excited chattering men. In the bows of each boat sat two marines in their red coats with their muskets loaded and bayonets fixed, and in their ears echoing their final orders, to the effect that if a single sailor succeeded in deserting while on shore every man among them would have his back well scratched with the cat.

An hour later the launch came back under sail, deep laden with her water casks full, and while the casks were being swayed out of her Mr. Midshipman Hooker came running up to Hornblower and touched his hat.

"The beef cattle and other supplies are coming down to the shore, sir," he said.

Hornblower had to struggle hard to receive the news as if he expected it. "How many?" he snapped; and the answer was more surprising still.

"Hundreds, sir. There's a Spaniard in charge with a lot to say, but there's no one ashore who can speak his lingo."

"Send him out to me when you go ashore again," said Hornblower.

It was Hernandez who came out to him in the same boat with the two tiny lateen sails in which Hornblower had been ferried across last night. They exchanged salutes on the quarterdeck.

"There are two hundred cattle awaiting your orders, Captain," said Hernandez. "I am afraid it will take longer to assemble the pigs. My men are sweeping the country for them, but pigs are slow animals to drive."

"Yes," said Hornblower.

"The women are out collecting the lemons, oranges and limes. But I am afraid it will be two days before we have them all ready."

"Ha-h'm," said Hornblower.

"The sugar is ready at El Supremo's mill, however. And with regard to the tobacco, señor, there is a good deal in store."

"Ha-h'm," said Hornblower again, suppressing just in time the cry of delight that nearly escaped him at the mention of tobacco.

"The coffee, the vegetables and the eggs will be easy to supply. But with regard to the bread— "

"Well?"

"There is a little wheat grown in the *tierra templeda*, your Excellency, but it rests still in the hands of the unenlightened. Would maize flour suffice?"

Hernandez' face was working with anxiety as he gazed at Hornblower. It was only then that Hornblower realized that Hernandez was in terror of his life, and that El Supremo's lighthearted endorsement of the requisitions he had made was far more potent than any stamped and sealed order addressed to a Spanish official. And then suddenly Hornblower remembered something he had forgotten to ask for, something far more important than the difference between maize flour and wheat.

"Very well," he said. "I will agree to use maize flour, but are there ardent spirits to be had here?"

"The people on this coast drink an ardent spirit with which you are perhaps not acquainted, your Excellency. It is distilled from the waste of the sugar mills, from the treacle."

"Rum, by God!" exclaimed Hornblower.

"Yes, señor, rum. Would that be of any use to your Excellency?"

"I will accept it in lieu of anything better," said Hornblower sternly. His heart was leaping with joy. It would appear like a miracle to his officers that he should conjure rum and tobacco from this volcano-riddled coast.

"Thank you, Captain, and shall we begin to slaughter the cattle now?"

"Very well," said Hornblower.

For the next two days the *Lydia's* boats plied back and forth between the beach and the ship. They came back piled high with joints of meat; the sand of the shore ran red with the blood of the slaughtered animals. On board the ship the purser and his crew toiled like slaves in the roasting heat, cramming the brine barrels with the meat and tugging them into position in the storerooms. Sacks of flour, casks of rum, bales of tobacco—the hands at the tackles sweated as they swayed these up from the boats. The *Lydia* was gorging herself full.

So obvious were the good intentions of those on shore that Hornblower was able to order that the boats which bore the victuals to the ship should return laden with cases of muskets and kegs of powder and shot. Hornblower had his gig hoisted out, and was rowed periodically round his ship inspecting her trim, in the anticipation that at any moment he might have to hoist up his anchor and beat out to sea to fight the *Natividad*.

He drove his men to work until they dropped. There was no time for enjoyment of the pleasures of land at the moment. The shore party did indeed cook their rations before a huge bonfire, and revel in roast fresh meat after seven months of boiled salt meat. But, with the characteristic contrariness of British sailors, they turned with revulsion from the delicious fruit which was offered them—bananas and papaws, pineapples and guavas, and considered themselves the victims of sharp practice because these were substituted for their regulation ration of boiled dried peas.

324

And then, late on the second afternoon, as Hornblower was on the beach conferring with Hernandez, and revelling secretly in the thought that he was free of the land if necessary for another six months, a horseman came galloping down the beach at full speed, waving his wide straw hat. Breathlessly this new arrival announced his news.

"A ship—a ship coming!"

He was so excited that he lapsed into the Indian speech, and Hornblower could not understand his further explanations. Hernandez had to interpret for him. "This man has been keeping watch on the top of the mountain up there," he said. "He says that he has often seen the *Natividad* before, and he is sure this is the same ship, and she is undoubtedly coming into this bay."

"How far off is she?" asked Hornblower.

Hernandez translated. "A long way, seven leagues or more," he said. "She is coming from the south-eastward."

Hornblower pulled at his chin, deep in thought. "She'll carry the sea breeze with her until sunset," he muttered to himself, and glanced up at the sun. "That will be another hour. An hour after that she'll get the land breeze. She could be here by midnight."

A stream of plans and ideas was flooding into his mind. Against the possibility of the ship's arrival in the dark must be balanced the Spanish habit at sea of snugging down for the night, and of attempting no complicated piece of seamanship save under the best possible conditions.

"Has the *Natividad* often come into this bay?" he asked.

"Yes, Captain, often," said Hernandez.

"Ha-h'm," said Hornblower, and tugged at his chin again. He had fought in ten single-ship actions. If he took the *Lydia* to sea and engaged the *Natividad* on open water the two ships might well batter each other into wrecks. At the best the *Lydia* would have a good many casualties, and she would expend much of her priceless ammunition. On the other hand, if he stayed in the bay and yet the plan he had in mind did not succeed—if the *Natividad* waited offshore until the morning—he would have to beat his way out of the bay against the sea breeze, presenting the Spaniards with every possible advantage as he came out to fight them. The

Natividad's superiority of force was already such that it was rash to oppose the *Lydia* to her. Could he dare to risk increasing the odds? But the possible gains were so enormous that by the time he had returned on board he had made up his mind to run the risk.

GHOSTLIKE IN THE MOONLIGHT, the *Lydia* glided across the bay. Hornblower had not ventured to hoist sail, lest a gleam of canvas might be visible to the distant ship at sea. The launch and the cutter towed the ship to the foot of the island at the entrance of the bay—Meanguera Island, Hernandez called it when Hornblower had cautiously sketched out his plan to him—and the anchor splashed into the deep water.

"Have that cable ready to slip, Mr. Bush," said Hornblower. "And call the boats alongside. I want the men to rest."

"Aye aye, sir."

"Masthead, there? What can you see of the enemy?"

"She's just come up over the island, sir. She ought to make the bay on this tack."

"Ha-h'm," said Hornblower. "Mr. Gerard, you have charge of the deck. I want Mr. Bush and Mr. Galbraith to come below with me."

"Aye aye, sir."

The ship was seething quietly with excitement. Everyone on board had guessed the captain's plan, even though the details of its execution, which he was now explaining to his lieutenants, were still unknown. In the two hours which had elapsed since the arrival of the news of the *Natividad's* approach, Hornblower's mind had worked busily at the perfection of his plan. Nothing must go wrong.

"That is all understood?" he asked finally; he stood, stooping under the deck beams in his screened-off cabin while his lieutenants fiddled awkwardly with their hats.

"Aye aye, sir."

"Very good," said Hornblower, dismissing them.

It would be nearly four hours before the *Natividad* reached the entrance, and before he could take any further action. Within five minutes he found himself pacing, stoop-shouldered, up and down

326

the tiny limits of his cabin, and checked himself furiously. Even though his professional reputation was to be at stake in four hours' time, he must show the ship that he could face uncertainty with indifference.

He called for Polwheal; and when Polwheal appeared he instructed him, "My compliments to Mr. Bush, and tell him that if he can spare Mr. Galbraith and Mr. Clay and Mr. Savage I would be glad if they would sup with me and have a hand of whist."

When Galbraith and the two midshipmen arrived, Hornblower compelled himself to play the part of the courtly host, while every word he uttered was designed to increase his reputation for imperturbability. He apologized for the shortcomings of the supper—the ship being cleared for action involved the extinction of all fires and the consequent necessity for serving cold food. But the sight of the cold roast chickens and pork, the golden cakes of maize, the dishes of fruit, roused Mr. Midshipman Savage's sixteen-year-old appetite and caused him to forget his embarrassment.

"This is better than rats, sir," he said, rubbing his hands.

"Rats?" asked Hornblower, vaguely. For all his appearance his thoughts were up on deck, and not in the cabin.

"Yes, sir. Until we made this harbour, rats had become a favourite dish in the midshipmen's berth."

"That they had," echoed Clay, carving himself substantial slices of cold pork and crackling. "I was paying that thief Bailey three-pence apiece for prime rats."

Desperately Hornblower jerked his mind away from the approaching *Natividad* and delved into the past when he had been a half-starved, homesick midshipman, and his seniors had eaten rats with gusto. He had never been able to stomach them himself, but he would not admit it to these boys.

"Threepence apiece seems a trifle dear," he said. "I can't remember paying as much as that when I was a midshipman."

"Why, sir, did you ever eat them?" asked Savage, amazed.

In reply to this direct question Hornblower could only lie. "Of course," he said. "I always maintained that a rat who had had the run of the bread locker made a dish fit for a king, let alone a midshipman."

"God bless my soul!" gasped Clay, laying down his knife and fork. The two boys blinked at their captain with admiration. This little human touch had won their hearts completely, as Hornblower had known it would. Now Hornblower had to make Galbraith feel at home, too.

"A glass of Madeira with you, Mr. Galbraith," he said, raising his glass. "I must apologize because this is not my best, but I am keeping my last two bottles for when I entertain the Spanish captain as our prisoner tomorrow. To our victories of the future!"

The glasses were drained, and constraint dwindled. Hornblower had spoken of "*our* prisoner" when most captains would have said "*my* prisoner". And he had said "our victories". Any one of the three junior officers would at that moment have laid down his life for this otherwise strict, stern captain—and Hornblower, looking round at their flushed faces, was aware of it and gratified.

Another midshipman, young Knyvett, came into the cabin. "Mr. Bush's compliments, sir, and the enemy is visible hull up from the masthead, sir. He says two hours ought to see her within range."

"Thank you, Mr. Knyvett," said Hornblower, dismissing him. The reminder that in two hours he would be at grips with a fifty-gun ship set his heart beating faster again. It took a convulsive effort to maintain an unmoved countenance. "We still have ample time for our rubber, gentlemen," he said.

Hornblower himself was a keen, good whist player; his close observation and his acute study of the psychology of his juniors were of great help to him. But to his officers without card sense— especially the midshipmen—Hornblower's card evenings were torment.

Polwheal cleared the table, spread the green tablecloth and brought the cards. One rubber ended quickly; there was almost dismay on the faces of the other three as Hornblower proffered the cards for cutting for a second one. He kept his face expressionless.

"You really must remember, Clay," he said, "to lead the king from a sequence of king, queen, knave. The whole art of leading is based upon that principle."

328

"Aye aye, sir," said Clay, rolling his eyes drolly at Savage, but Hornblower looked up sharply and Clay hurriedly composed his expression. Play continued—and to all of them seemed interminable. It came to an end at last, however.

"Rubber," announced Hornblower, marking up the score. "I think, gentlemen, that it is almost time that we went on deck." There was a general sigh of relief and a scraping of feet on the deck. But, "The rubber would not be over," Hornblower said dryly, "if Mr. Savage had paid attention to the score. I grant that if his finesse had been successful he would have won two more tricks, but—"

Hornblower droned on, while the others writhed in their chairs. Yet they glanced at each other with admiration for him in their eyes as at last he preceded them up the companion ladder.

Up on deck everything was deathly still as the crew lay at their posts. Bush touched his hat to the captain. "The enemy is still heading for the bay, sir," he said hoarsely.

"Send the crews into the launch and cutter again, with Mr. Gerard," replied Hornblower. He climbed the mizzen rigging to the mizzen topgallant yard. From here he could just see over the island; a mile away, with the moon setting behind her, he could see the *Natividad* close hauled across the entrance. There was small chance of her noticing, against the dark sky, the topgallant masts of the *Lydia*; and it was on the assumption that she would not that all his plans were based. She must go about soon, and her new course would bring her directly to the island. She would have to go about again to enter the bay, and that would be his opportunity. As he watched, he saw her canvas gleam brighter for a space and then darken again as she came round. He went down to the deck.

"Mr. Bush," he said, "send the hands aloft ready to set sail." The ship was filled with gentle noises as bare feet padded over the deck and up the rigging. Hornblower brought the silver whistle out of his pocket. "I am going for'ard, now, Mr. Bush," he said. "I shall try and get back to the quarterdeck in time, but you know my orders if I do not."

Hornblower hurried forward along the gangway, past the

329

forecastle carronades with their crews crouching round them, and swung himself over onto the bowsprit. From the spritsail yard he could see round the corner of the island; the *Natividad*, a glimmer of phosphorescent foam about her cutwater, was heading straight for him. All his excitement had vanished and his mind was making cool calculations of time and space. The Spaniard was coming very close. Now he could hear the babble of the Spanish crew. Then he heard orders being shouted; the *Natividad* was going about. He put the whistle to his lips and blew, and the whole of the *Lydia* sprang into activity. Sail was loosed from every yard simultaneously. The cable was slipped, the boats were cast off. Hornblower raced aft to the wheel as the *Lydia* gathered way and surged forward.

"Steady!" he called to the quartermaster. "Port a little! A little more! Now, hard a-starboard!"

So quickly had it all happened that the Spaniard had only just gone about and had gathered no way on her new course when the *Lydia* came leaping upon her out of the blackness behind the island and rasped alongside. Months of drill bore their fruit in the English ship. The guns crashed out in a single shattering broadside as the ships touched, sweeping the deck of the *Natividad* with grape. Overhead the topmen ran out along the yards and lashed the ships together. On deck the cheering boarders came rushing to the portside gangway.

On board the Spaniard there was utter surprise. One moment all hands had been engrossed with the work of the ship, and the next, the night had been torn to shreds with the flare of hostile guns, and now an armed, yelling host came pouring onto the deck. Hornblower had foreseen that the moral effect of a surprise attack would be intensified if the attackers made as much noise as possible. Not the most disciplined and experienced crew could have withstood the shock of that surprise. During the twenty years the *Natividad* had sailed the Pacific coast no enemy had been nearer to her than four thousand miles of sea.

Yet even then there were some stout hearts who attempted resistance. There were officers who drew their swords; on the high quarterdeck there was a detachment who had been served out with weapons in consequence of the rumours of rebellion on shore;

there were a few men who grasped capstan bars and belaying pins; but the upper deck was swept clear immediately by the wave of boarders with their pikes and cutlasses.

And on the lower deck the men sought blindly for leaders, for means of resistance. They were gathering together in the darkness ready to oppose the enemy above them when suddenly a new yelling burst out behind them. Gerard's two boats' crews had reached the *Natividad*'s port side, and prising open the lower deck ports, came swarming in, yelling like fiends as their orders bid them do. At this new surprise the resistance of the lower deck broke down completely.

CHAPTER V

Captain Hornblower was taking his usual morning walk on the quarterdeck of his ship. Half a dozen Spanish officers had attempted, on his first appearance, to greet him with formal courtesy, but they had been hustled away by the *Lydia*'s crew, indignant that their captain's walk should be disturbed by mere prisoners.

The captain had a good deal to think about, too—so much, in fact, that he could spare no time to rejoice in the knowledge that his frigate last night, in capturing a two-decker without losing a man, had accomplished a feat without precedent in British naval history. He wanted instead to think about his next move. With the capture of the *Natividad* he was lord of the South Sea. He knew that communications by land were so difficult that the whole trade—the whole life of the country—depended upon the coastwise traffic; and now not a boat could move without his licence. There was at least a chance now that with Alvarado's aid he might set the whole of Central America into such a flame that the Spanish government would rue the day when they had decided to throw in their lot with Bonaparte.

Then, with the prime part of his mission thus accomplished, there would be the other possibilities. The capture of the famed Acapulco galleon would at a stroke make him a wealthy man—

331

he could buy an estate in England then; could buy a whole village and be a squire, with the countryfolk touching their hats to him as he drove by in his coach. Maria would like that.

Hornblower tore his mind away from the contemplation of Maria snatched from her Southsea lodgings and settled in a country home. Forward, Sullivan, a red-haired Irish vagabond, was perched on a carronade slide with his fiddle; and round him a dozen sailors, their horny feet flapping on the deck, were setting to partners. Twenty-five guineas apiece, at least, the men would get as their share of the prize money for the capture of the *Natividad*, and they were already spending it in imagination.

He looked across to where the *Natividad* swung at anchor. Her waist was black with her crew. On her old-fashioned poop and quarterdeck he could see the red coats of his marines, and the carronades pointing down into the waist. Gerard, whom he had left on board as prize master, had served in a Liverpool slaver and knew well how to keep a ship full of hostile humanity in subjection. But Hornblower knew that soon he must make up his mind about what to do with the *Natividad*, and more especially with his prisoners.

He paced moodily up and down the deck until Midshipman Knyvett barred his way, touching his hat. "What the devil is it now?" snapped Hornblower.

"Boat alongside, sir. General Hernandez on board."

"Very good," said Hornblower, and went down the gangway to greet Hernandez as he came up the side.

Hernandez wasted no time on felicitations for the late victory. "El Supremo wishes to see you at once, Captain," said Hernandez. "My boat is waiting."

Dozens of captains in the British service would be infuriated at such a cavalier message, but Hornblower knew that it would be foolish to imperil his cordial relations with the shore. "Certainly," he said. "My duties leave me free at the moment." At least there was no need to dress up for this occasion. The capture of the *Natividad* was a clearer proof of his *bona fides* than any gold-hilted sword.

After giving final orders to Bush, Hornblower went ashore and mounted the horse which awaited him there, then rode along the avenue of dead men, up to El Supremo's house.

The appearance of El Supremo, sitting in his canopied chair on his dais, seemed for all the world to indicate that he had been sitting there, immobile, since the occasion four days ago when Hornblower had left him. "So you have already done what I wished you to do, Captain?" were his opening words.

"I captured the *Natividad* last night," said Hornblower.

"Then," said El Supremo, "you have done what I wanted." In the face of such sublime self-assurance there was no point in arguing. "This afternoon," he continued, "I shall proceed with my plan for the capture of San Salvador and the Captain General of Nicaragua. There are fewer difficulties before me now, Captain. The roads between here and San Salvador are not good. At one place the path goes up one hundred and twenty-seven steps cut in the lava between two precipices. It is difficult for a horse to make the journey, and an evilly disposed person armed with a musket could cause much trouble."

"I expect he could," said Hornblower.

"However," said El Supremo, "San Salvador lies less than ten miles from the sea, and there is a good road from the city to its port of La Libertad. This afternoon I shall sail with five hundred men in the two ships to La Libertad. Tomorrow evening I shall dine in San Salvador. By the way, you killed very few of the crew of the *Natividad*, Captain?"

"Eleven killed," said Hornblower. "And eighteen wounded."

"So you left enough to work the ship?"

"Ample, señor, if—"

"That is what I wanted. And, Captain, in addressing me do not use the expression 'señor'. I am El Supremo." Hornblower could only bow in reply. El Supremo's manner was like a stone wall. "The navigating officers are still alive?" he went on.

"Yes," said Hornblower; and, because he was anxious to keep trouble to a minimum, added with a gulp, "Supremo."

"Then," said El Supremo, "I will take the *Natividad* into my service. I will kill the senior officers and replace them with men of my own. The others and the common sailors will serve me."

There was nothing intrinsically impossible in what El Supremo suggested; Hornblower knew from experience that the Spanish Navy, old-fashioned as always, maintained a rigid distinction between the officers who worked the ship and the gentlemen who commanded it. And Hornblower had no doubt whatever as to what choice the seamen would make if asked to choose between death by torture and serving El Supremo. Nor could it be denied that to transport five hundred men in the *Lydia* alone would be difficult, to say the least, while the *Lydia* by herself would find it impossible to blockade completely all the thousand miles of coast—two ships would cause far more than twice as much trouble to the enemy in that way. Yet to hand over the *Natividad* meant starting an endless and probably unsuccessful argument with the lords of the Admiralty on the question of prize money. And he could not in honour hand over the Spanish officers to the death El Supremo had in mind for them. He had to think quickly.

"The *Natividad* is the prize of my King," he said. "Perhaps he would not be pleased if I let her go."

"He certainly would be displeased if he knew you had offended *me*," said El Supremo.

Hornblower was still thinking hurriedly. A little more opposition might cause this madman to order him out for execution, and if her captain were killed the *Lydia* would probably never reach home again. England would lose a fine frigate and a fine opportunity. He must sacrifice his men's prize money; he too would lose his share of it, the thousand pounds or so with which he had hoped to dazzle Maria. But at all costs he must keep his prisoners alive.

"The ship is yours, Supremo," he said; "she has been yours since my men first set foot on her deck last night."

El Supremo nodded, and then turned to Hernandez. "General," he said, "make arrangments for five hundred men to go on board the ships at noon. I will sail with them and so will you."

Hernandez bowed and departed. Hornblower made his next move at once. "Is the *Lydia*," he asked, "to have the honour of carrying El Supremo to La Libertad? My crew would greatly appreciate the distinction."

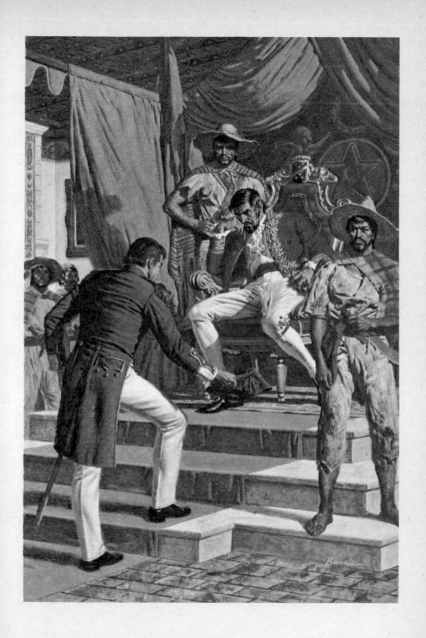

El Supremo considered for a moment. "Yes," he said, and Hornblower had to suppress the sigh of relief he was on the point of drawing. Once El Supremo was on board the *Lydia* it might be possible to deal with him with less difficulty.

El Supremo clapped his hands, and instantly a knocking at the brass-studded door heralded the arrival of the swarthy majordomo. He received in a single sentence orders for the transfer of El Supremo's household to the *Lydia*.

"Perhaps," said Hornblower, "you will permit me to return to my ship now to make arrangements for your reception, Supremo." He received another nod in reply. "At what time shall I be at the beach to receive you?"

"At midday."

On his return to the *Lydia*, the moment the twittering of the pipes had died away, Hornblower was giving his orders. "Have these men taken below at once," he said to Bush, pointing to the Spanish officers. "Put them in the cable tier under guard."

Bush made no attempt to conceal his surprise, but Hornblower wasted no time in explanations. "Señores," he said, as the prisoners came by him. "You are going to be harshly treated. But, believe me, if you are as much as seen during the next few days you will be killed. I am saving your lives."

Next Hornblower turned back to his first lieutenant. "Call all hands, Mr. Bush."

The ship was filled with the sound of horny feet pattering over pine boards.

"Men!" said Hornblower. "There is coming aboard today a prince of this country who is in alliance with our own gracious King. He is to be treated with respect. Every man will behave towards Señor El Supremo as he would to me. We shall be sailing tonight with his troops on board. You will look after them as if they were Englishmen. And better than that. You would play tricks on English soldiers. The first man to play a trick on any of these men I shall flog within the hour. Forget their colour. Forget their clothes. Remember only what I say to you. You can pipe down now, Mr. Bush."

Down in the cabin Polwheal was waiting faithfully with the

336

dressing gown and towel for his captain's bath, which ought according to timetable to have been taken two hours back.

"Put out my best uniform again," snapped Hornblower. "And I want the after cabin ready for a state dinner for eight at six bells. Go for'ard and bring my cook to me."

There was plenty to do. Officers had to be invited to the dinner and warned to be ready in full dress. Plans had to be made for the accommodation of five hundred men on board the two vessels.

Hornblower was just looking across to the *Natividad*, where she swung with her white ensign over the red and gold of Spain, wondering what steps he should take with regard to her, when a boat came running gaily out to him from the shore. The leader of the party which came on board was a youngish man of less than middle height, slim of figure and lithe as a monkey, with an expression of undefeatable good humour. He looked more Spanish than Central American. Bush brought him up to where Hornblower impatiently trod his quarterdeck.

Making a cordial bow, the newcomer introduced himself. "I am Vice-Admiral Don Cristobal de Crespo."

Hornblower looked the vice-admiral up and down. He wore gold earrings, and his gold-embroidered coat did not conceal the raggedness of the grey shirt beneath. "Of El Supremo's service?" he asked.

"Of course. May I introduce my officers—" The dozen officers introduced under resounding titles were barefooted, brutish Indians, the red sashes round their waists stuck full of pistols.

"I have come," said Crespo, amiably, "to hoist my flag in my new ship *Natividad*. It is El Supremo's wish that you should salute it with the eleven guns due to a vice-admiral."

Hornblower's jaw dropped. He was irked by the prospect of giving this ragged-shirted rascal as many guns as Nelson ever had, but with an empire at stake it would be foolish to strain at points of ceremony.

"Certainly, Admiral," he said with an effort. "It gives me great happiness to congratulate you upon your appointment."

"Thank you, Captain," said the vice-admiral. "Now may I ask where are the executive officers of the *Natividad*?"

"I greatly regret," said Hornblower, "that I dropped them overboard this morning after court martial."

"That is indeed a pity," said Crespo. "I have El Supremo's orders to hang them at the *Natividad*'s yardarms. Still, there is no help for it. I will go on board my ship, then. Perhaps you will accompany me so as to give orders to your prize crew?"

"Certainly, Admiral." Hornblower gave hurried orders for the saluting of the flag when it should be hoisted in the *Natividad*, and went down into the boat with the new officers.

On board the *Natividad* Crespo swaggered onto the quarterdeck. At a sign from him one of his officers hauled down the Spanish and British ensigns from the peak. It was a dramatic scene in the brilliant sunshine. The British marines stood in rigid line in their red coats. The British seamen stood by their carronades, matches smouldering, for no orders had yet relieved them of their duty. Gerard came over and stood beside Hornblower.

Crespo walked forward to the quarterdeck rail with its peeling gilt. The crew and the navigating officers herded in the waist listened dumbly to his uplifted voice. Hornblower, gazing down at them, saw that there would be small resistance to Crespo's missionary efforts.

To a man the crew were of non-European blood; presumably during the many years of the *Natividad*'s commission in the Pacific the original European crew had quite died out. Only officers had been replaced from Spain; fresh hands had been recruited from the native races.

In five minutes of brilliant speaking Crespo had won them all over. El Supremo, he said, was at the head of a movement which was sweeping the Spaniards from the dominion of America. Within the year the whole of the New World from Mexico to Peru would be at his feet. There would be an end of Spanish misrule, of brutal domination, of slavery in mine and field. There would be land, freedom and happiness for everybody.

Crespo had them all cheering wildly at the end of this speech. He came back to Hornblower. "Thank you, Captain," he said. "I think there is no more need for the presence of your prize crew."

Pulling back to his own ship Hornblower was startled by the

sound of a gun from the *Natividad*, instantly answered by another from the *Lydia*. He almost sprang to his feet in the sternsheets of the launch, but a glance over his shoulder reassured him. A new flag was now flying from the *Natividad*'s peak. Blue with a yellow star in the middle, he saw. The sound of the saluting guns rolled slowly round the bay; the salute was still being fired as he went up the *Lydia*'s side. Mr. Marsh, the gunner, was pacing up and down the foredeck mumbling to himself—Hornblower guessed at the jargon.

"If I hadn't been born a bloody fool I shouldn't be here. Fire *seven*. I've left my wife; I've left my home and everything that's dear. Fire *eight*."

Half an hour later Hornblower was at the beach to meet El Supremo, who came riding down, punctual to the minute, a ragged retinue of a dozen riding with him. El Supremo bowed and stepped straight into the launch; his suite introduced themselves, in a string of meaningless names, in turn as they came up to Hornblower. They were all nearly pure Indians; they all held the rank of general save for one or two colonels, and every little action of theirs indicated they were devotedly attached to their master.

At the gangway boatswain's mates and marines were ready to receive El Supremo with distinguished military formality, but El Supremo astonished Hornblower, as he was about to go up the ladder, with the casual words, "The correct salute for me, Captain, is twenty-three guns."

That was two more guns than His Majesty King George himself would receive. Hornblower stared for a moment, thought wildly of how he could refuse, and finally salved his conscience with the notion that a salute of that number of guns would be entirely meaningless. He sent a message hurriedly to Mr. Marsh ordering twenty-three guns, and he could hardly repress a grin as he thought of Marsh's certain astonishment, and the boiling exasperation in his voice when he reached—"If I hadn't been born a bloody fool I shouldn't be here. Fire *twenty-three*."

El Supremo stepped onto the quarterdeck with a keen glance round him, and then, while Hornblower looked at him, the interest faded from his face and he lapsed into his usual abstracted indifference. He looked over the heads of Bush and Gerard and the others as Hornblower presented them. He shook his head without a word when Hornblower suggested that he might care to inspect the ship.

"Dinner will be served shortly, Supremo," said Hornblower after an awkward pause. "Would you care to come below?"

Still without a word El Supremo walked with quiet dignity over to the companion and led the way down. At the entrance to the cabin where Polwheal and his stewards stood, El Supremo stopped for a moment and said the first words which had passed his lips since he came on board.

"I will dine alone here," he said. "Let the food be brought to me."

None of his suite saw anything in the least odd about his request. El Supremo might have been blowing his nose for all the surprise they evinced.

It was all a horrible nuisance, of course. Hornblower and his other guests had to dine in makeshift fashion in the gunroom mess, and his one linen tablecloth and the two last bottles of his old Madeira remained in the after cabin for El Supremo's use. Nor was the meal improved by the silence that prevailed most of the time; El Supremo's suite were not in the least talkative, and Hornblower was the only Englishman with conversational Spanish. Bush tried twice, valiantly, to make polite speeches to his neighbours, putting a terminal 'o' on the ends of his English words in the hope that so they might be transmuted into Spanish, but the blank stares of the men he addressed reduced him quickly to stammering inarticulation.

Dinner was hardly finished when a messenger arrived from the shore and was brought in by the bewildered officer of the watch who could not understand his jabbering talk. The troops were ready to come on board. With relief Hornblower put away his napkin and went on deck, followed by the others.

The men whom the launch and the cutter brought out plying steadily between ship and shore, were typical Central American soldiers, barefooted and ragged, swarthy and lank-haired. Each man carried a bright new musket and a bulging cartridge pouch, but these were what Hornblower had brought for them; most of the men also carried cotton bags filled with provisions. The crew herded them onto the main deck; they looked about them curiously and chattered volubly, but they were amenable enough, squatting in gossiping groups between the guns where the grinning crew pushed them.

When the last man was on board Hornblower looked across to the *Natividad*; it appeared as if her share of the expeditionary force was already embarked. Suddenly the babble on the main deck died away completely, to be succeeded by a silence surprising in its intensity as El Supremo came on the quarterdeck.

"We shall sail for La Libertad, Captain," he said.

"Yes, Supremo," replied Hornblower.

He was glad that El Supremo had made his appearance when he did; a few seconds later and the ship's officers would have seen that their captain was waiting his orders, and that would never have done.

"We will weigh anchor, Mr. Bush," said Hornblower.

CHAPTER VI

The voyage up the coast was completed. La Libertad had fallen, and El Supremo and his men had vanished into the tangle of volcanoes surrounding San Salvador, the city of the Holy Saviour. Once again in the early morning Captain Hornblower was pacing the *Lydia*'s quarterdeck, and Lieutenant Bush as officer of the watch was standing by the wheel rigidly taking no notice of him.

Hornblower was gazing round him, and filling his lungs deep with air as he walked. For a space he was free of El Supremo and the relief was inexpressible. At the moment there was just the gentlest wind abeam pushing the *Lydia* at three or four knots southwards towards Panama. Peeping over the horizon on the port side were the tops of the interminable volcanoes which formed the backbone of this benighted country.

Perhaps, Hornblower thought, El Supremo might accomplish his wild dream of conquering Central America; perhaps good communications might be opened across the Isthmus; perhaps someday a canal would be built. That would make a profound difference to the world. It would open up the Pacific to England by evading the difficulties of the journey round the Horn or by the Cape of Good Hope and India.

If, on the other hand, El Supremo's attempt upon San Salvador should fail, the *Natividad* would suffice to bring off what few might survive of his army. Hornblower felt justified in thinking that the *Lydia* could in no way influence the land operations and that the presence of his ship in the Gulf would hamper the transport of Spanish forces from Peru. The Admiralty would be glad of a survey of the Gulf and the Pearl Islands, and it was only right that the *Lydia*'s crew should be given a chance of winning some prize money among the pearl fishers; that would compensate them for the probable loss of prize money for the *Natividad*. Yet, for all these plausible arguments, Hornblower knew quite well that really why he had come this way was to get away from El Supremo.

A large flat ray, the size of a tabletop, suddenly leaped clear of the water close overside and fell flat upon the surface again with a loud smack, then vanished below, its pinky brown gleaming wet for a moment as the blue water closed over it. There were flying fish skimming the water in all directions. Hornblower watched it all, delighted. With a ship full of stores and a crew contented by their recent adventures he had no real care in the world. The Spanish prisoners whose lives he had saved from El Supremo were sunning themselves lazily on the forecastle.

"Sail ho!" came echoing down from the masthead.

The idlers thronged the bulwark; the seamen holystoning the deck surreptitiously worked more slowly in order to hear what was going on.

"Where away?" called Hornblower.

"On the port bow, sir. Lugger, sir, I think, an' standing straight for us, but she's right in the eye of the sun—"

"Yes, a lugger sir," squeaked Midshipman Hooker from the fore-topgallant masthead. "Two-masted. She's right to windward, running down to us, under all sail, sir."

"Running down to us?" said Hornblower, mystified. He jumped up on the slide of the quarterdeck carronade nearest him, and stared into the sun and the wind under his hand, but at present there was still nothing to be seen from that low altitude. Then, as the ship lifted, he saw a gleaming square of white rise for a second over the distant horizon and vanish again. At last, from the deck, the lugger was in plain view, running goosewinged before the wind, straight at the *Lydia*.

"She's flying Spanish colours at the main, sir," said Bush from behind his levelled telescope.

Hornblower had suspected so, but had not been able to trust his eyesight. "She's hauling 'em down, all the same," he retorted, glad to be the first to notice it.

"So she is, sir," said Bush, and then— "There they go again, sir. No! What do you make of that, sir?"

"White flag over Spanish colours now," said Hornblower. "That'll mean a parley. No. I don't trust 'em. Hoist the colours, Mr. Bush, and send the hands to quarters. Run out the guns and send the prisoners below under guard again."

He was not going to be caught unaware by any Spanish tricks. That lugger might spew up a host of boarders over the side of an unprepared ship. As the *Lydia's* gunports opened and she showed her teeth the lugger hove to just out of gunshot.

"She's sending a boat, sir," said Bush.

"So I see," snapped Hornblower.

Two oars rowed a dinghy jerkily across the dancing water, and a man came scrambling up the ladder to the gangway. Hornblower saw he wore the full dress of the Spanish Royal Navy, his epaulettes gleaming in the sun. He bowed and came forward.

"Captain Hornblower?" he asked.

"I am Captain Hornblower."

"I have to welcome you as the new ally of Spain," said the officer. "We have had the news for the last four days that last month Bonaparte stole our King Ferdinand from us and imprisoned him in France. He has named his own brother Joseph King of Spain. A junta government, acting in Ferdinand's name, has signed a treaty of alliance and friendship with His Majesty of

England. It is with great pleasure, Captain, that I have to inform you that all ports in the dominions of His Most Catholic Majesty, our rightful King, are open to you."

Hornblower stood dumb. It might be a ruse to lure the *Lydia* under the guns of Spanish shore batteries. Hornblower almost hoped it might be—better that than all the complications which would hem him in if it were the truth. The Spaniard interpreted his expression as implying disbelief.

"I have letters here," he said, producing them from his breast. "One from your admiral in the Leeward Islands, sent overland from Portobello, and one from the English lady in Panama."

He tendered them with a further bow, and Hornblower with a muttered apology fled below to study them in the privacy of his cabin.

The stout canvas wrapper of the naval orders was genuine enough. The two seals showed no signs of having been tampered with. He cut the wrapper open. The orders were brief—an alliance having been concluded between His Majesty's Government and that of King Ferdinand, Captain Hornblower was directed to refrain from hostilities towards the Spanish possessions, and, having drawn upon the Spanish authorities for necessary stores, to proceed with all dispatch to England for further orders. There was Rear Admiral Troubridge's signature—Hornblower had seen it before, and recognized it. It was a genuine document without any doubts at all. It was marked "Copy No. 2"; presumably other copies had been distributed to other parts of the Spanish possessions to ensure that he received one.

The other letter was sealed merely with a wafer and was addressed in a feminine hand. Hornblower slit it open.

17 August 1808   The Citadel,
                                                      Panama.

Lady Barbara Wellesley presents her compliments to the captain of the English frigate. She requests that he will be so good as to convey her and her maid to Europe, because Lady Barbara finds that owing to an outbreak of yellow fever on the Spanish Main she cannot return home the way she would desire.

Hornblower folded the letter and tapped it on his thumbnail in meditation. A crowded frigate sailing round the Horn was no place for females. Yet the woman seemed to have no doubt that her request would be instantly granted. The name Wellesley, of course, gave the clue to that. Two Wellesleys had been much before the public of late—the Marquis Wellesley, K.P., late Governor-General of India and now a member of the Cabinet, and General Sir Arthur Wellesley, K.B., the victor of Assaye and now pointed at as England's greatest soldier after Sir John Moore. Hornblower had seen him once, and had noticed the high-arched arrogant nose and the imperious eye. If the woman had that blood in her she would be the sort to take things for granted. An impecunious frigate captain with no influence at all would be glad to render a service to a member of that family. Maria would be pleased that he had been in correspondence with the daughter of an earl.

Hornblower locked the letters in his desk and ran up on deck, forcing a smile as he approached the Spanish captain. "Greetings to the new allies," he said. "Señor, I am proud to be serving with Spain against the Corsican tyrant."

The Spaniard bowed. "We were afraid, Captain," he said, "lest you fall in with the *Natividad* before you heard the news, because she has not heard it either. In that case your fine frigate would have come to serious harm."

"Ha-h'm," said Hornblower. This was more embarrassing than ever; he turned and snapped out an order to the midshipman of the watch. "Bring the prisoners up from the cable tier. Quickly!" The boy ran, and Hornblower turned back again to the Spanish officer. "I regret to tell you, señor, that by evil chance the *Lydia* met the *Natividad* a week ago."

The Spanish captain looked surprised. He stared round the ship, at the meticulous good order, the well set up rigging. "But you did not fight her, Captain?" he said. "Perhaps—"

The words died away on his lips as he caught sight of a melancholy procession approaching them along the gangway. He recognized the captain and the lieutenants of the *Natividad*. Hornblower plunged feverishly into an explanation of their

345

presence; but it was not easy to tell a Spanish captain that the *Lydia* had captured a Spanish ship of twice her force without receiving a shot or a casualty; it was harder still to go on and explain that the ship was now sailing under the flag of rebels determined to destroy Spanish power. The Spaniard, white with rage and injured pride, turned upon the captain of the *Natividad* and received confirmation of Hornblower's story. Bit by bit he realized that the whole of the Spanish overlordship of the Americas was in jeopardy, and as he realized that, a fresh aspect of the situation broke in upon him. "The Manila galleon is due to arrive at Acapulco next month!" he exclaimed. "The *Natividad* will intercept her."

One ship a year crossed the wide Pacific from the Philippines, never bearing less than a million sterling in treasure. Her loss would cripple the bankrupt Spanish government hopelessly. The three captains exchanged glances—Hornblower realized that this was why El Supremo had agreed so readily to the *Lydia* sailing southwestward. It would take the Spaniards months to bring around the Horn a ship capable of dealing with the *Natividad*, and in the interval El Supremo would enjoy all those advantages of sea power which Hornblower had foreseen for the *Lydia*. The rebellion would be so firmly rooted that nothing could put it down, especially as Spain was engaged in a life-and-death struggle with Bonaparte and would have neither ships nor men to spare.

"Very well," Hornblower announced abruptly. "I will take my ship back to fight the *Natividad*."

"Thank you, Captain," said the captain of the lugger, looking relieved. "You will call in at Panama to consult the viceroy first?"

"Yes," snapped Hornblower. In a world where news took months to travel, and where complete upheavals of international relationships were likely, he had learned now by bitter experience to keep in the closest contact with the shores.

"Then," said the officer, "I will bid you goodbye for the time. If I reach Panama first, I will be able to arrange a welcome for you. Perhaps you will allow my compatriots to accompany me?"

"No, I won't," rasped Hornblower. "And you, sir, will keep under my lee until we drop anchor."

346

The Spaniard shrugged and yielded. At sea one can hardly argue with a captain whose guns are run out and whose broadside could blow one's ship out of the water. The Spaniard had not enough intuition to guess that Hornblower still had a lurking fear that the whole business might be a ruse to inveigle the *Lydia* helpless under the guns of Panama.

CHAPTER VII

It was not a ruse at all. On the morning when the *Lydia* came stealing into the roadstead of Panama the only guns fired were the salutes. Boatloads of rejoicing Spaniards came out to greet her, but the rejoicing was soon turned to wailing at the news that the *Natividad* now flew El Supremo's flag, that La Libertad had fallen, and that Nicaragua was in a flame of rebellion. With his cocked hat and presentation sword Hornblower had made ready to go ashore and call upon the governor and the viceroy, when the arrival of yet one more boat was announced to him.

"Looks like an English lady in it, sir," said Gray, one of the master's mates, who brought the news. "She seems to want to come aboard."

Hornblower went on deck; a large rowing boat was coming alongside; at the six oars sat swarthy Spanish-Americans, bare-armed and straw-hatted, while in the stern sat a little Negress with a flaming red handkerchief over her shoulders, and beside her sat the lady Gray had spoken about. Even as Hornblower looked, one of the oarsmen caught the *Lydia*'s rope ladder, and the next moment the lady, timing the movement perfectly, swung onto it and two seconds later came on deck.

Clearly she was an Englishwoman. She wore a wide shady hat trimmed with roses and a grey-blue silk dress. Her skin was fair despite its golden tan, and her eyes were grey-blue, of just the same evasive shade as her silk dress. Her face was too long for beauty, to say nothing of her sunburn, and Hornblower told himself that any woman who could ascend a rope ladder in that fashion, unassisted, must be too masculine for his taste.

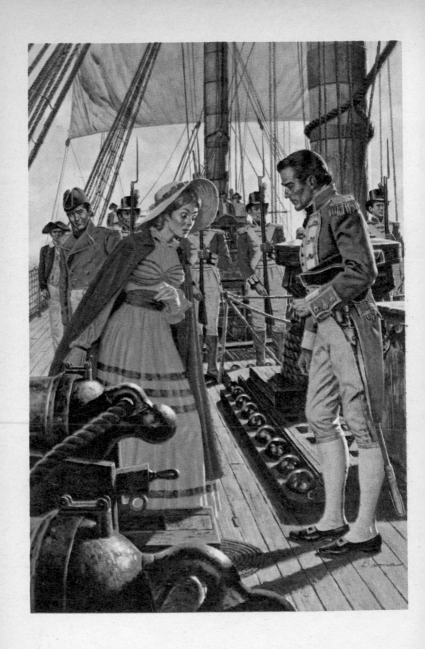

He held himself aloof as the visitor looked about her. A wild squawk from overside told that the Negress had not been as handy with the ladder, and directly afterwards this was confirmed by her appearance on deck, wet from the waist down, water streaming from her black gown onto the deck. The lady paid no attention to this mishap; Gray was nearest to her and she turned to him.

"Please be so good, sir," she said, "as to have my baggage brought up out of the boat."

Gray hesitated, and looked round over his shoulder at Hornblower, stiff and unbending on the quarterdeck. "The captain's here, ma'am," he said.

"Yes," said the lady. "Please have my baggage brought up while I speak to him."

Hornblower disliked the aristocracy—it hurt him nowadays to remember that as the doctor's son he had had to touch his cap to the squire. He felt awkward in the presence of the self-confident arrogance of blue blood and wealth, and it irritated him to think that if he offended this woman he might forfeit his career. Not even his presentation sword gave him confidence as she approached him. He took refuge in an icy formality. "Captain Hornblower, at your service, ma'am," he said, with a stiff jerk of his neck which might charitably be thought a bow.

"Lady Barbara Wellesley," was the reply, accompanied by a curtsy just deep enough to keep the interview formal. "I trust you received my note requesting a passage to England."

"I did, ma'am. But I do not think it is wise for your ladyship to join this ship." The unhappy double mention of the word ship in this sentence did nothing to make Hornblower feel less awkward.

"Please tell me why, sir."

"Because, ma'am, we shall be clearing shortly to seek out an enemy and fight him. After that we shall have to return to England round Cape Horn. Your ladyship would be well advised to make your way across the Isthmus. From Portobello you can easily reach Jamaica and engage a berth in the West India packet, which is accustomed to female passengers."

Lady Barbara's eyebrows arched themselves higher. "In my letter," she said, "I informed you that there was yellow fever in

349

Portobello. It was on the outbreak of the disease that I removed from Portobello to Panama."

"May I ask why your ladyship was in Portobello, then?"

"Because, sir, the West India packet in which I was a passenger was captured by a Spanish privateer and brought there. I regret, sir, that I cannot tell you the name of my grandmother's cook, but I shall be glad to answer any further questions which a gentleman of breeding would ask."

Hornblower winced and then to his annoyance found himself blushing furiously and stammering. "B-but we are going out to fight," he said. "It will be d-dangerous."

Lady Barbara laughed at that—Hornblower noted the pleasing colour contrast between her white teeth and her golden sunburn. "I would far rather," she said, "be on board your ship, whomsoever you have got to fight, than be in Panama with the yellow fever." Still Hornblower stammered and hesitated. "Soon, Captain," she continued, "I will come to think that I shall be unwelcome on board. I can hardly imagine that a gentleman holding the King's commission would be discourteous to a woman with my name."

That was just the difficulty. No captain of small influence could afford to offend a Wellesley. If he did he might never command a ship again. Furthermore, Hornblower at thirty-seven was still not more than one eighth the way up the captains' list anyway, and the goodwill of the Wellesleys could easily keep him in employment until he attained flag rank. There was nothing for it but diplomatically to wring advantage from his difficulties. "I was only doing my duty, ma'am," he said, "in pointing out the dangers. For myself nothing would give me greater pleasure than your presence on board my ship."

Lady Barbara went down in a curtsy far deeper than her first, and at this moment Gray came up and touched his cap. "Your baggage is all on board, ma'am," he said.

They had hove the stuff up with a whip from the main yardarm and now it littered the gangway—leather cases, ironbound wooden boxes, dome-topped trunks.

A new wave of irritation rose in Hornblower's mind. "There

350

will be no room in your cabin for a tenth of that baggage, ma'am," he snapped.

Lady Barbara nodded gravely. "I have dwelt in a cabin before, sir. The sea chest there holds everything I shall need on board. The rest can be put where you will—until we reach England."

Hornblower almost stamped on the deck with rage. He was unused to a woman who could display practical common sense like this. He turned on his heel and led the way below without a word.

Lady Barbara looked round the captain's cabin with a whimsical smile, but she made no comment.

"A frigate has few of the luxuries of an Indiaman, you see, ma'am," said Hornblower, bitterly. He was bitter because his poverty at the time when he commissioned the *Lydia* had allowed him to purchase none of the minor comforts which many frigate captains could afford.

"I was just thinking when you spoke," said Lady Barbara, gently, "that it was scandalous that a King's officer should be treated worse than a fat John Company man. But I have only one thing to ask for, and that is a key for the lock on the cabin door. It is not on my account, Captain. It is Hebe here, who will sleep on the floor of my cabin. I have to lock her in unless she is directly under my eye. She can no more keep from the men than a moth from a candle." The little Negress grinned widely at this last speech, and rolled her eyes at Polwheal, who was standing silently by.

"Very good," Hornblower said. "I will have the armourer make you a key, ma'am. Polwheal, take my things into Mr. Bush's cabin. Give Mr. Bush my apologies and tell him he will have to berth in the wardroom. See that Lady Barbara has all that she wants, and ask Mr. Gray with my compliments to attend to putting the baggage in my storeroom. You will forgive me, Lady Barbara, but I am already late in paying my call upon the viceroy."

STRETCHED FLAT ON HIS BACK in his new cabin, Hornblower began slowly to recover from the strain of a very trying day. It had begun with his cautious approach to Panama and it had ended so far with his unceremonious departure. Between the two had come Lady Barbara's arrival and the interview with the viceroy of New Granada.

The viceroy had been a typical Spanish gentleman of the old school. While full of approval for Hornblower's suggestion that instant action against the rebels was necessary, he had not been ready to act on it. He was obviously surprised at Hornblower's decision to sail from Panama on the same day as his arrival—he had expected the *Lydia* to stay for at least a week of fêtings and idleness. He had agreed that at least a thousand soldiers must be transported to the Nicaraguan coast, but Hornblower had had to use all his tact to persuade him to do it at once, to give his instructions from his very banqueting table.

The banquet had in itself been trying. Both because of the spiciness of the food and the pressing hospitality of the viceroy it had been hard to avoid drinking too much and Hornblower actively disliked the feeling of not having complete control of his judgment.

But he could not refuse that last glass of wine, seeing what good news from Europe had been brought to the viceroy's table. He sat up on his cot with a jerk. Weighing anchor had driven the recollection out of his mind. Good manners compelled him to go and communicate the news to Lady Barbara, seeing how closely it concerned her. He ran up on deck.

Lady Barbara was seated aft by the taffrail in a hammock chair, the Negress at her feet. Someone must have made that chair for her during the day; and someone had rigged up for her a scrap of awning. She seemed to be drinking in the cool air against which the *Lydia* was standing out of the Gulf close-hauled. On the starboard beam the sun was ready at the horizon, a disc of orange fire in the clear blue of the sky. There was serenity in Lady Barbara's expression, and she acknowledged Hornblower's bow with a smile.

"It is heavenly to be at sea again, Captain," she said. "You have given me no opportunity so far to tell you how grateful I am to you for taking me away from Panama. In Spanish America women are treated like Mohammedans. And Spanish-American food—"

352

The words recalled to Hornblower the banquet he had just endured, and the expression on his face made Lady Barbara break off her sentence to laugh so infectiously that Hornblower could not help but join in. "Will you not sit down, Captain?"

Hornblower had never once during his commission sat in a chair on his own deck, and he disliked innovations. "Thank you, your ladyship, but I prefer to stand if I may. I came to give you good news. Your brother, Sir Arthur, at the head of a large army, has been dispatched to Portugal to attack Bonaparte's forces."

"That is good news. I am prouder than ever of Arthur." Lady Barbara nodded a grave approval, and looked out to where the sun was sinking into the sea. To Hornblower the disappearance of the sun each evening into those placid waters was a daily miracle of beauty. They watched silently as the disc sank farther and farther. Soon only a tiny edge was left; it vanished, reappeared for a second like a glint of gold as the *Lydia* heaved up over the swell, and then faded once more. The sky glowed red in the west, but overhead it grew perceptibly darker with the approach of night.

"Beautiful! Exquisite!" said Lady Barbara; her hands were tightly clasped together. She was silent for a moment. "Yes. If my brother is victorious, the herd in England will be expecting him to lead the army into Paris by Christmas. And if he does not they will forget his victories and clamour for his head."

Hornblower resented the word "herd"—by birth and by blood he was one of the herd himself—but he was aware of the profound truth of Lady Barbara's remarks. She had summed up for him his opinion of the British mob and along with that went her appreciation of the sunset and her opinion of Spanish-American food. He actually felt well disposed towards her. "I hope," he said, ponderously, "that your ladyship was provided today during my absence with everything necessary?"

"Thank you, Captain. I was indeed. There is only one more thing which I should like to ask as a favour."

"Yes, your ladyship?"

"And that is that you do not call me 'your ladyship'. Call me Lady Barbara, if you will."

"Certainly, your—Lady Barbara. Ha-h'm."

Ghosts of dimples appeared in her cheeks, and the bright eyes sparkled.

"And if 'Lady Barbara' does not come easily to you, Captain, and you wish to attract my attention, you can always say 'ha-h'm'."

Hornblower stiffened with anger. He was turning on his heel, drawing a deep breath as he did so, and was about to exhale that breath and clear his throat when he realized that he must not make use of that useful and noncommittal sound. But Lady Barbara checked him with outstretched hand; even at that moment he noticed her long slender fingers. "I am sorry, Captain," she said, all contrition; "please accept my apologies, although I know now that it was quite unforgivable."

She looked positively pretty as she pleaded. Hornblower looked down at her. He realized that he was angry not because of the impertinence but because this sharp-witted woman had already guessed at the use he made of this sound to hide his feelings.

"There is nothing to forgive, ma'am," he said heavily. "And now, if you will forgive me in your turn, I will attend to my duties in the ship."

He left her there in the fast falling night and went below to his new cabin.

MORNING FOUND THE *Lydia* heaving and swooping lightly over a quartering sea. The captain was early afoot—indeed, his coxswain Brown had had apologetically to sand the captain's portion of the quarterdeck while he paced up and down it. Far away on the port side the black shape of a whale could be seen breaking the surface in a flurry of foam—dazzling white against the blue sea— and a thin plume of white vapour was visible as the whale emptied its lungs.

Gray, the master's mate, came aft to heave the log, and Hornblower checked in his walk to watch the operation. Gray tossed the little triangle of wood over the stern, and, log line in hand, he gazed fixedly with his boyish blue eyes at the dancing bit of wood. "Turn!" he cried sharply to the hand with the sandglass, and let the line run out freely over the rail.

"Stop!" called the man with the glass.

Gray checked the line and then read off the length run out.

"How much?" called Hornblower to Gray.

"Seven an' nigh on a half, sir."

The *Lydia* was a good ship to reel off seven and a half knots in that breeze, even though her best point of sailing was with the wind on her quarter. It would not take long if the wind held to reach waters where the *Natividad* might be expected to be found. The *Natividad* was a slow sailer, as Hornblower had noticed when he sailed in her company. If he met her in the open sea he could trust to the handiness of his ship and the experience of his crew to outmanoeuvre her and discount her superior weight of metal. If the ships once closed and the rebels boarded, their superior numbers would overwhelm his crew. Hornblower's busy mind, as he paced up and down the deck, began to visualize the battle, and to make plans for the possible eventualities.

The little Negress Hebe came picking her way across the deck, her red handkerchief brilliant in the sunshine, and before the scandalized crew could prevent her she had interrupted the captain in his sacred morning walk.

"Milady says would the captain breakfast with her," she lisped.

"Eh—what's that?" asked Hornblower, taken by surprise and then, as he realized the triviality for which he had been interrupted, "No no no! Tell her ladyship I will *not* breakfast with her, that I will *never* breakfast with her. Tell her you are *not* allowed and neither is she on this deck before eight bells. *Get below!*"

The little Negress nodded and smiled as she backed away. Apparently she was used to white gentlemen who were irascible before breakfast and attributed little importance to the symptoms. The open skylight of the after cabin was close beside him as he walked, and through it he could hear, now that his reverie had been broken into, the clatter of crockery, and then first Hebe's and then Lady Barbara's voice.

The sound of the men scrubbing the decks, the harping of the rigging and the creaking of the timbers were noises which he could tolerate, but this clack-clack-clack of women's tongues would drive him mad. He stamped off the deck in a rage. He did not enjoy his bath, and even the excellent coffee, sweetened (as he liked it) to a syrup with sugar, did not relieve his temper. Nor, most assuredly, did the necessity of having to explain to Bush that the *Lydia* was now sailing to seek out the *Natividad*, having already been to enormous pains to capture her and hand her over to the rebels who were now their foes.

"Aye aye, sir," said Bush gravely, having heard the new development. He was being so obviously tactful that Hornblower swore at him. "Aye aye, sir," said Bush again. Really what he wanted to say was some expression of sympathy for Hornblower in his present situation, but he knew he would be sworn at far worse if he said anything beyond "aye aye, sir."

As the day wore on Hornblower came to repent of his ill humour. The saw-edged volcanic coast was slipping past them steadily, and ahead of them somewhere lay a desperate battle. Before they should fight it, it would be tactful for him to entertain his officers at dinner. And ordinary politeness dictated that he should at this, the earliest opportunity, arrange that his guest should meet his officers formally. So he sent Polwheal across to Lady Barbara with a politely worded request that Lady Barbara would be so kind as to allow Captain Hornblower and his officers to dine with her in the after cabin, and Polwheal returned with a politely worded message to the effect that Lady Barbara would be delighted.

Six was the maximum number that could sit round the table; and superstitiously Hornblower remembered that on the eve of his last encounter with the *Natividad* Galbraith, Clay and Savage had been his guests. In the hope of encountering similar good fortune he invited them again. Bush was the sixth—the other possible choice was Gerard, and handsome Gerard had acquired such a knowledge of the world that Hornblower did not want to bring him into too frequent contact with Lady Barbara—solely, he hastened to assure himself, for the sake of peace and quiet in his ship.

The dinner was a success. At first, unsurprisingly, Clay and Savage were brusque and shy in Lady Barbara's presence, and then, when they had a glass of wine inside them, they moved towards the other extreme of over-familiarity. Even the hard-bitten Bush, surprisingly, showed the same symptoms in the same order, while poor Galbraith was of course shy all the time.

But Hornblower was astonished at the ease with which Lady Barbara handled them. She laughed away Clay's bumptiousness, listened appreciatively to Bush's account of Trafalgar (when he had been a junior lieutenant in the *Téméraire*) and then won Galbraith's heart completely by displaying a close knowledge of a remarkable poem called "The Lay of the Last Minstrel" by an Edinburgh lawyer, Walter Scott—every line of which Galbraith knew by heart, and which Galbraith thought was the greatest poem in the English language.

Hornblower contented himself with sitting back and watching as Lady Barbara conversed with a fearless self-confidence. Grudgingly he admitted to himself that she could talk to men as an equal, and yet could keep from her manner both invitation and hostility.

And when dinner was over and the officers rose to drink the health of the King, stooping under the deck beams (almost twenty-five more years would pass before a King who had been a sailor himself would give permission to the Navy to drink his health sitting), she echoed, "God bless him!" and finished her single glass of wine with exactly the right touch of lighthearted solemnity. Hornblower suddenly realized that he was passionately anxious for the evening not to end.

"Do you play whist, Lady Barbara?" he asked.

"Why, yes," she said. "Are there whist players on board?"

"There are some who are not too enthusiastic," replied Hornblower, grinning at his juniors.

But nobody had nearly as much objection to playing in a four with Lady Barbara, the more so as her presence might moderate the captain's dry strictness. The cut allotted Lady Barbara as the captain's partner against Clay and Galbraith. Clay dealt and turned up a heart as trump. Lady Barbara led the king of hearts, and Hornblower writhed uneasily in his seat. This might well be the play of a mere tyro, and somehow it hurt him to think that Lady Barbara was a bad whist player.

But as the game progressed his doubt changed to complete confidence in his partner, which was entirely justified. In the end, they made a slam even though their opponents held every trick in spades. Not since the *Lydia* left England had Hornblower had such a good partner.

And the next evening she displayed another accomplishment, when she brought out a guitar onto the quarterdeck and accompanied herself in the songs which she sang in a sweet soprano—so sweet that the crew came creeping aft and crouched to listen under the gangway. Galbraith was her slave, and the midshipmen loved her. Even the barnacle-encrusted officers like Bush and Crystal softened towards her, and Gerard flashed his brilliant smile at her and told her stories of his privateering days. Hornblower watched Gerard anxiously during that voyage up the Nicaraguan coast, and cursed his own tone deafness which made him find Lady Barbara's accomplished singing not merely indifferent but almost painful.

CHAPTER VIII

The long volcanic coastline slid past them day after day. With decks cleared for action and every man at his post they ran once more into the Gulf of Fonseca, but they did not find the *Natividad* there, nor in the roadstead of La Libertad. Had Crespo also received the news that they were now enemies, Hornblower wondered. Or would he be able to take the *Natividad* by surprise when finally he found her?

Storms awaited them in the Gulf of Tehuantepec. The *Lydia* began rising and swooping more violently than usual and a gusty wind was heeling her sharply over. It was just eight bells, and the watch was being called. Hornblower could hear the bellowings of the master's mates—"Show a leg! Lash up and stow!"—as he ran up to the quarterdeck. The sky was still blue and the sun was hot, but the sea was grey, now, and running high, and the *Lydia* was beginning to labour under her press of sail.

"I was just sending down to you, sir, for permission to shorten sail," said Bush.

Hornblower glanced up at the canvas. "Yes. Get the courses and t'gallants off her," he said.

The *Lydia* plunged heavily as he spoke, and then rose again, labouring, the water creaming under her bows. Under shortened sail she would ride more easily, but the wind on her beam was growing stronger, and she was bowing down to it as she crashed over the waves. Looking round, Hornblower saw Lady Barbara standing with one hand on the taffrail. The wind was whipping her skirts about her, and with her other hand she was trying to restrain the curls that streamed round her head.

"You ought to be below, Lady Barbara," he said.

"Oh no, Captain. This is too delicious after the heat we have been enduring."

A shower of spray came rattling over the bulwarks and wetted them both.

"It is your health, ma'am, about which I am anxious."

"If salt water was harmful, sailors would die young."

Her cheeks were pink under their tan, and her eyes sparkled. Hornblower could refuse her nothing, even though he bitterly remembered how last evening she had sat in the shadow of the mizzen rigging talking so animatedly to Gerard that no one else had been able to profit by her society. "Then you can stay on deck, ma'am, unless this gale increases."

"Thank you, Captain," she replied.

Hornblower turned away; he would clearly have liked to stay there talking, but his duty was with his ship. As he reached the wheel there came a hail from the masthead.

"Sail ho! Right ahead. Looks like *Natividad*, sir."

Hornblower gazed up. The lookout was clinging to his perch, being swung round and round in dizzy circles as the ship pitched and swooped over the waves. "Up you go, Knyvett," he snapped to the midshipman beside him. "Take a glass with you and tell me what you can see."

Soon Knyvett's boyish voice came calling down to him through the gale. "She's the *Natividad*, sir. I can see the cut of her tops'ls. On the same course as us. Now she's wearing round, sir. She must have seen us. She's heading up to wind'ard of us, close hauled, sir."

"Oh, is she," said Hornblower to himself, grimly. It was an

359

unusual experience to have a Spanish ship face about and challenge action—but he remembered that she was a Spanish ship no longer. And he was sure now that Crespo had somehow learned that the *Lydia* was no longer in the service of El Supremo.

He would not allow the *Natividad* to get the weather gauge of him, come what might. "Man the braces, there!" he shouted, and then to the man at the wheel: "Port your helm. And mark ye, fellow, keep her as near the wind as she'll lie. Mr. Bush, beat to quarters, if you please, and clear for action."

As the drum rolled and the hands came pouring up he remembered the woman aft by the taffrail. "Your place is below, Lady Barbara," he said. "Take your maid with you. You must stay in the cable tier until the action is over."

"Captain—" she began.

"Mr. Clay!" Hornblower rasped. "Conduct her ladyship and her maid to the cable tier. See that she is safe before you leave her. Those are my *orders*, Mr. Clay. Ha-h'm."

A cowardly way out, perhaps, to throw on Clay the responsibility of seeing his orders carried out. He knew it, but he was angry with the woman because of the sick feeling of worry which she was occasioning him. She left him, nevertheless, with a smile and a wave of the hand, Clay trotting before her.

For several minutes the ship was a turmoil of industry as the men went through the well-learned drill. The guns were run out, the decks sanded, the hoses rigged to the pumps, the fires extinguished. The *Natividad* could be seen from the deck now, sailing on the opposite tack towards her, obviously clawing her hardest up to windward to get the weather gauge. The two ships were nearing each other along the sides of an obtuse angle. Hornblower looked up at the sails and marked a slight shiver. "Steer small, blast you," he growled at the quartermaster.

The *Lydia* lay over before the gale, the waves crashing and hissing overside, the rigging playing a wild symphony.

"*Natividad* won't be able to open her lower deck ports!" gloated Bush beside him. Hornblower saw a cloud of spray break over the enemy's bows.

"No," he said heavily. He would not discuss the possibilities of the approaching action for fear he might be too talkative. "Mr. Gerard," he called down to the lieutenant in charge of the portside main deck battery. "See the matches in your tubs are alight."

With all this spray breaking aboard, the flintlock trigger mechanism could not be relied upon until the guns grew hot and the old-fashioned method of ignition might have to be used—in the tubs on deck were coils of slow-match to meet this emergency. He stared across again at the *Natividad*. She was flying the blue flag with the yellow star; Hornblower glanced up overhead to where the dingy white ensign fluttered from the peak.

"She's opened fire, sir," said Bush beside him.

Hornblower looked back at the *Natividad* just in time to see the last of a puff of smoke blown to shreds by the wind. The sound of the shot did not reach them, and where the ball went no one could say—the jet of water which it struck up somewhere was hidden in the tossing waves.

"Ha-h'm," said Hornblower. It was bad policy to open fire at long range. That first broadside, discharged from guns carefully loaded and aimed, was too precious a thing to be dissipated lightly. It should be saved up for use at the moment when it would do maximum harm.

"We'll be passing mighty close, sir," said Bush.

"Ha-h'm," said Hornblower. Still there was no means of telling which ship would hold the weather gauge when they met. It appeared as if they would meet bow to bow in collision if both captains held rigidly to their present courses. Hornblower had to exert all his willpower to keep himself standing still and apparently unemotional as the tension increased.

Another puff of smoke from the *Natividad*'s starboard bow and simultaneously a crash from the waist told where the shot had struck.

"Two men down at number four gun," said Bush, stooping to look forward under the gangway, and then, eyeing the distance between the two ships: "Lord! It's going to be a near thing."

Hornblower took a last glance up at the topsails. "Stand by, Mr. Rayner. Fire as your guns bear," he called. Second Lieutenant

Rayner was in command of the starboard side main deck battery. Then, from the corner of his mouth to the man at the wheel— "Put your helm a-weather. Hold her so!"

The *Lydia* spun round and shot down the lee side of the *Natividad* and her starboard side guns went off almost simultaneously in a rolling crash that shook the ship to her keel. The billow of smoke was blown away instantly by the gale. Every shot crashed into the *Natividad's* side; the wind brought to their ears the screams of the wounded. Only one single shot was fired from the *Natividad*, and that did no damage—her lower deck ports on this, her lee side, were closed because of the high sea.

"Grand! Oh, grand!" said Bush. He sniffed at the bitter powder smoke as if it had been sweet incense.

"Stand by to go about," rasped Hornblower. The well-drilled crew was ready at sheets and braces. The *Lydia* tacked about, turning like a machine, before the *Natividad* could offer any counter to this unexpected manoeuvre, and Gerard fired his battery into her helpless stern. The ship's boys were cheering in high piping trebles as they came running up from below with new charges for the guns. On the starboard side the guns were already reloaded; on the port side the guns' crews were thrusting wet swabs down the bores to extinguish any residual fragments of smouldering cartridge and ramming in the charges and shot. Hornblower stared across the tossing water at the *Natividad*. He could see Crespo up on her poop; the fellow actually had the insolence to wave his hand to him, while in the midst of bellowing orders at his unhandy crew.

The *Lydia* had wrung the utmost advantage out of her manoeuvre but now, by her possession of the weather gauge, the *Natividad* could force close action. Indeed, next moment the two-decker had swung round and was hurtling down upon them. Gerard stood in the midst of his battery gazing with narrowed eyes into the wind at the impressive bulk close overside. His swarthy beauty was accentuated by the tenseness of the moment and the fierce concentration of his expression. "Cock your locks!" he ordered. "Take your aim! Fire!"

The roar of the broadside coincided exactly with that of the

Natividad's. The ship was enveloped in smoke, through which could be heard the rattling of splinters, the sound of cut rigging tumbling to the deck, and Gerard's voice continuing with his drill. "Fire as you will, boys!" he shouted at last.

The next broadside crashed out raggedly, as the more expert gun crews got off their shots more quickly than the others; soon the sound of firing was continuous, and the *Lydia* was constantly a-tremble. At intervals through the roar of her cannon came the thunderous crash of the *Natividad*'s broadside—Crespo evidently could not trust his crew to fire independently with efficiency, and was working them to the word of command. He was doing it well, too; at intervals, as the sea permitted, her lower deck ports were opening like clockwork and the big twenty-four-pounders were vomiting flame and smoke.

"Hot work, this, sir," said Bush.

The iron hail was sweeping the *Lydia*'s decks. There were dead men piled round the masts, dragged there so as not to encumber the guns' crews. Wounded men were being hauled down the hatchways to the cockpit.

"Ha-h'm," said Hornblower, but the sound was drowned in the roar of the quarterdeck carronade beside him. It was hot work indeed, too hot. This five minutes of close firing convinced him that the *Natividad*'s guns were too well worked for the *Lydia* to have any chance against her overpowering strength broadside to broadside. He would have to win by craft if he was to win at all.

"Hands to the braces!" he yelled, his voice, high-pitched, cutting through the din of the guns. He made calculations with delirious rapidity. Throwing the main topsail aback a trifle allowed the *Natividad* to shoot ahead without taking so much way off the *Lydia* as to make her unhandy, and then the next moment Hornblower tacked his ship about. The *Natividad* came up into the wind in the endeavour to follow her opponent round and keep broadside to broadside with her, but the frigate was far quicker. Hornblower, keenly watching his enemy, tacked once more and shot past the *Natividad*'s stern on the opposite tack while Gerard, running from gun to gun, sent every shot crashing into the shattered timbers.

"Glorious! Damn my soul! Glorious!" spluttered Bush, leaping up and down on the quarterdeck.

Hornblower had no attention to spare for Bush's good opinion, although later he was to remember hearing the words and find warm comfort in them. As the ships diverged he shouted for the *Lydia* to go about again, but even as the helm was put over, the *Natividad* wore round to pass her to leeward. He watched her come foaming up; her bulwarks were riddled with shot and there was a trickle of blood from her scuppers. But Crespo was still on her poop—her guns were run out ready, and on this, her weather side, her lower deck ports were open.

"For what we are about to receive—" said Bush, repeating the hackneyed old blasphemy quoted in every ship awaiting a broadside.

Seconds seemed as long as minutes as the two ships neared. They were passing within a dozen yards of each other. Bow overlapped bow, foremast passed foremast and then foremast passed mainmast. Rayner shouted the order to fire. The *Lydia* lifted to the recoil of the guns, and then, even before the gale had time to blow away the smoke, came the *Natividad*'s crashing reply.

It seemed to Hornblower as if the heavens were falling round him. The wind of a shot made him reel; he found at his feet a palpitating mass which represented half the starboard side carronade's crew, and then with a thunderous crackling the mizzenmast gave way beside him. The mizzen rigging entangled him and flung him down into the blood on the deck, and while he struggled to free himself he felt the *Lydia* swing round as she paid off despite the efforts of the men at the wheel.

He got to his feet, dizzy and shaken. The mizzenmast was gone, snapped off nine feet from the deck. It had taken the main-topgallant mast with it, and masts and yards and sails and rigging trailed alongside and astern by the unparted shrouds. With the loss of the balancing pressure of the mizzen topsail the *Lydia* had been unable to keep her course on the wind and was now drifting helplessly before the gale.

At that very moment he saw the *Natividad* going about to cross his stern and repay, with a crushing broadside, the several unanswered salvoes to which earlier she had been forced to submit. His whole world seemed to be shattered. Ruin was all about him. He gulped convulsively, feeling a sudden sick fear of defeat.

But he knew, at the moment of his getting to his feet, that he must not delay an instant in making the *Lydia* ready for action again. "Afterguard!" he roared—his voice sounding unnatural to himself as he spoke—"Mr. Clay! Cut that wreckage away!"

Clay came pounding aft at the head of a rush of men with axes and cutlasses. As they were chopping at the mizzen shrouds he noticed Bush sitting up on the deck with his face in his hands— a falling block had struck him down, but there was no time to spare for Bush. The *Natividad* was coming down remorselessly on them; he could see exultant figures on her deck waving their hats in triumph. As her bowsprit went by he felt her reefed fore-topsail loom over him and then her broadside crashed out as gun after gun bore on the *Lydia*'s stern. As the shots struck home, he heard a scream from Clay's party beside him, felt a splinter scream past his cheek, and then, just as annihilation seemed about to engulf him, the smoke was borne away, the *Natividad* had gone by, and he was still alive and could look round him. The slide of the aftermost carronade had been smashed, and one of Clay's men was lying screaming on the deck with the gun across his thighs and two or three of his mates striving futilely to prise it off him.

"Stop that!" screamed Hornblower—the necessity of having to give such an order sent his voice up to the same pitch as that of the miserable wretch in his agony. "Mr. Clay, keep them cutting that bloody wreckage away!"

A cable's length away, over the grey-topped waves, the *Natividad* was slowly wearing round to deal a fresh blow at her helpless opponent.

"Foretop, there! Mr. Galbraith, get the headsails in!" Hornblower might, by juggling with the helm, get the *Lydia* to lie to the wind a trifle then, and hit back at his big opponent. But there was no hope of doing so while all this wreckage was trailing astern like a vast sea anchor. A glance showed him that the *Natividad* was already heading to cross their stern again. "Hurry up!" he screamed to the axe men. "You there, Holroyd, Tooms, get down into the mizzen chains."

He suddenly realized how high-pitched and hysterical his voice had become. At all costs he must preserve his appearance of imperturbability. He forced himself to look casually at the *Natividad* as she came plunging down on them, wicked with menace; he made himself grin, and speak in his normal voice. "Don't mind about her, my lads. One thing at a time. Cut this wreckage away, and we'll give them their bellyful after."

The men hacked with renewed force at the tough tangles of cordage. A new extravagant plunge on the part of the *Lydia* caused the wreckage to run out a little farther before catching again, this time on the mizzen stay, which, sweeping the deck, tumbled three men off their feet. Hornblower seized one of the fallen axes, and fell desperately on the rope as it sawed back and forth with the roll of the ship.

Then once more he was engulfed in the smoke and din of the *Natividad*'s broadside. The cries of the man under the carronade ceased abruptly, and Hornblower could feel the crash as the shot struck home in the *Lydia*'s vitals. But he was mesmerized by the necessity of completing his task. The mizzen stay parted under his axe; he saw another rope draw up taut, and cut that as well and then knew that the *Lydia* was free from the wreckage. At his feet lay young Clay, sprawled upon the deck, but Clay had no head.

A sudden breaking wave drenched him with spray; he swept the water from his eyes and looked about him. Most of the men who had been on the quarterdeck with him were dead, marines, seamen, officers. Simmonds had what was left of the marines lined up against the taffrail, ready to reply with musketry to the *Natividad*'s twenty-four-pounders. Bush was standing near the wheel which was manned by two quartermasters; not the same two quartermasters as had stood there when the action began.

Out on the starboard quarter the *Natividad* was wearing round again. Hornblower realized with a little thrill that this time he need not submit meekly to punishment. "Mr. Bush, we'll try and bring her to the wind," he called.

"Aye aye, sir."

He looked back at the *Natividad*, plunging and heaving towards them. "Hard a-starboard!" he snapped at the quartermasters. "Stand to your guns, men."

The crew of the *Natividad*, looking along their guns, suddenly saw the *Lydia*'s battered stern slowly turn from them.

"Fire!" yelled Gerard, his voice cracking with excitement. The *Lydia* heaved again with the recoil of the guns. "Give it her again, lads!" he screamed. "There goes her foremast! Well done, lads!"

The guns' crews cheered madly. In that sudden flurry of action the enemy had been hard hit. Through the smoke Hornblower saw the *Natividad*'s foremast bow forward; her main-topmast whipped and then followed it, and the whole vanished over the side. The *Natividad* turned instantly up into the wind, while at the same time the *Lydia*'s head fell off as she turned downwind despite the efforts of the men at the wheel.

Hornblower wiped the spray slowly from his eyes again. The gale screamed past his ears as the strip of grey sea which divided the two disabled ships widened to a full half mile, and then farther. Through his glass he could see the *Natividad*'s forecastle black with men struggling with the wreck of the foremast. The ship which was first ready for action again would win. He snapped the glass shut and turned to face all the problems which he knew were awaiting his immediate solution.

HORNBLOWER STOOD ON HIS QUARTERDECK while his ship, hove to under the main staysail and three-reefed main topsail, pitched and wallowed in the fantastic sea. It was raining with such violence that nothing could be seen a hundred yards away, and there were deluges of spray sweeping the deck, too, so that he and his clothes were as wet as if he had been swimming. Everyone was appealing to him for orders. At the moment it was Laurie, the purser's steward, who had been appointed acting surgeon.

"But what am I to *do*, sir?" he said pathetically, white-faced, wringing his hands. He had fifty wounded down in the grim dark cockpit, and all of them begging for the assistance which he had no idea of how to give.

"What are you to *do*, sir?" mimicked Hornblower scornfully.

367

"After two months in which to study your duties you have to ask what to do!" Laurie only blenched a little more at this, and Hornblower had to make himself be a little helpful and put some heart in this lily-livered incompetent. "See here, Laurie," he said, in more kindly fashion. "Nobody expects miracles of you. Do what you can. Those who are going to die you must make easy. You have my orders to reckon every man who has lost a limb as one of those. Give them laudanum—twenty-five drops a man, or more if that won't ease them. Tell 'em they're certain to get better and draw a pension for the next fifty years. As for the others, surely your mother wit can guide you. Bandage 'em until the bleeding stops. Put splints on the broken bones. A tot of rum to every wounded man, and promise 'em another at eight bells if they lie still. Get below, man, and see to it."

Laurie scuttled away below without a thought for the hell-turned-loose on the main deck. Here one of the twelve-pounders had come adrift, its breechings shot away by the *Natividad*'s last broadside. With every roll of the ship it was rumbling back and forth across the deck, a ton and a half of insensate weight, threatening at any moment to burst through the ship's side. Galbraith, with some forty men carrying ropes and mats, was trailing it cautiously from point to point in the hope of tying it or smothering it into helplessness. As Hornblower watched them, a fresh heave of the ship sent it thundering in a mad charge straight at them. They parted wildly before it, and it charged through them, its trucks squealing like a forest of pigs, and brought up with a shattering crash against the mainmast.

"Now's your chance, lads! Jump to it!" yelled Hornblower. Galbraith, running forward, risked limb and life to pass a rope's end through an eye tackle. He had no sooner done it than a new movement of the ship swung the gun round. "Mats there!" shouted Hornblower. "Pile them quick! Mr. Galbraith, take a turn with that line round the mainmast. Whipple, put your rope through the breeching ring. Quick, man! Now take a turn!"

Hornblower had accomplished what Galbraith had failed to do —had correlated the efforts of the men in the nick of time so that now the gun was bound and helpless. There only remained the ticklish job of manoeuvring it back to its gunport and securing it with fresh breechings. Howell the carpenter was at his elbow now.

"Four feet in the well, sir," said Howell, knuckling his forehead. "Making fast as well. Can I have more men for the pumps, sir?"

"Not until that gun's in place," said Hornblower grimly. "What damage have you found?"

"Seven shot holes, sir, below waterline. There's no pluggin' 'em, not with this sea runnin', sir. One clean through the third frame timber, starboard side. Two more—"

"I'll have a sail fothered under the bottom as soon as there are enough men to spare. Meanwhile, your men at the pumps will have to continue pumping," snapped Hornblower.

The first lieutenant and the boatswain were busily engaged upon the duty of erecting a jury mizzenmast. To sway up its fifty-five-foot length into a vertical position was going to be a tricky business—hard enough in a smooth sea, dangerous and prolonged out here with the Pacific running mad—but Bush and Harrison the boatswain were tackling it with resource and energy.

A sudden flurry of rain heralded the arrival of a brief clear spell. Braced upon the heaving deck Hornblower set his glass to his eye; the *Natividad* was visible again across the tossing grey-flecked sea. She was hove to as well, looking queerly lopsided in her partially dismasted condition. Hornblower could discover no sign of any immediate replacement of the missing spars; he thought it extremely probable that there was nothing left in the ship to serve as jury masts. In that case as soon as the *Lydia* could carry enough sail aft to enable her to beat to windward he would have the *Natividad* at his mercy—as long as the sea was not running high enough to make gunnery impossible.

He glowered round the horizon; at present there was no sign of the storm abating, and it was long past noon. With the coming of night he might lose the *Natividad* altogether. "How much longer, Mr. Harrison?" he rasped.

"Not long now, sir. Nearly ready, sir."

"You've had long enough and to spare for a simple piece of work like that. Keep the men moving, there."

Now it was the cook come to report to him—the cook and his

mates had been the only men who could be spared for the grisly work allotted to them. "All ready, sir," he said.

Without a word Hornblower strode forward down the starboard side gangway, taking his prayer book from his pocket. The fourteen dead were there, shrouded in their hammocks, two to a grating, a round shot sewn into the foot of each hammock. Hornblower blew a long blast upon his silver whistle, and activity ceased on board while he read, compromising between haste and solemnity, the office for the burial of the dead at sea: "We . . . commit their bodies to the deep—"

The cook and his mates tilted each grating in turn, and the bodies fell with sullen splashes overside while Hornblower read the concluding words of the service. Then he blew his whistle again and the bustling activity recommenced.

And now picking her way across the main deck below him came Lady Barbara, the little Negress clinging to her skirts. "My orders were for you to stay below, ma'am," he shouted. "This deck is no place for you."

Lady Barbara looked round the seething deck and then tilted her chin to answer him. "I can see that without having it pointed out to me," she said. "I have no intention of obstructing, Captain. I was going to shut myself in my cabin."

"Your cabin?" Hornblower laughed. Two broadsides from the *Natividad* had blasted their way through the cabin. The idea of Lady Barbara shutting herself up there struck him as being intensely funny. He laughed again and then, as an abyss of hysteria opened itself before him, controlled himself. "There is no cabin left for you, ma'am. I regret that the only course open to you is to go back whence you have come."

Lady Barbara, looking up at him, thought of the cable tier she had just left. Pitch-dark, with only room to sit hunched up on the slimy cable, rats scampering over her legs; the ship pitching and rolling madly, and Hebe howling with fright beside her; the tremendous din of the guns; the stench of the bilge, and the ignorance of how the battle was progressing. The thought of going back there appalled her. But she saw the captain's face, white with fatigue and strain under its tan, and she had noted that laugh with

370

its hysterical pitch, and the grim effort that had been made to speak to her reasonably. His coat was torn and his white trousers were stained—with blood, she suddenly realized. She felt pity for him, then. She knew now that to speak to him of rats and stinks would be ridiculous. "Very good, Captain," she said quietly, and turned to retrace her steps.

The little Negress set up a howl, and was promptly shaken into silence as Lady Barbara dragged her along.

CHAPTER IX

The crew of the *Lydia* had worked marvellously. The main deck was cleared of most of the traces of the fight. A sail stretched over the bottom of the ship had done much to check the inflow of water, so that with more men at work upon the pumps the level in the well was measurably sinking. The jury mast had just been fixed in position, and Hornblower leaned against the quarterdeck rail, sick with weariness, wondering dully how his men could find the strength to cheer as they put the finishing touches to this, their latest feat.

He found Bush beside him—Bush had a rag round his head, bloodstained because of the cut inflicted by the falling block. "Shall I send up the topmast and yards, sir?" he asked.

Hornblower looked round the horizon. The gale was blowing as hard as ever, and only a grey smudge on the distant horizon marked where the *Natividad* was battling with it. All the mad effort put into the work to get it done speedily was wasted. Hornblower could see that there was no chance of showing any more canvas at present, no chance of renewing the fight while the *Natividad* was still unprepared. It was a bitter pill to swallow. He could imagine the pitying smiles and knowing wags of the head at the Admiralty when he sent in his report, stating that the weather had been too bad to renew the action. It was a hackneyed excuse, like the uncharted rock which explained faulty navigation. Cowardice would be the unspoken comment on every side—at ten thousand miles' distance no one could judge of the strength of a storm. He could divest himself of some of his responsibility by asking Bush his opinion, but he turned irritably from the thought of displaying such weakness. "No," he said, without expression. "We shall stay hove to until the weather moderates."

There was a gleam of admiration in Bush's bloodshot eyes—Bush could well admire a captain who could make with such small debate a decision so nearly touching his professional reputation. "Aye aye, sir," he said, warned by the scowl on his captain's forehead not to enlarge on the subject. But his affection for his captain compelled him to open a fresh one. "If that's the case, sir, why not take a rest? You look mortally tired, sir. Let me send and have a berth screened off for you in the wardroom." Bush found his hand twitching—he had been about to commit the enormity of patting his captain's shoulder, and restrained himself just in time.

"Fiddlesticks!" snapped Hornblower. As if a captain of a frigate could publicly admit that he was tired! "It is rather you who need a rest," he added. "Dismiss the starboard watch, and turn in. Have someone attend to that forehead of yours first. With the enemy in sight I shall stay on deck."

After that it was Polwheal who came to plague him—Hornblower wondered ineffectively whether he came of his own initiative or whether Bush sent him up.

"I've been to attend to the lady, sir," said Polwheal. "I've screened off a bit of the orlop for her, sir. The wounded's mostly quiet by now, sir. I slung a 'ammock for her—nipped into it like a bird, she did, sir. She's taken food, too, sir—what was left of the cold chicken an' a glass of wine. Not that she wanted to, sir, but I persuaded her, like."

"Very good, Polwheal," said Hornblower. It was an enormous relief to hear that one responsibility at least was lifted from his shoulders.

"An' now you, sir," went on Polwheal. "I've brought you up some dry clothes and your boat cloak from the chest in your storeroom; it's all warm an' dry, sir—I'm afraid that last broadside spoilt everything in your cabin."

Polwheal could take much for granted and could wheedle the rest. Hornblower had anticipated dragging his weary form in his waterlogged clothes up and down the quarterdeck all through the night, but Polwheal unearthed Lady Barbara's hammock chair from somewhere and lashed it to the rail. Then he persuaded Hornblower to sit in it and consume a supper of biscuit and rum.

Finally, Polwheal draped the boat cloak about him and airily took it for granted that he would continue to sit there, since his determination was fixed not to turn in while the enemy was still close at hand.

And marvellously, as he sat there, with the spray wetting his face and the ship leaping and rolling under him, his head drooped upon his breast and he slept. But soon after midnight his sailor's instinct called him into wakefulness. Something was happening to the weather. He scrambled stiffly to his feet. The ship was rolling more wildly than ever, but as he sniffed round him he knew that there was an improvement. He walked across to the binnacle, and Bush loomed vastly out of the darkness beside him.

"Wind's shifting southerly an' moderating, sir," said Bush, peering into the darkness. "Black as the Earl of Hell's riding boots, all the same, sir."

Somewhere in the darkness, perhaps twenty miles from them, perhaps only two hundred yards, the *Natividad* was combating the same gale. If the moon were to break through the scurrying clouds they might be at grips with her at any moment. Yet in this present darkness, however much the gale might moderate, there was nothing they could do. Hornblower yawned elaborately.

"I think I shall sleep," he said, speaking with the utmost unconcern. "See that the lookouts keep awake, if you please, Mr. Bush. And have me called as soon as it grows lighter."

"Aye aye, sir," said Bush, and Hornblower went back to his boat cloak and his hammock chair.

He lay there for the rest of the night, unsleeping, and yet staying rigidly still so that his officers might think him asleep and admire the steadiness of his nerves. His mind was busy on the task of guessing what Crespo might be planning in the *Natividad*.

The latter was so badly crippled that probably he would be able to make no effective repairs while at sea. It would be much to his advantage to make for the Gulf of Fonseca again. There he could step a new foremast and send up a new main-topmast, and if the *Lydia* tried to interfere he would have the assistance of shore boats and possibly even of shore batteries. Moreover he could land his wounded and refill the gaps in his crew—even landsmen would be of use in a fight to a finish. Crespo was a man of sufficient flexibility of mind not to scorn a retreat if it were to his advantage. Yet making for the mainland would be dangerous in Crespo's opinion, for the *Lydia* could hem him in against the shore and compel him to fight before he arrived at his destination. Most likely he would reach far out to sea, clawing southward at the same time as much as he could, and make for the Gulf of Fonseca by a long detour out of sight of land. From the *Lydia*'s masthead, in clear daylight, a ship might be seen within a radius of as much as twenty miles. Hornblower plunged into further tortuous mental calculations as to the size of the circle in which the *Natividad* would necessarily be found at dawn.

Eight bells in the middle watch sounded; the watch was called; he heard Gerard come to take over the deck from Bush. The wind was dropping fast, although the sea showed no sign of moderating as yet. The sky was perceptibly lighter—here and there he could see stars between the clouds. Crespo would certainly be able to make sail now and attempt his escape. It was time for Hornblower to come to a decision. He climbed out of the hammock chair and walked across to the wheel.

"We will make sail, if you please, Mr. Bush."

"Aye aye, sir."

Hornblower gave the course, and he knew as he gave it that it might be quite the wrong one. Every yard that the *Lydia* was sailing now might be in a direction away from the *Natividad*. Crespo might at this very moment be heading past him to safety.

There would be some who would attribute his failure to destroy the *Natividad* to incompetence, and there would be not a few who would call it cowardice.

DAWN WAS APPROACHING, and already the stars were invisible overhead. The accustomed eye could pierce the greyness for a mile about the ship. Astern to the eastward, as the *Lydia* lifted on a wave, a grain of gold suddenly showed over the horizon, vanished, returned and grew. Soon it became a great slice of the sun, sucking up greedily the faint mist which hung over the sea. Then the whole disc lifted clear, and the miracle of the dawn was accomplished.

"Sail ho!" came pealing down from the masthead; Hornblower's calculations had been right. Dead ahead, and ten miles distant, the *Natividad* was wallowing along, her appearance oddly at contrast with the one she had presented yesterday morning. Something had been done to give her a jury rig. A stumpy topmast had been erected where her foremast had stood; her main-topmast had been replaced by a slight spar and on this jury rig she carried a queer collection of jibs, foresails and spritsails all badly set—"Like old Mother Brown's washing on the line," said Bush.

At sight of the *Lydia* she put her helm over and came round until her masts were in line, heading away from the frigate.

"Making a stern chase of it," said Gerard, his glass to his eye. "He had enough yesterday, I fancy."

Hornblower heard the remark. He could understand Crespo better than that: the man was quite right to postpone action. At sea nothing was certain. Something might prevent the *Lydia*'s closing with him; a squall of wind, the accidental carrying away of a spar, an opportune descent of mist. Crespo was merely exploiting the chance that the *Natividad* might get clear away; it was Hornblower's duty to see that the chance did not occur.

He examined the *Natividad* closely, ran his eyes over the *Lydia*'s sails to see that every one was drawing, and bethought himself of his crew. "Send the hands to breakfast," he said.

He remained, pacing up and down the quarterdeck, unable to keep himself still any longer. The *Natividad* might be running away, but he knew well that she would fight hard enough when he caught her up. Added to that, with a jury mizzenmast, and leaking like a sieve despite the sail under her, the *Lydia* was in no condition to fight a severe battle. Defeat for her and death for him might be awaiting them across that strip of blue sea.

Polwheal suddenly appeared beside him on the quarterdeck, a tray in his hand. "Your breakfast, sir," he said, "seeing as how we'll be in action when your usual time comes." As he proffered the tray Hornblower suddenly realized how much he wanted that steaming cup of coffee. He took it eagerly and drank thirstily. "Thank you, Polwheal," he said.

"An' 'er la'ship's compliments, sir, an' please may she stay where she is in the orlop when the action is renooed."

"Ha-h'm," said Hornblower. All through the night he had been trying to forget the problem of Lady Barbara, as a man tries to forget an aching tooth. The orlop meant that Lady Barbara would be next to the wounded, separated from them only by a canvas screen—no place for a woman. But the truth was that there was no place for a woman in a fighting frigate. "Put her wherever you like as long as she is not in reach of shot," he said, irritably.

"Aye aye, sir. An' 'er la'ship told me to say that she wished you the best of good fortune today, sir, an'—an'—she was confident that you would meet with the success you—you deserve, sir." Polwheal's stumbling revealed that he had not been quite as successful in learning this long speech as he wished.

"Thank you, Polwheal," said Hornblower gravely. He remembered Lady Barbara's clean-cut and eager face as she looked up at him from the main deck yesterday. "Ha-h'm," he said angrily. He was aware that his expression had softened, and he feared lest Polwheal should have noticed it. "Get below and see that her ladyship is comfortable."

The hands were pouring up from breakfast now; the pumps were clanking with a faster rhythm now that a fresh crew was at work upon them. The guns' crews were gathered about their guns, and the few idlers were crowded on the forecastle eagerly watching the progress of the chase.

"Do you think the wind's going to hold, sir?" asked Bush, coming onto the quarterdeck like a bird of ill omen. "Seems to me as if the sun's swallowing it."

There was no doubting the fact that as the sun climbed higher in the sky the wind was diminishing in force. The sea was still steep and rough, but the sky overhead was fast becoming of a hard metallic blue. It was growing hot.

"We're overhauling 'em fast," said Hornblower, staring fixedly at the chase so as to ignore these portents of the elements. A moment later he growled at the quartermaster at the wheel as the ship's head fell away in the trough of a wave, "Steer small, blast you."

"I can't, sir, begging your pardon," was the reply. "There aren't enough wind."

It was true enough. The wind had died away so that the *Lydia* could not maintain the two-knot speed which was sufficient to give her rudder power to act. "We'll have to wet the sails. Mr. Bush, see to it, if you please," said Hornblower.

One division of one watch was roused up to this duty. A soaking wet sail will hold air which would escape if it were dry. Whips were rove through the blocks on the yards, and seawater hoisted up and poured over the canvas. So rapid was the evaporation that the buckets had to be kept continually in action.

The *Lydia* crept, plunging madly, over the tossing sea and under the glaring sky. The *Natividad* was turning idly backwards and forwards, showing sometimes her broadside and sometimes her masts in line, unable to steer any course in the light air prevailing. Bush looked complacently up at his new mizzenmast, a pyramid of canvas, and then across at the swaying *Natividad*, less than five miles away. The minutes dragged by, their passage marked only by the monotonous noises of the ship. Hornblower stood in the scorching sunlight, fingering his telescope.

"Here comes the wind again, by God!" said Bush, suddenly. The *Lydia* plunged forward to the music of the water under her bows, while the *Natividad* grew perceptibly nearer. "It will reach him quickly enough. There! What did I say?"

The *Natividad*'s sails filled as the breeze came down to her. She straightened upon her course.

"'Twon't help her as much as it helps us," commented Bush. "We'll be trying long shots at her soon," he added.

"Mr. Bush," said Hornblower, "I can judge the situation without the assistance of your comments, profound though they be."

"I beg your pardon, sir," said Bush, hurt. He flushed angrily for a moment until he noticed the anxiety in Hornblower's tired eyes, and then stumped away to the opposite rail to forget his rage.

As if by way of comment the big main course flapped loudly, once, like a gun. The breeze was dying down, but the *Natividad* still held it. She was drawing away once more. Here in the tropical Pacific one ship can have a fair wind while another two miles away lies becalmed. Hornblower stirred uneasily. He feared lest the *Natividad* should sail clean away from him. The *Lydia* began to roll aimlessly to the send of the waves. Ten minutes passed before he was reassured by the sight of the *Natividad*'s similar behaviour. She was four miles away now—a mile and a half beyond the farthest range of any of the *Lydia*'s guns.

"Mr. Bush," said Hornblower. "We will tow with the boats. Have the launch and the cutter hoisted out."

Bush looked doubtful for a moment. He feared that two could play at that game. But he realized—as Hornblower had realized before him—that the *Lydia*'s graceful hull would be more amenable to towing than the *Natividad*'s ungainly bulk. It was Hornblower's duty to try every course that might bring his ship into action with the enemy.

So there began for the boats' crews a period of the most exhausting and exasperating labour. They would tug and strain at the oars, moving the ponderous boats over the heaving waves, until the tow ropes tightened with a jerk as the strain came upon them. Then, tug as they would, they would seem to make no progress at all, the oar blades foaming impotently through the blue water, until the *Lydia* consented to crawl forward a little and the whole operation could be repeated. Sometimes she yawed and sometimes she sagged, falling away in the trough on occasions so much that the launch and the cutter were dragged, with much splashing from the oars, stern first after her wavering bows, and then changing her mind and heaving forward so fast after the two ropes that the men, flinging their weight upon the oars, were precipitated backwards with the ease of progression while in imminent danger of being run down.

They sat naked on the thwarts while the sweat ran in streams down their faces and chests, unable—unlike their comrades at the pumps—to forget their fatigues in the numbness of monotonous work when every moment called for vigilance and attention, tugging painfully away until even hands calloused by years of pulling and hauling cracked and blistered so that the oars were agony to touch.

Hornblower knew well enough the hardship they were undergoing and he did his best to cheer them on. By careful measurement with his sextant of the subtended angles he was able to say with certainty at the end of an hour that their efforts had dragged the *Lydia* a little nearer to the *Natividad*. Lieutenant Bush was in agreement.

"*Natividad*'s hoisting out a twelve-oared boat, sir," hailed Knyvett from the foretop. "They're taking the ship in tow."

"And they're welcome," scoffed Bush. "Twelve oars won't move that old tub of a *Natividad* very far."

Hornblower glared at him, and Bush retired to his own side of the quarterdeck again. Hornblower was fretting himself into a fever. The endless clanking of the pumps, the rolling of the ship, the noise of the oars, were driving him mad, as though he could scream at the slightest additional provocation.

At noon he changed the men at the oars and pumps, and sent the crew to dinner—he remembered bitterly that he had already made them breakfast early in anticipation of immediate action. And then, at two bells, as he looked for the thousandth time through his telescope, he suddenly saw a disc of white appear on the high stern of the *Natividad*. The disc expanded into a thin cloud, and six seconds after its first appearance Hornblower saw a fountain of water rise no more than fifty yards from the *Lydia*'s starboard quarter. The *Natividad* was evidently trying the range.

"*Natividad* carries two long eighteens aft on the quarterdeck," said Gerard to Bush in Hornblower's hearing. "Heavy metal for stern chasers."

Hornblower knew it already. He would have to run the gauntlet of those two guns for an hour, possibly, before he could bring the brass nine-pounder on his forecastle into effective action. But it would cheer the men up to have a gun banging away occasionally instead of being merely shot at without making any reply.

"Mr. Gerard," said Hornblower. "Send for Mr. Marsh and see what he can do with the long nine forward."

Marsh came waddling up from the darkness of the magazine, and blinked in the blinding sunshine. He shook his head doubtfully as he eyed the distance between the ships, but he had the gun cleared away, and he loaded and trained it with his own hands, lovingly. As the cannon roared out, its report sounding flat in the heated motionless air, a dozen telescopes were trained on the *Natividad* to watch for the fall of the shot.

"Two cables' lengths astern of her!" yelled Knyvett from the foretop.

"Try again, Mr. Marsh," Hornblower said. As he spoke there came a crash forward as one of the *Natividad*'s eighteen-pounder balls struck home close above the waterline. Hornblower could hear young Savage down in the launch hurling shrill blasphemies at the men at the oars to urge them on—that shot must have passed just over his head. Hornblower knew now that there would be a long and damaging interval before the *Lydia* could hit back with effect. He balanced the arguments for and against continuing to try and close with the enemy while Mr. Marsh was squinting along the sights of the nine-pounder, and his flexibility of mind crystallized into sullen obstinacy. He had started the action; he would go through with it to the end, cost what it might.

The nine-pounder went off as though to signal this decision. "Just alongside her!" screamed Knyvett triumphantly.

"Well done, Mr. Marsh," said Hornblower, and Marsh wagged his beard complacently.

The *Natividad* was firing faster now. Three times a splintering crash told of a shot which had been aimed true. Then suddenly a thrust as if from an invisible hand made Hornblower reel on the quarterdeck, and his ears were filled with a brief rending noise. A skimming shot had ploughed a channel along the planking of the quarterdeck. A marine dropped his musket with a clatter and clapped his hands to his face, with the blood spouting between his fingers.

"Are you hurt, sir?" cried Bush, leaping across to Hornblower.

"No." Hornblower turned back to stare through his glass at the *Natividad* while the wounded man was being dragged away. For a second he was puzzled. The *Natividad*'s stumpy foremast and

380

mainmast were coming into view. The rowing boat was now pulling the ship laboriously round so that her whole broadside would bear. Not two, but twenty-five guns would soon be opening fire on the *Lydia*.

Hornblower felt his breath come quicker. He was compelling himself to appear lighthearted and carefree. "They're waiting for us now, lads," he said. "We shall have some pebbles about our ears before long. Let's show 'em that Englishmen don't care."

The men cheered him for that, as he expected and hoped they would do. He looked through his glass again at the *Natividad*. She was still turning, very slowly, but her masts were fully separate from each other now, and he could see a hint of the broad white stripes which ornamented her side.

Forward he could hear the oars grinding away as the men in the boats laboured to drag the *Lydia* to grips with her enemy. Across the deck a little group of officers—Bush and Crystal among them —were academically discussing what percentage of hits might be expected from the Spanish broadside. They were cold-blooded about it in a fashion he could never hope to imitate with sincerity. He did not fear death so much—nor nearly as much—as defeat and the pitying contempt of his colleagues. The chiefest dread at the back of his mind was the fear of mutilation. An ex-naval officer stumping about on two wooden legs might be an object of condolence, but he was a figure of fun, nevertheless. Hornblower dreaded being a figure of fun. It was a thought which set him shuddering while he looked through the telescope. So horrible did it seem that he did not stop to think of the associated details, of the agonies he would have to bear down there in the dark cockpit at the mercy of Laurie's incompetence.

The *Natividad* was suddenly engulfed in smoke, and seconds later the air around the *Lydia* was torn by the hurtling broadside.

"Not more than two hits," said Bush, gleefully.

"Just what I said," said Crystal. "That captain of theirs ought to go round and train every gun himself."

"How do you know he did not?" argued Bush.

As punctuation the nine-pounder forward banged out its defiance. Hornblower fancied that his straining eyes saw splinters fly amidships of the *Natividad*. "Well aimed, Mr. Marsh!" he called. "You hit him squarely."

Another broadside came from the *Natividad*, and another followed it, and another after that. There were dead men laid out again on the *Lydia*'s deck, and the groaning wounded were dragged below.

"It is obvious to anyone of a mathematical turn of mind," said Crystal, "that those guns are all laid by different hands. The shots are too scattered for it to be otherwise."

"Nonsense!" maintained Bush sturdily. "See how long it is between broadsides. Time enough for one man to train each gun. What would they be doing in that time otherwise?"

Crystal started to answer, but a sudden shriek of cannonballs over his head silenced him for a moment.

"Mr. Galbraith!" shouted Bush. "Have that main-t'gallant stay spliced directly." Then he turned triumphantly on Crystal. "Did you notice," he asked, "how every shot from that broadside went high? How does the mathematical mind explain that?"

"They fired on the upward roll, Mr. Bush. Really, Mr. Bush, I think that after Trafalgar—"

Hornblower longed to order them to cease the argument which was lacerating his nerves, but he could not be such a tyrant as that. "Mr. Bush," he asked, "at what distance do you think the *Natividad* is now?"

Bush considered. "Three parts of a mile, sir."

"Two thirds, more likely, sir," said Crystal.

"Your opinion was not asked, Mr. Crystal," snapped Hornblower. Even at two thirds of a mile the *Lydia*'s carronades would be ineffective. She must continue running the gauntlet.

Though it was long past noon it was still terribly hot under the blazing sun. The men at the guns were silent now, Hornblower noticed—for long they had laughed and joked at their posts, but they were beginning to sulk under the punishment. That was a bad sign. "Pass the word for Sullivan and his fiddle," he ordered.

The red-haired Irish madman came aft, and knuckled his forehead, his fiddle and bow under his arm.

"Give us a tune, Sullivan," Hornblower ordered. "Hey there,

men, who is there among you who dances the best hornpipe?"

There was a difference of opinion, apparently. "Benskin, sir," said some voices. "Hall, sir," said others. "No, MacEvoy, sir."

"Then we'll have a tournament," said Hornblower. "Here, Benskin, Hall, MacEvoy. A hornpipe from each of you and a guinea for the man who does it best."

In later years it was a tale told and retold, how the *Lydia* was towed into action with hornpipes being danced on her main deck. It was quoted as an example of Hornblower's cool courage, and only Hornblower knew how little truth there was in this.

Then later in that dreadful afternoon there came a crash from forward, followed by a chorus of shouts and screams overside. "Launch sunk, sir!" hailed Galbraith from the forecastle, but Hornblower was there as soon as he had uttered the words.

A round shot had dashed the launch practically into its component planks, and the survivors were scrambling in the water, leaping up for the bobstay or struggling to climb into the cutter.

"We're close enough now for the enemy to feel our teeth," Hornblower said loudly. The men who heard him cheered. "Mr. Hooker!" he called to the midshipman in the cutter. "When you have picked up those men, kindly starboard your helm. We are going to open fire." He came aft to the quarterdeck again. "Hard a-starboard," he growled at the quartermaster. "Mr. Gerard, you may open first when your guns bear."

Very slowly the *Lydia* swung round. Another broadside from the *Natividad* came crashing into her before she had completed the turn, but Hornblower did not notice it. He had brought his ship within four hundred yards of the enemy. The period of inaction was over.

"Cock your locks!" shouted Gerard in the waist. "Take your aim! Fire!"

The smoke billowed out amid the thunder of the discharge, and the *Lydia* heaved to the recoil of the guns.

"Give him another, lads!" shouted Hornblower through the din. Now that action was joined he found himself exalted and happy, the dreadful fears of mutilation forgotten. In thirty seconds the guns were reloaded, run out and fired—again and again and again. Five broadsides from the *Lydia*, and Hornblower reckoned only two from the *Natividad*. At that rate, the *Natividad*'s superiority in numbers of guns and weight of metal would be more than counterbalanced. At the sixth broadside a gun went off prematurely, a second before Gerard gave the word. "Steady, there!" Hornblower shouted. "I'll flog the next man who fires out of turn."

"Good old Horny!" piped up some unknown voice forward, and there was a burst of laughing and cheering.

The smoke was banked thick about the ship already so that from the quarterdeck it was impossible to see individuals on the forecastle, but in this unnatural darkness one could see the long orange flashes of the guns despite the vivid sunshine outside. Hornblower found Bush beside him.

"*Natividad*'s feeling our fire, sir," he roared through the racket. "She's firing very wild. Look at that, sir."

Of the broadside fired only one or two shots struck home. Hornblower nodded happily. This was his justification for running the risks involved in closing to that range. To maintain a rapid fire, well aimed, amid the confusion of a short-range naval battle called for discipline and practice of a sort that he knew the *Natividad*'s crew could not boast.

He looked down through the smoke at the *Lydia*'s main deck. Something—the concussion of the guns, a faint breath of air, or the send of the sea—was causing the *Lydia* to turn away a trifle from her enemy. The guns were having to be trained round farther and farther so that the rate of firing was being slowed down. He raced forward, running out along the bowsprit until he was over the cutter where Hooker and his men sat staring at the fight. "Mr. Hooker, bring her head round two points to starboard." The men bent to their oars and headed their boat towards the *Natividad*. Hornblower ran back to the quarterdeck.

"It's my belief we've hit them hard, sir," commented Bush. He tried to look through the eddying smoke, even fanning ridiculously with his hands in the attempt—a gesture which, by showing that he was not quite as calm as he appeared to be, gave Hornblower an absurd pleasure.

384

Crystal came up as well. "It's my belief that there's a light wind blowing." He held up a wetted finger. "There is indeed, sir. A trifle of breeze over the port quarter."

There came a stronger puff as he spoke, which rolled away the smoke in a solid mass over the starboard bow and revealed the scene as if a theatre curtain had been raised. There was the *Natividad*, looking like a wreck. Her jury foremast had gone the way of its predecessor, and her mainmast had followed it. Only her mizzenmast stood now, and she was rolling wildly in the swell with a huge tangle of rigging trailing over her disengaged side. Abreast her foremast three ports had been battered into one; the gap looked like a missing tooth.

"She's low in the water," said Bush, but on the instant a fresh broadside vomited smoke from her battered side, and this time by some chance every shot told in the *Lydia*, as the crash below well indicated. The smoke billowed round the *Natividad*, and as it cleared the watchers saw her swing round head to the wind, helpless in the light air. The *Lydia* had felt the breeze. Hornblower could tell that she had steerage way again. He saw his chance on the instant. "Starboard a point," he ordered the quartermaster at the wheel. "Forward, there! Cast off the cutter." The *Lydia* steadied across her enemy's bows and raked her with thunder and flame.

"Back the main tops'l!" ordered Hornblower.

The men were cheering again on the main deck, through the roar of the guns. Astern the red sun was dipping to the water's edge in a glory of scarlet and gold. Soon it would be night.

"She must strike soon. God! Why don't she strike?" Bush was saying, as at close range the broadsides tore into the helpless enemy, raking her from bow to stern. Hornblower knew better. No ship under Crespo's command and flying El Supremo's flag would strike her colours. He could see the golden star on a blue ground fluttering through the smoke.

"Pound him, lads, pound him!" shouted Gerard.

With the shortening range he could rely on his gun captains to fire independently now. It was growing darker and the flashes of the guns could be seen again, leaping in long orange tongues from the muzzles. High above the fast-fading sunset could be seen the first star, shining out brilliantly.

The *Natividad*'s bowsprit went, and then the mizzenmast fell as well, cut through by shots which had ripped their way down the whole length of the ship.

"She must strike now, by God!" said Bush.

As if in reply to him there came a sudden flash and report from the *Natividad*'s bows. Some devoted souls had contrived to slew a gun round so that it would bear right forward, and were firing into the looming bulk of the *Lydia*.

At every second the range was shortening. In the dwindling light, when their eyes were not blinded with gun flashes, Hornblower and Bush could see figures moving about on the *Natividad*'s deck. They were firing muskets now, as well. The flashes pricked the darkness and Hornblower heard a bullet thud into the rail beside him.

"The closer we are, the quicker we'll finish it," said Bush.

"Yes, but we'll run on board of her soon," said Hornblower. Conscious of an overmastering weariness, he roused himself for a further effort. "Call the hands to stand by to repel boarders," he said, and he walked across to where the two starboard side quarterdeck carronades were thundering away. Their crews were so hypnotized by the monotony of loading and firing that it took him several seconds to attract their notice. Eventually they stood still, sweating, while Hornblower gave his orders. Then they loaded the two carronades with canister and waited, crouching beside the guns, while the two ships drifted closer and closer together.

The actual contact was unexpected, as a sudden combination of wind and sea closed the gap with a rush. The *Natividad*'s bow hit the *Lydia* amidships with a jarring crash. There was a pandemonium of yells from the *Natividad* as a dark mass of her men swarmed forward to board. The captains of the *Lydia*'s carronades sprang to their lanyards.

"Wait!" shouted Hornblower. His mind was like a calculating machine, judging wind and sea, time and distance, as the *Lydia* slowly swung round. With hand spikes and the brute strength of

386

the men he trained one carronade round and the other followed his example, while the mob on the *Natividad*'s forecastle surged along the bulwarks waiting for the moment to board. The two carronades came right up against them. "Fire!"

A thousand musket balls were vomited from the carronades straight into the packed crowd. There was a moment of silence, and then the pandemonium of shouts and cheers was replaced by a thin chorus of screams and cries—the blast of musket balls had swept the *Natividad*'s forecastle clear from side to side.

For a space the two ships clung together in this position; the *Lydia* pounded away with a dozen guns almost touching the *Natividad*'s bow. Then wind and sea parted them again. From the *Natividad* came not a gun, not even a musket shot.

"Cease firing," Hornblower shouted to Gerard. The guns fell silent, and he stared through the darkness at the vague mass of the *Natividad*, wallowing in the waves. "Surrender!" he shouted.

"Never!" came the reply—Crespo's voice, he could have sworn to it, thin and high-pitched. It added two or three words of obscene insult.

Hornblower could afford to smile at that, even through his weariness. He had fought his battle and won it. "You have done all that brave men could do," he shouted. Then something caught his eye—a wavering glow of red about *Natividad*'s vague bows. "Crespo, you fool! Your ship's on fire! Surrender, while you can."

"Never!"

The *Lydia*'s guns, hard against the *Natividad*'s side, had flung their flaming wads in among the splintered timbers. The tinder-dry old ship would be a mass of flames soon. Hornblower's first duty was to his own ship—when the fire should reach the *Natividad*'s magazine she would become a volcano of flaming fragments, imperilling the *Lydia*.

"We must haul off from her, Mr. Bush," said Hornblower, speaking formally to conceal the tremor in his voice. "Man the braces, there."

The *Lydia* swung away, clawing her way up to windward of the flaming wreck. Bush and Hornblower gazed back at her. There were bright flames spouting from the shattered bows—the red

387

glow was reflected in the heaving sea around her. And then, as they looked, the flames vanished abruptly, like an extinguished candle. There was nothing to be seen at all, nothing save darkness and the faint glimmer of the wave crests. The sea had swallowed the *Natividad* before the flames could destroy her.

"Sunk, by God!" exclaimed Bush, leaning out over the rail.

HORNBLOWER STILL SEEMED TO HEAR that last wailing "Never!" during the seconds of silence that followed. Yet he was perhaps the first of all his ship's company to recover from the shock. He put his ship about and ran down to the scene of the *Natividad*'s sinking. They picked up a few men—two were hauled out of the water by men in the *Lydia*'s chains, and the cutter found half a dozen swimmers; that was all. As they stood on the *Lydia*'s deck in the lantern light with the water streaming from their ragged clothes and their lank black hair, they were sullen and silent.

"Never mind, we'll make topmen of them yet," said Hornblower, trying to speak lightly. Fatigue had reached such a pitch now that he was speaking as if out of a dream.

"Aye aye, sir," said the boatswain.

Anything was grist that came to the Royal Navy's mill—Harrison was prepared to make seamen out of the strangest human material; he had done so all his life, for that matter.

"What course shall I set, sir?" asked Bush, as Hornblower turned back to the quarterdeck.

"Course?" said Hornblower, vaguely. "Course?" It was hard to realize that the *Natividad* was sunk, that there was no enemy afloat within thousands of miles. It was even harder to realize that the pumps, clanking away monotonously, could hardly keep the leaks in check, that the *Lydia* still had a sail stretched under her bottom and stood in acute need of a complete refit.

At last it came to him that now he had to make fresh plans. He must report his success at Panama, as soon as possible; perhaps he could refit there. He had to force his tired brain to think again. He went wearily down to his cabin and found the splintered chart cases amid the indescribable wreckage, and he pored over the torn chart, laying off a course that would carry the *Lydia* to Panama.

He came up on deck again and gave the course to Bush. Then Polwheal materialized at his elbow, with boat cloak and hammock chair. Hornblower allowed himself to be wrapped in the cloak, and he fell half fainting into the chair. His head sank on his breast and he slept and he snored through all the din which the crew made in their endeavour to get the *Lydia* shipshape again.

CHAPTER X

W hat awoke Hornblower was the sun, which lifted itself over the horizon and shone straight into his eyes. He rose from his chair, stretching himself painfully, for all his joints ached with the fatigues of yesterday. Bush was standing by the wheel, his face grey and lined and strangely old in the hard light. Hornblower nodded to him and received his salute in return; Bush was wearing his cocked hat over the dirty white bandage round his forehead. Hornblower would have spoken to him but all his attention was caught up immediately in looking round the ship. There was a good breeze blowing and the *Lydia* could only just hold her course close hauled. The jury mizzenmast seemed to be standing up well to its work, but every sail that was spread seemed to have at least one shot hole in it—some of them a dozen or more. On the leeside gangway was a long row of corpses, each in its hammock. Hornblower flinched when he saw the length of it.

The dead on deck outnumbered the living. Bush seemed to have sent below every man save for a dozen to hand and steer, which was sensible of him, seeing that everyone must be worn out with yesterday's toil; yet one man out of every seven on board would have to be employed at the pumps until the shot holes could be plugged.

There were still evident many other signs of yesterday's battle. The decks were furrowed and grooved in all directions, and there were shot holes in the ship's sides with canvas roughly stretched over them. The port sills were stained black with powder; on one of them an eighteen-pounder shot stood out, half buried in the tough oak. But on the other hand an immense amount of work had been done, and apart from the weariness of her crew, the *Lydia* was ready to fight another battle at two minutes' notice. Hornblower felt thankful that he had had seven months to train his crew into its present state of readiness and discipline.

But he felt a prick of shame, too, that so much should have been done while he slept lazily in his hammock chair. "Very good indeed, Mr. Bush," he said, walking over to him; yet his natural shyness combined with his feeling of shame to make his speech stilted. "I am both astonished and pleased at the work you have accomplished."

"Today is Sunday, sir," said Bush, simply.

So it was. Sunday was the day of the captain's inspection, when he went round examining everything, to see that the first lieutenant was doing his duty in keeping the ship efficient. Hornblower could not fight down a smile at this ingenious explanation. "Sunday or no Sunday," he said, "you have done magnificently, Mr. Bush. I shall say so in my report to the Admiralty."

"I know you'll do that, sir." Bush's weary face was illuminated by a gleam of pleasure.

"They may make much of this in England, when eventually they hear about it," continued Hornblower.

"I'm certain of it, sir. It isn't every day of the week that a frigate sinks a ship of the line."

It was stretching a point to call the *Natividad* that—sixty years ago when she was built she may have been considered just fit to lie in the line, but times had changed since then. But it was a very notable feat that the *Lydia* had accomplished, all the same. Hornblower's spirits began to rise. "What's the butcher's bill?" he demanded. There was another criterion which the British public was apt to apply in estimating the merit of a naval action, and the Board of Admiralty itself not infrequently used the same standard.

"Thirty-eight killed, sir," said Bush, taking a dirty scrap of paper from his pocket. "Seventy-five wounded. Four lost when the launch was sunk. Clay was killed in the first day's action—" Hornblower nodded; he remembered Clay's headless body

390

sprawled on the quarterdeck "—and John Summers, master's mate, was killed yesterday; Donald Scott Galbraith, third lieutenant, Lieutenant Simmonds of the Marines, Midshipman Savage, and four other warrant officers wounded."

"Galbraith?" said Hornblower. That piece of news prevented him from beginning to wonder what would be the reward of a casualty list of a hundred and seventeen, when frigate captains had been knighted before this for a total of eighty killed and wounded.

"Badly, sir. Both legs smashed below the knees."

Galbraith had met the fate which Hornblower had dreaded for himself. The shock recalled Hornblower to his duty.

"I shall visit the wounded at once," he said, and checked himself and looked searchingly at his first lieutenant. "What about you, Bush? You don't look fit for duty."

"I am perfectly fit, sir," protested Bush. "I shall take an hour's rest when Gerard takes over the deck from me."

"As you will, then."

Down below decks in the orlop it was like some canto in Dante's *Inferno*. It was dark; the four oil lamps whose flickering, reddish yellow glimmer wavered from the deck beams above seemed to serve only to cast shadows. The atmosphere was stifling. To the normal stenches of bilge and the ordinary noises of a ship were added the stinks of seventy-five sick men crammed together, and the sounds of their groaning and sobbing, blaspheming and vomiting.

Hornblower found Laurie standing aimlessly in the gloom. "Come round with me and make your report," he snapped.

They approached the first man in the row, and Hornblower drew back with a start of surprise. Lady Barbara was there; the wavering light caught her classic features as she knelt beside the wounded man, sponging his face as he writhed on the deck.

Hornblower was shocked to see her engaged thus. The day was yet to come when Florence Nightingale was to make nursing a profession for women. "Don't do that!" he said hoarsely. "Go away from here. Go on deck."

"I have begun this work now," said Lady Barbara indifferently.

"I am not going to leave it unfinished." Her tone admitted no possibility of argument. "The gentleman in charge here," she went on, "knows nothing of his duties. This poor man has a splinter of wood under his skin. It ought to be extracted at once."

She displayed the man's bare chest, hairy and tattooed. Under the tattooing there was a horrible black bruise, stretching from the breastbone to the right armpit, and in the muscles of the armpit was a jagged projection under the skin; when Lady Barbara laid her fingers on it the man writhed and groaned with pain. "Are you ready to do it now?" she asked of the unhappy Laurie.

"Well, madam—"

"If you will not, then I will. Don't be a fool, man."

"I will see that it is done, Lady Barbara," interposed Hornblower. He would promise anything to get this finished.

"Very well, then, Captain." Lady Barbara rose from her knees, but she showed no sign of retiring in a decent female fashion. Hornblower and Laurie looked at each other.

"Laurie," said Hornblower, harshly, "get your instruments. Now, Williams, we're going to get that splinter out of you. It is going to hurt you."

Throughout the painful and bloody business Lady Barbara's lips were firmly compressed. She watched Laurie's muddled attempts at bandaging, and then she stooped without a word and took the rags from him. The men watched her fascinated as with one hand firmly behind Williams' spine she passed the roll dexterously round his body and bound the fast-reddening waste firmly to the wound. "He will do now," she said, rising.

Hornblower spent two stifling hours down there in the cockpit going the rounds with Laurie and Lady Barbara, but they were not nearly such agonizing hours as they might have been. One of the main reasons for his feeling so unhappy regarding the care of the wounded had been his consciousness of his own incompetence. Insensibly he came to shift some of his responsibility onto Lady Barbara's shoulders; she was so obviously capable. When they had gone round every bed, he turned to her. "I don't know how I can thank you, ma'am," he said. "I am as grateful to you as any of these wounded men."

"There is no gratitude needed," said Lady Barbara, shrugging her slim shoulders, "for work which had to be done. Now, we must have air down here. Perhaps those men who can be moved can be brought on deck?"

"I will arrange it, ma'am," said Hornblower.

Lady Barbara's request was strongly accented by the contrast which Hornblower noticed when he went on deck—the fresh Pacific air, despite the scorching sunshine, was like champagne after the solid stink of the orlop. He gave orders for the immediate re-establishment of the canvas ventilating shafts which had been removed when the decks were cleared for action, and for certain of the wounded, to be selected by Lady Barbara Wellesley, to be brought up on deck.

So that on board HMS *Lydia* that morning divisions were held and divine service conducted a little late, after the burial of the dead, with a row of wounded swaying in hammocks on each side of the main deck, and with the faint echo of the horrible sounds below floating up through the air shafts.

THE FORTNIGHT WHICH ELAPSED before the *Lydia* neared Panama went far to reduce her list of wounded. Some of the men were by then already convalescent, but shock and exhaustion had relieved the ship of many, and now gangrene was relieving her of still more. Every morning there was the same ceremony at the ship's side, when two or three hammock-wrapped bundles were slid over into the blue Pacific.

Galbraith went that way. He had borne not only the shock of his wound, but also the torture to which Laurie submitted him when, goaded by Lady Barbara's urgent representations, he had set to work with knife and saw upon the smashed tangle of flesh and bone which had been his legs. He had even bade fair to make a good recovery. Then, suddenly, the fatal symptoms had shown themselves, and Galbraith had died five days later after a fortunate delirium.

Hornblower and Lady Barbara drew nearer to each other during those days. Lady Barbara had fought a losing battle for Galbraith's life to the very end, had fought hard and without sparing herself. Hornblower would never forget her calm quiet voice, hiding the torment in her face, as she sat soothing the dying boy, who was babbling feverishly and clutching her hands, under the impression that she was his mother. And for Hornblower himself, it was unexpectedly painful when Galbraith died. Hornblower always looked upon himself as a man pleasingly devoid of human weakness. It was a surprise to him to find his voice trembling and tears in his eyes as he read the service. Now when his eyes met Lady Barbara's on deck or across the dinner table, there was a new understanding between them.

The *Lydia* was one day's sail from Panama, and the Pearl Islands were just in view over the port bow, when the *guarda costa* lugger which had encountered them before came running downwind and hove to a couple of cables' lengths away. A few minutes later the same smart officer as had boarded once before from the lugger came clambering onto the *Lydia*'s deck.

Looking curiously about him he approached Hornblower. "Good morning, Captain," he said, bowing profoundly. "I see that your fine ship has been recently in action. I hope that your Excellency had good fortune in the encounter?"

"We sank the *Natividad*, if that is what you mean," said Hornblower.

"Then, sir," said the Spaniard, "I have a letter to give you." He felt in his breast pocket, but with a curious gesture of hesitation—

Hornblower realized later that he must have had two letters, one to be delivered if the *Natividad* were destroyed and the other if she were still able to do damage. The letter which he handed over, when he was quite certain which was which, was worded with a terseness that implied (having regard to the ornateness of the Spanish official style) absolute rudeness, as Hornblower was quick to realize.

It was from the Viceroy of Peru, informing Hornblower that by orders of His Most Catholic Majesty, whose forces had already routed those of the rebel Don Julian Alvarado, who called himself the Almighty, the *Lydia* was formally prohibited from entering into any port of Spanish America.

Hornblower re-read the letter, and while he did so the dismal clangour of the pumps, drifting aft to his ears, made more acute the worries which instantly leaped upon him. He thought of his battered, leaking ship, his sick and wounded, his weary crew and attenuated stores. And more than that: he remembered his supplementary orders from England regarding the effort he was to make to open Spanish America to British trade.

"Can you explain this most unfriendly behaviour, sir?" he asked. "I cannot understand how any civilized man could abandon an ally who has fought his battles for him and is in need of help solely because of those battles."

The Spaniard was haughty, even brazen. "You came unasked into these seas, sir," he said. "There would have been no battle for you to fight if you had stayed in those parts of the world where your King rules. The South Sea is the property of His Most Catholic Majesty, who will tolerate no intruder upon it."

"I understand," said Hornblower. He guessed that the new orders had come out to Spanish America now that the government of King Ferdinand had heard of the presence of an English frigate in the Pacific. The retention of the American monopoly was to the Spanish mind as dear as life itself. There was no length to which the Spanish government would not go to retain it, even though it meant offending an ally in the midst of a life-and-death struggle with the most powerful despot in Europe. To the Spaniards the *Lydia's* presence hinted at the coming of a flood of British traders, at the drying up of the constant stream of gold and silver on which their government depended.

But however badly Hornblower was being treated, his innate caution restrained him from speaking his thoughts. There was nothing to be gained by causing an open breach.

"Very good, sir," he said. "My compliments to your master. I will call at no port on the Spanish Main. Please convey to His Excellency my lively sense of gratitude at the courtesy with which I have been treated. And now, sir, I must, much to my regret, wish you good-day and a pleasant journey. I have much to attend to."

The Spanish officer looked at him sharply, but Hornblower kept his face immobile while bending his spine with studied courtesy. He could only return Hornblower's bow and walk back to the ship's side.

The *Lydia* rolled heavily, hove-to, on the swell, while her captain resumed his pacing of the quarterdeck, eyed furtively by those officers and men who had guessed at the bad news this latest dispatch contained.

First of all, Hornblower must decide about the ship's stores and water. Six weeks back he had filled his storerooms and water barrels. And since that time he had lost a quarter of his crew. Even allowing for the necessary refit, there was enough food to last them (now that all need for secrecy had disappeared) to St. Helena. That was satisfactory. But refit he must. The *Lydia* could not hope to survive the storms of Cape Horn in her present condition. The work could not be done at sea, and the harbours were barred to him. He must do as old buccaneers did and find some secluded cove where he could careen his ship.

Neither the mainland nor those Pearl Islands on the horizon would be suitable, for the Spaniards had settled round every navigable bay—besides, the lugger was still in sight and watching his movements. Hornblower went below and got out his charts: there was the island of Coiba, which the *Lydia* had passed yesterday. His charts told him nothing of it save its position, but it was clearly the place to investigate first. Hornblower laid off his course and then went on deck again. "We will put the ship about, if you please, Mr. Bush," he said.

397

CHAPTER XI

Inch by inch His Britannic Majesty's frigate *Lydia* crept into the bay, and Hornblower took his eye from the ship's course to study the bay before him. There were mountains all round it, but on the farther side the slope down to the water was not nearly as steep, and on the water's edge, at the foot of the dazzling green which clothed the banks all round, there was a hint of golden sand which told of the sort of bottom which he sought. It would be shelving there, without a doubt, and free from rock. "This seems very suitable," he said to Bush.

"Aye aye, sir. Made for the job," said Bush.

"Then you may drop anchor. We shall start work at once."

It was terribly hot in that little bay in the deserted island of Coiba. The lofty mountains all about cut off any wind that might be blowing, and at the same time reflected the heat to a focus in the bay. On land, in the breathless jungle, it was even hotter.

Before she could be beached, the *Lydia* had to be lightened. And also, before she could be laid defenceless on her side, the bay had to be made secure from all aggressors. Tackles were rigged, and the two-ton eighteen-pounders were swayed up from the main deck and one at a time were ferried to the headlands, where Rayner and Gerard were ready to work with parties preparing emplacements. Powder and shot for the guns followed, and then food and water for the garrisons. At the end of thirty-six hours the *Lydia* was a hundred tons lighter, and the entrance to the bay was so defended that any vessel attempting it would have to brave the plunging fire of twenty guns.

In the meanwhile another party had been working like furies on shore above the sandy beach. Here they cleared away a section of forest, and dragged the fallen trees into a rough breastwork; and into the rude fort thus delimited another party brought up further supplies, guns and shot, until the *Lydia* was a mere empty shell rolling in the tiny waves of the bay. The men stretched canvas shelters for themselves as protection against the frequent tropical showers which deluged on them, and for their officers they built rude timber huts—and one for the women as well.

The captain of a ship that is no ship, but only a mere hulk helpless in a landlocked inlet, cannot feel a moment's peace. Under the strain of the responsibility which he bore, and having in mind the need for haste, Hornblower flogged himself into working harder and harder, so that the days passed in a nightmare of fatigue, during which the minutes he could spend with Lady Barbara were like the glimpses a man has of a beautiful woman during delirium.

He drove his men hard from earliest dawn as long as daylight lasted, but they did not grudge him the efforts he called for; he was so little prepared to spare himself. Sleeping on beds of sand instead of in their more comfortable hammocks, working on solid earth instead of on board ship, hemmed in by dense forest instead of engirdled by a distant horizon—all this seemed only to stimulate and cheer them. Down the cliff face there tumbled a constant stream of clear water so that they were allowed as much fresh water as they could use, and to men who for months at a time had to submit to having a sentry standing guard over their drinking water this was an inexpressible luxury.

Soon, on the sandy shore and as far as possible from the canvas-covered powder barrels, there were fires lit, over which was melted the pitch brought from the boatswain's store. The *Lydia* was hove over and the carpenter applied himself to the task of setting her bottom to rights. The shot holes were plugged, the strained seams caulked and pitched, the missing sheets of copper were replaced by the last few sheets which the *Lydia* carried in reserve. For four days the bay was filled with the sound of the caulking hammers at work, and the reek of melting pitch drifted over the water as the smoking cauldrons were carried across to the working parties.

At the end of that time the *Lydia* was hove off, and, still empty, was towed across the bay until she lay at the foot of a high cliff where one of the batteries was established—the shore was steep enough here to allow her to lie close in. At this point Lieutenant Bush had been busy setting up a projecting gallows, a hundred feet above, and vertically over, the ship's deck. After many trials, the *Lydia* was manoeuvred until she could be moored so that the stump of her mizzenmast stood against the plumb line which Bush dropped from the tackles high above. Then the tackles set to work, and the stump was drawn out of her like a decayed tooth. Next, the seventy-five-foot main yard had to be swayed up to the gallows, and then hung vertically down from them; if it had slipped it would have shot down like some monstrous arrow and would have sunk her for certain. But it was lowered, inch by inch, until its solid butt came at last solidly to rest in its step upon the keelson.

Back at her anchorage, the *Lydia* could be ballasted once more, with her beef barrels and water barrels, her guns and her shot, save what was left in the entrance batteries. Then, steady upon her keel, she was re-rigged and her topmasts were set up again until she was as efficient a ship as when she had left Portsmouth newly commissioned.

It was then that Hornblower could allow himself to draw breath and relax. He was like a man released from a sentence of death when he trod the *Lydia*'s quarterdeck once more.

At this very moment the guns from the entrance batteries were being ferried out to the *Lydia* one by one. Already he had a broadside battery which could fire, a ship which could manoeuvre, and he could snap his fingers at every Spaniard in the Pacific. It was a glorious sensation, he turned and found Lady Barbara beside him, and he smiled at her dazzlingly. "Good morning, ma'am," he said. "I trust you found your cabin comfortable again?"

Lady Barbara smiled back at him—in fact she almost laughed, so comical was the contrast between this greeting and the scowls she had encountered from him during the last two weeks. "Thank you, Captain," she said. "It is marvellously comfortable. Your crew has worked wonders to have done so much in so little time."

Quite unconsciously he had taken both her hands in his, and was standing there holding them, smiling all over his face. Lady Barbara felt that it would only need a word from her to set him dancing. "We shall be at sea before nightfall," he said, ecstatically.

She could not be dignified with him, any more than she could have been dignified with a baby; she knew enough of men and affairs not to resent his previous preoccupation. Truth to tell, she

400

was a trifle fond of him because of it. "You are a very fine sailor, sir," she said to him, suddenly. "I doubt if there is another officer in the King's service who could have done all you have done on this voyage."

"I am glad you think so, ma'am," he said, but the spell was broken. He had been reminded of himself, and his cursed self-consciousness closed in upon him again. He dropped her hands, awkwardly, and there was a hint of a blush in his tanned cheeks. "I have only done my duty," he mumbled.

"Many men can do that," said Lady Barbara, "but few can do it well. The country is your debtor—my sincerest hope is that England will acknowledge the debt."

The words started a sudden train of thought in Hornblower's mind; it was a train he had followed up often before. England would only remember that his battle with the *Natividad* had been unnecessary. A more fortunate captain would have heard of the new alliance between Spain and England before he had handed the *Natividad* over to the rebels, and would have saved all the trouble and loss which resulted. A frigate action with a hundred casualties might be glorious, but an unnecessary action with a hundred casualties was quite inglorious. No one would stop to think that it was his obedience to orders and skill in carrying them out which had been the reason of it. He would be blamed for his own merits, and life was suddenly full of bitterness again.

"Your pardon, ma'am," he said, and he turned away from her and walked forward to bawl orders at the men swaying an eighteen-pounder up from the launch.

Lady Barbara shook her head at his back. "Bless the man!" she said to herself, softly. "He was almost human for a while."

CHAPTER XII

The rumour had gone round the crew that the *Lydia* was at last homeward bound. The men's heads were full of England. The pressed men thought of their wives; the volunteers thought of the joys of paying off. They had flung themselves with a will into the labour of warping out of the bay and they had chattered and played antics like a crew of monkeys when they dashed aloft to set sail. Now the watch below was dancing and setting to partners through the warm evening while the *Lydia* bowled along with a favourable breeze over the blue Pacific.

Only the captain kept himself solitary, in his cabin. Uncertain and gloomy about the lives that had been lost and about the reception that awaited him in England, he was unable to bring himself to join the merry parties on the quarterdeck whose gay chatter drifted down to him through the skylight.

Later that night Lady Barbara and Lieutenant Bush sat talking in the moonlight beside the taffrail. "Aye, ma'am," Bush was saying. "He's like Nelson. He's thinking all the time—you'd be surprised, ma'am, to know how much he thinks about."

"I don't think it would surprise me," said Lady Barbara.

"That's because you think, too, ma'am. It's us stupid ones who'd be surprised, I meant to say. He has more brains than all the rest of us in the ship put together, excepting you, ma'am. Of course, he's short with me sometimes, the same as he is with everyone else, but that's only to be expected. I know how much he has to worry him, and he's not strong. I am concerned about him sometimes, ma'am."

"You are fond of him."

"Fond, ma'am?" Bush's sturdy mind grappled with the word, and he laughed self-consciously. "I suppose I must be. I hadn't ever thought of it before. I like him, ma'am, indeed I do."

"That is what I meant."

"The men worship him, ma'am. Look how much he has done this commission, and the lash not in use once in a week. That is why he is like Nelson. They love him not for anything he does or says, but for what he is."

"He's handsome, in a way," said Lady Barbara—she was woman enough to give that matter consideration.

"I suppose he is, ma'am, now you come to mention it. But he's shy, ma'am. It's that which always surprises me about him. You'd hardly believe it, ma'am, but he has no more faith in himself than—than I have in myself, ma'am, to put it that way."

402

"How strange!" said Lady Barbara. She was accustomed to the sturdy self-reliance of her brothers, unloved and unlovable leaders of men, but her insight made her comment only one of politeness —it was not really strange to her.

"Look, ma'am," said Bush, suddenly, dropping his voice. Hornblower had come up on deck. They could see his face, white in the moonlight, as he looked round to assure himself that all was well with his ship, and they could read in it the torment of bitterness which was depressing him.

"I should be grateful if you could try to take him out of himself a little, ma'am, begging your pardon. Perhaps—"

"I'll try," said Lady Barbara, "but I don't think I shall succeed where you have failed. Captain Hornblower has never taken a great deal of notice of me, Mr. Bush."

FORTUNATELY LADY BARBARA'S INVITATION to dine, which Polwheal conveyed to his captain the following day, arrived at a moment when Hornblower was just trying to emerge from his black fit of depression. He read how Lady Barbara had been informed by Mr. Bush that the *Lydia* was about to cross the equator, and that she thought such an occasion merited some mild celebration. If Captain Hornblower would give her the pleasure of his company at dinner she would be delighted. Hornblower wrote back to say that he had much pleasure in accepting.

Yet even in this prospect there was some alloy. Hornblower had always been a poor man, and at the time when he commissioned the *Lydia* he had been at his wits' end about where to turn for money in the need for leaving Maria comfortably provided for. In consequence he had not outfitted himself satisfactorily, and now, all these months later, his clothes were in the last stages of decay. The coats were all patched and darned; the epaulettes betrayed in their brassy sheen the fact that they had begun life merely coated with bullion; and he was conscious that his white duck trousers, made on board the *Lydia*, had none of the fashionable appearance to which Lady Barbara was accustomed.

He was on the verge of sending a message to Lady Barbara to say that he had changed his mind and would not dine with her that evening, until he thought that if he did so, Polwheal would guess that it was the result of his realization of his shabbiness and would laugh at him (and his shabbiness) in consequence. He went into dinner and had his revenge upon the world by sitting silent and preoccupied at the head of the table, blighting with his gloomy presence all attempts at conversation, so that the function began as a frigid failure. Then Lady Barbara suddenly began talking lightly and captivatingly, and led Bush into describing his experiences at Trafalgar—a tale she had heard, to Hornblower's certain knowledge, twice at least already.

The conversation became general, and it was more than Hornblower's flesh and blood could stand, to stay silent with everyone else talking in such an animated fashion. Against his will he found himself entering into the conversation, and an artless question from Lady Barbara about Sir Edward Pellew inveigled him into it completely, for Hornblower had been both midshipman and lieutenant in Pellew's ship, and was proud of it.

By the end, the dinner had served its purpose admirably, making it possible for Hornblower to meet Lady Barbara's eye again on deck. He had forgotten his shabby coat and shapeless trousers; and, mercifully, his mind was no longer so acutely troubled by the memory of Galbraith and Clay and the other dead.

The days that followed were happy indeed. The routine of the *Lydia* progressed like clockwork. During the heavenly nights when the ship's wake showed as a long trail of fire on the faintly luminous water, Hornblower and Lady Barbara learned to talk together, endlessly. She could chatter about the frivolities of the vice-regal court at Dublin, and of the intrigues which could enmesh a governor-general of India. He could tell, in return, of months spent on blockade with Pellew, combating storms off the ironbound Biscay Coast—a monotonous toilsome life as fantastic to her as hers appeared to him. He could even tell her, as his self-consciousness dwindled, of the ambitions which he knew would seem to her as trivial as those of a child yearning for a hobbyhorse; of the two thousand pounds in prize money which he had decided would be all that he would require to eke out his retirement pay.

404

And yet she listened without a smile, with even a trace of envy in her calm face, as the moon shone down on them.

They could talk of books and of poetry. She heard him with patience, even with approval, as he talked of Gibbon (the object of his sincerest admiration), and in turn she won his grudging approval of an ungainly poem called "The Rime of the Ancient Mariner", although he maintained sturdily, in the last ditch, that its only merit lay in its content, and that even then it would have been infinitely better had this Coleridge fellow been assisted by someone who knew about navigation and seamanship.

Lady Barbara had, from the time of her first arrival on board, found pleasure in Hornblower's society. Now they had formed a habit of each other, as though they were insidious drugs, and were vaguely uneasy when out of sight of each other. The voyage had been monotonous enough, as the *Lydia* held steadily southwards, for habits to be easily formed; it had become a habit to exchange a smile when they met on the quarterdeck in the morning—a smile illumined by secret memories of the intimacy of the conversation of the night before. It was a habit now for Hornblower to discuss the ship's progress with Lady Barbara after he had taken the noon sights, a habit now for him to drink coffee with her in the afternoons, and especially was it a habit for them to meet at sunset by the taffrail.

There, in the warm darkness, they could sit silent together, watching the mastheads circling amid the stars with the rolling of the ship, listening to the faint orchestra of the ship's fabric, and their thoughts paralleling each other's so that when eventually one of them spoke it was to harmonize completely with what was in the other's mind. At these times Lady Barbara's hand, like any healthy young woman's, was at her side where it could be touched without too great effort. But Hornblower seemed unconscious of it. She would see his face lifted to the stars, peaceful and immobile, and she found pleasure in giving herself credit for the change in it from that evening when she had talked with Bush and seen Hornblower's torment.

Meanwhile, the *Lydia* ran steadily south, until the evenings grew chill and the mornings misty, until the blue sky changed to grey and the first rain they had known for three weeks wetted the *Lydia*'s decks, and the west wind blew more blustering and searching, so that Lady Barbara had to wrap herself in a boat cloak to be able to sit on deck at all. Those evenings by the taffrail came to an imperceptible end. For the first time Lady Barbara saw Hornblower dressed in tarpaulins and sou'wester, and she thought how well those hideous garments suited him. There were times when he would come into the cabin, his eyes bright and his cheeks flushed with wind, and she felt her pulses leap in sympathy with his.

She knew she was being foolish. She told herself that this weakness of hers only arose because life in close contact with Hornblower for four continuous months was bound to make her either love him or hate him—and as there was no room for hatred in her system the other thing was inevitable. On board ship one saw things in a false perspective, she informed herself; trifles assumed an exaggerated importance. Just as toothache tended to disappear when something occurred to distract the mind, so would this heartache of hers disappear when she had other things to think about. It was all very true; but strangely it made not the least difference to her present feelings.

They had reached the region of westerly trade winds now. Every day they roared harder and harder, and every day the sea rose higher. There were two or three days when the *Lydia* logged over two hundred and forty nautical miles from noon to noon. All Lady Barbara could do was to brace herself in her cot while the ship tossed and rolled as though at any moment she would turn over, while Hebe (who never succeeded quite in overcoming her seasickness) moàned in her blankets on the deck and her teeth chattered with the cold. No fire could be kept alight; nothing could be cooked, while the groaning of the ship's timbers swelled into a volume of sound comparable with that of an organ in a church.

At the very climax of the voyage, the freakishness of Cape Horn weather allowed them just one pleasurable morning of sunshine before a gale fell on them with a sudden shriek. They ran before it all the afternoon, and at evening Lady Barbara could tell by the motion of the ship (so experienced a sailor had she become) that Hornblower had been compelled to heave her to. For thirty-six hours the *Lydia* remained hove-to, while the heavens tore themselves to pieces around her and Lady Barbara found it hard to believe that men had ever succeeded in sailing a ship westward round the Horn.

ON THAT VOYAGE THE CHANGE in conditions after rounding the Horn was most dramatic. It seemed to Lady Barbara almost as if one day they were labouring along over grey seas with waves running as high as the yardarms, and the next they were enjoying blue skies and gentle breezes. In fact they were leaving the Antipodean autumn behind them, and the northern spring was coming down in the track of the sun to meet them.

It seemed the most natural thing in the world that as night fell Lady Barbara should find herself seated as ever by the taffrail, and just as natural that Hornblower should loom up in the half-light and should accept her unvaryingly polite invitation to a seat beside her.

Yet to Hornblower—and to Lady Barbara—things were not the same as they had been in the Pacific. Hornblower felt a tension he had not felt before. Perhaps the rounding of the Horn had forced it home upon him that even sailing-ship voyages must end sometime. Perhaps because he had been thinking of England, the image of Maria had been much before his eyes of late; Maria, short and tubby with the black silk parasol which she affected; or Maria in her flannel nightshift and curl papers. It was disloyal to think of Maria like that; rather should he think of her as she was that feverish night in the Southsea lodgings, her eyes red with weeping, struggling bravely to keep her lips from trembling while little Horatio died of the smallpox in her arms and little Maria lay dead in the next room. "Ha-h'm," said Hornblower, harshly, and he stirred uneasily in his seat.

Lady Barbara looked at his face in the starlight. It bore that bleak, lonely expression which she had come to dread. "Can you tell me what is the matter, Captain?" she asked gently.

Hornblower sat silent for some seconds before he shook his

head. No, he could not tell her. For that matter he did not know himself; introspective though he was, he had not dared to admit even to himself that he had been making comparisons between someone short and stout and someone tall and slender, between someone with apple cheeks and someone with a classic profile.

Hornblower slept badly that night, and his morning walk which followed was not devoted to the purpose for which it had originally been destined. He could not keep his mind upon the ship's problems, which he was accustomed to solve at this time. He was too unhappy to think connectedly.

He was tempted to make advances to Lady Barbara; that, at least, he could admit to himself. He wanted badly to do so. He had been nearly a year cooped up in the *Lydia*, and a year's unnatural living bred strange fancies. Strangest of all was the suspicion that possibly Lady Barbara would not repulse him. Yet whether he offended her, or whether he seduced her, he was playing with fire. On the other hand, supposing, as was just conceivable, the Wellesleys could tolerate the seduction of their sister—supposing that, confronted with a *fait accompli*, they resolved to try to make the best of things. No, that was not conceivable at all. And to Hornblower it was a dreadful thing to toy with a woman on board his ship. It was contrary to the Articles of War—worse, it was undignified, subversive of discipline, dangerous.

And then all these cold-blooded considerations were swept away to nothing in a white-hot wave of passion as he thought of Lady Barbara, slim and lovely, understanding and sweet. He stood by the rail staring unseeing over the blue sea with its patches of golden weed, conscious of nothing save the riot in his own body and mind. He had only just regained his self-control when Lady Barbara came on deck.

"I spent last night dreaming dreams," she told him.

"Indeed?" said Hornblower, awkwardly. He, too, had been dreaming.

"Yes," said Lady Barbara. "I was dreaming mostly of eggs. Fried eggs, and buttered eggs. And cabbage—plain boiled cabbage. My dreams were not extravagant enough to run to a

purée of spinach, but I almost attained to a dish of young carrots. And behold, this morning Hebe brings me my black coffee and my weevily maize bread."

Lady Barbara's laugh whisked away Hornblower's passion for a space, and her fine naturalness acted upon his state of mind like an open window on a stuffy room. The crisis was staved off for a few more days—golden days, during which the *Lydia* kept the southeast trades on her beam and reached steadily across the South Atlantic for St. Helena.

The wind did not fail her until the very evening when the lookout at the masthead caught sight of the tip of the mountaintop just as the light was fading from the sky, and his cry of "Land ho!" told Hornblower that once more he had made a perfect landfall. All day long the wind had been dying away, and with the setting of the sun it dwindled to nothing, tantalizingly, just when a few more hours of it would have carried the *Lydia* to the island.

It may have been the mere fact of this respite working on Hornblower's subconscious mind which precipitated the crisis; for undoubtedly Hornblower had a lurking fear that the call at St. Helena might well bring about some undesired alteration in affairs on board the *Lydia*. On the other hand, the thing was bound to happen, and perhaps coincidence merely allotted that evening for it. It was coincidence that Hornblower should come into the main cabin in the half-light at a moment when he thought Lady Barbara was on deck, and it was coincidence that his hand should brush against her bare arm as they stood cramped between the table and the locker and he apologized for his intrusion. She was in his arms then, and they kissed, and kissed again, giddy with passion. Then a roll of the ship forced him to let her go, and she sank down upon the locker, and she smiled at him as she sat so that he came down on his knees beside her, his head on her breast.

She stroked his hair, and spoke to him with the endearments which her nurse had used to her when she was a child—it was hard to find words that would tell him of her love for him. "Your hands are beautiful," she said, spreading one of them on her own palm, and playing with the long slender fingers. "I have loved them ever since Panama."

410

Hornblower had always thought his hands bony and ugly. He looked at her to see if she were teasing him, and when he saw that she was not he could only kiss her again—her lips were so ready for his kisses.

Hebe's entrance made them part; at least it made Hornblower spring up, to sit bolt upright and self-conscious, while Hebe grinned at them slyly Lady Barbara remained quite unruffled.

"Go away, Hebe," she said, calmly. "I shall not need you yet."

And she turned back to Hornblower, but the spell was broken. He had seen himself in a new light, grovelling furtively on a couch with a passenger. He was blushing hotly, already angry with himself.

"What are we to do?" he asked feebly.

"Do?" she replied. "We are lovers, and the world is ours. We do as we will."

"But—" he said, and again, "but—" There was a cold fit on him; he wanted to explain to her the complications he could see hedging him in, and how the captain of a ship was not nearly as much his own master as she apparently thought; but it was hopeless. He could only stammer, his face averted.

She put her hand on his chin and made him turn to her. "Dear," she asked. "What is troubling you? Tell me, dear."

"I am a married man," he said, taking the coward's way out.

"I knew that. Are you going to allow that to interfere with—us?"

"Besides—" he said, and his hands flapped in the hopeless effort to express all the doubts which consumed him.

She saw the look in his face, and rose abruptly. Her blood and lineage were outraged at this. However veiled her offer had been, it had been refused. She was in a cold rage now.

"Please have the kindness, Captain," she said, "to open that door for me."

She swept out of the cabin with all the dignity of an earl's daughter, and if she wept when in the privacy of her own cabin, Hornblower knew nothing of it. He was pacing the deck above, up and down, up and down, endlessly. For him, this was the end of a dream.

CHAPTER XIII

Early next morning, following a fair wind, the *Lydia* made her number among the shipping at St. Helena, and the sound of her salutes rolled slowly round the bay. Hornblower was caught up in the current of naval routine, and he would be too busy for some time to have a word with Lady Barbara even if she condescended to allow him one. He did not know whether to be glad or sorry.

Within the hour, Rear Admiral Sir James Saumarez received Hornblower in the quarter gallery of his flagship, the *Téméraire*. He listened courteously to Hornblower's brief report, and there was a gleam of approval in his fierce blue eyes when he heard that the *Lydia* had sunk a fifty-gun two-decker in a ship-to-ship duel.

"You can accompany me and the East Indian convoy to England," he said, at the end. "I will send you written orders later. And now, sir, perhaps you will give me the pleasure of your company at the breakfast party at which I am about to be host?"

Hornblower knew that it was ill to raise objections to a suggestion by an admiral, but he simply had to raise one. "There is a lady on board the *Lydia*, sir," he said, and when the admiral's eyebrows went up he hurriedly began to explain Lady Barbara's presence to him.

The admiral whistled. "A Wellesley!" he said. "And you brought her round the Horn? We must tell Lady Manningtree of this." He led the way unceremoniously into the lofty admiral's cabin. There was a long table with snowy cloth, glittering with crystal and silver, and by the table there stood chatting a little group of men and women, beautifully dressed. The admiral made hurried introductions.

Lady Manningtree was a short and dumpy woman with good humour in every line of her face. "Captain Hornblower has brought Lady Barbara Wellesley with him from Darien," said Sir James, and plunged into rapid explanation.

Lady Manningtree listened in perfect horror. "And you have left her there? On that little ship?" she said. "The poor lamb! She must not stay there another moment! Sir James, you must excuse me. I will not have a moment's peace until she is comfortably in the cabin next to mine on board the *Hanbury Castle*. Sir James, would you be so good as to order a boat for me?"

She left in a whirl of apologies, a fluttering of petticoats and a perfect torrent of objurgations, mainly directed at Hornblower.

"When women take charge," said Sir James philosophically, after she had departed, "it is best for the men to stand from under. Will you sit here, Captain?"

Curiously, Hornblower could eat almost nothing of that delicious breakfast. There were heavenly mutton cutlets. There was coffee with fresh milk. There were fruits and vegetables, all the things Hornblower had dreamed about when his thoughts had not been occupied with Lady Barbara, and now he could only eat a mouthful here and there. Fortunately his lack of appetite went unnoticed because he was kept so busy answering the questions which were rained on him, about Lady Barbara, about his passage round the Horn, and about his adventures in the Pacific. After a time, the loquaciousness against which Hornblower was usually on his guard led him into eloquence. He told of the long duel in the lonely Pacific, the labour, the slaughter and agony, up to the moment when, leaning weakly against the quarterdeck rail, he had known triumph at the sight of his beaten enemy sinking in the darkness. He stopped self consciously there, suddenly fearful that he had been boasting, and looked round the table from face to face. It was with amazement that instead of expressions of disapproval he saw what he could only consider admiration.

Still, he was glad when the party showed signs of breaking up and he was able to say goodbye to Sir James and the rest of the company.

The admiral's barge was still hooked onto the *Lydia*'s chains when he returned to her. He went on board; Lady Barbara's baggage was piled on the gangway waiting to be swung down into the barge. Down in the main cabin could be heard a continuous chatter of female voices. Lady Manningtree and Lady Barbara were sitting there deep in conversation; obviously one topic led to another so enthralling that they had forgotten the barge, forgotten the waiting baggage, forgotten even about breakfast.

Lady Barbara was wearing a gown which Hornblower had not seen before, and a new turban and veil. She was very obviously the great lady now. To Hornblower's startled mind she seemed as she stood up to be six inches taller than when he saw her last. And clearly Hornblower's arrival, breaking the thread of their conversation, constituted for them a signal for their departure.

"Lady Barbara has been telling me all about your voyage," said Lady Manningtree, buttoning her gloves. "I think you deserve a world of thanks for the care you have taken of her. Nevertheless, it is high time that she enjoyed a little more comfort than you can offer her here."

Hornblower managed to gulp out a few words regarding the superior arrangements for passengers on board an Indiaman.

"I don't mean to imply that it is your fault, Captain," protested Lady Manningtree, hastily. "I'm sure your frigate is a very beautiful ship. But frigates were never made to carry females. And now we must say goodbye, Captain."

Hornblower bowed and allowed her to pass before him. Lady Barbara followed.

"Goodbye," she said. Hornblower bowed again as she went down in a curtsy. He was looking straight at her, but somehow he could see no detail of her face—only a white blur. "Thank you for all your kindness," said Lady Barbara.

The barge left the ship's side, and rowed steadily away. She was all blurred, too, a vague patch of red and gold.

HORNBLOWER FOUND Bush beside him. "The victualling officer's signalling, sir," he said.

Mercifully, Hornblower's duties were clamouring for his attention. As he turned away from the ship's side, he found himself remembering the admiring faces round the breakfast table. And then he remembered that he would soon be seeing Maria again. He was glad about that. Overhead the sun was shining brightly, and before him rose the steep green slopes of St. Helena.

C. S. Forester

Cecil Scott Forester was born in Cairo in 1899, moving to London with his family when he was only a few years old. He went to school at Dulwich College, and then studied medicine at Guy's Hospital—but failed to qualify since he was unable to recognize a single human bone in his anatomy examination!

His first successful novel, a murder mystery called *Payment Deferred*, was written when he was only twenty-four. It was put on the stage in 1931, with Charles Laughton in the lead, and was later filmed.

Meanwhile however, and quite by accident, the landlubber novelist had turned to writing about the sea. In 1927, rummaging along the shelves of a secondhand bookshop, he had come upon a bundle of old naval magazines which provided exact, practical documentation for the sailing of a British ship of the line in Nelson's day. Fascinated, he contrived a voyage on board a coffee trader to South America, and it was on this journey that he worked out the first of his many Horatio Hornblower stories.

In later years he was to write many other, different sorts of books—*The African Queen*, *The Ship*, and *Brown on Resolution* are among the most successful. He worked in Hollywood as a scriptwriter and was also a foreign correspondent for *The Times*. Nevertheless, such was the enormous popularity of his sailing stories that his name is always linked primarily with that of Captain Hornblower.

This did not wholly please him. Forester often felt the same kind of exasperation with his hero as Conan Doyle felt with Sherlock Holmes. Indeed, it is probable that he would have killed Hornblower off, had he not been aware of the public outrage this would cause. It is significant perhaps that when he died, in 1966, he left a short story locked in a London vault, telling of the captain's last days, with instructions that it was not to be published until after his own death. He dared not let Hornblower die before himself.

HOME
BEFORE DARK

a condensation of the book by
SUE ELLEN BRIDGERS

Illustrated by Tom Hall

Published by Alfred A. Knopf

Stella Mae Willis had lived most of her fourteen years out of a battered station wagon, moving with her family from one fruit-picking station to the next. When her father suddenly decided to take them all back to the tobacco farm where he grew up, Stella discovered for the first time what it was to have roots. Her uncle provided a shack for the family, tumbledown perhaps, but a *home*. But coming home, Stella soon learned, had its special difficulties. There was Rodney trying to impress her with his fancy car. And Toby, her first real friend. . . . Then, just as Stella was settling in, tragedy struck, shattering the precarious structure of her new life. Suddenly having roots and a house of one's own were no longer enough.

A moving novel of youth and innocence, full of the beauty of America's farmland and the love and hope of the people who live there.

Chapter One

THE dusty white station wagon turned off the highway onto a narrow asphalt road that shimmered with steam and sunlight, then lurched at the downshift and, sucking air under its belly, roared into third.

In the back seat, Stella pressed her palms against the lumpy, ragged cushion and tried not to sway into the territory claimed by her brother William, who dozed next to her. She strained her neck forward to see where their daddy was taking them.

"Hold on," he said, too late. The baby, Lissy, had already slid off her pallet in the luggage space into the narrow corridor of hard, hot floor at four-year-old Earl's feet. Now she wailed her baby cries.

"Hush up," their mother, Mae, said from the front seat. To Stella she seemed propped up against her will between the door and a bundle of household goods that separated her from her husband. The wind from the window caught her butchered, unkempt hair and parted it neatly as she turned wearily to stretch over the back of the seat.

Lissy had already stopped crying and was playing with Earl's feet. The baby pushed her wet fingers between Earl's toes, and he giggled, writhing against the hot window.

"Stop that, Lissy," Mae said halfheartedly. "Earl, you get outa her way."

"There's nowhere else for him to go," Stella answered.

At fourteen Stella was thin and fair, with the dingy, fading pallor of intermittent sunburns to her skin. She looked like a discarded doll, with dry fiber hair, that had been endowed with human eyelids which were puffy and red from hours of restless sleep in the car. Now she leaned over the back seat and lifted Lissy to pull her into her lap. She loved the plump, responsive body of the baby, who seemed to want cuddling even in the heat.

"She's so hot," Stella whined softly. "We're all so hot."

"Another couple of miles," James Earl said. "Mae, can you clean 'em up a little?"

"With what?" Mae asked irritably. She rummaged through an old straw bag and came up with a handkerchief. "Here," she said to Stella. "Do what you can."

Stella wiped Lissy's forehead and mouth and her thick red cheeks. Then she sat the baby down on the seat between herself and William, and went after Earl, who scooted against the stacked boxes and bags in the luggage space.

"My face ain't dirty," he said, holding out his hands to her in defense. Stella rubbed them hard with the sticky cloth.

"Your face is too dirty to bother with," she said emphatically, growing excited at having even this tiny chore to do after so many miles of nothing. She handed the cloth to William, and he spit into it and wiped his mouth and cheeks.

"Lord knows, you're all a sight," Stella said to them, including her parents in her verdict.

"Look," James Earl said. The town was easing up on them, one house at a time, until suddenly, almost without warning they felt, they were at its center and James Earl was pulling out of the traffic lane and into a gray stucco service station.

The other children scrambled around inside the rusted station wagon while Stella pushed against the door, which finally screeched open. The children dropped out, one after another, onto the greasy concrete.

"Anybody needs to go, now's the time," James Earl said, heading toward the station, where a man stood staring out at them.

"Tell 'em I'll pump it, Daddy," Stella called, already twisting off the gasoline cap.

420

"It's my turn," William yelled, racing for the pump.

"You take Earl to the bathroom. It's Stella's turn," James Earl said, and watched while she rescued the pump from William, stuck the nozzle in, and pushed the lever. James Earl went on into the station, bought five soft drinks, and rummaged through the candy cartons, picking four different kinds of candy and then crackers for Mae and a bag of peanuts that he poured into his own Pepsi bottle. He brought the candy and drinks to the car and, having delivered breakfast, went back into the air-conditioned office and leaned against a glass case, looking out the window at his family.

Mae leaned against the station wagon drinking her soft drink. Holding Lissy in one arm, she lifted the bottle to the baby's mouth and poured the cola in. The child writhed in her arms, and the cola spewed down her chin and clothes. Mae didn't seem to notice but went back to her drinking, her thin neck moving rhythmically as she swallowed. The children were eating, too, jaws working resolutely on the candy. James Earl knew that at times eating was the only thing that mattered to them. That and sleep.

"Where you headed?" the station attendant asked while counting out James Earl's change.

"This is it," James Earl said almost shyly. "Been living in Florida, all over Florida if you're wanting the truth, for the past sixteen years. Name's Willis. James Earl Willis."

"By God, you're Newton's brother," the man said excitedly. "You headed out to the farm?"

"Yeah," James Earl said. "I'm on my way home."

The land itself was home to him. James Earl, who remembered from sixteen years ago what was planted where and who planted it, drove slowly. The smaller children sat quietly in the back, not knowing they were almost there. They had ridden for a long time, for years it seemed, and they just knew they'd never get there.

Stella sat up straight, looking at everything. She had never heard much about this place they were going to, her daddy's home. Having never had a home herself, she was always surprised when he'd begin remembering aloud something from his childhood. But just when she was really interested, he'd stop himself short.

421

"Lord, it was so long ago," he would say. "I don't remember, Stella." But he'd say it looking at Mae instead of her. It was her mother that didn't want him to remember, who didn't want to hear.

"How much longer is it, Daddy?" Stella asked softly.

"Just a couple of miles," James Earl said. "I used to walk this road into town. Your great-granddaddy owned a lot of this land once, but by the time I came along he'd lost most of it. We had enough to make a good living, though."

Stella caught the growing excitement in his voice. "Did you live in the same house all the time, Daddy?" she asked, almost afraid to imagine something so remarkable as that about him.

"Sure I did, honey. The same house my daddy grew up in. We had it modernized, of course. I remember helping your granddaddy put in the hot-water heater. That very night Mama ran a wash-tub of hot water, and I took a bath in the kitchen. I can remember the look on Mama's face to this day. She was just beaming."

"And your room had a fireplace, didn't it?" Stella asked, trying to remember all the scattered bits of his life she'd stored away.

"Yeah. Almost every room had a fireplace, but we didn't light the bedroom fires except when we were sick. We stayed in the parlor or in the kitchen in the wintertime. When Mama sent me up to bed, I can tell you I went in a hurry. You don't mess around in that kind of cold. The bed would be icy and my teeth would be chattering—you've never felt anything like it, Stella."

"I'd like to, though," she said.

"A house brings things with it, that's a fact," James Earl said. "But somehow I've forgotten most of the everyday things and just remember what was special to me. Like that bath when we first got running hot water." He gave Stella a glancing smile.

"I wish I had a house to stay in—" she started.

"Hush up," Mae said, and Stella knew to be quiet. She leaned back and shut her eyes to study the house she was imagining.

"When we get there, I'll go in first," James Earl was saying to Mae. "You and the kids just stay in the car. We can't all go in right off."

"I know," Mae said without understanding.

"Newton's probably married by now. After all, he's twenty-six."

422

James Earl paused a moment and watched the road intently, as if he envisioned his brother in the steamy air before him.

He turned to Mae again, but she was looking at the fields. The thick green, leafy tobacco plants seemed foreign to her. It was a dry, dusty jungle without the sweet citrus smell or the low open space of bean fields that meant home to her. He'll stay forever, she realized with sudden clarity, or he won't stay at all.

They came upon a thick wood, and the trees, heavy with summer, darkened the car and diluted the hot wind that blew in on them through the open window. Suddenly the woods cleared and sunlight made them blink.

"Here it is," James Earl said, stopping the car.

Mae looked at him. The house and the brother didn't matter. All that counted for her was in the station wagon, was next to her gripping the wheel and looking tearful. She hadn't expected to see him weakened by love so soon.

"Look at it," James Earl said sharply, and she turned abruptly toward the window.

The house was big and white, with a deep front porch and tall narrow windows. It looked like what it was—the old homeplace made modern by succeeding generations. The front had been extended past the porch on both sides, and the extensions were of old brick with small square windows and shutters. The original clapboard was now aluminum siding.

"Oh, Daddy, it's so beautiful," Stella said, leaning forward between her parents. "It's just like I knew it would be."

The boys began pushing to get out. "Wait," Mae said angrily. Her command seemed as unreasonable to her as it did to them.

"I'll be back in a minute." James Earl slipped out of the car.

Mae wanted to cry, trapped as she was in the station wagon. Instead, she looked down at her skinny, unshaven legs, holding back her tears while he disappeared into the porch shadow and the house. She couldn't for the life of her watch him go.

James Earl's brother, Newton, let them move into an empty tenant house at the end of a lane that ran beside the homeplace back into the farmland.

"It's not much," Newton said during dinner that noon. He seemed unable to hide his surprise at seeing the faces crowding his table, and so his own face was contorted between smiles and worried looks. "We put a bathroom in it a few years back, but with help so short nobody's lived there in over a year now."

"It'll be all right, Newt," James Earl said. "You've done fine with the whole place, and I know I'm not bringing anything to this arrangement but two hands and a back." He looked at his children, who ate quickly and silently. Around this table, they looked like liabilities to him. His eyes settled on Stella. "Stella likes to work. Don't you, honey?"

She stared up at him, her fork in midair. She was being called on to perform in public for the first time other than in truck-stop restaurants, where she was sometimes appointed to negotiate for extra packets of catsup and sugar. She had a flair for these dramatics, having played the role first as a chubby blond toddler to whom nothing could be denied. Then, as she had grown older, becoming thin, almost frail, she had learned that plaintive eyes and a pouting mouth could be as profitable as a cherubic face. Perhaps the waitresses, thin and plaintive themselves, saw the determination in her eyes and thought to themselves, What's ten cents' worth of catsup if it helps this kid make it?

But now Stella hesitated, wondering what the unpracticed answer could possibly be. "I like picking," she said finally. "I like picking oranges and peaches, too, because they smell good." It seemed important that she and James Earl prove themselves.

Anne, Newton's wife, was refilling the serving dishes. "Have some more," she kept saying.

They all looked half starved to her. Mae seemed ill at ease, painfully incapable of anything but embarrassment. The younger children, with their stares and scrawny bodies, looked like mouth-moving statues. Only Stella seemed to have a spark.

Anne stopped at the girl's chair and passed a basket of biscuits over her shoulder, touching Stella gently with the back of her hand as she did. Stella turned quickly and gave Anne a little smile.

"Good biscuits," she said. "Aren't they good biscuits, Daddy?" She turned back to the table.

"Good as Mama ever made," James Earl said, "and that's saying something."

"Mama don't make no biscuits," William said solemnly. They sounded like the first words out of the ten-year-old's mouth.

"Not your mama." James Earl laughed. "My mama."

They were silent—James Earl, Newton, Anne—conjuring up the memory of the mother in the kitchen, kneading, serving, blessing. In the silence, the others struggled to catch the mystery of the woman's presence and absence, but imagination failed them and they went back to eating.

"As soon as you get settled in the house, we'll make some biscuits, Mae," Anne said.

"I thank you," Mae said softly, without looking up from her plate. There was no one she could look at.

Since the tenant house wasn't furnished, Newt went into the attic, where he had stored some old family furniture, and came up with a kitchen set, a sofa and two beds, an extra mattress, and the crib James Earl and Newton had slept in. James Earl recognized the extra mattress, with its quilted yellow roses.

"That was Mama's," he said. "I remember it was the first mattress I ever saw that wasn't plain ticking."

"Mama killed herself, you know," Newton said abruptly.

The attic was unbearably hot. In the yard below, James Earl could hear the children playing red rover. He turned away from the mattress and leaned against the jamb of the open window, looking down at his children. "I guess I thought she just died," he whispered finally. "Without any pain or anything."

"She had cancer," Newton said more gently. "But I guess she knew she could live like that a long time. Anne was here that day. She found her. Mama used a revolver I'd given her six or seven years before."

"I thought she just died," James Earl said again. The words seemed so absurdly childish that he wanted to snatch them back.

"We didn't know where you were, so I wrote letters to general delivery at the places on the cards you sent Mama. She kept them in a box on her dresser."

"I got a letter in Orlando a month or so later. Too late." James Earl breathed in the fresh air from the attic window.

Newton started to wipe dust off a table with a dirty rag. "You know, James Earl," he said, "what I really regret is that I didn't understand what Mama was going through. But then, maybe we don't understand any suffering but our own. Mama and I got to where we didn't talk very much; so when the time came, I don't reckon she could tell me how bad it was. I couldn't have listened, either, or said the right things if I had. I learned something from it, though. That's why I want to be open with you right now."

"We had some good times, didn't we, Newt?" James Earl sat down on a chair and looked at his brother.

"I guess we did. I thought you were the greatest thing on two feet." Newton grinned. He had a familiar, almost childishly shy expression on his fleshy face, and for a moment he looked like James Earl's memory of him—roly-poly, laughing.

"I don't remember much now, though," Newton continued, his features turning into a more masculine face, still fleshy, but strongly defined. "I could always see where I stood in the family. It wasn't just being the youngest. It was being so different from you. You could always do everything better than I could.

"I was glad when you quit school and joined the air force. I thought, Now it's my turn. I worked hard here, and Daddy lived to see me make money farming. It's mine, you know, except for those acres on the far side of the pasture. They belonged to Mama outright, and she willed them to you. The house, everything else, Daddy left to Mama for her lifetime and then to me."

"Seems fair."

Newton looked at him closely. James Earl's face was narrow and painfully drawn, his nose too short and flared, his jawline weakening. His face seemed to have slipped a little, missing the mark of youth he'd once had. He needed a haircut, too. Rusty curls fell down onto his shirt collar.

"Looks like a damn hippie," Newt had said to Anne earlier that afternoon, and she'd smiled and kissed him gently, urging him with her fingers on his shoulders to relax and take strength from her.

Now things were different. There was no Anne to comfort him.

426

Only a gaunt, disturbingly old but ungrown brother across the stifling attic from him. "I just want you to understand. I—we're—glad you've come. Help is scarce and I need you to get the crop in, but I want you to know where you stand."

"I didn't come expecting anything," James Earl said softly. "I just needed to be here, to show Mae and the kids, to see for myself." He brushed his hand across his disheveled hair. "Can you cut hair?" he asked. "I hate like hell to go to town like this."

"I've got some pruning shears." Newton laughed. He felt suddenly happy. "Now let's start hauling this stuff down. We can get most of it over to the house before supper."

THE house was only half painted. Coming down the path, Mae and Stella saw the painted half first, and Mae's heart thumped. Suddenly, without thinking, she took Stella's swinging hand. Stella was no more accustomed to being touched than her mother was to touching, and her impulse was to pull away and explore a kind of bursting freedom she felt in her own body.

She can't hold me back anymore. This is where I'm going to live, Stella thought. There won't be any stuffy old car to sit in half the day, while houses go by and I'm wondering what it's like to be living somewhere, anywhere, where I can get to know people who aren't leaving tomorrow.

The house was before them, a shotgun house with a kitchen attached to the back of the side porch, and another low porch on the front. Mae walked slowly and Stella stayed back with her, although she wanted to run and jump on the porch, push open the door, step inside. It's her house, too, Stella thought. Probably the best house she's ever had.

Mae tightened her hand around Stella's thin fingers. "I know it's a handout," she said softly, "but it's all right, ain't it?"

"Sure it is," Stella said. "We can do lots of things to it. Anne's got magazines about what to do in houses to make them nice. I saw some of them. Pretty rooms with books and statues and wallpaper, like Anne has."

"We can't do none of that," Mae snapped.

They reached the porch and stood in front of the house, looking

427

at the one side gleaming in its coat of paint and the other side, defeated, weather-beaten brown.

"We can get some more paint. I bet I can paint it right by myself," Stella said, hardly surprised at the house's double nature.

"We can't do nothing like that," Mae said again. "This is Newton's house. You remember that, Stella. Everything you can see belongs to your daddy's brother." Looking at the house had taken the life out of Mae, and she released Stella's hand slowly, as if she'd died standing there.

"You coming in?" Stella felt clammy with excitement and couldn't help hoping that her mother would let her explore the house alone, free from the doubts that always seemed to color Mae's thinking.

"You go ahead." Mae sat on the porch, out of the sun.

The door swung open without a creak, and Stella stepped inside. Because the room was bare, it seemed very large to her. In her mind it was an empty, dusty world of filtered light waiting for her to clean it up and fill it with her whole life. She walked slowly into the next room and then the next, through shades of brown and gray and sun-bright white, down the narrow side porch into the kitchen and tiny bathroom. Then she turned and, looking back at where she'd been, saw how good living there could be.

She had been born a squalling knot of tight, unexplainable longings that screamed "I will be" to a world that seemed to ignore her, that gave her no safety but the battered shell of an automobile and an armrest on which to pound her silent anger. Now she had a place to store the secret Stella and draw her longings out slowly, carefully, one by one, and keep them safe. She would never desert this place, never let it slip away as her daddy had. They could all vanish, and she would stay, inside walls that didn't move in the dark or carry her somewhere as strange and unwelcoming as the last place she'd been.

"Stella Mae!"

"Here." She came into the middle room, where her mother stood with her hands over her face, as if she were afraid to look.

"Come and see," Stella said. "It's real nice. The kitchen has spigots, and there's a little bathroom with a shower bath in it."

Mae moved her hands and looked at the empty room. Her face was stricken, contorted with what seemed to be physical pain.

"We're going to stay, aren't we, Mama? Can't we stay forever and ever?" Stella begged, knowing the answer but wanting it out in the open, clearly visible, where she could fight it better.

"There ain't no forever," Mae said. "We keep moving 'cause that's what we can do."

"Not me," Stella said, filling the little house with her voice until the dust seemed to stir. "I'm never leaving."

Mae stood in the middle of the handout house and let loose the tears saved up across Georgia and South Carolina, held back in the stinking, oily heat of the station wagon and in the gardenia-scented, air-conditioned space of Anne Willis' living room. Spilling down her trembling cheeks and chin, they said what she could never have found words to say, for she knew that what was a beginning for her child was a final, desperate failure for herself.

JAMES Earl went to work in the fields, priming tobacco next to the tenants until his shoulders ached so painfully that he couldn't straighten up.

"Them sand lugs is the worst," Silas Brown said, seeing James Earl squatting in the next row, his face hidden behind the sticky foliage of the tobacco plants. Silas was grinning. He always grinned, even when he was serious. It gave him a stupid, lively look that made people feel good.

James Earl grinned back. He'd known Silas when they were boys, and coming home had been as much coming home to people like Silas as to anything. The house, the land, the tenants who farmed it, the very air he breathed was home to him. He raised his shoulders slowly, trying to find a position that didn't hurt.

"Tomorrow you gonna die out here," Silas said. "Sure as the sun comes up, these here lugs gonna kill you. Tell you what, though. I'll send Toby down to the house tonight with some of Synora's salve. You rub it in good and it'll take the fire right out. Out of everything, if you want to know the truth."

Silas laughed, his chuckle rising slowly until it ripped his mouth and showed even, yellow teeth. He was bent double over the plants. "You better keep from being sore, if you expect them wages."

Wages, James Earl thought, leaning forward to pull a damp, heavy leaf out of the dirt. The wages were nothing for a man thirty-two years old. Tobacco prices weren't what they used to be, either.

It's like I've been moving and standing still all these years, he thought. But now I'm home, and tenant wages or not, I'd rather be in this dirt than anywhere else I've been.

"James Earl!" It was Silas halfway down the row. "Time to eat." Silas dropped his leaves into the burlap-sided cart and yelled up the land to his son, Toby. "Come get this mule outa here!"

Toby, his dark hair slick with sweat, puffed up the dusty road to where the mule stood hitched to the truck. "Dinnertime, Daddy," he said, jumping onto the back of the truck.

"You ain't tellin' me nothin' I don't already know, boy." Silas still grinned, but his expression was somehow different, almost shy, when he spoke to his only child.

Toby took the reins and clucked to the mule, while James Earl and Silas started down the road on foot.

"That boy is what counts for me," Silas said, watching his son's straight, muscular body leaning forward, balancing his bare feet with the rumbling sway of the truck. "I ain't never goin' count for nothin'. But Toby. He's got brains."

So Silas is looking toward the future, James Earl thought. As for himself, he'd never been concerned beyond the next picking station, had never given much thought to what would become of his children, whose futures had always seemed beyond his imagination. He knew he would have stayed on the road forever were it not for this compulsion to see his home and brother again. He hadn't come for the kids. He could have let them grow up in an automobile, without ever knowing what roots meant. How could he have lived so completely in the present and not realized that his children deserved a chance as much as Toby did?

James Earl and Silas walked slowly along in the dust of the truck, the noon sun burning into their aching shoulders. In the distance James Earl saw Stella's thin blond figure dart out from under a barn

430

shelter and jump onto the truck next to Toby. The dust was like a curtain between him and his daughter, and at that moment he would have brushed it away if that meant seeing what her life would be like if they stayed or if they went. Stella balanced precariously next to Toby, and James Earl came in slowly behind them, knowing that at least today life was good to her.

Already she had Toby for her first real friend. The day after their arrival, Silas and Synora had come shyly to the back door, Toby behind them, to welcome James Earl home. The first thing James Earl had noticed was how bashful Toby was about meeting Stella, who didn't hold shyness among her attributes. She had jumped right off the porch, practically into the poor boy's arms, in her excitement at finding somebody near her own age.

"This is Stella," James Earl remembered saying. "She's been wondering what she was going to do around here."

"I work all day," Toby had said, as if that would save him from her.

"Doing what?" Stella asked.

"Trucking tobacco, putting up sticks. Whatever Mr. Newton says to do."

"I guess I'll be doing that, too," Stella said.

"Girls don't truck tobacco. You'd have to drive a mule."

"I can do it if Uncle Newton says I can." Stella plopped down on a patch of grass, while the grown-ups settled on the steps.

"You know how to drive a mule?" Toby asked, still standing.

"No, but you didn't always know how."

Toby must have known he was losing, because he changed the subject. "What grade are you at school?"

"The eighth, I guess. Last year I didn't get to go much. Mama stayed sick for the longest time after my baby sister was born. But this year I'm going every single day. What grade are you in?"

"Ninth," Toby said happily. He was confident about school.

"Uncle Newton says I can ride the bus. Do you ride the bus?"

"I'm not sitting with a girl, if that's what you're thinking."

"I'm just making conversation, Toby Brown, so you won't be standing there like a knot on a stick."

"Yeah, well, I got to get going," Toby said, edging away.

"I'll see you in the morning!" Stella called after him. "What time do you start work?"

"Six," Toby said, obviously hoping to discourage her.

"Oh, I'm always up by then," Stella replied.

And of course she was, if for no other reason than that Toby had inadvertently challenged her.

Now James Earl saw them tying up the mule and racing off toward the house. "Looks like they'd be tired," he said to Silas.

"Work's still fun to them," Silas said, "and if they're lucky, it always will be. I can't think of nothin' better to spend my time doing."

"But you want something different for Toby," James Earl said.

"Yeah. Something better."

"That's what I want for Stella, too," James Earl said, knowing that it was true.

Chapter Two

STELLA, wrapped in a towel, her hair and shoulders glistening with water from the shower, was standing in the middle of the kitchen when Toby knocked on the screen door.

"You in there, Stella?" he called.

"I'm not dressed, Toby," she said, coming close to the door so he could see the towel. "I'm dripping wet."

"I brought another batch of salve. Mama says you all must be eating the stuff, it goes so fast." Toby smiled. "She's as proud as a peacock. None of the Willises ever used her salve before. You planning to let me in?"

"I'll be back in a minute." She sauntered across the kitchen and into the bathroom.

When she came out on the porch dressed in shorts and a wrinkled shirt, Toby was sitting on the steps. Stella sat down next to him and began combing her hair.

"You got the cleanest hair in Montreet County," he said. "You're goin' wash it out if you aren't careful."

"That's stupid, Toby. Anne's got magazines just for ladies that tell all about hair and skin and pretty clothes. They say you can't wash your hair too much. Besides," she said, striking what she

432

thought was a magazine pose, "just because you don't ever wash yours . . ."

"I'm as clean as you are," Toby said. "I just don't wash unless I'm dirty."

"You're just mouthing off." Stella jumped up and walked into the yard. "I'm going to paint this house, Toby. You wanna help?"

"I've been trucking tobacco all day and you're asking me if I want to paint a house?" Toby came over and looked at the weatherboards with her.

"We could make it nice, Toby," she said. "Newton'll buy the paint, and there's brushes already at his house."

"You got a ladder?" Toby asked reluctantly.

"I can get one."

"You got turp and stirrers?"

"I can get 'em. Please, Toby."

"You gotta pay me," Toby said stubbornly.

"Toby, you're as hateful as a rattlesnake." Stella stamped off down the path, yelling, "I'll paint the house myself."

"Stella!" Toby took off after her. "Stella!" The dust stirred around his feet and legs, coating him with gray powder.

"You're getting me dirty," Stella said angrily when he'd caught up. She wouldn't look at him, but marched resolutely on.

"I'll help you, Stella," Toby said. "Saturday, I'll help you."

She didn't answer, and he saw her cheeks were flushed, suddenly fuller and more soft. Her hair was drying in white wisps around her face.

"I can do it myself," she repeated, refusing to look at him.

Toby gave up and stood in the path while Stella tramped on into the woods. "Stella," he called when she was almost out of sight, "please let me paint the house!"

"All right!" the answer came, and Toby, somehow the victor, went home.

EARLY Saturday morning they started painting. They were still at it that afternoon, when Silas and James Earl were going into town with Newton. Mae and Toby's mother were up at the house helping Anne slice and sugar peaches to be served up pink and icy from her freezer in winter, and the children played in the yard, where William was pulling Lissy and Earl around in a rusty wagon.

Toby hung on to the ladder and watched Newton's pickup disappear down the road, leaving him at the mercy of Stella, who was turning into a tyrant with a personal slave.

"You're missing a place, Toby," she said from the ground, where she'd gone to inspect his work.

"I'm resting," Toby grumbled. "I ain't missing nothing."

"Well, you are," Stella argued. "I know your intentions are the best, Toby, but you're too close to see what you're missing."

"Now I should grow my arms, I reckon, so I can stand down there with you and paint up here," Toby said.

"You can't take a bit of criticism, can you, Toby? Not one little bit. Or advice, either."

Toby couldn't really complain about Stella. She had painted more than he had. Of course, being on the rickety ladder handicapped him. He watched her steady, dauntless strokes. She could do anything she set her mind to, and he liked her for it.

"When we get through, let's hitch a ride into town," Toby said. "We could get a grape soda and sit around awhile."

Stella looked up, her face splattered with white freckles of paint. "You asking me to town?" she whispered.

"Yeah. You got to get that paint offa you first, though. I'm not taking you anywhere like that."

"You don't look like much yourself," Stella said gaily. "You've got paint on your head." She painted more quickly. "What else can we do?"

"Well, we'll just see what's happening, look around in Grover's Department Store, sit in the soda shop. Nothing much."

"Sounds real good to me," Stella said. "Thanks, Toby."

The tone in her voice forced Toby to look down. He felt suddenly flustered, warmer than the afternoon sun could make him. It was a heat deep inside and it told him that maybe he didn't have to go it alone now. It seemed possible that here was someone who could know he'd read hundreds of books from the school library, and that the librarian borrowed special ones from the high school library just for him. Perhaps he could tell her that his mind wan-

dered in class because he knew more details of history than the teacher did.

Here was Stella Willis, a girl as poor as himself but with a family name that had always been respected in the town; a girl with spunk and temper, whom he didn't pretend to understand but nevertheless felt he could risk trusting. He had made her happy, and he felt like crying with joy himself. Instead, he worked carefully, as if painting the house were very important to him.

"It'll be finished in thirty minutes," he said after a while. "You go on and get cleaned up."

"I'm not leaving till it's done," Stella said. "You've got to move the ladder one more time."

"I can do it. You go ahead." Toby climbed down.

"We're doing this together," Stella said, taking his paint can while he moved the ladder a couple of feet.

Toby settled the ladder against the corner of the house and climbed up quickly. His heart was suddenly racing and his legs trembled as he tried to fix his knees against the rungs for support.

I'm worn out, he thought. But he knew he wasn't. He was trembling because of Stella. She was too close. He could reach down and touch her head, the bright crown of hair she wore. He felt keenly the risk of making a fool of himself. He saw how truly alien she was to him, how little he knew about her.

STELLA wore a dress into town, a light blue sleeveless one with a white collar and tiny pearl buttons down the front. Anne had given the dress to her after collecting outgrown clothes from among her friends in town. Stella knew the dress was a hand-me-down, but it looked new and it was the only dress she had.

They got a ride with Anne. Stella rode in the front seat of the yellow Buick, while Toby sat in the back.

"You take care of her now, Toby," Anne said, looking at him through the rearview mirror. "Take her around a little and introduce her to the young people in the soda shop." She smiled at Stella. "You tell them she's Newton's niece," she added to Toby.

Toby looked out the window. He was flying, and the fields spinning by seemed to blur into the sky. Stella must feel all the things

436

I feel, he thought. Suddenly he wanted to lean forward and touch her shoulder so she'd turn to him.

"I'll let you out here," Anne said, stopping the car in front of a grocery store. "You find Newton and get a ride home tonight," she added. "I don't want Stella down here when it gets dark."

"Yes, ma'am." Toby slipped out of the car in time to open Stella's door.

Stella looked at him with surprise and got out, grinning. "Thanks, Anne," she said. "We'll be all right."

She started down the sidewalk, then stopped and waited for Toby to join her. She was smiling and bouncing along on the balls of her feet, as if every second wasted were more than she could bear. "Where we going first?" she wanted to know.

"Let's get a drink," Toby said. "And maybe play the jukebox."

"You've got money for the jukebox?"

"Maybe one song," Toby said sheepishly.

"Oh, Toby, this is the nicest day. First we got the house looking pretty and now we're downtown by ourselves. I just can hardly believe it!"

Neither could Toby.

RODNEY Biggers, sixteen on March 12 and carrying his driver's license between an I WILL NOT SMOKE pledge card and a ten-dollar bill in his wallet, sat at the soda-shop counter and stirred his cola with a plastic straw. He was bored, and watching the swirling reddish brown liquid gave him something to do.

He'd already put a quarter in the jukebox and pushed "Fire and Rain" twice. He liked that song, especially the sad way James Taylor sang it. Rodney had heard a girl say right here in the soda shop that the song was about taking drugs. She'd read it in *Time* magazine, so Rodney believed her.

He'd never read *Time* magazine. The only things he ever read that weren't school assignments were the joke pages in the copies of *The Reader's Digest* at his mother's beauty shop. Anyhow, he liked "Fire and Rain" no matter what it was really about, because to him it meant feeling low and restless, and that was how Rodney felt most of the time.

"You finished with that?" Elsie the countergirl asked him, nodding at the warm cola. She wanted to clean up.

"Nope, I'm not finished with it," Rodney said, spinning a black plastic ashtray that stood on the counter.

The advertisement written in white letters on the face of the ashtray read JEAN'S BEAUTY SHOP—CUT, CURL, COLOR—NIGHT APPOINTMENTS. Night appointments at his mother's shop meant Rodney cooked supper for himself and his daddy. He really liked to cook, so he didn't mind that. Jean Biggers wasn't much in the kitchen anyway; the food she prepared ended up smelling like waving lotion or hair spray. The smells about her, the lacquered sheen of her black hair, the dyed tips of her fingers were the things that consciously annoyed him. They were such unnatural things, and they embarrassed him.

Right now, his daddy was out on the farm paying off the hands so they could come into town and spend a week's wages, and his mother stood on aching feet in white crepe-soled shoes behind the head of some talker. She didn't just fix the outside of heads, she liked to say, she listened to the inside. As a philosopher, his mother was matched locally only by the preacher at the Free Will Baptist Church, who claimed that there wasn't a thing he hadn't heard at least once and nothing at all that surprised him.

Rodney heard his mother's customers' secrets one by one; she had a way of letting them slip out, as if she couldn't remember what was told her in confidence and what wasn't. She ended up telling everything to his daddy. He'd heard it all before, too.

But from the time he was a little boy, Rodney had found himself listening intently and remembering these modern horror tales. He never repeated his mother's stories, because he wouldn't be able to tell about family fights or binges or men running around without turning all shades of red and then repenting on his knees afterward, when his conscience would get to him about the sin of gossip, which he knew was a sin no matter what his mother said.

Rodney knew he would never fall into sin, because he appreciated the trouble it would bring him. He'd been baptized in the church, which had certainly washed away any sins he could have accumulated before the age of ten. Since then, he'd known where temptation lurked and avoided it so carefully that he was barely sociable. He intended never to drink, steal, or fornicate, and he protected himself from the sin of unclean thoughts—his own fantasies—by attributing them to what he'd heard rather than to any originality on his own part. Rodney rarely if ever had an original thought anyway—except when he was cooking, where he eagerly concocted his own mayonnaise and barbecue sauce.

Despite his cooking skills and the minimal exercise he got, he'd managed to stay thin through puberty. He scrubbed his face with medicated soap and shaved occasionally, so he always looked clean. His mother could afford to buy him nice clothes and she did, although he refused to wear some of her purchases. She liked flashy colors and wide-legged, cuffed pants. Finally, Rodney had consented to a pair of candy-striped jeans and a red knit shirt, which he always wore on Saturday afternoons.

When Stella and Toby entered the soda shop, Stella saw Rodney first because she was looking at everything. Toby, who'd seen Rodney in his outfit Saturday after Saturday, didn't even notice him until Stella started tugging at his arm and nodding toward the counter where Rodney sat. "Who's that?" she whispered.

"It's just Rodney Biggers," Toby muttered, although he was pleased that the first person they'd seen was somebody he knew.

"Let's sit at the counter," Stella said loudly, and sat right down next to Rodney Biggers.

The stool had once been a spinner, but now it leaned precariously on its pedestal, and Stella put her arms on the counter to keep from slipping off. Toby sat next to her and ordered two grape sodas, while Stella looked at Rodney. She stared at him openly, not bothering with sidelong glances, while Rodney studied his fingernails.

"I'll have a grape soda, too," he said to Elsie. He pushed the watery cola away as though it didn't belong to him.

"Rodney, whatcha know, buddy?" Toby said, and Rodney found himself forced to look straight at Stella and then past her to Toby.

He grinned too widely. "Nothin' much," he said, and thumped the lever on the straw dispenser so heavily that two dropped out.

"This is Stella, Mr. Newton Willis' niece," Toby said.

Stella flashed Rodney a smile. "Toby is the nicest person," she said, in a strangely sophisticated voice. "This morning he helped me paint our house and now he's brought me to town."

Rodney thought the conversation was already beyond his grasp, and he looked around Stella at Toby. "Whatcha know?" he said glumly.

"We're going to look in the stores some, just mess around all afternoon," Stella answered happily. She sipped her soda daintily. "I bet you're in high school."

Rodney puffed up. "Yeah. I'm a sophomore," he said proudly.

"No kidding," Stella said. "And you know Toby?"

"We were in junior high together two years ago," Toby said. "Rodney's sixteen. He's got wheels."

Rodney felt as if he were watching his own creation.

"No kidding. You've got a car?" Stella bounced on the rickety stool, and Toby grabbed her arm to keep her from falling off.

"It's Mama's," Rodney admitted. "But I've got it today. It's right out front there. A baby-blue Impala with factory air." He was grinning uncontrollably.

"Where you going in it?" Stella asked.

"I don't know," Rodney said, beginning to deflate.

Most Saturdays he let the car sit down the street at the beauty shop. All week he thought about where he'd go during the weekend, but when Saturday came, his plans always seemed not worth the trouble. He often used having to run errands for his mother as an excuse for not doing anything more exciting. He had to keep himself available.

"You could just ride around and look at things," Stella said.

"Look at what?" Rodney became more dumb by the minute. Girls generally ignored him so completely that he was totally unprepared for conversation with someone like Stella.

"At anything. At everything!" Stella was exasperated and turned to Toby. "Could we go for a ride in Rodney's car with him?"

"I guess so," Toby said slowly. He wanted to ride around and listen to the radio, but the idea frightened him a little. Suddenly he felt responsible for Stella, whose strong-mindedness seemed likely to override his judgment.

"Please, Toby." She was patting his arm anxiously. It came so

440

easy to her, this intimacy with which he had to take such tremendous care. But what could he do?

"You want to show Stella around?" he asked Rodney. "Maybe over to Lawrence and back?"

"Yeah. I reckon so." Rodney was scared to death.

Minutes later Stella sat in the middle of the front seat strapped in by a seat belt, because that was one of Jean Biggers' rules. The strap made Stella feel good, more secure than she'd ever felt in the rumbling old station wagon. Now she felt cared for, and so she sat up straight, looking prim and detached from the excitement the two boys were trying to hide.

"This is the nicest day," Stella said to both of them.

"Everybody buckled in?" Rodney asked, like a pilot instructing his passengers above the roar of his engines. "Everybody ready?"

He turned slowly out into the traffic.

LAWRENCE—15 MILES read the intersection sign. It was Rodney's longest road trip.

SITTING in the Impala at the Dairy Queen west of Lawrence, Toby knew they'd be too late to find Newton in town and get a ride home.

Out under one of the umbrellas on an aluminum bench, Stella sat licking a chocolate-covered custard that Rodney had bought her, while Rodney sat across the table watching her. He had ordered himself a cone and had offered one to Toby, but Toby had refused and stayed in the air-conditioned car, which had been, for a few minutes, cooler than outside. Now he wished he'd gotten out with them and let Rodney buy him an ice cream, too. Frustrated by his inability to act, Toby watched them. He could see Rodney's mouth moving, he was learning how to talk to a girl. Stella was listening intently, as she had on their way to Lawrence.

Rodney had driven slowly, as if he were a tour guide. He had even explained to her about tobacco warehouses when he didn't know a thing about them, Toby thought. What did Rodney ever do but come to Lawrence the first day the tobacco market opened each year and just follow his daddy around, looking? Toby had seen him while he, Toby, was unloading graded leaves from the truck,

441

sweat dripping into his eyes, and Silas saying, "Hurry up, boy, fore the bidding starts."

And the bidding: the loud stream of numbers going higher and higher, splitting Toby's head with the roar of money. Oh, he could tell Stella about the warehouse: the concrete floor that always chilled his bare feet no matter how hot the air was, the smell of motor oil and bourbon, the rich, yes rich, smell of tobacco. There were men there wearing overalls and diamond rings, and men smelling like a barbershop, in spectator shoes and slick dress suits. He'd seen a man once handling a roll of hundred-dollar bills that could have been ones for all the man seemed to care. He waved them in his hand, and Toby envisioned one, just one, floating down to his own feet and the man saying, "Keep it, son."

Toby could tell her about other, more private times, too. He could tell her how the sky looked on nights when he lay in a tobacco truck under the stars, not because Newton needed him there but because he wanted the feeling of being completely alone, just Toby Brown and the barn owls and the old cat sleeping at his feet and so many stars the sky seemed on fire.

He could say all that only if he and Stella were alone, sitting on the steps of the house they'd painted.

"Don't you want anything?" Stella was asking through the car window.

"Nope," Toby said lazily. "We better get back, though. Mr. Newton's more than likely already gone home."

"Rodney'll take us, won't you, Rodney?" Stella straightened up and smiled at Rodney. She already knew she had a way with him, and she climbed into the car without waiting for his answer.

"We'll take the back road home," Rodney said when they were all strapped in.

He turned through a residential section that Toby hadn't even known existed and drove very slowly past houses, most of them large and brick, with small fruit trees in the yards that showed how new they were, and built-in sprinkler systems that made the new grass as green as moss. Some real estate firm had bought this land from a bankrupt farmer and sold quarter-acre lots for thousands of dollars.

"This is the prettiest place I've ever been," Stella said.

"That's the Lawrences' house." Rodney nodded toward a brick colonial. "They're the same family of Lawrences that founded this town. Tobacco rich, they are. You'd never know it, the way Mr. Lawrence is always smiling and joking."

"And you know him?" Stella asked.

"Sure. I see him all the time. Even been in that house."

"You've been in there?" Stella was straining to look back at the house as if it were a castle about to vanish.

"Well, in the kitchen. Daddy and me went there on business."

"Why, Rodney, you're just—well, amazing, that's what."

Rodney had awed himself, and he watched the road closely while a blush crept up his neck. Toby was silent, feeling the sudden separateness that had arisen between himself and Stella.

At home in the driveway, Rodney stopped the car and Toby got out. Dusk was falling and the lights were on at Newton's.

"I'll go tell Mr. Newton we're back," Toby said to Stella.

"Okay," she said, not moving to get out. "See you tomorrow."

Toby went around the house to the back door, away from them, where he pressed the bell hard. A breeze was coming up, a cool, light wind that could bring a summer storm with it.

"Well," Anne said through the screen. "You're home all right?"

"We got a ride up with Rodney Biggers," Toby said humbly. "Stella wanted to ride in his car. He's real careful."

"It's all right, Toby. We weren't ready to call the sheriff yet. But next time you arrange to come home with Newt. I'll make that clear to Stella."

"Yes, Miss Anne," Toby said, turning into the darkness. He didn't think there'd be a next time.

Chapter Three

MAE pulled the stopper out of the kitchen sink and stood the baby up while the soapy water gurgled around her chubby feet and down the drain. Lissy's body was tanned except for beneath her diaper, and there she seemed so vulnerable and white that Mae hurried to wrap her in a towel and take her in her arms.

There had been little time for affection in Mae's life. She'd never grown accustomed to touching people when she was a child, and so when her own children came, she didn't know how to cuddle them without feeling conspicuous and foolish. But now that closeness didn't mean four in a bed or packed into the car, she was beginning to find pleasure in Lissy. Lissy was the prettiest of her children, better-looking by far than Stella, who had a sharp, aggressive face that told Mae she could never be satisfied.

That look of arrogance about Stella frightened Mae. Add the house—this stability James Earl seemed to relish—to Stella's determination, and Mae felt a growing fear, a pain in her joints that could move up her body until it finally stopped her heart.

All her life Mae had wanted to hide, and her migrant existence had meant she could. There were so many people on the road that nobody noticed you. But now Stella wanted to be noticed, and her needing that already made her dangerous to Mae.

Like painting the house. She'd been determined and she'd done it. Even gotten that boy of Silas' to help her, and now she's off somewhere with him, finding something else to do.

Not that Mae worried about Stella taking care of herself. What she didn't like was that Stella was always giving her something to think about. She wouldn't be ignored, even when she wasn't there.

Why couldn't Stella leave everything alone? Too often lately, Mae could see James Earl in her as clear as day. Sometimes seeing Stella forced her to acknowledge that she hadn't known James Earl when he was a boy, hadn't followed the path that led him to Florida and into the diner where she was waiting tables during the wait-over between orange and tomato picking. God knows, she remembered him a lot of times since—not just how he looked in that airman's uniform, as blue as sapphires he seemed. True blue. Well, he'd turned out all right, too.

When she'd hated the air force base, that concrete-block apartment building they had to live in, he had turned down reenlistment, although other people thought he was crazy. He'd gone on the road with her, battling the highway like it was the enemy he'd been trained to fight.

He hadn't minded the work, either. He was a farm boy, knew

444

the soil. And even when the babies grew in her, one after another as regular as a time bomb, he hadn't been angry or complained, but had just moved on from place to place—strange shack towns that got familiar just because one field looked like another.

Sure, maybe she wouldn't have lost those other babies if they'd lived in a house and she'd seen a doctor regularly. But she didn't like doctors. The one that came when she miscarried last had seemed mad at her because the blood wouldn't stop. Doctors. All spruced up in white like they expected the whole world to be clean and shiny, too.

Still, she hadn't given any thought to James Earl having a home or a family like this. Newton and Anne were grabbing folks, who believed in taking what they could get. Like all this furniture from their attic. Why hadn't they sold it or given it away? No, they kept things. And they'd keep Stella.

Mae had seen Anne fitting that blue dress, which did improve Stella's looks even if it was a hand-me-down. Anne wanted to take Stella over, Mae thought. But Mae wouldn't let go easily.

They're taking James Earl, too, she thought suddenly, and squeezed the baby to her breasts. Sure as the world they're taking him, and I'll be left with nothing.

Outside, she heard voices. Stella and a strange high-pitched voice she couldn't put a face to.

So Stella was making friends. She had said she would. Mae remembered the first day they'd come down here to this house, and how Stella had said she'd never leave. She remembered herself crying, and now she felt the tears coming again.

Why can't I be like Stella? she wondered. Why can't I fit in and not have this bad feeling like we're doing something terrible staying here? I ought to be glad for what Anne's doing. Anne had never been condescending, had never seemed sorry they'd come.

"But I've got to get outa here," Mae whispered into Lissy's hair.

Her children had never been so clean before, had never eaten sweet corn or broccoli from a garden. They'd never been to an indoor movie or to church. But still, with a desperation that clung heavy in her chest, Mae Willis wanted to go. Not back to any place she'd ever been, not back to the field shacks or the one-room apartments in sultry cities, but away from a life that would require something of her, make her somebody, if she would only let it. She smothered the soft head of her baby in her arms, wishing she could take the good things life was offering her.

STELLA heard them in the night. Lying on the flowered mattress, her body flat and straight next to Baby Earl, who slept beside her, she listened to the sounds in the next room. It was a strange feeling to be separated from her parents, with only Earl to share her bed and William on the cot across the room, which seemed tremendous to Stella. Spilled with moonlight from the open window and the door that led onto the side porch, it gave her such a feeling of lightness and space that she wanted to stretch herself and roll on the bed, laughing aloud with delight.

From the next room, separated by the plasterboard wall and a half-closed door, sounds crept toward her. Stella lay very still, listening more closely than ever before, because the sounds seemed different from those which had long been a part of her nights.

The wall between Stella and her parents made the difference. Before, she would hear words. Now the words were inaudible; they had become moans banging into a thin wall.

The bed creaked loudly, then James Earl was up and passing through her room. His body was white and shining in the door light as he went down the porch and into the kitchen. Stella didn't move. Through the open door of her parents' room she could hear her mother talking. She listened, straining to hear the words, and finally they came to her, barely audible in the darkness: "O Jesus, let me keep him," her mother was saying.

Stella held her breath. She felt air moving; the screen door opened and James Earl leaned over her. His cool hand touched her cheek, her hair. Stella struggled to be still and felt the sheet being gently laid across her stomach.

"God loves you, Stella," James Earl whispered. It was a fact, the way he said it.

James Earl went softly across the floor and back to his room. The bed creaked again as he eased in next to Mae, who lay still, her prayer, heavy with a fear of losing him, still quivering on her lips.

446

He was good to her because he was a good man. That one thing she understood. His gentleness was as inherent as the blue marble of his eyes, the shape of his wiry hands. Mae shut her eyes, but the tears rimmed her lashes and she muffled a trembling sob.

James Earl, already half asleep but stirred by her sigh, rolled into her, his head against her thin shoulder. His warm breath fell on her breast. It was a gentle breeze, but it chilled her through the long night.

IN EARLY June, just weeks before James Earl and his brood came, Anne Willis met with the high school principal and resigned from her teaching job because she was expecting a baby.

The pregnancy had been planned. Conception in late winter; birth in the fall. A baby weaned by the time school started again the next year, in case she wanted to teach again that soon. She really couldn't imagine not working. She liked being as busy as she'd been when she was teaching and remodeling the house at the same time. She'd hardly found time then for the monthly social gatherings of their church group, and she'd enjoyed saying so.

Just being a Willis could have kept Anne busy. Her life hinged on her reputation as a wife, decorator, and social planner, and she did everything well, with such efficiency that the other wives were helpless beside her. Yet they liked her.

Anne, for herself, knew she could do anything confidence would allow, and having Newton Willis fall in love with her had given her such a sense of accomplishment that the possibilities of her life now seemed limitless.

Not that she hadn't always believed that good things were waiting in the wings. She had recognized all the turning points, had felt herself becoming pretty and then blossoming, until finally, in her sophomore year of college while she was serving up spaghetti in the church kitchen, Newton Willis asked her out.

She was wearing a white crepe blouse and a light blue pleated skirt that night, and she lifted the steaming spaghetti carefully onto the plates with two forks and then passed them down to DeeDee Johnson, who ladled the sauce on and passed them through the serving window to a table in the recreation room.

Anne was wearing her best clothes because she knew Newton Willis would be there, but now with the steam from the spaghetti pot rising in her face and tiny sprigs of hair curling crazily about her damp head, she almost hoped she wouldn't see him. For a month, since the last church supper, when she'd sat next to him, she'd been half expecting him to call her. He'd implied as much when they'd finished the meal and she rose to help in the kitchen.

"Do you have to?" he'd asked, as if he didn't want the time with her to end.

"I promised," she said breathlessly. She'd hoped he'd say more, something like, How long will you be? But he didn't, only stood up and said, "Well, I'll see you later."

Anne had taken his parting words literally, so for a week she jumped when the phone rang, until her initial excitement fell slowly into a dull memory of her longing to go out with the best-looking boy in Montreet County.

Now she glanced through the serving window and saw his mother, tall and thin, her graying hair curled tightly around her weathered face. It was the hollow, bony face of a farm woman that smiled almost unwillingly, as if pleasure embarrassed her.

Behind her stood Newton. They stopped in front of the plates of food, and Anne saw his mother begin to smile slowly, the wrinkles of her cheeks moving up to the hollows of her eyes. Newton was saying something to her and the girl serving them. The girl and Newton laughed, and his mother continued to smile, her face coloring under a lingering summer tan.

Anne stood staring at them through the window, until suddenly Newton's glance caught hers, and for a second they looked at each other through the steam from the spaghetti pot. Anne quickly turned away, and when she looked again, the Willises were gone.

Anne lifted the pasta resolutely. So Newton Willis wasn't interested. So what? She was just nineteen and had almost three years left in college. She had time, and if it wasn't Newton Willis, there'd be someone else, probably somebody with a college degree.

Newton Willis wasn't going to college, not that that mattered when you'd inherited a nice farm and were smart enough to make money from it. People were already talking about what kind of

448

success Newton was headed for. He took night courses in farm management at the technical school and worked hard all day. At twenty he was turning the place to a profit.

"And, thank God, Hannah is living to see it," people said, remembering the hard times since James Earl went off, leaving old Willis and Newton to do all the work, with Newt just a boy and old Willis practically an invalid after his stroke.

Hannah had suffered and grown old and thin, sickly herself under the strain of not being able to do anything about her husband and her sons but watch. James Earl never came back, not even for his daddy's funeral; and Newton had to give up things, like playing baseball when he was the best hitter Montreet High ever had, because somebody had to work those spring afternoons. Those things had hurt Hannah, and she'd looked on helplessly, doing the little chores mothers do when they want to make up for things they can't change. She cooked Newt good hearty dinners, and let him take the car whenever he wanted. She never asked him for anything or nosed into his business. The only thing she would have asked of him was that he go to church, and he did that without being asked.

All in all, Newton Willis was practically perfect, and very attractive besides. That's what Anne Atwood was thinking when he came into the hot kitchen, his dark hair brushed carefully across his forehead and his skin smelling of English Leather.

"Hi." He was standing next to her at the stove.

"Be careful," Anne said. "DeeDee's dangerous with that sauce."

DeeDee giggled. "You better get out of here, Newton."

"Not till Anne says I can drive her home," said Newton.

"I have to clean up afterward."

"I'll do it for you," DeeDee said.

"She'll do it for you," said Newton.

"Well . . ." Anne hesitated for effect. "Well, all right then."

"Now get outa here, Newton Willis. We're busy," DeeDee said with a silly laugh.

"See you later," Newton said into Anne's ear, and was gone.

"Newton Willis could have any girl in Montreet County," Dee-Dee said, as happily as if he'd asked to take her home.

I wonder what will happen? Anne thought. She had always

known what her life was about. She'd even reserved a place for Newton Willis, in case he was interested. We'll date a few times and that'll be the end of it, she thought, knowing all the time that given the chance she'd spend the rest of her life with him.

RODNEY rode with his left elbow jutting out the window and his right hand gripping the top of the wheel. Pressing his foot on the accelerator, he felt the blue Impala pick up. The speedometer's red arrow edged toward sixty and Rodney smiled. The feel and power of the car were beginning to have an exhilarating effect on him as he sped along the country road toward the Willis farm.

During the past two weeks Rodney'd driven the car down this road more times than he could count; now he leaned back, almost stretching. He was happy. Gradually his summer was taking shape without his doing a thing but making himself available. Stella Willis seemed to be taking care of the rest.

Like the first time he'd taken her for a ride after their jaunt to Lawrence. She'd sat on her feet, the seat belt hanging to the floor, putting what she wanted first without regard for regulations. The rules were meaningless for Stella.

"Let's open the windows!" she'd shouted over the radio.

Rodney had never driven without the protection of closed windows, and now she wanted to strip it away and let the smells and sounds of summer blow in around him with the wind.

"Sure," he said finally, because no other answer came to him. He switched off the air conditioner and Stella bounced on the seat, her arm out the window, her hair flying all the way to Lawrence.

Now it was Saturday again, and Rodney had the car and ten dollars he intended to put to good use. Just the day before yesterday he'd been sitting on the Willises' front porch between Stella and Toby, eating the blackberries she and Toby had picked, and he had felt a pang of jealousy that told him he had to do better than just taking her to the soda shop. What really galled him was that she seemed to have the same kind of good time with Toby she had with him. And Toby was always around. Of course, he knew Toby was no threat to him—it was just age and their living nearby that made Toby her friend.

450

Besides, long before school started he intended to be going steady with Stella, even though she was just in junior high. There wasn't anything wrong with a two-year age difference. If the truth were known, Stella acted older than Rodney felt.

Still, his concern about Toby had caused Rodney to do some careful planning about this particular afternoon.

TOBY, coming across the field of green oats toward Stella's house, saw the Impala pull in. He stopped to watch Rodney, wearing a new blue outfit, emerge from the car and go up the concrete blocks to the front porch. Stella was waiting there, and they sat down together on the porch glider Anne had given them.

Toby had been on his way to see Stella, but now he wouldn't go. What good would it do? Every time Rodney came, Toby felt left out, no matter what he and Stella had been doing. He could feel Stella's attention edging away—politely, he thought, so she wouldn't hurt his feelings outright, but nevertheless slowly, purposefully moving toward Rodney Biggers. Toby turned away.

"We're going into town," Silas said when Toby was back in his own yard. "You comin'?"

"Yeah." Toby slumped on the porch, his back to the post.

"Somethin' ailin' you, boy?" Silas asked.

"Just blues," Toby said, not wanting to lie to his father. Somehow he knew a lie, even a little one, would break a link between them that could never be repaired.

"A bright boy like you ain't got no use for blues," Silas said. "Come on into town. Live it up some."

"Daddy, when school starts, I think I'll try out for the choir," Toby said. "I've been thinking about doing more things this year, and Miss Brasher at the church says I've got a clear voice."

"That's fine, son, just as long as you keep up your grades. You've got to get some of that awards money for college. There ain't no other way."

"I know it, Daddy. But I need to get around some, too."

Across the field, dust rose and spun into the air. "Rodney Biggers's taking Stella off somewhere," Toby said coolly.

"Yeah. He's hot for that girl, all right. James Earl better be

451

watching out," Silas said. "And you better, too, son. I see you mooning around her. Hell, I like Stella. But she's a Willis, Toby. You got to remember that, and what's fitting is for people like the Willises and the Biggerses to be under the same bit of moonlight."

Toby stood up to stop the talk. "I'm coming with you," he said.

"We're getting a ride with James Earl in that vehicle of his," Silas said. "Probably have to push the damn thing."

They started down the path. I'm not going to care about Stella Willis, Toby thought. There's other fish to fry, and I got better things to do with my time. But where the hell was Rodney taking her? And how long would it be before he didn't care?

STELLA sat in the dark car with Rodney, sensing that he wanted her to get out. But she'd had a good time and didn't want it to end. Full of Kentucky Fried Chicken, then popcorn and cola at the movie theater, she leaned back against the seat and smiled. "It was a lot of fun," she said softly. "It was the best time I've ever had."

"We could go again," Rodney said, sighing heavily. He was satisfied with the evening, too. They'd seen John Wayne at the movies, and that always made Rodney feel good, left him believing he could ram some heads together if he had a mind to.

I could kiss Stella if I wanted to, Rodney thought, remembering John Wayne.

Stella was leaning back, resting as if she never intended to get out and go into the dark house before her. She looked like she wanted kissing, as if she had planned it to happen next. He had thought about it, too. Ever since he'd known Stella, he'd thought about kissing her, and the idea scared him.

Stella sighed. Her face was turned slightly toward him, so he could see the little smile of pleasure that edged her lips. He knew better than to kiss a girl in a car. That was one of his mother's rules. "Kissing in cars leads to other things, and the lesson you learn comes too hard and too late," she had said. So Rodney found himself wishing Stella would get out and go up on the porch, where he could kiss her properly—well, decently, at least.

Stella moved suddenly and Rodney started. "What's the matter?" he asked, panic-stricken at being caught with his thoughts.

452

"Nothing," she said. "I guess I better go on in." She sighed again, then pushed down the door handle.

"Okay." Rodney slipped out quickly and went around the car to help her out, but she was already standing in the moonlight, as if she were waiting, biding her time. Rodney stood between the car and the porch, feeling foolish.

Finally, Stella came toward him. "I really did have a good time," she said when she reached him.

He took her arms at the elbows quickly, feeling the delicious life beneath her soft flesh.

"Oh, Lord," he said, pulling her against him. Even before he could find her mouth, her arms went around his neck, where prickly heat lay in rough powdered patches. His lips felt hers gently, and he thought suddenly that she was smiling and that her lips were imprinting a soft moist smile on his mouth. Then he felt her arms tighten and her smile relax, so that against his mouth her lips fell open and the warm tip of her tongue ran softly against his teeth, then moved away as quickly as it had come. She let go her arms and mouth in one instant that left him absolutely abandoned. "Night, Rodney," she said softly, and went up the steps.

He stood there empty, drained by his first kiss of all expectation, of all John Wayne theatrics. No lights went on in the house. Stella had disappeared. It might have never happened except for the trembling in his legs and the knotted muscle of his heart. He went stumbling to the car and sat down heavily behind the wheel. Mechanically he started the engine and drove home.

STELLA knew the knock on the pane was Toby without seeing his face. She sighed and began rebuttoning her dress when what she wanted to do was ignore the tapping and fall into bed. She wanted to feel the kiss on her mouth all night, and now she would have to destroy it with words to Toby.

She opened the door and went out onto the side porch where he was sitting. "What is it?" she asked.

"I needed to see you. It's important," Toby said.

"What is?" She sat down next to him, still unwilling, but curious. The kiss, her dreams, had already been destroyed.

"Where've you been?" Toby asked.

"We went to Kentucky Fried Chicken and to the picture show."

"I saw Rodney kissing you."

"You ought to be home in bed. It's late."

"You kissed him. You were all tangled up with him."

"I was no such thing. Besides, it's none of your business, Toby. What makes you think it's your business anyway?"

"I just saw it, that's all."

"Well, you shouldn't be over here in the middle of the night worrying yourself about it."

"It's not worrying me."

"Okay, then what's so important? You said there was something important."

"He don't love you," Toby said. "You're the first girl ever looked twice at Rodney Biggers."

"You go on home, Toby Brown," Stella said, standing up. "You don't know nothing about Rodney and me."

"He don't care about you, that's all," Toby said stubbornly. "I'm just telling you the truth."

"And you know all about it, I reckon," Stella said. "You been places and had girl friends and kissed them all lots of times."

Toby got up. "I never kissed nobody," he said slowly. "I've never been places or had girl friends. I've never done anything in my whole life that counts, but just one thing. I love you, Stella. I really do." He jumped off the porch and, before she could answer, disappeared into the wooded darkness.

STELLA was back in the little bathroom, her face making a pale pout in the mirror, her thoughts on Toby, because she knew he was out there in the night, wandering probably.

Stella pulled her hair back, and fine yellow wisps slipped from her hand and framed her face. Her pink nightgown, a gift from Anne, had a lacy collar, and with her free hand Stella pulled up the collar until it stood around her thin neck. She looked like somebody now; she knew she was changing. She let her hair fall and turned down the collar.

I'm supposed to grow up, she thought. I'm supposed to like boys

454

and go places with them. I'm supposed to let Rodney kiss me and kiss him back if I want to.

Even Anne, who knew all about growing up from psychology books, had explained that to her. Anne wanted Stella to understand how natural it all was. Natural, she kept saying, as if she were trying to convince Stella without being convinced herself. Stella couldn't imagine Anne and Newton necking or going to bed together. Still, Anne was pregnant. Anne had explained that, too, had called it "being in the family way." But Stella had seen more about making and having babies than Anne Willis could have ever explained, no matter how many books she read. Stella knew the bad things, like the despairing look of a woman carrying a child she didn't want and couldn't afford.

She'd seen two babies born—Baby Earl, who'd kept Mae screaming for hours until finally a doctor, looking tired and disgusted, had come. She'd seen Lissy born, too—Lissy, who had slipped into her own hands—these two trembling white hands that now clutched the folds of a nylon nightie. Lissy had come so quick, and Stella, alone and stunned by the birth cry of a newborn baby, had had to do something and so had done everything. She had done things Anne Willis couldn't even imagine.

But this situation with Toby—it was something new that needed explaining. Toby had said he loved her, and at that moment, with the memory of a mouth against hers, she had thought he meant he wanted to kiss her like Rodney had. But he hadn't even come near her. He'd slunk off in the dark like he was ashamed.

Well, he ought to be, Stella thought. After all, Toby's the best friend I've ever had. So what he meant when he said he loved me was that he wants good things for me, like Daddy does when he kisses me and says, "God loves you." That's what Toby meant.

She went down the porch into the bedroom and lay down on the bed next to Baby Earl. The moon was behind the woods now, so the house was very dark. Suddenly she was very lonely. Tears sprang into her eyes and she wished she hadn't sent Toby away. She wished she had him near, with his hand to hold. Baby Earl moved restlessly. Stella let him move in against her, and when she had wrapped him in her arms, she went to sleep.

Chapter Four

ANNE Willis watched the Impala's taillights fade into the night and turned her head back toward the tenant house, which remained dark. In her own darkness, she leaned against her bedroom windowsill and thought about Stella. Fourteen years old and just beginning life. Already going off with boys, coming home late, and nobody up to make sure she comes in at all. Nobody but me.

Newton lay asleep across the room, his face buried in the pillow.

Anne felt protective of Stella. There was a wildness in her, a spirit that Anne had never had and which attracted her. How she admired the way Stella took on life, flipping her head at it as if beckoning a challenge. Stella was brimming with strength, and Anne wanted to turn that willfulness to some good purpose.

She leaned closer to the window and caught in the moonlight the shadow of someone moving. Toby roving around, stuck on Stella, not knowing he's trapped in a land he'll never own. She could see to it that Toby went to college, though. She and Newton had already decided if Toby couldn't get a good scholarship, she and Newton would pay for his tuition and books if Silas could supply the rest. She wanted Toby to succeed. His mind gone static would be such a terrible waste.

But I'll have to talk to Mae about him, she thought. She's so stupid, she'll never see, not about Toby or Rodney Biggers.

Anne went back to bed and slipped under the sheet next to Newton. He didn't stir, and she moved closer to him.

THE bedroom next to Anne and Newt's had been designated the nursery, and on the weekdays when there was no tobacco ready for barning, Stella went up to the big house to help Anne get ready for the baby. James Earl offered to return the crib he and Newton had slept in and that now was Lissy's, but Anne wouldn't hear of it. She wanted everything new and shiny, so she took Stella into Lawrence and they picked out furniture and material and paint. Anne let Stella pick out an outfit, white trimmed in yellow, so either a boy or girl could wear it home from the hospital.

"She's spending too much time up there," Mae said to James Earl one day. "She's bothering 'em."

"No, she ain't. Newton told me just yesterday how much Anne's enjoying Stella's helping her. When you get right down to it, Stella knows more about babies than a lota folks."

"Not about what Anne's doing, she don't. Stella knows about makin' 'em and the pain of gettin' 'em into the world, but she don't know a thing about furniture and all that."

"Then she's learning something," James Earl said. "It ain't hurting nothing, Mae." He stirred his mashed potatoes with his fork.

Mae sat down across the table with Lissy on her knees. "Anne says Stella's too young to go off with that Biggers boy," she said, holding a glass of tea up to the baby's mouth.

"What'd you say to her?" James Earl stopped eating.

"I said I didn't know." Mae sniffed and put the baby on the floor. "I can't talk to Anne. You know that."

"Stella's smart. She knows better than to get into trouble."

"Well, Anne says Toby Brown likes her too much, too. She says we ought to know about it."

"Hell, Mae, Toby's as good as they come. Anne's worrying about things ain't hers to worry about. Stella's nothing to worry about."

"She ain't perfect, James Earl. She's growing up, got the pip and all. She could get a baby." Mae blew her nose.

"Stella's all right," James Earl said. He got up and went to the back door. "Stella's all right, you hear?"

"I hear," Mae said when the screen had banged shut.

RODNEY Biggers' mother had been known to say that habitual sin could begin looking virtuous. That was sort of what happened to Rodney. Not only that, now he wanted to get more expert at sin.

At first just the sight of Stella Willis had him shivering. Then touching her made his heart race; then came kissing—quick tongue kisses that got longer and longer. For a while, kissing was all Rodney thought about; then kissing wasn't enough.

"Rodney's getting itchy," Jean Biggers said to her husband. "He's going off with that Willis girl three or four nights a week, and I can just tell he's getting itchy."

"So?" Mr. Biggers said over his *Farm Journal.* "Every normal boy gets itchy."

"I tell you, Frank, it's getting serious. Rodney thinks he's in love, and we both know what that can lead to."

"He's had a good upbringing. I trust him to behave himself."

"You ought to have a talk with him," Jean said. "You ought to make sure he understands everything."

"Jean," Mr. Biggers said, "there's nothing I could possibly tell Rodney that you haven't told him already."

STELLA stood next to her mother under the barn shelter and handed bunches of tobacco to Synora, who tied them quickly on the stick with twine that ran from a ball hanging on a post. For the past two weeks, since the night Toby had seen her kissing Rodney and had told her he loved her, Toby had avoided her. When he brought the full truck into the shelter, he didn't look at her, but joked with the black girls on the other side of the wagon. Stella knew that sooner or later she and Toby would have to come to terms with each other, but at the moment she was living in the pleasure of helping Anne plan for the baby and being Rodney Biggers' girl. So she ignored Toby's subtle glances in her direction.

All day she stood there handing tobacco, barefoot, in her faded shorts, an old T-shirt of Newton's, and her first bra.

Anne had taken her into the only ladies' store in town a few days ago, back into a little room with a brass and velvet chair in it and a tremendous mirror on the wall. Then she'd said, "Take off your dress and try this on."

She'd held out a brassiere, dangling it by the lacy white straps. Stella had stood motionless, stunned by the sheer beauty of it, and then reached out and touched the tiny blue flower in the middle. "Am I big enough?" she'd whispered.

"I think so. We'll try it and see," Anne had said gaily, unable to hide her own delight at Stella's excitement.

Stella had undressed quickly and slipped the bra on, turning toward the mirror, looking at herself. "It fits," she'd said breathlessly. "I fill it up!" She laughed and grabbed Anne and hugged her for the first time, dancing her around in the tiny room.

"You can wear it home," Anne had said, laughing with her.

Stella had put on her clothes and felt completely, newly dressed, not yet hampered by the contraption around her chest, but made freer than ever by this undeniable fact of her growing up.

So now she wore the bra under Newton's T-shirt and knew that everybody, Toby included, could see it.

Toby noticed the bra, the white outline of it clear as day through the shirt, and he turned away, not wanting to see that she was changing. Every day she grew farther away from him. Under the shelter, he watched her slyly and then sometimes bluntly just to see if she'd look him in the eye, challenging her to face what he'd told her about himself. Loving Stella was the hardest thing he'd ever done, and he longed to have her know that, not because it was a weakness in him, but because he believed it showed his strength. He could love her and leave her alone, which was something Rodney Biggers obviously couldn't do. Rodney was there almost every night, kissing her, mauling her, taking her God knows where in that car of his. Rodney was using her, learning from her and on her, whether Stella would admit it or not.

THE dawn was wet. Dew lay heavy on the grass when James Earl crossed the yard to Newton's back door and slipped into the kitchen. Newt leaned over the sink, half a waffle dripping with syrup in his hand.

"Breakfast," Newt said, shoving the rest of the waffle in his mouth. "You eat yet?"

"Coffee's all I wanted," James Earl said, sitting down at the table. He hunched his shoulders as if he were shivering, although the morning was already warm.

"Want some more?" Newt offered, and poured James Earl a mug.

"You ever feel cold right down through your bones?" James Earl said, embracing the mug with his fingers.

"Yeah," Newton said. "When I've been tramping in those woods for three hours in twenty-degree weather and ain't seen one squirrel."

James Earl laughed, although his brother wasn't really affecting his seriousness. "I've been that kind of cold, too," he said solemnly.

459

"One time Daddy and me went deer hunting up near Smithfield, Virginia. He was in one blind and I was in another. I just about froze my tail off and didn't see a deer all day. Finally I went over to see if Daddy wasn't ready to call it quits, and there he was, nursing a bottle of whiskey and as warm as toast. Couldn't of hit a buck if one had stopped ten feet in front of him."

Newt laughed, but then, seeing that the recollection of their father seemed to trouble James Earl, became quiet. Their father seemed to Newton to have always been an old man—not tottering as he had been in those last years after a stroke broke his mind, but humorless, arbitrary, unaffectionate toward his sons, as if he believed love was a weakness they should all conquer.

Newton didn't like this memory of his father, so he turned his attention back to James Earl. "Something bothering you?"

"I need to talk to you," his brother said slowly.

"The season's almost over," Newt said. He moved back to the sink and stood looking at the sun, which was spreading itself across the horizon like apricot nectar. "Two more weeks and we'll have the tobacco in. Then the women'll have to get to the grading."

"Mae don't know a thing about grading," James Earl said.

"She can learn," Newt said. "And Stella can take off sticks."

"Well, I was gonna ask you about our staying on a few weeks," James Earl said. "I figured with the tobacco about in, you wouldn't be needing us much longer."

"I need you as long as you need me," Newt said, still looking at the sky, imagining himself the parent not just of the baby Anne was carrying but of his brother as well. It was a responsibility he didn't want, yet he knew acutely that it was his. He was afraid he couldn't be different from his father, for at that moment he also felt the possibility of love being a weakness.

"Come winter there ain't enough to do. I know that," James Earl was saying. "You'll be supporting us and I don't want that."

"There's potatoes to dig, Jimmy," Newt said. "Then there's the combining. I combine oats for just about everybody in the county. And there's the livestock to take care of and burning off the fields. There's enough to keep you and me and Silas busy till Christmas. Then, before you know it, it's seedtime again."

460

"I can go now, Newt," James Earl said. "I mean, after the tobacco's ready for market, before school starts and Stella gets all ripe to go, we can be gone. You say that's best and I'll go."

"Stella wants to go to school in town," Newt said impatiently. "And you're thinking about taking her off in that station wagon that probably wouldn't get ten miles down the road anyhow." Newton turned and looked at his brother. "Anne's having a baby in September. The tobacco looks darn good. Life seems to be starting all around us, Jimmy. What makes you want to back off from it?"

"I'd like to stay, Newt. God knows, it's time for me to stay somewhere. I just need for you to say it's all right. Come spring I can plant that acreage Mama left me, if that's all right by you. Maybe make something on my own."

"Hell, yes, it's all right." Newton sat down and pulled on his brogans. He could feel the growing complexity of his life like the tangled laces Baby Earl played with.

"James Earl," he said, as his fingers sought the knot and it unraveled miraculously between his fingers, "all those years you were gone, when Mama was dying and even before that, when things were bad with Daddy and I couldn't do all the things kids think they've got to do to be somebody, I hated you for going off. Even knowing your going gave me a chance to make something of myself didn't stop me from feeling what I did. I didn't understand then how responsibility and making something of yourself go so close together. But things worked out. I got Anne, something I hadn't even dreamed about. I got lucky with the weather, and the crops came in good. Gave me time to learn about the land and make enough to get some new equipment, like that combine machine that's been making money ever since.

"Then you come home. And darn it, James Earl, if you weren't dragging your tail when you came in here. I put you in that tenant house and I thought to myself, I ain't my brother's keeper. You went out and got married and got them children, and you're responsible for 'em. But then I started seeing something. All the time I've loved you. And now I love them all, even Mae, who can't look me in the face to this day, because they're yours and you're mine and together we're all that's left of the Willises."

"Thanks, Newt," James Earl said. His voice was quavering beyond his control. He stood up and went to the back door, unable to look at his brother.

"It's gonna be a scorcher," Newton said, following him outside. He stopped next to James Earl on the steps and looked up at the sky. "But we might get rain by afternoon."

The dew was drying. Across the grass they went, Newton's hand resting lightly on his brother's shoulder. Under his brother's hand, James Earl felt the chill leaving him.

AT ONE thirty, only a little while after they'd gone back into the fields from dinner, the sky split open. Lightning, a blazing butcher knife among the windblown black clouds, cut jagged slices in the stirred-up sky, and rain poured from the slits as the men raced for the shelters. The women, already there at work, stopped their bunching and tying and sat down, squatting against the barn's worn side, where they talked slowly among themselves to squelch their fear of the storm.

Mae was under the shelter, too, but she stood with the side of her head against the wall and stared at her bare black feet. She was the only white woman there except for Stella, who sat on the packed dirt playing ticktacktoe with another girl. They drew the game quickly, ignoring the chilling rain and the thunder that shook the building sporadically.

Toby was there, too, but he stood away from the girls and watched them play. Down the lane under the next barn shelter, Mae could see James Earl and Silas smoking against the barn wall. She made a quick count of her children: Stella, William in an empty tobacco truck next to his daddy, Baby Earl easing up behind Stella like a bandit taking his victim by surprise, Lissy down the road in the house, sleeping through the storm, Mae hoped.

She could account for them all, and yet she couldn't accept them in this setting. The rain had brought with it a torrent of her own feelings, and she felt how much she despised the gummy feel of tobacco juice on her hands, the tenant house where her baby slept and where she had a bathroom, electric lights, and oil heat for when winter came.

462

Winter, she thought resentfully. I can't stay here through the winter. I just can't.

A gust of wind brought a sudden spray of water against her back. "You're getting wet, Miss Mae," Toby was saying to her.

"I'm going in the barn," she answered sharply, knowing she had become so stationary that even these people could interfere with her thoughts.

To escape them, she stepped over the boards into the dark. The barn held the sweet aroma of cured tobacco.

"Smells just like money," Newton liked to say.

And how Mae longed to look him in the face and spit out words that fermented like vinegar in her brain. I despise your damn tobacco, she wanted to say. And your house and your wife and your voice that takes my children away because it bribes them, yes, bribes them with toys and fancy ideas when none of this is really theirs. We don't want what you can give us, Newton Willis.

But she would never say that because she knew it wasn't really true. The kids and James Earl did have wants. Already the word was spreading through the vocabularies of children who had never known they needed anything beyond what was already there—a blanket, some milk, a body next to theirs in the dark.

The interior of the barn was pitch-black, as dark and cool as the inside of the car at night when they were heading for the next picking station. She could sleep best with the whirring of the engine, the rippling highway that rocked her as if she were a baby herself, carrying her wherever it wanted her to go.

Toby followed Mae to the door, and a sudden flash of lightning showed him how the chain attached to the ceiling vent wasn't hooked to the wall as it usually was, but had been slung over the rafter directly above Mae's head. The sight of the chain—metal in the electric air—terrified him.

His mouth was opening to say, Come from under there, Miss Mae. But while the words were still on his tongue, the barn was aglow with lightning. The chain burned brightly, shooting flame to Mae, who was white and glaring, a burning outline of herself.

Toby was falling, feeling the scorch on his own body, smelling the sear of skin and hair, tumbling onto the ground that shook with thunder. When he hit the floor, he was already scrambling up, shaking his head violently. His vision blurred as he tried to focus on Mae, who seemed suspended between the chain and the ground, silent, stock-still, as if paralyzed.

Toby lunged at her with the only tobacco stick he could find, and it tore into his hand as he swung frantically. Mae toppled over in a heap on the barn floor, the current suddenly as still as death.

Stella was there. All his life Toby would remember that. She was there screaming and the women were screeching and the thunder was clapping. Everybody was running. Toby held Stella, who had appeared in the frame of white door light as Mae fell. His arms pressed her against his chest as he poured all his energy into his trembling limbs to keep her safe, because suddenly she was weaker than he.

"She's dead," Silas said over the body.

James Earl, dripping rain from his skin and clothes, knelt there, while the black women held on to his sons and Toby held his daughter. He caressed the hot body of his wife tearlessly until Newton came and lifted him under his arms like a child and set him on his feet. Then Silas led him out through the drizzling rain to the house where Lissy still slept.

But Stella stayed and Toby held her limp body, which seemed boneless, melting into his own, until her weight was more than he could bear and he sank to the ground, still holding her, and she sank with him. They sat huddled together near the canvas-covered body of her mother until Newton returned with a quilt to wrap her in, with Anne running after him, calling to the women to carry the children up to the big house.

Then an ambulance came, and still Stella stayed in Toby's arms and watched, as though she were gathering every detail concerning a death. When Anne tried to loosen her from Toby's grasp, her grim refusal contorted her cheeks and mouth as she whispered hoarsely into Toby's chest, "No . . . no."

So after everyone had gone, she sat in Toby's arms, and he kissed her white neck gently and cradled her head against his chest with

464

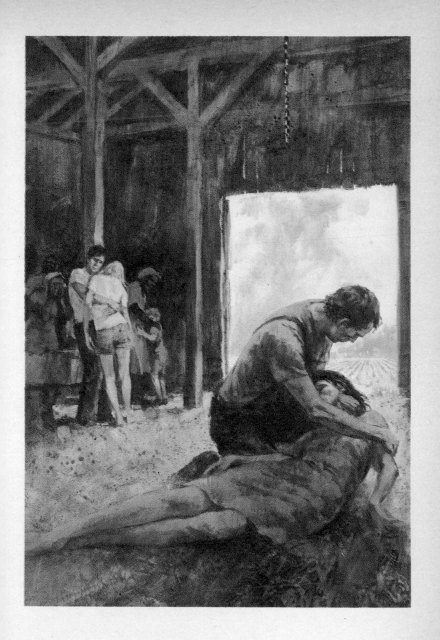

an unsteady hand. The searing smell about his body held him as closely as he held Stella. His eyes watered and his arms ached. But then the reality of Stella touched him, and he let himself go in a dream of holding her forever.

When she finally stirred, it was as if from sleep, and she pulled herself away from Toby impatiently. Silently she searched the darkness above her head until she made out the chain that had been burned away from the ceiling vent and now hung loosely over the rafter.

"Lift me up," she said coldly.

Toby hoisted her into the air until her hands grasped the chain and she sent it clanging to the ground. Then he let her down so that their heads were together.

Stella put her cheek against Toby's. "Do you think people want to die?" she whispered. "Do you think she wanted it to happen? She didn't like it here, you know."

"Don't go," Toby said, putting his arms around her again. "Stay here with me. I'll take care of you."

"I'm going to the house to see about Daddy. He needs me now." She moved away. "Don't you come with me," she said.

Toby stood in the barn door and watched her leave, her whole form white in the night. Then he went back into the barn and picked up the chain, now charred and gritty beneath his fingers. He felt how completely the metal in his hand had changed Stella's life—more than she knew yet.

All his senses were still keyed to her physical presence, the feel of her skin and hair, the fluttering of her body in his arms. She had needed someone, and he had been her comfort, at least for a while. But he needed comfort, too. His body hurt. His mind still shook in waves of shock at the sight of Mae's electrified form. He had seen someone die. He had done all he could to save her, and it hadn't been enough.

He stepped outside the barn, dropped the chain into an empty nail keg, and went slowly home, a shadow among so many. The grit from the charred chain stuck in his scratched palm, and he rubbed his hand on his shirt slowly, as if to brand himself with failure.

466

Chapter Five

YOUNG Enright the undertaker waited by his front door to lead the Willis family down the hall to the last visiting room of his funeral home.

Enright didn't really like the business he'd inherited from his father. He had already endured a frustrating childhood of infuriating Enright jokes. "Enright sure gets them in right" was the classic, corny example of small-town humor that he had to bear. He had, of course, considered other occupations and had wanted to teach, but in the end the money to be had in the family business had swayed him. He'd gotten used to burying people just like he'd gotten used to Enright jokes.

The Willises received special treatment—the last room, so no one could gawk at them; a discount price on the coffin, because Enright knew James Earl didn't have any money and because he'd already been paid more than he deserved on other Willis funerals. He'd phoned Jean Biggers, who came and tried to do something with the woman's hair when there was nothing much that could be done. She'd finally done old-fashioned finger waves that at least made the brittle, singed hair lie down.

"She just mighta been pretty once," Jean had said to Enright when she'd finished and was packing up her supplies.

"Yes," Enright whispered. "Well, we did what we could."

Now he watched from the shadow of his front door as the Willises came up the walk—Newton and James Earl first, with Newt carrying Baby Earl, and James Earl holding William's small hand firmly. Enright could see that James Earl was holding on for dear life and that the boy, his arm bent awkwardly in his father's grasp, didn't know what was happening.

At that moment James Earl was the weaker of the two, because he did understand and was feeling his loss. He was a man with no place to turn, because his comfort was finally, undeniably gone. His hot, clutching hand squeezed his helplessness into his son. Newton was like a giant beside them.

They came up the steps. The men nodded to Enright as they passed, and then he could see Anne and Stella coming slowly, the

467

baby girl waddling between them. "Come on in," he said softly, giving Anne and Stella his sympathetic smile.

They all stood waiting, as if they could wait forever. He had to lead them, to force them gently in to face the dead woman, whose body they had all known in one way or another.

The body was all he could speak for, and Enright stopped inside the room to let them pass and move silently toward the casket. He had learned to discern how the corpse looked to the mourners from their sighs, stifled moans, tiny throaty sobs. Now there was silence.

"Mama don't have hair like that," William said at last. His voice seemed to come through a microphone, transmitting Enright's failure.

"Shush," James Earl said, still clutching the boy's hand.

"She looks pretty, though," Stella said.

James Earl turned away. His head was down and his body shook. Newton put his broad muscular arms around his brother.

"Don't let the children see you like this, Jimmy," he said.

James Earl straightened up and looked at Enright. "She looks real nice, Fred," he said, his voice warbling in his throat.

"Yes," Enright said. "A lot of people have come, James Earl. You've got a lot of friends here." He nodded toward the register next to the door.

"That's real nice," Newton said. "You want to stay here a while longer, Jimmy? Anne and I can take the kids on out."

"No," James Earl answered, and then turned back toward the casket, as if his own negative response had told him what this really meant. "Stella," he said while he stared at Mae, "you ready to go home now?"

Stella nodded. She was standing close to the casket, looking at her mother's face, studying the finality of death.

"Mama's soul's with Jesus," she said to Baby Earl and Lissy, who stood next to her, neither of them tall enough to see into the casket. "That's just Mama's shell, like a snail's shell," she said, quoting what Anne had told her. "Mama doesn't live in there anymore."

"Where's Mama?" Baby Earl asked on his tiptoes. He was trying to peep over the edge of the casket.

468

"With Baby Jesus," Stella said. "She's his mama now, too."

Earl turned away satisfied.

"Well, let's go," Stella said. "Anne, I'll carry Lissy. She's getting tired." She bent over and picked up her sister, and carrying the baby that was now hers, she led the way down the corridor.

THE first thing Stella noticed, the very first thing that showed itself in the summer glare that made everything look hot and wilting, was the hole itself. A frame had been set into it to support the casket, but the metal rods and rope didn't hide the emptiness of the hole or the clear, smooth dirt sides of it. She had expected something less methodical, a gently sloping hollow in the ground like turned earth to plant something in.

There is a difference in planting and burying, she thought, watching the casket being slid across the metal and ropes so that it was suspended above the deep hole, hovering there like it was unwilling to be let down.

Men were putting flowers around the box, covering up what was happening, as if they could smooth over this day. Stella shuddered, her insides as cold and clammy as the inside of the hole must be. Across the sprays of carnations and gladioli she saw Toby, and the sight of him made her feel better.

There was a crowd: people she'd never seen before, friends of Newton's, people like Miss Maggie Grover, who had known her daddy when he was a boy. Rodney Biggers was there, too, with his parents, his mother lacquered and shining in her summer clothes, his father slouching, not able to stand up against the heat. They all sweltered while the preacher read, and Stella pressed Lissy's hand just to make sure she herself could feel. Nobody cried.

It was over. The people moved away and then came closer. They were grasping hands and saying words that made no sense to her. Maggie Grover was hovering over her, whispering something Stella didn't catch. Then Rodney Biggers was at her side.

"I'll come out to see you," he stammered. "When can I come?"

What was he talking about? Stella bent down and picked up Lissy. "What do you want?" she asked Rodney. He was a blur in front of her, and she wished he'd move away to give her room.

469

"I just want to come and see you," Rodney said again.

"Well, do it then," she said, and clutching Lissy tightly, she turned away and started toward the black Lincoln where Enright stood holding the door open for her.

"We can come back later," he said as she got in.

"What for?" she asked.

"I saw you there," she said to Toby that night when he came and sat on the side porch, his bare feet dangling above the grass. He had come without asking, just in case she needed him.

And she did. Looking at him, Stella realized she had always needed somebody like Toby, solid, stationary, and predictable.

"You knew I'd be there." Toby looked into the woods.

Stella sat down next to him and put her hand on his arm. "There were all those people I didn't know, and there was you."

"And Rodney Biggers," Toby said.

"He's nice, Toby," Stella said, still touching his arm. "I know you don't like him much, but he's nice to me."

Why did she want him to understand? Why did she want him to be patient and listen? Neither of them knew. It just seemed as if that must be the way it was if they were to go on from here, if they were ever to be close again the way they were the day they painted the house and went to town.

But we didn't come home together that day, Toby remembered. Rodney Biggers had brought them and stayed. He'll probably stay, him or somebody like him, for the rest of our lives.

Although he felt the rage beneath his crawling skin, Toby knew he had to face the fact that he didn't belong in Stella's world, that his family had nothing behind it but a past of working somebody else's land. He wished his father had gone north years ago when there were good factory jobs for the asking. He wished they'd abandoned the South forever. What had it ever done for them?

But Silas didn't think he could handle the worry of city living or working on his own, so Toby had learned to say, "Yes, sir," or "Yes, Miss Anne," like he didn't have a mind at all.

He spit out those words for his parents' sake, but he'd never doubted that he could change his life when he was old enough

470

and smart enough. He believed with angry determination that economic and educational poverty (that's what his civics teacher called it) were all that stood in his way. He would be seen and heard someday.

Stella moved closer to him now and sighed, her hand on his shoulder, her arm lying heavily on his back. "I'm glad you were there. It wasn't like I thought it would be. Nothing was—not the way Mama looked or the things the preacher said or that hole they put her in. Especially that hole. It looked too big and deep, like you couldn't climb out of it if you fell in. You'd just be down there forever." She leaned closer, resting her head against his shoulder so that she was embracing him. He couldn't move. Now Stella was in control, and he was lifeless, suspended in a motionless dream.

"I think Mama stood there waiting to get struck down," she said without bitterness. She sighed again and leaned heavily against him. It was as if she remembered the comfort he'd once given her and was returning to it. "I think she let it happen because she didn't like it here. And now she's in this ground forever."

Stella spoke carefully, and the finality of her words seemed to defeat her. "Oh, Toby," she whispered into his neck. "Oh, Toby."

He was kissing her. At first his mouth felt tight and hot, but then her lips seemed like water on his, her face like a pool he could dip into. She was kissing him, pushing his breath away. She seemed to struggle against him, fighting to get closer. And then he heard the alien sound—the crunch of footsteps—as if it were a warning he had been expecting.

Still holding Stella, he opened his eyes as a slouching form disappeared around the corner of the house. He heard the whirring of an engine, saw the dim splash of headlights, listened for the distant rumble of the car falling into darkness. And still he held Stella Willis to him, as if his life depended on it.

AT NIGHT, when the house was hushed with breathing and the feathering of moth wings against the screens, James Earl lay awake.

He didn't see how his children could sleep so peacefully when their mother had been dead only two weeks. But they had gone

471

to bed dry-eyed, and Anne said that in the daytime they asked for Mae only occasionally: Baby Earl when he stubbed his toe and held the hurt up to the wrong woman; Lissy more often.

Stella and William were working with him in the packhouse, not crying or asking, not seeming to expect anything from him. He was grateful for that. He'd never given them much, and now he seemed to have even less to offer.

Yet he knew his life was taking on some kind of normality that he couldn't comprehend. He still wanted to grieve aloud as he had those first few days, when his hurt had been like a knife wound—no, not like a slit that could seal itself and finally disappear, but more like a gunshot wound, irreparable, open to the air, and streaming his lifeblood. He didn't want his hurt to heal quickly, because he was more afraid of guilt than of pain.

How could he have loved her, had these children from her, and then forgotten so soon? That's what he thought in the daylight, when Silas would say, "Let's go in to dinner," and James Earl would head toward his own house, forgetting—how could it be?—that Mae wasn't there.

But in the night he remembered. Walking in from the packhouse at twilight, he remembered because the coming darkness brought thoughts like goblins to haunt him, and he was afraid to be alone. What will I do? he would wonder. What will become of us?

Newton seemed to think things could stay the same, but James Earl knew better. Anne was having her baby soon; her back and legs ached from standing too much and from lifting Lissy. When the packhouse work was finished, Stella could take on the cooking and cleaning, even the washing if Anne would let her use the machines in her utility room. Soon Stella and William would be in school, and he would be doing whatever had to be done—more than likely digging potatoes, feeling the earth growing chill in his hands and his fingernails filthy with the rich soil of his home—now Mae's home, too. Newt thought it could be like that and so did James Earl in the daylight, but at night . . .

At night he washed under the shower spray in the dark, because he couldn't stand to look at his body in the harsh light that made shadows as black and deep as a bottomless pit. And all the time, as the hot spray splattered his skin, he was crying. He longed for Mae then, while their children, his life without her, slept and he was alone with a body that still needed her and didn't seem to know she wasn't there in the bedroom, half asleep and waiting.

MAGGIE Grover, proprietress of Grover's Department Store, saw them coming into church, James Earl in the lead holding Baby Earl by the hand, and then the other boy, then Stella carrying Lissy, who ought to have been in the nursery downstairs. Maggie moved her head a little, not intending to make her beckoning obvious. James Earl saw the bobbing of her white straw hat, and he turned into the pew where she sat alone like a sentry.

She had, in fact, invited him to church in that biting tone of hers. Yesterday, after she'd rung up his purchases and given the children each a box of Chiclets, she'd said bluntly, "They ought to be going to church, don't you think, James Earl?"

James Earl had looked surprised, as if the thought were new to him, although Anne had tried to get them to church all summer; but Mae wouldn't go, and he wouldn't go without her. Now all that was changed. And Maggie's words and the half-embarrassed expression on her face when she heard her own reprimand had nothing to do with religion or what the children needed, but with Maggie Grover herself, proprietress of the store, middle-aged, single, a woman who sometime during the past weeks had given thought to James Earl Willis.

"Maybe we will," he said pleasantly. He felt strangely strong, newly masculine. Looking at her primness, her narrow fragility in a summer cotton shirt and skirt, he felt a surge of attractiveness in himself. It was a new feeling, one laid to rest when he'd married Mae, and now he realized that with her death it had been reborn.

"Maybe we will," he repeated, this time boldly.

"Just you think about it." She put her hand to her throat in a nervous gesture she'd fought for years. Mama used to say she had a neck like a goose, just one of the painfully true things Mama used to say.

Now they sat down the pew from her with James Earl closest, only room enough for a child between them. He set Baby Earl

473

there and pulled William closer to him, so they were all close together, although the church was roasting hot and other people were spreading out, trying to get cool. Anne and Newton entered from the door next to the pulpit, coming from their Sunday school class, and James Earl gave them an embarrassed grin and the children waved shyly, grateful for familiar faces. The children were wearing their funeral clothes and looked stiff and grown. Anne and Newton passed them quickly, while Maggie Grover held a bulletin in her gloved, perspiring hand and prayed that her neck wasn't growing red under the imagined stares behind her.

What had she been thinking of, she wondered, to say such a thing to James Earl when it was none of her business whether they came to church or not? Of course, it was for the children's sake, she remembered. She tried to decipher her motives more carefully, so that she could join in the sermon and the hymns and prayers unchallenged by her own private thoughts. But James Earl Willis, a widower—a man—was too close, and she couldn't think beyond that fact. That he was a man and that she, deep through the unbroken thread of her femininity, was a woman.

After the service James Earl, with Baby Earl pulling at his pants leg and Lissy squirming in his arms, stood next to Maggie on the church porch. The six of them hesitated there, away from the noon sun, as if they expected something to happen. James Earl shifted Lissy's weight and saw for the first time that they were with him— his four children and a woman—all he needed in his life if he could stay and work his little bit of land.

The woman stood silently, wondering what to do next. It seemed to her that her life had changed, that sitting next to James Earl Willis in church this once had altered her future so that she was dependent on him. She waited.

For more than two months she'd been watching him, from the moment he'd parked that terrible old station wagon in George's service station. She'd seen him coming into town with Newton and Silas. She'd seen the girl, Stella, in Rodney Biggers' car, seen Mae once walking alone, sneaking up the street in broad daylight like she wished it were night and she could disappear into it. And, of course, she'd seen Mae dead.

474

She had stood a long time and looked at the face, worn out and heavily made up, with those silly finger waves. She'd wanted to memorize the face—to remember it—in the specific way that someone studies a person they intend to impersonate. Even then she was conscious of what newly grew in the back of her head—a flower of her future with James Earl Willis—where loneliness had long ago settled like a gigantic, rooted weed.

Looking at Mae, she'd wondered how he could have married that woman, who could never have been pretty, when he'd always been such a handsome boy, full of jokes and good times. She remembered James Earl well, remembered him in the store, trying on boots and things when he was a boy and she not so much older than he but already helping Papa because there was no one else to do it. And besides, what else did she have, even then?

She had studied Mae's face, aware that she could, if luck were with her, take her place in James Earl's bed in her big old house where she lived alone with too much emptiness. She had a great deal to offer a man like him—money, a house and business, the mothering of his children, a body eager to be given.

Now, on the church porch, she summoned a courage that seemed to be fleeting and said to him, "Alice, who cooks for me, she'll have plenty of dinner if you want to bring the children and come on over to the house." She hesitated and slid her tongue lightly across her upper lip. "It would give Anne a rest."

James Earl knew what she was saying better than she did. He grinned sheepishly into the sunlight. "Kind of you, Maggie," he said. "We'd like that."

Charm, hidden in years of indecision and drudgery, edged his voice. Never had he been so sure of the course before him. He took Maggie's arm with his free hand and marched with his brood down the steps, nodding and smiling until he reached Newton.

There he stopped and said close to his brother's face, "We're going down to Miss Maggie Grover's house for some dinner," and winked. By God, he winked without meaning to.

And then they went down the street toward Maggie's rambling house, leaving the station wagon in front of the church and every head on the church lawn turned in their direction.

AFTER DINNER, WHERE the children had shown off the table manners learned from Anne and where James Earl had eaten heartily, without the queasy stomach that should accompany the beginning of a courtship, they went out on the front porch and sat down in the matching rockers that had belonged to Maggie's parents.

The sun was coming in at them, and Lissy lay down on the glider and went to sleep without a word. She seemed especially content and James Earl sighed, letting the sound come out evenly, showing his contentment, too, while the older children raced into the side yard, where an ancient swing hung from an oak tree.

"That was yours, wasn't it?" James Earl asked. "I remember coming by here years ago and swinging in that swing. I guess everybody in town's sat in that swing sometime or other."

"Yes," Maggie said. "But not anymore. Children don't come by, although I get a new rope every few years just in case. People ride too much. Have you noticed that, James Earl? We used to walk everywhere we went because Papa didn't like to get out the car." She stopped abruptly. It's wrong to tell him about the past, she thought. It'll only remind us both of things best forgotten.

But the idea had caught on in James Earl's head. "Do you remember, Maggie, when the bank building was painted brick red, and almost before the paint was dry, somebody wrote on it with white paint? 'So long, it's been good to know you,' it said. That was Bobby Turner and me, just days before I went to Texas. A childish prank is what it was," he explained, suddenly wary about her understanding him.

Maggie was smiling. "Bobby Turner confessed," she recalled. "But he didn't say you were with him. You were gone by then anyhow, but the sheriff—it was Tyler then—he made Bobby go out and paint over it in broad daylight in front of the whole town."

"I worried about it," James Earl said. "But it was a thing that boys will do. Earl and William'll probably do something like that someday."

The boys were flying in the swing, William standing and Baby Earl crouched between his legs. It looked dangerous.

"Y'all be careful!" James Earl called in a voice that carried across the yard.

476

"I'm watching out, Daddy!" Stella called back, her voice full of careless laughter.

Maggie was looking out at the children, the boys flung in the air outside the foliage of the oak, their bodies thin and defenseless against the blue and white sky. "My whole life has been in this town, in this house," she said quickly, as if she had to get the words out before the tears started.

"It's as good a place as any," James Earl said, not looking at her. He didn't want to see her face.

"Papa died ten years ago, and of course you remember we'd been without Mama for years before that. Ten years I've been alone in this house, and at the store, too, because who can you trust, James Earl? Who can you depend on?" Maggie sniffed into a tissue that had been crumpled in her fist since dinner.

"You're a nice-looking woman, Maggie," James Earl said as lightly as he could. "You should of gotten married, found a man to take care of things for you."

"Nobody asked me." Maggie blew her nose. "Not that I didn't get courted some, but you see, Papa didn't want me to move away. I was all he had, and by the time he died, I was thirty—I'm forty years old, James Earl—and nobody asked me."

Lissy was stirring, and James Earl moved quickly to keep her from falling off the glider. She awoke in his arms and put her face against his chest.

"I guess I better get these kids on home," he said. "Thank you for the dinner, Maggie."

"I'm glad you came," Maggie said. She stood up and leaned against the porch railing.

"Stella!" James Earl called. "We got to get going!" He turned back to Maggie and held Lissy between them. "I'd like to come by sometime, Maggie, if you don't mind. I get sorta lonesome now."

"You come by anytime," Maggie said. She was beginning to smile. "We remember each other, James Earl," she said boldly, "if that matters any."

The children were waiting on the walk, and James Earl joined them with Lissy holding on to his neck. Together they went down the street and out of Maggie's sight to the rumbling old car.

Chapter Six

TOBY knew something was going to happen. Kissing Stella had been an act of finality akin to old Mrs. Willis' suicide or even Mae's death. He knew it could create a chain of events that would hurt him, but while he was kissing her and all through the night, he didn't really care.

At home in his bed, he lay in the warm darkness remembering Stella's face, the touch of her hand on his shirt. Just thinking about Stella made his whole body ache with longing. He held back the fear that rushed him like a fever and turned his face into the pillow. Whatever happened, he wouldn't panic.

THEY found him on Saturday in the pool hall. He was standing against the wall, watching the players shoot, when he saw two boys come in and start toward him, not really menacing, but smiling as if they had won the door prize and he was it. Toby didn't know their names, but he knew they were much older than he was. They introduced themselves.

"I'm George. This is Lucien. And you're Toby Brown," one of them said, latching his thumbs into his front belt loops.

"We're friends of Rodney Biggers'," Lucien said, chuckling. He had been drinking beer, and the smell lay in the cool, smoky air between them. "Rodney don't come in places like this."

"Rodney ain't worth two cents," George said.

"Sure he is. One thing Rodney's got is money."

The boys punched at each other, laughing.

Toby wished they'd get on with it. "This ain't no party," he muttered finally, while the boys laughed.

"You damn right it ain't," Lucien said, his laughter stopping as abruptly as it had begun. "Rodney says you ain't a nice boy. In fact, he says you put your trashy hands on his girl. He sent us in to get you to come with us."

The hollow noise of the pool balls breaking drifted across the room. The men playing pool didn't look up. Most of them had a day's wages on their game. "All right," Toby said.

He had planned to fight. Knowing this or something like it would happen, he had spent the week planning strategy, thinking about escapes or even killing someone. But now he was weaponless, brainless, his mind telling him over and over the one thing he knew to be true: they could kill him if they wanted to.

Outside, the sunlight made him blink, and he thought for a second how light could be a destructive thing. He thought of Stella's hair, a sun cap on her head, then of the lightning that had charred the chain.

Night is better, he thought, climbing into the waiting car. He closed his eyes, finding darkness and feeling the car move as Rodney Biggers turned the Impala onto the back road to Lawrence.

NOBODY called the sheriff. The people who found him, a black couple coming to the edge of the woods where their still was hidden, didn't want the law around. Besides, it wouldn't have done any good.

In the boy's pants pocket they found a wallet with his name in it. They laid him on the kitchen table, and while the wife slit his shirt and tried to wash the dirt and blood off his face and chest, the man went to the nearest white people's house, where he used the telephone. He knew to call the minister.

By the time the preacher arrived, Toby was coming to. His chest and arms hurt so he couldn't breathe deeply and he couldn't talk. His pulse pounded in his face and his lips showed the imprint of his teeth in marks that continued to bleed even though the woman wiped at them gently, trying not to hurt him.

"It's Silas Brown's boy," he heard the man saying to the minister. "Somebody near beat him to death."

"Don't move, son," the preacher said as he neared the table.

"I don't think nothin's broken," the woman said. "Maybe some cracked ribs. I reckon he ought to see the doctor, though."

"No," Toby whispered. "Home. Newton Willis' place."

"That might be the best thing," the man said to the preacher. "Mr. Willis oughta decide about this."

"Help me get him in the car," the preacher said.

The man picked Toby up and carried him to the car. The woolly

479

fabric of the seat itched his skin, but he couldn't complain. Don't talk, he thought. Don't think. Don't do anything. Tears ran from the corners of his eyes along the edge of his hair to his ears, stinging his raw cheeks, and his mind was as blank as the empty sky before the coming of dawn.

ON THE second day he started running a fever. Anne leaned over him, her bulging stomach close to his bruised face, and put her hand on his forehead.

"Fever," she said to his mother, Synora, who stood across the cot from her in the kitchen of the big house. Synora was holding a mason jar of her special salve. Toby's face was smeared yellow with it, and it stung his nostrils and watered his eyes. Or was he still crying? He couldn't tell.

Sometimes he thought tears just came for no reason, or because his body was weeping for itself. Only once had he consciously cried since the afternoon in the preacher's car. That was yesterday when Anne let Stella into the kitchen for a minute, and he opened his eyes a little to see her.

She was a blur of white and silver, a streak of lightning above his head. He closed his eyes to blink away the tears, but the blur wouldn't focus. "Stella," he whispered.

"Don't talk," a voice said back to him. "Anne won't let me stay if you talk. Rodney did this. I know he's responsible." The voice seemed angry, and he knew part of the anger was directed at him.

"I know you won't tell," she said. "Because that would mean telling why he did it. He saw us, didn't he? I thought I heard a car that night, but I didn't suspect it to be Rodney. Why should I? I didn't have plans to go anywhere with him. It was the day of Mama's funeral, wasn't it? Well, he shouldn't of been there." She sighed impatiently. Whispering didn't suit her anger. "I could kill him with my bare hands. I would, too, except that people would know, Toby. We can't let that happen. I mean, Newton and Anne, what would they think?"

The voice stopped abruptly. Then she was gone.

Toby wanted to answer her, to have her understand that he wasn't ashamed, but he knew already that what he felt didn't

480

matter. Stella was ashamed. All his pain focused on her regret, and he hated her for it. He began to cry, not just tears, but deep chest sobs that wrenched his body and left him exhausted.

"He's delirious," he heard Anne saying. "Newton, we'll have to take him to the hospital."

THE only place for people without insurance in the hospital was a ten-bed ward with portable screens between the patients. Newton signed the financial guarantee, and a black orderly wheeled Toby into the room and lifted him onto a bed. The orderly put a thin blanket over him, and instantly Toby felt warm.

After a long time the doctor came. He was a big man and he held Toby's limp hand while talking to Anne and Newton. "Pulse and blood pressure okay. His skin ruptures seem to be doing all right." He smiled at Anne. "You've been doing a good job."

"But the fever," Anne said anxiously.

"Well, he's pretty badly battered up. Probably needs some ribs taped. We'll make X rays. The fever is from a low-grade infection. This many skin abrasions generally need an antibiotic. You'll be all right, son," the doctor said, patting Toby's hand.

Toby felt them moving away.

"Who the hell did that to him?" he heard the doctor asking.

"I don't know," Newton answered. "I wish to God I did."

MAGGIE Grover could imagine James Earl in the store. While her lucid, businesslike mind told her he knew nothing about dry goods and probably not much more about hardware, her imagination spun an elaborate picture of him behind the counter greeting customers and in the stockroom with the salesmen ordering nails and Rototillers and cast-iron frying pans.

She'd keep the dry goods if he couldn't manage it all right away. She could order shoes, dresses, material, without even looking at the samples. Her customers weren't influenced by fashion any more than she was. They wore whatever she had to sell.

Maggie was a wealthy woman, and yet the thought never entered her head that she could give up the store, which left her with fierce headaches and fits of exhaustion at the end of the day.

It kept making money even with inflation, and she had to look out for herself. There was no one else to take on the burden of her aging. Until James Earl came, she'd spent considerable time contemplating her final years, and she intended to have enough money for the best nursing home in the county, if it came to that.

Maggie had taken care of her mama when she was barely out of her teens, making a haggard slave of herself racing from the store where Papa needed her to the house where Mama lay as white as a ghost. Mama had had a heart attack and was afraid to move, even after the doctor had said a little exercise might be the best thing.

"He's trying to kill me," her mama would say about the doctor. "He's trying to get me up so I can fall dead." She died anyway, lying there trying not to let her heart beat too much, resenting all of them, saving herself as best she could because she wanted to live to see Maggie married and with children.

What did money matter when it meant living and dying like her parents had? Maggie thought. They seemed to have existed just because living was there to do, not because there was any joy in it. Maggie had felt that way, too, until she found joy in the form of James Earl Willis. One whole day hadn't passed since that Sunday dinner before there he was, leaning across her counter, saying, "Maggie, where you keep the bandages, thermometers, and such?" He sounded worried, and angry at something, but also familiar, like he could let her know his feelings.

"What's the matter?" she asked while she put gauze, tape, and a thermometer in front of him.

"It's Toby Brown. Somebody near killed him Saturday. Yesterday when we got home, Synora had brought him up to Anne's house, she was so worried. Now Anne's got him in the kitchen, trying to bandage him up. We think he's running a fever, though, so he'll more than likely end up in Lawrence in the hospital."

"Why would anybody do that?" Maggie asked.

"I don't know," James Earl said. "But whoever it was, I'll kill 'em if I ever get my hands on 'em."

Maggie felt dizzy. The power in his voice sent her brain spinning. Already she loved his rage. She could imagine him strangling the culprit with the giant hands that now thumped the counter in heavy, blunt fists. Strangely, the picture didn't frighten her at all, but spread, hot and smoldering, inside her skin.

"I hope he'll be all right," she whispered.

"I reckon he will." James Earl's anger was subsiding. "I meant what I said about coming to see you, Maggie," he said gently. "I could come Wednesday night, if that's convenient."

"Wednesday is fine," she said. "Could you come for supper?"

"That's kind of you, Maggie, but I'd better be seeing to the children since Anne's so busy with Toby. I could be there around eight, though." He collected his purchases and handed her the money.

She had wanted to say, Don't pay. Everything here is yours. But she couldn't, and so she made change. "Here, wait," she had said as he was going out the door, "Take this to the children." It was a bag of bite-sized chocolate bars.

"Why, thank you, Maggie," he said. He was smiling. The smile came just for her, and she smiled back.

"I'll see you on Wednesday," she said.

"On Wednesday."

SHE thought Wednesday would never come, with two hot August nights between that bothered her sleep and made her stomach quiver when she tried to swallow. She forced herself to eat. She was too thin already. She couldn't come to James Earl as gaunt and deathlike as Mae had been.

In the store, her mood shifted from despair that she knew nothing about fashion and therefore had no new dress to wear, to euphoria that she could offer him the house, the pride of the town when he was a boy. He would remember that. The furniture was all the same, the curtains the same elaborate style her mother had liked; the kitchen appliances and bathroom fixtures were serviceable relics. The house was old, Maggie knew, but it had quality.

Now she stood at the door watching James Earl come up the porch. Alice had already gone home after setting out the sherry bottle and sliced pound cake. They would be alone.

"James Earl." She led him into the parlor, feeling that this time she was truly leading him into her life, without the buffer of the children. She felt both frightened and relieved that they were finally beginning this adventure of knowing each other again. He sat in her father's chair; she sat on the end of the sofa closest to him. They were silent, immobile.

"How is Toby?" she asked finally.

"In the hospital. The doctor says he'll be okay." James Earl sighed and tapped his fingers on the armrest.

He's bored, she thought. Already I'm losing him. "And Stella?" she asked in desperation, remembering how he'd seemed to love the girl more openly than the other children.

"She's upset about Toby, I reckon. Anne let her see him one time, and the whole rest of the day she just moped around. That ain't like Stella. She's got spunk and a word for anything." He was relaxing. The strain of loneliness was loosening.

"There's something I want to say to you, Maggie," he said, so quickly she felt her breath leaving in one gigantic gasp. "It's about Mae—and, well, about you and me. Mae's been gone less than two months—it's more like one month, I guess—but for me, it's been years, Maggie. Years of being sad and pretending I know what to do with the children—with my life, for that matter.

"I haven't been able to figure things out very well yet. All those years we were on the road, I didn't have to think beyond getting the car to run and having us a place to sleep at night. But since I've come home, things are getting complicated, like there's more to deal with in a man's life than I thought.

"And here you are, Maggie, complicating things more. Without meaning to, of course, and I'm grateful for your kindness to me and the children. The truth is, Maggie, I'm wanting to court you. I can even see us getting married someday. I wanted to tell you that, so we'd understand each other right off. You might not want any part of me, and if you don't, you'd best be blunt and say so, because otherwise, I intend to court you, Maggie, as best I can."

She was certain her heart had stopped beating. She shut her eyes, feeling herself float off on a tremendous wave that could lift her forever if she let it.

"James Earl," she said without opening her eyes, "there's sherry on the tray over there. Let's have some."

He put the stemmed goblet in her hand, and she gripped it as delicately as she could, feeling his closeness, because James Earl had sat down on the sofa next to her, their thighs touching. She sipped the sherry. It was sticky and hot, and the liquid oozed down her throat and then up into her head.

"I won't stand in the way of your courting me," she said slowly. "And as for marriage, that will come if it will. I told you already nobody ever asked me. You know my secrets, James Earl, and I trust you to handle them with care."

"You can, Maggie." He put his hand on her knee, and she lay her own hand over his, pressing gently.

"I know nothing about love," she said after a while. "No, that's not true. I think I know a great deal about love, but nothing about sex. Maybe I'm too old."

"And maybe," James Earl said, "when we're young we know too much about sex and too little about love."

Maggie turned to him, her eyes shining with the wine, and put her hands on his face tentatively, not as if she were afraid, but as if wanting to savor the moment. "What a lovely thing to say."

Her fingers reached his mouth, and he kissed them softly.

"I never thought I'd have children, even someone else's. I'd given up on ever being wanted. And now there's a chance for there to be people in this house, children who can grow up and come back to it. This house has been needing that for such a long time, and so have I."

Drained of emotions, they leaned into each other's arms and stayed there, as still as the shadows in the silent room and the ghosts that had been laid to rest in both of them.

RODNEY Biggers sat on Stella's front porch, while the sweat ran down his back and collected in a soggy stripe above his belt. All week he'd worried about this initial meeting with Stella, knowing he couldn't avoid running into her, wishing he could be with her just like before, because he missed her.

Rodney had a fundamental belief in punishment that had never been disproved. Because the terrible thing that had happened to Toby Brown was his responsibility, he had half expected an overt, divine punishment—an automobile wreck that killed his parents, the house burning down. Since no signs of disaster had appeared, he now contemplated a more subtle kind of retribution: Stella would tell on him.

But Rodney hadn't come to shut her up. After all, he still envisioned walking her to the soda shop after school and driving her home in the car. Yet with Toby in the hospital, Rodney had a sense that his dream was impossible. He was scared. He hadn't intended for Lucien and George to hurt Toby so bad. A warning was what he'd intended, but once those guys had started getting in licks, he couldn't stop them. They'd hit Toby until it wasn't fun anymore, and there was nothing Rodney could do. He paid them five dollars, too. Five dollars was all it took to hire what could have amounted to a killing.

Rodney pressed his palms into the splintered arms of the weather-beaten chair. He wished Stella would come out so he could get this talk over with. He'd been planning to pretend that he didn't know a thing about Toby, but while waiting for Stella, he realized that she probably knew he was the cause of it and would throw it in his face like a dirty dishrag.

The screen door swung open, and there she was in that blue dress, looking like she'd just arrived from heaven.

"Daddy said you were out here," she said wearily, and sat down on the glider without looking at him. "I couldn't believe my ears."

Rodney sucked in his breath and gripped the arms of the chair. "I've been planning to come ever since your mama died," he began.

"You came, Rodney. Don't you lie to me on top of everything else." Stella's voice was as cold as the waves of sweat on his skin, and he shuddered. He had lost her.

"Toby's in the hospital. Newton took me to see him. He looks better now. At least he's not as swollen. His face was so hurt, Rodney. All week I've been thinking he won't look the same ever again, so when I saw him today, I wanted to cry with relief. He's going to look the same. But you're always going to look different to me, no matter how fancy your clothes get or how many new cars you drive. You're gonna look like a skunk, Rodney, because what you did to Toby is so stinking and hateful and yellow that I'll remember it every time I look at you."

Rodney was crying. "I didn't mean for it to be so bad," he sobbed. "I didn't want anything but for him to leave you alone."

"I'm not telling anybody," Stella said. "Neither is Toby. But I'll never forget. Not ever. I don't want you coming here again."

Her voice wasn't like he'd ever heard it before. There was calmness in it and purpose and such a lack of regret that Rodney felt as if the past month with her had been a dream.

"Just get off this porch, Rodney Biggers," she was saying. "You just stay off my property."

Rodney stumbled off the porch and into the car. Protected by his seat belt, the drone of the air conditioner, the soothing voice of a disc jockey wishing him a happy day, he pulled out onto the road, while Stella sat with folded hands, as if she were in a church pew having her life explained to her.

WHEN Toby came home from the hospital, Stella was waiting for him. "They're here!" she cried when the car carrying Newt, Silas, and Toby started up the road. She could hear Synora bustling in the kitchen, finishing a meal that had taken all morning to cook.

Stella jumped off the porch as the dust settled and Toby crawled out of the back seat. He looked like a ghost, much whiter and thinner than he'd seemed in the hospital. He came slowly up the steps and sat down on the first chair he came to.

"He's tired out," Synora said worriedly, standing at the screen door. "Just riding home's wore him down."

"That's to be expected, Synora," Silas said. "You feed him good and he'll be the same old Toby in a few days."

"Well, dinner's ready." She touched her son's shoulder.

"You staying around?" Toby asked Stella.

"Your mama invited me, if that's all right with you."

"Yeah." He smiled. "I've been missing you."

"Me, too."

"You all come eat," Synora urged.

"I got to get my wind back, Mama," Toby said. "You and Daddy go ahead. We're coming in a minute."

"I was so scared when you went to the hospital," Stella said when Synora and Silas had gone inside. "Even that day I went to see you

487

and I could see you were all right, I was still scared. My heart was breaking because you were so sick and I was the cause."

"No, Stella."

"Rodney came. He had the nerve to drive out here and sit on my front porch like nothing had happened. I told him I didn't want to see him ever again. And that's the truth, Toby."

"You all come on and eat!" Synora called.

"We're spoiling your mama's celebration," Stella said.

Toby stood up, stumbling a little, and Stella caught his arm. He leaned against her, wishing he had all the strength loving her took. "We can be friends," he said finally. "Even if you change your mind about Rodney Biggers, we can try."

JAMES Earl's world moved in slow motion. Although August had ended, he felt the days lengthening, had time on his hands, and the future seemed to move tediously, just outside his grasp. Stella and William were in school, riding the bus which stopped for Toby and them in front of Newton's house. He could hear them even before he was up; Stella already in the kitchen fixing sandwiches for the lunch boxes, coaxing William against dawdling, laughing, yelling sometimes when her patience wore thin.

The days were all good for Stella now that Toby was well, and she fluttered about, clucking at Baby Earl and Lissy, telling James Earl what needed doing around the house, poring over her lessons.

James Earl wanted to grab life as Stella had, and yet old worries bogged him down so that sometimes he regretted having come home at all. If they were still on the road, he would think, Mae would be alive, time wouldn't be bothering him; only the weather and how many days they could stay in one place. Mae never could stand more than a week in one place.

But here they were, stationary, and he the worse for it. He didn't know what had gotten into him, talking to Maggie Grover like he had, although every time he went there he liked her better. Sitting evenings in her parlor, he felt alive, fearless. He wanted to hurry up and marry her if he was going to.

Now that he knew her better, he believed he was beginning to love her. She assured him of permanence and comfort. Oh, hell,

488

it was more than that. He loved her already, even knowing that love was sometimes painful—you lose people and you hurt and you think the hurt will never stop, and sometimes it doesn't.

He'd seen Maggie Grover six times in three weeks. He would have been there every night if he could have gotten away without Anne and Newton knowing where he was going. He hadn't told them yet, knowing they would think it was too soon for him to be courting. Even Maggie brought the subject up too frequently to suit him, always protesting that she didn't care a whit what people thought and then adding a "but" that told him they shouldn't go out for supper yet or to the movies. They hadn't even sat in church together since that first Sunday.

But last night he'd tried to straighten the situation out. At least he could talk to Maggie; she seemed to grasp his meaning better than Mae had, as if their sharing of roots gave Maggie a special understanding of him.

He was kissing her good night—they were to the stage where he kissed her at the door—and while she was in his arms, he had said, "I want to marry you, Maggie, soon as it's fitting."

She had moved back a little to collect herself. He could see the back of her head, her shoulders down to her waist, in the mirror above the hall table. The back of her summer print dress was wrinkled, and James Earl was struck by the thought that where she couldn't see, the other side of herself, she wasn't prim—but somehow careless and unprotected.

"I want to marry you, too," Maggie said softly.

"Anne's having the baby late this month. We could get married after that."

"I just don't know, James," she said. "It's very soon."

"And you care about that?" he asked, unable to resist touching her again. Once she was back in his arms he knew he would have his way. He put his hands on her shoulders, caressed her neck with his fingers, then cupped her face in his hands.

She was trembling. Power pressed into his muscles, and he had to resist pulling her roughly against his chest.

"Folks here have never had reason to talk about me. I guess it's about time they did."

"Early October, then," James Earl said, his face close to hers.

"Early October." She nodded.

"Show me where you live, Maggie," he whispered.

There was no place more secret than that. But she took his hand and led him softly up the wide steps into the hall dimly lighted with frosted sconces, past the room where her mother had died, past the useless nursery, into the hidden space where, amid the clutter of her child life, the doilies and sachets, photographs and heavy scrolled furniture, she was truly herself.

At first James Earl felt himself the intruder. Then he saw in Maggie's silent face the beginning of her welcome, a softening blush that told him she was more sure than he. This would be their room, their bed. In Maggie's face James Earl saw her willingness to share it with him.

The bed was high, with a faint smell of bath powder in it. The smell alone was intoxicating, but soon James Earl felt heady with the pleasure of loving a woman who responded out of her own happiness. Already he had begun to love her strength, the resilience that let her abandon the bitterness she once harbored in her lonely past; now he loved her tenderness as well.

And Maggie, knowing the tangibleness of James Earl for the first time, held him close until she felt her heart would break with loving him.

COMMITTED now, he must tell Newton and Anne, face the discord his family could bring to his new harmony. Today, he thought. Then I'll tell Stella, because she must know everything I feel as honestly as I can tell her.

"I'm courting Maggie Grover," he said to Stella that night, after he'd endured Anne's silent stare and Newton's embarrassed backslapping. The other children were in bed, and he sat across the kitchen table from Stella.

Stella looked up from her book. "But she's old, Daddy. She's older than you." There was a hint of accusation in her voice.

"I know that, honey, but we've known each other since we were children. We're good friends."

"You still miss Mama a lot, don't you?" Stella closed her book.

The question seemed to be more empathy than accusation, and James Earl struggled to find an honest answer. "Yes, I miss her," he said. "Don't you?"

"Yes, but in a different way from you. I know that."

"Then you'd understand if I wanted to marry Maggie someday. She's got that big old house, the store. She could help bring up William and Earl and Lissy. They need a woman, and we can't expect Anne to take care of us forever."

"I can bring them up. You and me together can do it."

"You wouldn't like doing that all the time, Stella. Soon you'll have friends at school and you'll be wanting to hang around at the soda shop and go places."

"But this is our house," Stella argued. "We can stay here as long as we want to."

James Earl felt suddenly tired. "This is a tenant house, Stella. When I was a boy, I wouldn't have set foot in a house like this." He bent his head and rubbed the back of his neck with his hands. The hands were scraped and callused, the nails rimmed with dirt. "Don't you understand? Maggie Grover is offering us everything you've ever dreamed about."

Stella studied the hands. He was saying that time in the store would ease his shoulders, dry up his sweat, put pounds around his narrow waist.

"I love you, Daddy," she said.

James Earl's fingers relaxed on his neck. "We'll be getting married in October, I guess," he said. "After Anne's baby comes. It'll be a little wedding in Maggie's house, with just Newt and Anne and you children there. Then Maggie and me, we'll go away for a couple of days—on a honeymoon." He grinned because the word embarrassed him. "Then we'll be back living at Maggie's."

Stella envisioned that house, dark and cool, with heavy furniture and dull rugs, and goblets of such heavy crystal she could barely lift them. She looked at her father. He was calm now. Nothing churned in him as it did in her, so Stella couldn't tell him what she knew was true.

She wouldn't leave this little house for Maggie Grover's leaden world. She wouldn't set her feet off this land or desert the flowered

491

mattress of a grandmother she'd never known. The brute force of them all combined couldn't make her. For she knew, as surely as her mother had known the road to be her home, that this shotgun frame house was where her life was. She wouldn't leave it.

Chapter Seven

BY THE middle of September, James Earl and Maggie Grover were being seen in public. Anne, who had worried at first, put the social considerations as far back in her mind as she could and began thinking how much easier Maggie Grover was making her own situation. Anne certainly hadn't wanted the responsibility of James Earl's children, especially with her own baby to think about. But now the children would be in Maggie's house, three miles away, and she would see them on Sundays. Sharing Sunday dinner could turn out to be a good idea, she thought—she really didn't want Newt and James Earl to lose their renewed family ties. She wanted to love James Earl's children, and now she saw the best way to do that was to let Maggie Grover have them.

Of course, there was still the problem of Stella, who said nothing about the marriage and therefore said a lot. Stella was silent only when she was worried. Like when Toby had been so bad off. It had been almost as if Stella knew something she couldn't bring herself to say. And yesterday, when she did say something, she was snappy and irritable.

They were talking about the baby, but Anne could see Stella's mind drifting off. "What is it, sweetheart?" she asked.

"Oh, nothing." Stella turned to look out the nursery window. "I was just thinking about Mama. She shouldn't have had so many babies—some of them died, you know. They were too little to be born. And Lissy, well, she came so quick that Mama bled and bled. I kept scrubbing and wiping, but I just couldn't keep up with it."

"You poor thing," Anne murmured.

"We managed." Stella's voice became strident so abruptly that Anne was startled. "We had hard times. But we had good times, too. Days when the sky was so pretty and the fields smelled so good. I wanted those days to go on forever.

"And then sometimes we'd have money and could fix the car up or buy something special. Everything we did made me know there was more to do. Just because I never went anywhere important, like fancy restaurants or picture shows, that didn't mean I thought I wouldn't ever go. I always, every minute, had hope."

So Stella had exploded at her, and Anne had felt a moment of grief that Stella wasn't her child. "When you move to Maggie's, I want you to come back often," she said. "You can help with the baby. You'll be special to it, you know. You'll be the baby's cousin."

"I'm not going to Maggie's," Stella said.

"Why, Stella!" Anne put down the baby clothes she'd been folding. "Whatever are you thinking of?"

"I'm going to stay in the little house. Newton will let me. He just has to."

"That's for your daddy to decide, Stella. Not Newton."

"Well, I won't go unless you and Newton lock me out. And you wouldn't do that, would you?"

Stella looked as if she were about to cry, and Anne felt a flood of emotion in herself. But her practical nature ran too deep for her to ignore the reality of what Stella was saying.

"But you can't stay in that house all alone," she protested.

"You and Newton are right here. And Toby's just across the field. I won't be alone."

"But why, Stella? When you can live in that wonderful house in town, close to school, where your friends can visit?"

Stella was quiet. She knew she could never make Anne truly understand. "You don't know what a house means to me, Anne," she said finally. "When we were on the road, the six of us in that station wagon, it was us against everybody and everything else. There wasn't a place to go where things belonged to us, where we could keep safe a little bit of ourselves. Everything we had went in the car, and all we had was each other.

"But now I have a house with screens on the windows and doors that lock. Even if the wind blows hard, I can be safe in it." She stopped, overcome by what she knew she couldn't say.

"But you can have that at Maggie's," Anne argued. "Surely you see that all together in one place you could be happy."

493

"I can't depend on that," Stella said coldly. "Do you think I can depend on Daddy? Or on Maggie Grover? I don't even know that woman, and here she is telling me everything she's got is mine. That's exactly what she said, and I guess she thinks she means it. But, Anne, that little house is all I really have, and I can't give it up. You'll explain that to Newt, won't you?"

"I'll try, Stella," Anne said. "But the truth is I don't understand it myself."

THE next time Stella saw Anne she was in a hospital bed, wearing a lacy bed jacket that Stella had seen her pack but couldn't believe anybody short of a movie star would wear.

Stella had marched down the hall of the hospital next to Newt, proud that she was old enough to come upstairs while the other children had to sit in the lobby. Before they reached Anne's room, Newton took her to the nursery window where the babies were lined up in boxlike beds, each wrapped in a pink or blue blanket.

"Which one?" Stella asked, and Newton craned his neck to read the cards taped to the bassinets until he found one that read WILLIS BOY.

"That's him," Newton said, and Stella laughed out loud because she was so excited.

The baby was sleeping, his hand a minute fist beside his cheek. "He's so tiny," Newton whispered, awed by his child.

Stella was remembering Lissy—hot, slippery, squirming in her trembling hands. Now here was a baby so clean, the room so bright, the nurse so sterile in her white smock and mask, that Stella wondered how they could have survived at all in the shacks and car, on the edge of dusty fields, with Mae's watery milk their life food.

They went to see Anne. She looked soft, fragile, as precious as the baby, and Stella wanted to kiss her, to touch her purity.

"I talked to Newton and to your daddy," Anne said. "You can stay in the house awhile. Just awhile."

"I'll help you with the baby," Stella said exuberantly. "Every afternoon I can help you."

"And I'll get you a new dress to wear to your daddy's wedding," Anne said. "Jonathan can wear the outfit you picked for him."

494

"We'll all be there," Newton said. "The whole Willis family. You're part of that, Stella."

"You'll let me stay forever, won't you, Newton?"

"We'll see, Stella," he said, but he was smiling. "We have to think about your daddy. He's going to miss you."

"If I'd been in Daddy's place, I'd never have left home," Stella said. "And once I'd come back, I'd never leave again."

THE wedding was planned for Saturday afternoon so Maggie and James Earl could be back in town to open the store on Tuesday morning. Maggie had made the momentous decision to close the store on Saturday afternoon and Monday without even asking James Earl. Once they were married, she'd leave the store to him. She really did trust James Earl's decision making, except, of course, where Stella was concerned. She couldn't believe her ears when he told her he was leaving that child out in that house alone. She knew Newton and Anne were nearby, but a lot of things could happen to a child, or even to an adult, for that matter.

Besides, Maggie knew more than James Earl did about loneliness. She could tell Stella about living alone in a house where you heard voices talking in empty rooms just because you wanted to talk to somebody so bad. Sometimes Maggie went to sleep with the television on just for the comfort of the voices.

And aside from the loneliness and danger Stella was subjecting herself to, there were Maggie's feelings to consider. James Earl hadn't seemed to think she should be upset that one of his children wasn't going to be in this house for her to mother. Of course, she knew Stella would be the child to bring her problems if any of them did, although she wasn't really afraid of having a teenager in her charge. Since Stella had abruptly broken off with Rodney Biggers, there didn't seem to be a problem with boys—unless Toby Brown was a problem, and she doubted that. Well, she just didn't know. She had too many other things to think about.

A decorating firm from Lawrence had been upstairs for two weeks working on the empty bedrooms for the children, and she'd told them to decorate a room for a fourteen-year-old girl while they were at it. Outside, there was the window washing and some work on the lawn, although the yard seemed to be decorating itself; the maples were bright, the chrysanthemums still in bloom. She had had a new rope put on the swing and decided on a spot near the kitchen window for a sandpile. The furnishings were to remain the same. Maggie wanted the rooms to be the way James Earl had first seen them. For herself she had shopped in Lawrence for new clothes and had bought a smoke-blue shantung suit to be married in. She was packing her bag slowly and then daily rearranging it, spreading sachets among her lingerie, fingering the lace and crisp new fabrics.

After the rehearsal on Friday evening, she and James Earl went with Newton and Anne to a restaurant in Lawrence, where she ate flaming shish kebab and drank champagne. The next day she felt light-headed, even at noon, when she locked the store and walked slowly home to a house that would be empty for the last time. She lounged in the bathtub, hearing Alice below in the kitchen, where sandwiches were being arranged on her mother's silver trays. She heard the bakery truck from Lawrence arriving with the cake, and the florist with the flowers she'd ordered for the dining-room and the parlor.

STELLA was ready long before James Earl, and so she sat on the side porch staring at the gray autumn sky. While she waited, Toby came and sat beside her. She smoothed her skirt. The dress was a rosy color, and it reminded her of peach groves.

"That's a new dress," Toby said. "It sure is pretty."

"It's for the wedding. We're having cake and punch at Maggie's house. Then we're supposed to throw rice at Daddy and Maggie when they get into Newton's car to go off. We'll all come back here until Maggie and Daddy get back Monday afternoon. Then the children will go over there."

"You still staying here?" Toby asked.

"Of course I am." She tried to suppress the excitement in her voice. "We'll still get on the bus together every morning. And after school we can study together because there won't be Lissy and Earl to take care of."

"I don't know," Toby said slowly. "I've joined the glee club,

496

and I'm thinking I might work on the school paper this year. I might not be coming home on the bus so much."

"I'll be all right alone," Stella said. She toyed with her collar.

He knew he'd hurt her. Ever since he'd heard that she planned to stay in the tenant house, he'd been afraid of hurting her, while still wanting to protect himself. He sensed that she shouldn't depend on him, any more than he should depend on her. Yet he loved her still, could even fantasize about living in the house with her; an impossible idea, he knew, not only because of the Willises and his parents but because loving her was so impossible.

"I think you ought to move into town with your daddy, Stella," he said slowly. "I guess staying out here seems like fun, like acting all grown up. But you'll be lonesome."

"I don't think it's one bit fun, Toby," Stella said. "But this house belongs to the Willises, and Maggie's house belongs to her. I don't mind Daddy marrying her. He needs somebody. But what I need is right here. It's this house and this farm."

"It's just land," Toby argued. "I don't understand what you're expecting from it."

"I expect to take care of myself, Toby, and you can stay late after school every single day if you want to."

"It's time we were going," James Earl said through the screen door. His face looked ruddy and young as he grinned out at them. "This is no time to be late, girl," he said.

Stella stood up. "I never owned anything in my life," she said to Toby, "but someday I will, if I don't start letting things slip away right now. Don't you see that?"

She went down the steps and around the corner. When she was out of sight, Toby leaned against the porch post and shut his eyes. He could see her still. The vision of her, not just today but every memory he'd saved up, came to him. Stella that first day, standing before the half-painted house. Stella under the barn shelter, handing tobacco. Stella between himself and Rodney Biggers, and then in his arms after the accident. In his arms again after the funeral, this time really there with him, aware of him as surely as he had been aware of Rodney Biggers. He would keep on loving her. He just hoped that didn't mean giving up himself.

ANNE WAS PLAYING Mendelssohn's "Wedding March" on the old mahogany piano. From the corner of her eye she could see Maggie, in her shantung suit, reach the bottom of the stairs. She was carrying a bouquet of orchids, and her graying hair shone as if she'd put a touch of bluing in it. She's almost pretty, Anne thought.

James Earl was standing in front of the mantel next to the minister, and while looking at Maggie, at how downright good-looking she was when she fixed herself up, he had a flashing memory of Mae. He closed his eyes, fighting off the remembrance of her face. He had not tried to understand Mae in the deep, thoughtful way he wanted to know Maggie. Somehow he could feel confident that Maggie would be with him as long as he lived. She was so stationary. He could moor in her and live quietly, easily, without the rumbling of car engines in his head.

Maggie was next to him and she took his arm heavily, leaning on him because she wanted to give him the sense of oneness she felt. The minister was speaking; she was answering. James Earl was answering, too. She had sat on a church pew through at least a hundred weddings and heard these same words, but until today she'd heard her own failure and loneliness in them.

Anne was playing the piano again. Newton was kissing her cheek. The children were locking around her, even Stella, who had always seemed so aloof. James Earl was holding Lissy between them, and Maggie kissed the child and then leaned closer to put her face against James Earl's. She'd never touched him in front of people before, but she didn't feel embarrassment, only a joy that throbbed so intensely she thought she might cry.

"Let's have some champagne," she said, and drew the children into the dining room with her. "They can have a taste, can't they, James?" She heard gaiety in her voice, and she smiled at all of them while Newton poured the golden bubbles into her mama's crystal goblets. She handed the first glass to Stella.

Stella cupped both hands under the bowl of the goblet. She heard Newton booming a toast, saw her daddy gulping the champagne and laughing. He seemed right at home in Maggie's dining room, where the chandelier sparkled and the chairs were heavy with brocade.

498

"To the children," Maggie was saying in a loving tone. Her voice was almost singing. "May they fill this house with laughter."

Stella sipped the champagne. Bubbles flew into her nose. The cold liquid caught fire in her chest. It was delicious. Her family was beautiful, even Maggie. The gold ring on her finger shone with newness, no scratches on it, no dull places. Her daddy wore a ring like it. Stella had never seen him wearing jewelry. He is different now, she thought. We are all so different. She wanted to dance, to hold out her peachy skirt and balance herself miraculously on her toes, or sing, or hug everybody.

"It was the prettiest wedding I've ever seen," she said to Maggie. Her mind wandered forward and backward, flashing the past beside the present. She had never been to a wedding before, had never drunk wine, or heard a toast. What had Newton said? "A long and happy life"? Yes, that was it. Was such a thing possible? In her young life only bad things had lasted long—childbirth, rainy spells, highways. The happy moments had been gone too quickly. But perhaps Newton was right. Here there was no rushing, no speed to take her from memory to memory so fast they became blurs. She felt a calm she had never known, and she began to cry. Tears washed down her cheeks.

"Why, Stella!" Anne said.

"It's the champagne," Newton advised, and sat Stella down on the parlor sofa. Through the archway she could see the family about the table, nibbling, drinking, laughing. And as she watched them, Stella's grief and her joy culminated in one gigantic, tremulous sigh.

THERE had never been an autumn like this one. The dogwoods that edged the pines near Stella's house turned red as blood. The days were still as the sun moved farther away into a haze of changing seasons. Finally the wind came, turning the pines into giant brooms that brushed endlessly across the sky.

Stella listened from inside her house, where she slept beneath an accumulation of Anne's blankets. Nightly she plugged in the electric heater Maggie had given her from the store. Maggie had wanted her to take two, but Stella had refused. The oven in the kitchen would keep that part of the house warm, and she had

closed off the other rooms so that she lived in the last bedroom and scampered down the chilly porch to the kitchen and bath.

She had lived there alone for only a week when Newton had Silas and Toby up there to board in the side porch. Now her passageway was close and dark. She didn't like it very much because she missed sitting there, with the woods so thick and protective. But that wasn't the kind of protection Newton and James Earl thought she needed.

They were all keeping her as safe as they could, when what they really wanted was to carry her down to Maggie Grover's house and lock her in a pink-wallpapered room that had white furniture, and a bedspread with ruffles down the sides. She'd seen that room when she was depositing Lissy in a nursery that looked as fine as Jonathan Willis'. She had stood in the doorway, with Maggie behind her, and felt she must grab hold of the doorjamb to keep from being pushed in and the door slammed behind her. The windows were too high for escape; the world would be suddenly, irrevocably, too far outside her reach. But Maggie hadn't pushed her. No, Maggie Grover Willis had been silent, as if she understood what little result her voice would have.

Then Stella had wanted to step in. She'd wanted to tell Maggie that the room was beautiful and that she was grateful, although she couldn't live there. But those words seemed beyond her, and so she turned away from the room and hurried out of the house, because suddenly she could imagine it being her home.

Still, she was glad to be in the little house. Toby had done all the things he'd said he would—joined the glee club, worked for the school newspaper, had a role in the freshman-class play. She got off the bus every morning at the junior high, leaving him to ride on to bigger, better things at the high school. Usually she didn't see him again until the next morning, when he'd be waiting in front of Newton's house to catch the bus again.

One afternoon after school she'd gone downtown instead of home, and outside Maggie's store she'd caught a glimpse of Toby. There was a girl with him—a high school girl wearing a dress too nice for school, and shoes with wedge heels. Stella had ducked into the store as if she'd escaped a hailstorm.

"What ails you, girl?" James Earl had said, seeing her panting behind the door.

"Nothing," she breathed. "I was just running." She walked down the aisle and into the shoe department. "Daddy, do you have any shoes with wedge heels on them?"

"Now wouldn't I look foolish walking around like that?" James Earl laughed from his place at the cash register, where he could watch the store and the street at the same time. He seemed so much in the center of things now that Stella felt a need to put him a little off-balance.

"I mean shoes for me." She pouted, sitting down on one of the two chairs in the shoe department. "Everybody's wearing shoes with wedge heels, and here I am in these dumb old loafers."

James Earl left the cash register and sat down on the fitting stool in front of her. "Now I know what seventh-grade folks are wearing. Don't I sell it to 'em?"

"No, you don't," Stella said. "The girls I know go to Lawrence shopping. They say Maggie's clothes came off the ark."

She expected him to be angry, but he was smiling. "Well, hell-fire, they ain't far from wrong. Just this morning a salesman was by with blouses. Here he comes with these things that button up the front. So I say to him, 'Where's the pullover kind? Those turtle-necks, and ones without a collar at all. That's what folks are wear-ing.' Well, I can tell you he was surprised. Maggie'd been buying the same blouses for the last ten years. So I did some ordering, not spending any more than she does, but getting something girls like you will be wanting."

Stella saw the excitement in her daddy's face. He had discovered he could buy and sell, and it pleased him. "Well," she said, "when you get those chunky-heeled shoes, you let me know."

"Yes, ma'am. I sure will." James Earl slapped his knees. "Now how about you hanging around here for supper? Maggie's home with the children already, and Alice is frying chicken."

Generally, Stella found a way of avoiding going to Maggie's. She didn't like to sit in the big old kitchen, where the food smelled so good her stomach jumped and churned through the prayers. But outside, the afternoon waned, the wind was taking on a chilly look, and she didn't really want to go home and eat Anne's leftover soup. "All right," she said finally.

"I wish you'd stay with us, Stella," James Earl said. "You've got a room right there waiting."

"I know, Daddy, but not yet. I can't come yet."

"Well," he said, getting up. "You can help me close this place. It'll be five o'clock before we know it. Maggie wants us to bring ice cream home, too."

Stella unfolded the white cover sheets and put them over the bolts of cloth. The store became eerie, the floorboards creaked, and the long aisles seemed to float in their gowns like drifting ghosts.

"You just got that sweater?" James Earl asked, slipping into a new plaid jacket. "You better be wearing your coat these days. Temperature drops every night. It could snow anytime now."

"Oh, Daddy." Stella watched while he turned out the lights.

When they arrived at the house, there was a fire laid in the parlor, and even before calling to Maggie and the children, James Earl stopped to light it. From other visits Stella knew there were bonds growing between Maggie and her daddy. They showed themselves in the ritual lighting of fires at twilight; the way he hoisted Lissy onto his shoulders to take her up to bed; the expression on Maggie's face when he swung the baby under the hall chandelier; her relaxed smile when Lissy was safe in his arms again.

"Well, hello," Maggie said to them from the parlor door. "I smelled the fire." She came into the room and rested her hands on James Earl's chest for a moment. "Stella, how wonderful to have you! The children miss you, you know. We all do."

Stella could feel the aura of love, the warmth of the fire around her. "Daddy asked me to stay for supper," she said.

"We're having chicken, too," Maggie said. "But look here, that ice cream's melting. Take it into the kitchen, dear, and I'll get the children washed up."

Stella held the cold sack against her sweater. The hallway seemed shorter than before, not a shadowy passageway but a lived-in place with light to illuminate both the way and the framed photographs that spoke of Maggie's past.

In minutes they would all be around Maggie's table. She would

503

be looking at the children, who seemed already to have forgotten the fields and shacks, the battered station wagon. And that was just as well, Stella thought. Not everybody is supposed to remember. Just some of us. Someday I guess I'll understand why.

After supper, Stella got into the new car James Earl had bought with Maggie's money, and they whizzed out of town.

"I don't want to see you downtown without a coat again," James Earl said. "You ain't used to this kind of weather."

"I promise to wear a coat," Stella said to silence him. The night moved around her. The car was dark and warm, and she tried to think which way it was taking her—forward or backward. Back to the farm, she decided finally. Back where I belong. Then Maggie's house must be forward. Could it be that they were all moving forward but her?

"Daddy, tell me about Grandmother Willis."

"There ain't much to tell. Mama was one of those people folks like, but there isn't a lot to tell about. What I remember best are things I can't describe, like the way her apple cobbler tasted or the sound she made when she laughed. Sometimes you sound like her—both when you're laughing and when you're mad."

"When she killed herself, was she mad then?"

"Maybe she was, in a way. Her sickness gave her a lot of pain, and she knew she'd never get better. I suppose she was being stubborn, like you can be, Stella. She died her way, not somebody else's." He turned the car up the path and the lights beamed on Stella's house. "I guess you're living your way and not anybody else's," he said. "But I admit it hurts me. I always thought we got along pretty good together."

"We did, Daddy. We still do." Stella eased the car door open. Cold air swept against her legs. "I'm glad you're happy. I'm glad for all of us." She raced toward the house, with a black shadow of herself moving in the headlights.

When the car had pulled away, she turned on the heater and sat in her dark bedroom. The orange glow of the electric coils played in the air, warming her. She didn't want to go to bed, so after a while she got up and put on the coat her daddy had demanded she wear.

504

She couldn't remember a night as cold as this one. The moon was very bright, and the two houses closest to her seemed very near. Both of them were dark, like shadows set into hedges and shrubbery. Outside, she walked down the field toward Toby's house. He was there asleep, dreaming maybe about the girl in the expensive dress or about college. He was beyond her reach now. She had put him there by some strange, almost foreign idea that he was not as good as she was.

She stood in the field hoping a light would come on, hoping Toby would know she had come. But there was nothing but the night around her, the moon moving, the wind stirring in the pines.

Back in her little house, she undressed and climbed into bed. Her mind was spinning with the memory of the dinner at Maggie's. They were happy. All of them. Maybe she should go to live in town. She could try it for a while, as long as she knew she could come back to the farm whenever she wanted to. Maybe Toby would walk her home sometimes and come into Maggie's kitchen. She wanted him to see how big that kitchen was and how her room looked and how the chandeliers glittered, not to brag about them but to share them with him.

But maybe that couldn't be. There was an overpowering sense of past in Maggie's house that would awe Toby just as it awed her. Still, if she were to move there, it would have to be a house he could come to. It would have to be a place where she belonged.

Chapter Eight

RODNEY Biggers sat on a stool in the soda shop, watching Toby Brown out of the corner of his eye. The kids Toby was hanging out with were all from good families. Rodney wished he knew why, in high school, where everything was so difficult for him, Toby Brown had gotten popular.

Now he watched the girl next to Toby lean closer to him in the booth, as if she intended to whisper something to him. But she didn't. They just looked at each other and started smiling, as if they were someplace else and the jukebox wasn't blinking its lights and Elsie wasn't fussing over cola spilled on the floor.

"This ain't your pigpen," Elsie was saying to one of the kids as she slapped the wet string mop to the floor tiles.

The kids laughed, and Rodney felt sudden empathy with Elsie, thwarted in her effort to do her dreary job halfway right. After all, Rodney hadn't wanted anything but Stella Willis. But somehow his one great effort to keep her had backfired and given Toby Brown a mysterious new start. Rodney felt sure the "accident" had resulted in Toby being able to abandon himself to whatever life offered. Now he seemed willing to take his chances with people; a risk Rodney never felt equipped to take.

"Whatcha know, Rodney?" someone was saying.

Rodney looked up to find Toby standing next to him. "What do you want?" he blurted.

"Nothing, man. Just speaking to you." The kids were ganging around them. "Want to come take a ride with us? Charlene here, she's got her daddy's car."

Charlene took hold of Toby's arm. "He doesn't want to come, Toby. He's still mooning around over that little Willis girl, aren't you, Rodney?"

"Shut up about Stella," Toby commanded. "She's not in this, Charlene. You want to come, Rodney?"

"No," Rodney gasped. "I got to get over to the shop."

The other kids laughed and began drifting to the door.

"I guess you got reason to be scared of me," Toby said as he moved away.

Oh, Lord, he was going to start bawling. Rodney faked a sneeze and wiped his eyes and face with his handkerchief.

"You're coming down with something," Elsie accused. "Why don't you go on home?"

Rodney slid off the stool. "You remember a couple of months ago somebody beat up Toby Brown? Well, I know who did it."

"Shut your mouth, boy," Elsie said. "I don't want to hear that kind of rot."

So nobody wanted to know. Already the incident was buried, locked deep like the scars on Toby Brown's ribs. Maybe even Toby was forgetting, maybe even Stella was. Rodney felt the tears stinging. He would be the one to remember. Only he. Alone.

506

THE WEEK AFTER Thanksgiving, when the frost had settled on the countryside and the windows of the little house were icy and rattling with winter wind, Stella left school during the lunch break and walked slowly to Maggie's, taking a long, chilling, inconspicuous route that made her arrive at the kitchen door just after James Earl had returned to the store.

Alice was in the kitchen, and she hardly seemed surprised at Stella's shivering form in the doorway. "Miss Maggie's putting Lissy to bed," she whispered. "You go on up there if you want to."

Stella dropped her coat on a chair and slipped down the hall. She could hear Maggie singing. Her voice warbled slightly, like a child learning a new tune, but a haunting quality in the husky sound made Stella pause on the stair and listen intently. The voice struggled on the notes. Soft *s*'s hung in the air, and rising with them was a sound that caught Stella's ear so purely that she felt tears springing to her eyes; she knew she was hearing the sound of love. Never had she heard it so clearly before. It was music—richly, harmoniously, undeniably true.

"Maggie," she whispered at the half-closed door. There was a moment of silence, and then the song continued softly, moving across the room toward her. The door opened slightly, and she saw Maggie smile and then put her finger across her lips.

Maggie eased through the slit in the doorway and drew Stella silently into the next room, which Stella realized, with a sudden gasp, was the pink and ruffled place Maggie had created for her.

"Lissy's asleep," Maggie said in a whisper. "She usually goes right off without a fuss, but today little Earl is spending the afternoon with a nursery school friend and she misses him." She let go of Stella's hand. "Sometimes I think they miss more than we realize. It's so easy to forget that their worlds are very small, and so every single thing is important to them. I mean, sometimes I forget that I'm not really their mother. . . ." She paused, as if she'd just realized who she was speaking to.

"Oh, Stella," she said quickly. "Whatever is the matter? It's too early for school to be out."

"I got a pass," Stella said. "I pretended to be sick." She smiled a little, feeling good that she could tell Maggie the truth.

"You pretended?" Maggie tried to look displeased.

"Yes, I wanted to see you." Stella sighed and looked at the room. "This is so pretty," she said. "It's almost too pretty, you know. If somebody really lived here, they might mess it up."

"Oh, no," Maggie said. "What it needs is somebody living in it. This room has always been needing you, Stella."

Stella sat down gingerly on the bed. "I came to tell you something, Maggie." She paused, believing she must control her courage, direct it carefully into the words she wanted to say. "I've been thinking about this ever since Daddy married you and I wouldn't come here with him after you fixed up this room, and Daddy had begged me and I knew you were hurt about it. I didn't want you to be hurt, Maggie, but somehow I felt good about it, too. I knew it meant you cared about me—about all of us.

"But, you see, at first I saw what belonged to you as yours—just yours—and I couldn't see you sharing it with us. I couldn't trust your giving us things. I didn't think you cared about us that much. Loving never seemed to have anything to do with giving before. Daddy and Mama never had anything to give. None of us ever owned anything until we came back to Daddy's home and Newton gave us that little house. But, somehow, I felt like it had always been ours. That land out there belonged to us no matter what anyone said. Daddy was born to it, and I was born to Daddy; so the land and the house were mine. They truly belonged to me, and I belonged to them."

Stella stopped and looked at Maggie, who was looking straight at her and listening.

"I love it so much, Maggie. I thought nobody could understand but me, and so I've never tried very hard to say it. Now I know I hurt you and Daddy by staying in the only place I felt I belonged.

"But somehow, lately, I've started to think you'd understand, because your house and the store—the things you've been giving Daddy and all of us—belonged to you even before you were born. It's like a tree's root deep in the ground. You can't see it, but you know it's there, because the tree is there. So I came to tell you that I'm sorry I couldn't leave my place and come here, and I want to say that I think I will someday. Sometime, maybe soon, I think I can leave my little house and not be giving it up, because what I feel about it will come with me."

Stella didn't know when she had begun crying, but suddenly Maggie's arms were around her, steadying her trembling shoulders.

"I can love you, Stella," Maggie said softly. "And I know about holding on to what belongs to you. That was all I knew until I found your daddy. Then I learned there were better things than being brave and pretending to like a life that's hard and lonely. It's not always easier to love people more than things, but I've learned it's worth the risk." She smoothed Stella's hair with her hand. "You must be tired out, walking all the way from school on a windy day like this. I bet you skipped lunch, too."

Stella nodded, unable to speak.

"Then you lie right down on this bed, and I'll go and get you some hot chocolate and a sandwich. I think I'll have something myself." She smiled and patted Stella's hand. "You don't have to be afraid of this room," she said gently. "Remember, it's just a place, and places don't really own people, do they?"

The autumn sun was golden in the room. I can't stay, Stella thought, but her eyes were closing. Not yet. I can't.

When she awoke an hour later, the room was still rosy, hazy with midafternoon, but it didn't look the same to her. There was no threat in it; no demon to capture her separateness and make her one with Maggie Grover's world if she didn't choose to be. There was still the farm and the woods and the house beyond, and before that afternoon waned into twilight she went back to it.

THE Sunday after the new year began, Stella awoke early. She had her suitcase packed and by the door, ready to be carried away with her. But what had awakened her so suddenly wasn't the excitement and dread of moving to Maggie's house, but a brightness in her room that was too white and glaring for sunlight alone.

Even before she reached the window, she knew what it must be. The field beside the house was covered with snow. The trees were gloriously frosted. She dressed quickly and went out into the yard, where she pulled her shoulders up against the breathtaking cold. The snow still fell lightly, as if it were finishing the lace on a gigantic white spread. Flakes touched her hair and coat, but melted almost before she could see them.

Toby was jumping the gullies in the field. "I was coming to wake you up," he called breathlessly.

"I think I felt it in my sleep that this had to be a special day," Stella said when he reached her. "Anne and Newt are taking me to Daddy and Maggie's for dinner, and I'm staying."

"Yeah." Toby kicked into the snow. "I'm going to miss you."

"You'll come to see me, won't you, Toby? I want you to."

"Sure, I'll be around."

"I mean it, Toby. I couldn't stand it if I thought you wouldn't come."

"I'll come," Toby said. "I promise."

HE WAS already gone when Newton came out and called to Stella and she carried her suitcase to the car. The little house looked so empty from where she stood, although she knew the things from the attic were still there—her grandmother's mattress, the dishes and linens. And yet, Stella knew the house had long been empty, so when she was snug in the car and they were turning away toward the town, she didn't look back, not out of any trembling emotion, but because she knew where the future was.

The town came to them slowly, one house at a time, until suddenly, almost without warning, Stella felt, they were before the ancient house, where smoke and light and snow mingled like the magic of life itself. "Well," she said, "we're here."

Then the door was flung open, and as the house's warmth slammed into her with arms and legs and milky breath, she could hear the house itself saying, "We're here."

510

Sue Ellen Bridgers

Sue Ellen Bridgers was born and raised in North Carolina, in the heart of the tobacco-rich country she describes so lovingly in *Home Before Dark*. Her own father was a tobacco farmer—and a born raconteur. "My family definitely has a penchant for storytelling," she says in her lilting Southern accent, "but I'm the first to switch from the oral tradition to writing."

Until recently Mrs. Bridgers wrote mostly short stories. *Home Before Dark* is her first novel, and springs from her recollections of growing up in a small, Southern town. "When I was a child," she explains, "transient children sometimes made brief stops in my school, and I always felt curious about them. They were silent children, aloof, and probably ill at ease because they were so far behind in their studies, and I suppose they knew they wouldn't be there long enough to improve much. They were mysterious, and although they knew less than most of the local children academically and socially, they were far more aware than we were about many things. They were at once childlike and very old. I tried to capture that element of inconsistency with Stella.

"In *Home Before Dark*," the author continues, "I also tried to explore the idea of family. The family unit has a greater potential for hurting or helping a person than any other social group. It is a very vulnerable place."

Sue Ellen Bridgers lives in Sylva, North Carolina, with her husband (a lawyer) and their three children. She is currently at work on her second novel.